WHAT *the*
FOCACCIA!

Ginger Jones is a fiery redhead with a love for chocolate, spicy food and swimming al fresco. She collects chintzy china teacups, drinks loose leaf Darjeeling and loves fifties fashion.

Most of her writing time is spent in the company of Lulu, her Schnoodle, who has helped and hindered the creation of her books in equal measure.

Ginger loves comic writing. Her influences are Caitlin Moran, Helen Fielding and Nora Ephron. Having previously written for the stage, she finds the live buzz of theatre exhilarating and enjoys nothing more than finding fringe venues she never knew existed.

She and Lulu look forward to penning many more novels together. You can find them both via:

🐦 @GingerJ53270983
📷 @redhotscribbler
f @GingerJonesRedHotScribbler

WHAT the FOCACCIA!

Ginger Jones

ZAFFRE

First published in the UK in 2023 by
ZAFFRE
An imprint of Bonnier Books UK
4th Floor, Victoria House, Bloomsbury Square, London, England, WC1B 4DA
Owned by Bonnier Books
Sveavägen 56, Stockholm, Sweden

A CIP catalogue record for this book is
available from the British Library.

ISBN: 978-1-83877-844-6

Also available as an ebook and an audiobook

1 3 5 7 9 10 8 6 4 2

Typeset by IDSUK (Data Connection) Ltd
Printed and bound in Great Britain by Clays Ltd, Elcograf S.p.A.

Zaffre is an imprint of Bonnier Books UK
www.bonnierbooks.co.uk

To Stephane V,
who knows a lot of the world, and even more about fashion;
des façons, des contrefaçons, des caleçons.

And to Marianne and Jonathan who unwittingly travelled
with us on that day.
Thank you for inviting me to co-write that
very first pantomime x

CHAPTER ONE

House of Horror

'An inclusive range gives you more. More confidence. More comfort. More choice.' I direct my eyeline at Flora, who does her very best to concentrate on my pitch in spite of the onslaught of multi-coloured plastic balls being pelted at her head.

'Great start!' Zhané claps excitedly over the hullabaloo, her leather jacket getting caught in a giant plastic cobweb as she lowers her three-year-old from the cargo net.

Trying to ignore the ear-splitting roar of shrieking toddlers and the faint smell of wee, I reach for my phone, my hand brushing against something warm and soggy which, upon greater inspection, looks to be a regurgitated custard cream. Nice. It was Zhané who suggested we meet at The House of Horrors play barn to practise my pitch, not just as a means to entertain Leo, but also as a way of getting me to focus.

'If you can deliver your pitch in a giant ball pit of screaming kids, you can get through it anywhere,' she reasoned, and she's right – getting through the opening sentences whilst Baby Shark is booming over the speakers to drown out the shrieks and squeals of a hundred or so preschoolers as they collide on crash mats, face plant into giant slabs of sponge and shake machines full of small rubbery zombies behind you is indeed a great test of stamina.

'Go on.' Zhané grins, scraping her curls into a ponytail to reveal sensible stud earrings – most unlike the Zhané I know and love, who favours five-inch heels for the nursery drop and has embraced a whole new wardrobe since divorcing Mandla, self-diagnosed sex addict and father of her child, 'flaunt it' her new motto. As though reading my mind, she reaches for her earlobe. 'My tortoiseshells got caught in the cargo net last time.'

'OK.' I sling the soggy custard cream into the gaping mouth of a friendly witch, and try to call to mind the notes I have spent way too long finessing over the last few days, because let's be honest; this pitch is not just important; this pitch is *everything*. If Aart ter Horst, or 'The Horse' as he's affectionately known amongst fashionistas, is wowed by my designs tomorrow, House of Dreams may just commission my collection, and Curvaliscious could not only be a made-up word on my hard drive, but an actual, living breathing size-inclusive clothing range and a life-long dream fulfilled.

I inhale sharply. 'They say size doesn't matter, but as a Plus Size woman, let me tell you, it matters enormously. Did you

2

know that the average woman in the Western World is a size 44 and is considered Plus Size?'

'No,' Flora says with what's coming across as rehearsed incredulity or has she too put her fingers on a semi-digested biscuit?

I go on. 'If the average woman is Plus Size, what does that make women who are larger than average? Plus Plus?'

'XXL?' Flora suggests, her face alight with the glow of a praised school prefect.

'The questions are supposed to be rhetorical, Flor!' Zhané casts her a thousand-yard stare.

'I just thought . . .' Flora's words ebb away as a sea of nursery kids perform a giant conga on a cobwebbed rope bridge above us, crumbs, spittle and primal joy raining down on us in the jam-packed arena of soft-play. 'Eugh, did someone just *spit* on us?' Her eyes widen with horror.

I love Flora. I've loved her since the day we sat next to each other in Maths and she sorted me out with an emergency tampon, and I've continued to love her since she hit the big time with a dating algorithm based on cohabiting compatibility (CoCo for short), and has singlehandedly facilitated the blossoming of romance and the propagation of the human race across the Western hemisphere (apart from her own). But there is one thing that Flora doesn't do very well and that's anything icky. Mess. Dirt. Vomit. Child spit or any bodily fluid is enough to turn her stomach and if this situation is difficult for me, you can bet your last Jaffa Cake it'll be a zillion times more difficult for a woman who bleaches our bath three times a week and insists that we steam-clean the carpets fortnightly – a compulsion Mr Salim, our landlord, seems to be very happy with, but one that makes it difficult to flatshare with her at times.

'The size-inclusive market is growing faster than any other area of the fashion market, but it's not growing fast enough. If the average woman is Plus Size and yet only 21 per cent of the European clothing market serves women size 44 and upwards, aren't we missing a trick?'

'Yes!' Flora squeals, her baby blue eyes fizzing with excitement, Zhané dead-eyeing her with a look that could sever limbs.

Bracing myself as a three-year-old torpedoes into my head from an adjacent slide, I clear my throat in an attempt at gravitas. 'And also . . . What are all these women wearing?'

'I don't . . .' Flora trails off, pulling an imaginary zipper across her mouth.

'You're smashing it!' Zhané says, removing Leo's fingers from her nostril. 'Now go in for the kill!'

'Kill. Kill,' Leo echoes and I feel my insides turn all warm and mushy. He may be slobbery and obstructive, but with his mop of curly black hair, huge eyes and rosy brown cheeks, he's enough to melt the most cold-hearted of humans.

'Bring it home, Roma.' Zhané's eyes narrow like a leopard stalking its prey, and that's what I love about her – she's a straight-talking, cut-to-the-chase, get-on-with-it kind of a girl. No grey areas. No bullshit. I guess, since having Leo, there's precious little time for hesitation; life as a single working parent being one long string of decisions that need to be made under pressure and on the spot without agonising over making the wrong choice. Go in for the kill and move on.

Bolstered by the support of friends who have known me since school and ridden the highs and lows of my experimentation with fashion over the years – they should really have ditched me when I made the three of us salmon pink sixth form prom ball gowns with ruffle layered underskirts that caused considerable chafing – I conclude my speech, holding up an imaginary champagne glass and raising my voice over the repeated refrain of Grandpa Shark (doo-doo, doo-doo).

'Research says the Plus Size market is due to grow at a pace of 5 to 6 per cent each year and that is why I believe that my inclusive range is the future. As a passionate and dedicated employee of House of Dreams, I would therefore like to ask for your consideration of Curvaliscious as part of next year's catalogue. Not only would it mean a great deal to me personally to see my concepts become a reality within the fashion house I love working for, but it also makes great business sense. Curvaliscious: it's now or never!' I thump my fist down for effect, feeling like one of those alpha businesswomen on *Dragon's Den* minus the pile of banknotes and power lipstick, only for a scuffed yellow ball to catapult into my nose, my nostrils prickling with the onset of pain.

'What kind of investment?' Zhané untangles Leo's leg from the cargo net behind her. 'Don't be afraid to tell them exactly what you want, Roma. Remember, they need you, too. Symbiosis. Think of the sea anemone and the hermit crab.'

I wonder whether I've misheard. It's difficult to pick out words when an inflatable ghost woooohs every time someone enters our inflatable House of Horror.

'They must have taught you about the sea anemone and the hermit crab in biology?' Zhané goes on.

Flora's face looks as blank as mine does.

'We had a whole lesson on it in Year 7. You know, the hermit crab sticks its scavenged shell to a sea anemone and both it and the sea anemone live happily ever after. It's Romeo and Juliet for sea creatures, the hermit crab getting protection from the sea anemone's stinging tentacles and the sea anemone feeding off the titbits left behind by the crab.'

I'm still not sure exactly where she's coming from and now can't get the word *titbit* out of my brain, which is doing mental acrobatics, trying to decide whether it's 'tid' or 'tit'.

'Mutual benefit,' Zhané says with an air of exasperation. 'You need to walk away with a deal, and they need to walk away excited. After all, it's a collaboration.'

'Right.'

Leo sneezes, a thick trail of snot running down his face, which Zhané mops up with a wet wipe.

Thinking quickly, Flora rearranges her facial expression from one of unbridled disgust into that of a synchronised swimmer for Zhané's benefit and fiddles with her fringe, which is such a lovely icy blonde I question why I didn't go for something a little lighter than the dark cherry red I plumped for in the haircare aisle of Sainsbury's last night.

Scooping Leo up and attaching him to her hip, Zhané fixes me with a grin. 'You've got this, Roma. Plus Size or whatever, your clothes rock and so do you.'

Despite flinching at having the word 'Plus Size' played back to me (Doesn't it imply 'bigger than normal', which suggests that parameters have been set for what is and isn't an acceptable shape and size for a woman?), an involuntary smile spreads across my face at the thought of a lifelong ambition achieved, but before I can get too swept up in getting ahead of myself, the soft-play supervisor is announcing that time is up for everyone with a pink wristband.

Like Aphrodite rising from the sea (or Plus Size thirty-year-old on a heavy period, trying not to dislodge her moon cup), I emerge, with a warm glow of pride, from the House of Horrors ball pit and wade towards an exit just about big enough for an Oompa Loompa. I've got something special here and I can't let it slip between my fingers. I allow myself a private moment of reflection to enjoy the sense of satisfaction that comes with knowing I've produced an entire summer collection of Flora & Fauna designs with an assortment of price tags. Something for everyone. And I mean *everyone*, no matter their size.

From House of Horrors to House of Dreams. Move over Stella McCartney – Ramona Matthews means business.

CHAPTER TWO

The Horse

Dressing for a fashion pitch comes with its own pressures. Just as all decent hair stylists are expected to have an attention-grabbing, state-of-the-art cut and colour, it is inconceivable that a respectable costumier should be anything short of immaculately presented. A clothes horse for your own designs, you effectively need to flaunt your wares with an elegance and seduction befitting of an A-list celebrity, neither of which come easily with menstrual bloating and a bra that is losing its underwire.

I've been obsessing over what would make the biggest impact ever since I was invited to pitch two weeks, three days and five hours ago (not that I'm counting), deliberating between my macaw crêpe de Chine midi dress with ruffle trim and gathered hem – one of the five dresses included in my Fauna & Flora summer collection, or my peony print, lantern-sleeved cotton blouse coupled with tailored cream culottes. Conceding that the feathers of each macaw clash with my freshly dyed cherry red hair and that the peonies don't quite work either, I plump for a wrap dress I designed earlier this year – bold, green ferns on strong, cream canvas – cool, calm, collected and a little bit Indiana Jones meets Boden.

Checking myself out in the mirror and stepping into my beige suede stilettos (at five foot three you need every trick in the book to elongate the leg), I tie a matching fern-print silk scarf around my neck and supplement with yellow gold jewellery. What was it my teacher at textiles college used to say? *Let the clothes do the walking but the accessories the talking.*

'You look amazing!' Flora says, planting a mug of steaming hot coffee on my dresser and kissing me on the cheek. 'Good luck and let us know how you get on!'

With a swish of her silk scarf, she waltzes out of the room and heads out to oversee another day of online matchmaking, the loose glass panel clanking in the door as she clicks it shut – one of the many repairs our landlord has promised he'll get onto ASAP.

My phone jingles with an incoming message.

Fabrice

> Good luck, kitten! Look hot and make them eat it.

A smile plays on my lips. Fabrice is up there with Zhané and Flora as one of the most important people in my world. I may not have known him for quite as long, but it feels like forever, and I can't imagine life without him. Whilst the girls are my confidantes, Fabrice is my inspiration and I admire him like no other. They say you can count your inner circle on one hand, but for me, it's three fingers. Quality over quantity and all that. Not that I mix them a great deal, Zhané and Fabrice both citing each other as 'fine in small doses', so it tends to be either the girls or him solo.

Ramona

Is it normal that my sphincter is like a feeding baby bird on steroids?

Fabrice

Eugh! And please ask The Horse if he's hung like one.

Ramona

Eugh! back atcha!

Fabrice

Coming to my gig tonight, Vivienne? (Because watching Polly Darton try out her new material ahead of DragFest is JUST the sort of place a young thing like you will want to celebrate Curvalicious getting commissioned!)

A rush of warmth fills my core. Fabrice has called me Vivienne ever since we met at my student union bar where he performed as Britnerella and belted out 'Oh baby, baby' from a giant silver marshmallow and likened me to a younger Vivienne Westwood, God rest her soul, when backstage I offered to make him the turquoise, wing-shouldered air hostess outfit Britney wore in her *Toxic* video. Both making the costume and carrying the subsequent nickname have always been a privilege. And although Fabrice may be ten or twenty years my senior – with the amount of makeup he wears, it's difficult to tell and there's no way I'm asking – we seem to have an awful lot in common, especially when he performs as Polly Darton down at Pandora's Box drag bar on a Friday evening. As he frequently tells me, us big girls with big dreams have to look out for each other.

Ramona

Like I'd be anywhere else x

Half an hour later, I arrive at my workplace on the first floor at House of Dreams' back office in East London's Shoreditch, a converted warehouse which overlooks what's left of Spitalfields Market. A quick check of my Curvaliscious prototypes sees me spreading them lovingly across my cutting table one at a time as though they are sick children and I am the Florence Nightingale of textiles. Double- and triple-checking that everything is as it should be, I take a deep breath as the hands on the clock advance towards nine thirty. And exhale. Right, no time for procrastination. Or is there? Opening my laptop, I glance through my notes:

11

- The Rule of Thirds
- Body elongation
- Curve enhancement
- The importance of flesh-coloured heels

I shake out my fingers and try to stop the jackhammering of my heart. There's an awful lot to remember and The Horse is known for being a bit of an arsehole so I'm not expecting an easy ride, but I have prepared for this and cannot afford for nerves to get the better of me. Heading out of the building to the main head-quarters over the road with a clothes rail of outfits and a squirming stomach, I think of Fabrice, a warm glow infusing me: all I need to do is look hot and make them eat it, right? I smooth down my fern-print wrap dress and take a deep breath as I wait for the green man at the pedestrian crossing to appear. Then, dragging the rail down a side alley, I reach our state-of-the-art headquarters and gaze up at the construction looming over me – five seemingly precariously arranged floors balanced one on top of the other and jutting out at different angles to give the effect of an abandoned Jenga tower – and have the distinct sensation that the entire structure is going to collapse upon me, window by window.

Inside, I feel as though I'm an outsider, a stranger rather than an employee. My heels tap across the marble as I head across the expansive foyer to the main reception where three women – who look as if they've been cloned from the same person with their identical sleek, dark ponytails and a splash of scarlet lipstick – sit side by side between two displays of giant orchids twisted into eye-wateringly expensive arrangements. This place has never made me feel at ease and today is no different. Approaching the OTT marble counter, I give the underwire of my bra a surreptitious hoist, flatten my new cherry-red fringe against my forehead and take a deep breath.

'Hi,' I say, smiling at the nearest receptionist. 'I've got an appointment to see the – the . . .'

She looks at me in a way that suggests I've been lobotomised, pity and impatience battling it out on her forehead, but all I can think of is 'The Horse'. What *is* his proper name? 'Sorry, I've got an appointment to see the . . .' Horse. Horse. 'Aart The Horse.'

'Aart *ter* Horst, perhaps?' she perseveres.

'Absolutely.' I plaster a smile on my face, papering over the cracks of humiliation.

Mercifully, the tumbleweed moment is quickly broken when a tall woman with an isosceles triangle-shaped torso comes strutting towards me, slim arms dangling from square shoulders alongside a waist so tiny, its circumference is about the same size as my wrist.

'Ramona?' She runs her dark eyes over me with the apathy of someone who is merely tolerating life. 'This way, please.'

I follow her into the lift where we stand shoulder (mine) to waist (hers), in the two-person great glass elevator which rockets up to the fourth floor with a wobble and a whiz as my pitch freecycles around my head until we arrive with a bump, my heart somewhere in my mouth and sweat forming under my arms. I take a deep breath. The sooner I'm in, the sooner I'm out.

My isosceles friend leads me down a wide corridor I've never seen before, where huge black-and-white photographs of catwalk models sporting the latest fashion dominate the walls. Bold. Eye-catching. Intimidating. At the end of the corridor hangs a huge painting of Oscar de la Renta posing next to one of his sketches in a blue pinstriped suit and paisley cravat. I look into his oil eyes and feel hollow inside. An imposter. A fraud. I chew the inside of my cheek and give myself a talking-to as the wheels of my portable clothes rail squeak and judder. Vera Wang didn't become a fashion designer until she was forty and Christian Dior didn't make it until he was forty-one, I reason, so I mustn't allow myself to feel over-whelmed – after all, I have just as much right to be here as anyone else. Even so, my nerves jangle and tiny palpitations have started up in my chest.

I reach the meeting room, the door swinging open to release the scent of Levantine spice and sharp grapefruit, revealing no other than my archnemesis and fashion's greatest pain in the arse, Setayesh. I don't think I've had a single meeting at work where Setayesh and I haven't clashed over the cut of a kimono or a poncho print. Fabrice reckons she's dangerous and that I should avoid her at all costs, citing her as The Devil in Lycra ever since she belittled him at his own drag show by standing on stage in a skintight Lululemon catsuit pulling out his bra padding in front of a live audience – disrespect in the highest regard – and although he and I are on the same page, avoiding Setayesh is like avoiding getting wet in the shower: she's everywhere, pouting and pos-ing, pretending and posturing, in meeting rooms, corridors, the ladies toilets, and now here in front of me, her minuscule frame wrapped in what looks to be black patent cling film, showing off long bare legs that culminate in six-inch diamanté fuck-me shoes. Her slim, toned arms push a chrome clothes rail furnished with her Babes in the Woods summer collection; a small selection of teeny, tiny dresses designed for teeny, tiny women with the proportions of a Barbie doll.

She looks me up and down, the corner of her mouth curling up with an air of disgust as her eyes travel to my nude suede shoes. 'Oh, it's *you* in next, is it?'

My heart plummets and my mouth dries. I thought this was a one-woman race, my Fauna & Flora collection having piqued the interest of a number of influential big-hitters at House of Dreams who have helped to set up this pitch with The Horse. This was supposed to be a 'show him what you're made of and he is sure to commission your collection' meeting, not a competition. Just how many other people are in this race?

Setayesh turns back to the people in the meeting room. 'Thank you for having me.' Then swooshing her long mane of silky black hair over her shoulder, she looks back at me. 'I wondered who the other contender was.'

The back of my neck itches, my shoes start to feel unbearably small and I've somehow, all of a sudden, lost the ability to swallow. It's me against Setayesh?

'Come in!' The dulcet tones of the gruff Dutchman I know to be The Horse chime out.

Taking a deep breath, I sidestep Setayesh, flashing a fake smile (I do, after all, need to keep her on side as she's the one who has to sign off my timesheets) and try not to choke on the fumes of her perfume as I enter the boardroom. Reflected in the floor-to-ceiling mirror behind, The Horse sits at the end of a mahogany boardroom table, sipping an espresso from a small paper cup held by trembling hands like a jaded rock star – think

Rod Stewart at sixty. His leathery face is bronzed, the faint tan line of goggles around his eyes suggesting a weekend of glacier skiing – either that or he's been on the sunbed. An eruption of wiry white facial hair sprouts from his chin, elongating his face into that of . . . well, a horse.

Rising to his feet, he shows off an expensive white shirt and a thin black tie. As I advance towards him, I feel my eyes involuntarily travelling to his black suit trousers and lingering around his crotch – not because I want to gawp at his groin but because it's impossible not to, the cotton clinging so closely to his meat and two veg that they're almost propping them up on display as though they're his main feature. I think I can safely answer Fabrice's question.

'Good morning.' His voice is the sort of gravelly that comes from too much coffee and not enough sex. He reaches over to shake my clammy hand, pulling me into his chest to deliver a kiss to each of my cheeks and I realise I have forgotten how to breathe – not just because I'm being pressed against his promi-nent package (which I swear is all sock after all – sorry, Fabrice) and his breath carries a whiff of last night's alcohol, or because he's the rock star of fashion and the man to impress, but because of the enormity of the moment.

'Donatella Ricci is over from Milan.' The Horse gestures, twid-dling the gold signet ring on his pinkie with his thumb as his whole body spasms for a split second before regaining its original form.

'Ciao.' The immaculately dressed woman next to him stands to give me a firm handshake whilst making no attempt to con-ceal that she's looking me up and down. She wears thick-framed tortoiseshell glasses and a scarlet dress tapered to her waist with red lacquered nails and lipstick to boot; judging by the way she's glancing at the Armani watch on her wrist, she clearly doesn't suffer fools gladly.

'And our third member of the panel . . .' The Horse nods to a teenage boy dressed in a House of Dreams' dinner suit from last year's 007 collection, the twisted, misaligned collar more James May than James Bond, who shuffles from foot to foot as he waits his turn to greet me. 'This is Jens.'

'Hi,' he says with an eagerness in his eyes that reminds me of Flora's Jack Russell. He has a baby face, delicate features that look as though an artist may have painted them on as an afterthought and can't be any older than eighteen – the boy, not Flora's Jack Russell.

'My nephew's over from Amsterdam and I just thought, as he has an eye for fashion, that he'd make a good judge. Right, we'll give you five minutes to prepare.' The Horse goes on in that gravelly voice of his, plucking a filterless cigarette out of his jacket pocket and jabbing it at the huge plasma screen set up at the end of the room. 'That's for your storyboard.' Then, just when I think he's about to impart some meaningful words of wisdom, his facial muscles flinch and his whole body twitches like a puppet on a string that has been collapsed, his knees crumpling and his shoulders twisting only to be yanked back into action a moment later, and I am left slack-jawed, watching him walk out of the door as though nothing has happened.

Since the start of my employment three years ago at House of Dreams, I've heard loads of things about The Horse – how he's been a party animal for decades, how he's signed some of the biggest names in the industry over the years, how he likes champagne for breakfast and cocaine sprinkled on his cornflakes, but this is the most time I've spent in his presence and he's truly fascinating to watch. Still, mustn't get distracted.

Wheeling my clothes rail in from the corridor and glancing at the diminutive proportions of the three mannequins in the corner of the room, I wonder how this is going to work out. They were supposed to have arranged three Plus Size mannequins for me – Setayesh said it was all confirmed. Of course, had I known that Setayesh was competing with me, I would never have relied on her, though would she really stoop that low? Panic rises in my chest as I wander over to the wire-frame models, my stomach dropping further when I see just how small they really are.

'I think these ladies might need bigger bones if they're to wear Curvaliscious clothes.' I try to remain light and breezy but the waver in my voice betrays me.

To illustrate the point, I ease my watermelon cotton sundress off its hanger and lower it over the mesh frame, but it doesn't matter how many times I adjust the straps, the dress falls clean off in spite of its cinched waist.

'You could pin it?' The boy offers a shrug of the shoulders, sucking in his cheeks and running his fingers over the hem of the kaftan as he does so.

'I think that might defeat the whole purpose. This is a size-inclusive range and isn't supposed to fit snugly around . . .' I want to say 'around a skeleton' but think better of it. 'Around something like this.'

Donatella stands with her hands on her hips and shakes her head in frustration. 'We don't have another mannequin. It's these or nothing.'

My throat constricts, despair pooling in my gut. 'Unless . . .' I say, directing them out of the door with my eyes whilst undoing the top button of my dress. Desperate times call for desperate measures and all that.

Three minutes later, I am wearing the watermelon backless sundress and the sting of degradation that comes from having to take my own clothes off in an office boardroom, knowing that anyone could have walked in at any moment. Sweaty and shaky, I try to regain my inner calm but it's difficult to *'look hot, and make them eat it'* when you're all fingers, thumbs and jangling nerves.

'Come in!' I anchor the soles of my feet to the floor and tell myself I have every right to be here: Setayesh may be able to wear a bin bag and still look the epitome of goddess glamour, but her designs are not for everyone. I look at the Barbie-doll proportioned dress she has left at the back of the room and decide that they're hardly for *anyone*, but it does little to stop my guts from churning and, as the door opens and my interview panel resume their positions around the table, I burst into nervous hiccups. Not just dainty almost-not-there feminine hiccups, but violent, manly, body-tremor gulps which come out thick and fast and I can't for the life of me contain.

I inhale deeply, swallowing what has to be my last and final hiccup. 'Thank you so much for giving up your time today, *hicc*!' My shoulders jolt. 'Sorry, I've got a violent case of . . . *hicc*!' My whole body jerks.

'Il singhiozzo.' Donatella smirks, and I can't quite tell whether she's amused by the situation or stifling a laugh at my expense.

19

The Horse scratches at his beard and studies me as though I am a new species that he is unable to classify. Either that or he thinks I'm mimicking his body spasms. Oh Jesus. I redden at the thought.

'Take your time,' he says, extracting an apple from his pocket, polishing it against his thigh and biting into it like a hungry . . . well, horse.

'Hicc.'

'Hold your breath.' The Horse demonstrates by holding a leathery hand over his chest and inhaling sharply.

'Hicc.' I shudder.

'Drink the water,' Donatella says.

'Pull your knees up to your chest and lean forward,' Jens says, taking it upon himself to demonstrate the brace position you're supposed to adopt if your airplane crash lands, his leather chair spinning in a circle as he screws himself up into a human ball of gangly limbs.

'Maybe I should just go for it,' I say, feeling the red-hot rush of blood and self-loathing to my cheeks. 'Today, I would like to introduce you to Selina, Carmella and Lucia.' I gesture to the two dresses hanging on the rail and then to the third, which I am wearing. 'They are big people with big dreams. All of them enjoy fashion and want the latest and greatest in women's clothing – but do you know how many times Selina has been told to stick to black to camouflage her curves and slim down her body shape? Do you know how many times Carmella has gone to the shops and walked away with jewellery or a scarf, because there is nothing in her size? And do you know how badly Lucia wants that fern-print wrap dress she saw on the front cover of *Vogue* but will never own it because it isn't available in sizes larger than a size 18? These women are frustrated. They're bored. They have money to spend but they just can't spend it.'

Donatella clasps her fingers together and nods. 'Very good.'

'Where are these people?' The Horse peers around the room, all furrowed brow and showmanship.

Heat travels to my cheeks. 'I'm currently dressed as Selina, but am happy to change into the others if we've time. Sorry, it's just without the mannequins . . .'

He exhales with frustration. 'Continue.'

'Selina, Carmella and Lucia are happy in their own skin. They don't aspire to be a single-digit size. They enjoy life and want to wear glamorous jumpsuits and pretty dresses like everybody else. They don't want to camouflage their lumps and bumps, they want to—'

'Lumps and bumps?' Donatella's eyes narrow.

The Horse's nephew mimes an hourglass figure with his hands.

Buoyed by Donatella's affirming nod, I go on. 'They want to celebrate their curves.'

The Horse's brow crinkles with confusion. 'Are we celebrating or camouflaging?'

A nervous laugh escapes me. 'We're celebrating.'

'By camouflaging?'

'We're definitely not camouflaging.' My throat constricts as I desperately try to claw my way back to my storyboard which is rapidly fraying around the edges and starting to unravel entirely.

'What is this made of?' The Horse reaches to touch the edge of the culottes lying on the table in front of him.

'That is a cotton and polyester blend. Light enough for the summer and robust enough for spring,' I say, relieved that I can escape the shackles of my pitch.

The Horse interlaces his fingers and folds them back until his knuckles crack. 'When you say size-inclusive, what size are you looking to go up to?' he says.

'At least a 56 in European size – 28 in UK size. In petite and tall.'

A collective gasp fills the room, The Horse sharing a horror-stricken look with his nephew before turning to Donatella, who gives a shrug of the shoulders and reaches for a boiled sweet, her gold bracelet clanking against the glass bowl sitting on the centre of the table. 'I like the designs.' She glances at The Horse before returning her attention to me, handing me a gold-embossed business card. 'And I think Giovanni would like them, too.'

My heart swells with hope. Giovanni Columbo is the CEO at House of Dreams and you don't get higher up the chain than that. His word is final. Thank God for Donatella Ricci!

'Surely there's not much market for size 26?' The Horse says, tapping his expensive pen against his expensive notebook.

I press the soles of my feet into my shoes and dig deep. 'Size is a spectrum just as a rainbow is, and a rainbow doesn't stop at indigo, does it?'

'Very true!' Donatella grins.

Plastering a smile on my lips, I try to ignore the rush of desperation that whiplashes through my veins. 'My point is that there's a whole bunch of women out there who have nothing to wear and it is our motto at Curvaliscious that "Nobody should go undressed".'

'Nobody *is* going undressed.' The Horse lets out a sigh of exasperation and closes his leatherbound notebook with dramatic gusto.

Time slows as I watch my dreams slide away, my toes curling up inside my shoes and my brain departing my head to board some sort of out-of-body experience. With clammy palms, I reach for my glass of water, my head woozy with fifty million thoughts. It's time to ditch the pitch and speak from the heart.

'Squeezing yourself into clothes that are too small is not a good look and neither is it good for morale. I just want nice clothes that fit me. Not black tents or floaty smocks. I want to wear what's fashionable, what's fun. I want an invitation to the party. I want to feel sexy.'

I feel the tears welling up inside me as The Horse gets out of his seat, walks over to me and helps me out of mine whilst rubbing my back as though I am a faithful but overweight Labrador. He then places his hands on my shoulders and stands square on, his grey-blue eyes interlocking with mine. 'It's great that you feel so passionately about this, Ramona. Truly, it is. It's great that you want to make a difference for all the women in the world, but I need to be honest with you. The designs are a little too . . . big.'

My blood runs cold.

'And far too pedestrian for House of Dreams,' Jens adds for good measure.

Each word is a bullet through my heart.

The Horse blinks and twitches. 'You need to invest more time in seeing what's out there. Attend fashion shows. See the latest haute couture on the catwalks.'

'Don't feel like you've got to hold back,' I say, making eye contact with the carpet.

'Thank you,' The Horse says, irony lost. 'Because at the end of the day, this is House of Dreams. Not House of Nightmares, so I'm afraid it's a "no" from us.'

No? Did he just say no? A piercing ringing starts up in my left ear and my legs no longer feel stable enough to support my weight. As I scrabble around for my clothes rail and drag it over the carpet and out of the room, I fight to hold back the tide of tears that are on their way but it's no use, and by the time I'm out of the room and back in the corridor, I am full-on sobbing and shaking as I hobble towards the fire escape, tripping over the dresses in front of me.

The Girlz

Ramona

Completely bombed in front of The Horse. Total disaster. Need to rock in the foetal position and lick my wounds for a bit. Love you both xx

Flora

I'm sure it's not as bad as all that. Treat yourself to a new handbag and the world will be a better place xxx

Zhané

> Fuck The Horse. What does he know? I still see your name in lights, Roma. The universe isn't quite ready for you yet but give it a chance and it'll get there. Chin up and know that you are loved xxx

Through the blurry sting of tears, I read my texts, a discombobulated mess of distress, defeat and disappointment . . . and yet, at the same time, I thank my lucky stars that I've got friends who care.

Mum

> So come on then, Rambo. How did it go?

Now what the hell do I tell my parents?

CHAPTER THREE

Pandora's Box

Fabrice touches up his lipstick in the rear-view mirror and gives his Dolly Parton wig a pat and a primp. 'I'm on stage at seven so I'll have to get my foot down.' He turns the key in the ignition of his cartoonish mint-green Nissan Figaro, which looks more like an accessory than a mode of transport, and we make our way out of House of Dreams staff car park. 'You're going to have to start talking at some point, Vivienne.'

I close my eyes, reliving the horror of the pitch, the teenage boy ushering me out of the boardroom with a glass of water and a box of paper tissues, Setayesh loitering down the corridor, her eyes sparkling with delight upon hearing about my car-crash meeting, and her acrylic nails running over her well-defined collarbone in mock sympathy.

'Vivienne?' He slides the gearstick into first gear.

I look out of the window, my stomach hollow with defeat. 'How is it that Setayesh can look like some sort of action heroine tomb-raider goddess in a bin bag whilst I can wear a really nice jumpsuit and look as though you've just hired me to unblock the drains?'

'Is this really about Setayesh?' he says, tapping an errant silver-studded, pink-feathered lash against his eyelid with one hand and steering with the other. 'It's not decided yet, Vivienne. You never know. Signora what's-her-name might have just had the final say and didn't you say she was supportive?'

'It'll be The Horse who has final say and it's clear he's going to pick Setayesh's collection over mine so . . .' I watch as he plucks a dusky-pink bomb-shaped bottle out of the driver's door pocket and applies three short, sharp blasts of Agent Provocateur to his blond nylon locks. 'I just don't get how she always gets—'

Fabrice slams his hand against the steering wheel. 'Setayesh is like a fondant fancy. She looks highly desirable but beneath the sugar coating, she has no substance. All cherry. No cake.'

I turn to look at him and let out a laugh in spite of myself. Whatever would I do without Fabrice? Thank God I have a flamboyantly dressed, six-foot drag queen to keep me grounded. 'You know, I didn't even get to pitch. Not properly. I couldn't even showcase my designs because they didn't have a mannequin big enough. And meanwhile, bloody Setayesh . . .' I waft away the talcum powdery smell of Agent Provocateur that catches in my throat, wondering what it might feel like to be all cherry and no cake and deciding I might rather like it. 'I swear to God she never passed on the message about Plus Size mannequins.'

And before I know it, I'm rattling away, explaining in graphic detail what happened between the walls of the boardroom and thinking up gratifying ways of slagging off Setayesh. 'Honestly, she was practically wearing a tattered rubble sack and still had the sophistication of an A-list celebrity on a red carpet.'

'The bitch,' Fabrice concurs.

'The cow.'

'The Devil in Lycra!' He throws the perfume bottle onto the back seat and moulds the padding in his bra into two perfect lumps with one hand whilst the other remains firmly on the steering wheel. 'Now let's get you that pink gin.' He presses his foot against the accelerator with gusto and immediately has to brake, given the traffic through Islington.

A nervous bout of hiccups takes hold of me as we drive through Archway and shows no signs of abating by the time we've reached Highgate, each jolt a fresh wake-up call to the career purgatory I am now living in; the opportunity of a lifetime pissed up the wall.

The sky turns a dark charcoal grey and rain starts to hammer down, punishing the pavements, cars ploughing through puddles the size of ponds. God knows how I'm going to feel in the morning but pulling up outside the entrance to a grubby burlesque joint in the arse end of East Finchley, just around the corner from Fabrice's flat, I feel full of self-hatred, my stomach hollow with guilt.

'No time for moping,' Fabrice says, holding onto his wig as he cranes his neck to get out of the car, dropping his lipstick in the gutter and watching it sail towards the drain in a gulley of rainwater. 'Polly Darton does not entertain negativity.'

How is it that Fabrice is always totally together, be it as himself or Polly? Nothing ever fazes him. Nothing derails him. It's as if he lives life on a higher spiritual plane which has granted him immunity to all the worries of the world. Since I've known him, he has lost his mother, his partner and consequently his mind, but never has he lost his mojo.

Hauling myself out of the low seat of the car and rearranging my resting bitch face into something I hope looks effusively supportive, I pull up the collar of my jacket and follow Fabrice past an overturned dustbin and down a dark alley that stinks of urine. Shielding his blond curls with his jacket, he negotiates the back entrance, trampling through discarded chicken bones, cabbage leaves and used teabags. I follow, the gritty gunk of PG Tips spongy beneath the soles of my shoes, all the way round to the rear of the building where a dim light hangs over a set of concrete steps, PANDORA'S BOX lit up in hot pink neon. He scrambles up the stairs two at a time and opens the door. 'Come the fuck on then, slowcoach!'

Inside, the air is musty. It takes a moment for my eyes to adjust to the dark before I can make out an old wooden staircase and the entrance to the Ladies loo. We head down into the basement, the soles of my shoes sticking to each lager-coated stair as I flick rainwater out of my hair and dry my face on my sleeve.

'Hi, beautiful!' A tall drag queen with ebony skin and liquid green eyes greets Fabrice at the bottom of the stairs with a shot of vodka.

'This is my friend, Vivienne.' Fabrice inches me forward. 'Vivienne, this is Queen Bea. Propmaker and set designer extraordinaire by day, songstress by night.'

'Hi.' I shake Queen Bea's hand, awestruck at just how beautiful she is. 'My real name's Ramona.'

Fabrice gives Queen Bea's black velvet evening gown the once-over. 'You didn't go for the gold sequined number?'

'Couldn't fit in it.' Queen Bea sniffs. 'Only made for skinny bitches.'

'Still, looking gorgeous as ever.' He gives her shoulder pad an approving squeeze.

'Thanks.' Queen Bea puts one hand on her hip, accentuating her curves and flashing a broad set of aspirational dentistry.

Being thrust between two drop-dead gorgeous, enigmatic drag queens is like being the only one sober at a party. It's not just their exquisite beauty and intimidating femininity that make me feel drab and boring, but the confidence they exude – their personalities clever, bitchy and full of sass – everything a woman aspires to but worries about being either 'too little' or 'too much'.

Fabrice takes the shot glass from Queen Bea. 'Get her up dancing,' he says, brushing a nylon tendril out of his face with the back of his hand and gesturing at me. 'She needs cheering up.'

'I . . .' My words die in my throat. The remorse incurred from flunking a pitch and losing out on a major fashion deal does not incite the desire to dance, whoop or leap around a drag bar in joyful celebration.

Fabrice ushers me through to the bar. 'I'll be with you in two shakes of a fake breast.'

With its Wetherspoons' carpet, shadowy booths and defunct glitterball, Pandora's Box is everything an underground burlesque venue should be, the smell of spilt booze and stale sweat mingling to form a fragrance of guilty pleasure that oozes from its bricks and mortar. I run my fingers over the threadbare ruby-red velvet-lined walls and imagine bygone times when its décor was soft and plush, its visitors a mix of jazz enthusiasts and its profits at an all-time high. A dozen or so black-and-white photographs make up a hall of fame in a mismatched arrangement next to the entrance to the bar – actors, dancers, comedians, compères, burlesque performers – but it's the drag queens that catch my eye; loud, proud, beautiful women in all their finery. Glitter gowns. Fishnet stockings. Long and leggy. Chic and stylish. Flamboyant and fun. Even in monochrome, they look colourful.

I edge my way along the bar, eyeing the seating options with suspicion. I hate high stools. Every time I have to mount something taller than a chair, I'm reminded of the unsuspecting Indian elephant I was forced onto as part of a jungle trek in Thailand, my bikini bottoms sliding down every time the mahout tried to push me up, much to the amusement of my fellow travellers, the whole experience humiliating to the very core. Gingerly, I press my hands against the cold, metallic surface of the bar and heave myself up until I am at eye level with a rainbow of spirits lined up on the shelf behind. I really need something different right now. Something I wouldn't ordinarily choose. Something not *me*, because at the moment I don't want to be the slightest bit *me*. I plump for a Blue Curaçao vodka because it's blue, and that's how I'm feeling.

'Mona?'

I turn around to see Flora, closely followed by Zhané.

'Well, we couldn't leave you solo, could we!' Zhané shrugs, helping herself to a handful of peanuts set out on the bar.

The barman fixes us each a Blue Lagoon and directs us to a narrow booth Fabrice has had set aside. Three Blue Lagoons later, my friends are still at stalemate, Zhané suggesting I demand a reschedule of my pitch meeting as I couldn't deliver it properly without the mannequins whilst Flora concedes that I should let this one go. Eventually, we reach a compromise, agreeing that I should sleep on it and see how I feel in the morning. So deep are we in conversation, I don't notice the bar filling with people until the humdrum of chatter is so loud it's like being in the standing kop at a football match. I close my eyes, my imagination haunted by the thought of Setayesh splashed all over the billboards, modelling her summer collection, all pert buttocks and toned arms – *'It's amazing what Nightclub BodyPump can do for triceps, Ramona!'*

My phone jingles with the arrival of mail, and there it is: the inevitable letter of rejection.

From: Aart.terHorst@houseofdreams.com
Subject: Curvaliscious by Ramona – proposed designs

Hi Ramona,

Thank you for sharing designs from your Curvaliscious range with us. Our commissioning team was highly impressed with your set of prototypes and the fabric samples.

It is with a heavy heart, however, that we've decided that a Plus Size range will not align to our strategic vision of mass market growth and have therefore chosen to commission Setayesh Akhtar's Babes in the Woods summer collection. Whilst we strongly support body inclusivity and wholeheartedly support the idea of featuring Plus Sizes, we are, at the end of the day, a high-volume worldwide fashion house and our business model is built on profit margin potential. As much as we love your proposal, we feel it is a little niche for our brand.

We wish you the best of luck and please do keep in touch, should you have something a little more all-inclusive.

With warmest regards,
Aart ter Horst

Head of Commissioning
Global Fashion Design
House of Dreams

A little more inclusive? It feels as though I've been stabbed through the chest and am unable to breathe through perforated lungs. Blood drains from my face and an acidic taste forms in my mouth that won't go away even when I swallow. How can you be all about body inclusivity whilst claiming that a Plus Size range is too exclusive? And House of Dreams specialise in Haute Couture, which isn't and will never be mass market. What total bullshit. Fire burns inside my chest. Well, I tell you what: Aart ter Fucking Horst can bloody well stick it up his mainstream-sized arse.

'What's up?' Zhané detects my shift in mood.

I show them the email, despair and despondence vying for pole position in a race of emotions that are shooting through me – anger, disappointment, frustration, but overall an overwhelming sense of loss. This was my one shot at it.

'Too exclusive?' Flora frowns.

'Fuck,' Zhané concludes. 'Who's his boss?'

'His boss?' I peer into my cocktail. Does a man like The Horse even have a boss? 'I don't know. I mean, The Horse is the global head of fashion design commissioning, he's on every executive decision-making board I know of.'

'Give us your phone.' She holds her hand out in my direction.

'What do you want with my—'

'Everybody's got a boss. Even the guy at the top has to report to shareholders, especially in a place as big as House of Dreams.' She takes my handset, holds it up to my face to unlock the screen and starts scrolling. 'Here we go. Giovanni Columbo. Chief executive officer. Shit the bed, he's hot!' She waves my phone in front of my face, showing a monochrome photograph of our impeccably coiffed, immaculately styled CEO – the most senior person in the organisation and therefore entirely unapproachable.

I rub my head in the palm of my hand. 'He would never reply to someone like me!'

'Well, screw him then.' Zhané inflates her chest and spreads her fingers out across the table. 'There must be plenty of other fashion houses out there who would love your designs, Roma. What about Gucci? Or Pucci? Prada or Fendi? Versace? Armani?' She rakes her bottom lip with her top teeth and cocks her head to one side. 'How come they're all Italian?'

'Because Italians know how to dress,' Flora adds helpfully. 'I had an Italian boyfriend once and let me tell you, never did I have to march him to the shops and hint that he invest in something other than jeans and a T.'

34

I hold on to the edge of my seat. If only the room would stop spinning for a moment.

'Mona, you OK?' Flora strokes my arm.

'OK, here's what you do.' Zhané's face looms towards me. 'You make a list of all the major fashion houses in Italy. You identify the commissioning manager or whatever they're called and you phone each of them, telling them that you're in town and insisting on a face-to-face.'

'You realise they're all based in Milan?' I say, blowing bubbles into my Blue Lagoon through my straw, the coiled paper dissolving into mush in my mouth.

Zhané looks me straight in the eye and I immediately sober up a notch. 'You know there's this concept called air travel?' she says. 'You need to get on a plane, meet them in the flesh and show them that your clothing is not just a concept or digital design, but a living, breathing range of essential apparel every woman needs to feel good in.'

Essential apparel. Every woman needs. To feel good in. My head spins as I try to commit it all to memory.

'Roma?' Zhané shakes me. 'Are you even listening?'

My neck flushes with heat and I can hear my heartbeat in my ears. I'm just not sure I've got it in me to hotfoot it to Milan and demand meetings. I'm just not the ball-breaking type. When Zhané walks into a business meeting, she commands the room. I've seen her in action. Statement shoulder pads. Bold lipstick. Don't-fuck-with-me leather belt. A panther to my pussycat. If I could be more Zhané this might work, but I'm an introvert at heart and it'll just come across as odd. No, worse than that, desperate.

We order another round of drinks and watch as a one-woman whirlwind of sequins, glitter and nylon hair takes to the stage in a floor-length gown and the kind of platformed six-inch heels synonymous with strip joints. With a flick of the wrists and a toss of blonde curls, Fabrice's transformation is complete, and Polly Darton is now well and truly in the house.

'Ladies and Gentlemen, good evening! I'm Polly Darton, your hostess. Good to see you're all looking hot dot com dot org dot co dot UK tonight, because here in Pandora's Box we don't have room for ugly. No, here in Pandora's Box, we're all about making the most of what we've got—'

'Show us your tits!' A man in double denim heckles from the back.

Polly raises her chin and looks down her nose, a perfect, straight structure that has always contributed to her elegance, snarling as she drags the microphone stand across the stage. 'I think we've already got one tit too many in here without me getting mine out, sweetheart.'

Unflappable. Off the cuff. Amazing. I admire my friend like no other. She's the only person I know who has a fail-safe way of putting any douchebag back in his box. If only I could have channelled a bit of Polly in my pitch meeting today.

'One's bigger than the other!' Double denim strikes again.

Polly flashes a saccharin smile. 'Every girl's got wonky tits, sir. It's a fact of life. Have you never seen a lady in her birthday suit?'

Unfazed. Unsurprised. Unstoppable.

'So tonight's show is a set I've prepared for DragFest, which is being held in France this year. Has anyone here been to DragFest?' She swishes a blonde curl out of her face.

Flora springs up and whistles through her fingers.

'It's the best!' Polly effuses. 'I intend to get very dressed up and very drunk, and promise you all a round of drinks if I win!'

'Fancy a shag?' Double denim stands and jeers, beer sloshing down his sleeve.

Polly looks over to the bar staff. 'Can we get some crayons and a menu for this guy to colour in, please.'

'Come on,' he slurs.

'Seriously, sir.' She shields her eyes with a gloved hand. 'Your bus leaves in ten minutes, be under it.'

The crowd erupt into applause as the inimitable intro to Dolly Parton's '9 to 5' starts up in the background. Backs straighten, drinking pauses and the energy in the room shifts to a heightened buzz of whoops and claps as Polly Darton takes the microphone from the stand and launches into song, effortlessly customising her own lyrics, and firing them one at a time at Mr Double Denim like a musical rocket launcher, the room dissolving into laughter. The atmosphere is electric and yet the words are sliding over me like water and as the next two or three songs fly by, all I can think about is House of Dreams rejecting me and my curves. It almost feels personal, a volcano of rage bubbling inside me. How is it that you can feel ten feet tall one moment and nothing the next?

'Let's give a big round of applause to my bestie, Ramona!'

To my horror, the whole song has passed me by and everyone is staring at me and I can't quite catch up with what's happening as Flora ushers me out of our booth and towards the stage, my limbs somehow complying. And before I know it, there I am on stage, opening and shutting my mouth in front of everyone like a goldfish trapped in a very small tank.

Polly lowers her mouth to the microphone. 'Ramona here is a very talented fashion designer. She makes such gorgeous clothes that are available in sizes for bigger girls like me.' She turns to me, gazing through long, sweeping eyelashes. 'Come tell our audience about your clothes.'

I step backwards, crossing my arms back and forth fitfully in front of my chest, a cold sweat forming on my brow. I don't want to talk about this now or ever again and certainly not on stage in front of a bunch of strangers. All eyes are on me and I feel like I'm back in my primary school nativity play reprising the role of Innkeeper and have forgotten my lines. My stomach squirms. I run my tongue over my lips, the taste of citrus lingering in my mouth and suffer an out-of-body experience as Polly sticks the microphone in front of me, my hand somehow accepting it and lifting it towards my chin.

'One woman's jumpsuit splendour is another woman's jump-suit horror,' I slur into the mic as the room spins around me at a hundred miles an hour, the crowd swooshing and blurring into one mass of multi-coloured madness. 'We are all different shapes and one size does *not* fit all.'

'Too true!'

I go on, lifted by a few whoops of encouragement and a shed-load of alcohol. 'I work as a fashion designer and recently pitched size-inclusive apparel to a major fashion house. You know what they said? They said it was too exclusive. But I'll show them. I'll show them what they're missing out on when I get on that plane to Milan and show my designs to their competitors.'

Through blurred vision, I can just about make out Flora crossing and uncrossing her hands in front of her throat but why she's trying to do the macarena whilst I'm kicking ass up here is a mystery to me. Everyone else seems to be spellbound by my emboldening speech about . . . about . . . I can't for the life of me remember what it's about, but whatever it is it's going down a storm and I am 'on it like a car bonnet' etcetera, etcetera and . . . that's it . . . 'Curvaliscious is not dead yet,' I blurt out, all the while twerking next to Polly.

I never twerk.

I have never twerked in my life.

I am not a twerker and yet here I am twerking on stage as part of a drag act like my life depends on it.

'Pur-lease!' Polly eyes me with disdain. 'That is sooooo 2020.'

'No!' I slap at her wrists. 'Twerk-shaming is like slut-shaming, which is like body-shaming. They say they're body inclusive,' I slur into the microphone. 'But they're not really. They don't care. Nobody cares, really. Apart from me.' I stifle a sob. 'I care. And I'm going to make size-inclusive clothing a thing. I'm going to put it on the map. Just you watch!'

Tears are now sliding down my cheeks, but I am determined to see this through. Drawing my hand to my chest, I stare into the distance in what I hope looks like a prime-ministerial pledge from a down-to-earth do-gooder, channelling a blend of both Barrack and Michelle in what is both an uplifting and authentic address.

'I will fly to Milan and I will convince those major fashion houses that . . .' I try to remember Zhané's inspirational speech from earlier. What was it again? 'Curvaliscious is not just a living, breathing digital design.' No, that doesn't sound quite right. 'Everyone needs to feel good essentially. And it's essential. I mean the clothes, the clothes are essential. You have to try the culottes. Even *I* look good in the culottes, which you'd think would be the worst thing possible for someone of my shape but let me tell you . . . a hidden elasticated waistband can save the day.' I twang the material around my middle with gusto.

'Ladies and Gentlemen, put your hands together for my brave friend, the new Vivienne Westwood, Ramona Matthews!' Polly shunts me off stage with the back of her heavily bejewelled, silk-gloved hand and sends me staggering back towards my booth.

The introduction to 'Just Because I'm a Woman' starts up and, as I turn back to see Polly stepping up to the microphone for her next number, I resolve right there, in the alcohol-addled fug of Pandora's Box, that I *will* fly to Milan and demand that Curvaliscious gets taken seriously. I will step up, step out, an Obama amalgam of gentle but firm persuasion and win the battle. Of course, I will.

So why am I crying into my drink?

The next day, my head is a collision of thoughts, all of them painful and none of them removable by Ibuprofen. I wake to the smell of my own stale breath and a lavender fabric softener I associate with my grandma but is actually Fabrice's. I smile, which makes my face hurt. Febreze, they apparently used to call him at the last place he worked. And whilst I love the smell of lavender, I do not love it in this context.

'Morning, Sleepyhead.' Fabrice nudges the door open with two mugs of steaming hot tea and places them on the bedside table. Rolling up the sleeves of his sweatshirt, he opens the window, a blast of cold air whipping through the curtains and blowing the two paracetamol capsules he has lined up next to me onto the carpet.

'Did I really say I was going to take Curvaliscious to Milan?' I groan, pulling the bedcovers over my head.

'And you twerked.' He relishes in reminding me.

'Nooooo.' I massage my temples with my index fingers. Everything hurts. And then flashbacks of last night start coming to me in tiny fragments. The failed pitch. The rejection letter from The Horse. His comment about size-inclusive clothing being too exclusive. A fresh wave of anger rips through me. Getting up on stage. Twerking. Oh God, did I really twerk? And then some very patchy memories of Zhané and I hunched over my phone looking at flights. Wasn't I going to track down any commissioning agent attending the world's most prestigious haute couture fashion show, la Gala di Milano? Wasn't I going to build a spreadsheet? Wasn't I going to put together a pitch package and demand time with them all? Oh God. I clutch my head in disbelief. I can't even order a coffee in Italian, let alone pitch a range of size-inclusive apparel.

'They wouldn't let you in a cab so your friends helped me carry you back here.'

'*Carry?*' I wince, my head pounding.

Handing me a mug of tea, he perches on the edge of the bed, his back straight, shoulder blades symmetrical and hips perfectly aligned with his knees – a posture I have always envied. 'Isn't it about time you got the conversation with your parents out of the way before you start thinking about Milan?'

'What conversation?' I frown – also painful – my fingers finding an earring embedded in my hair.

'They want to know how the pitch went yesterday. Your phone has been flashing like billy-o.'

41

I gather up my phone and see a whole bunch of texts stacked up in preview mode, asking how the pitch went and whether it's too early to crack open the champagne. My heart drops like a stone and all I want to do is hide under the duvet and fall asleep until it's dark again, but to my horror, Fabrice only goes and selects my mum's name from my list of FaceTime favourites. 'Time to rip off the Band-Aid!'

A crackle, a bleep and I'm through. I wipe the dried spittle off my chin and comb my fingers through my hair in a bid to look presentable, my scalp aching with hypersensitivity.

'Hi Mum.' Wind whistles in my ears and it takes me a couple of seconds to realise that this is not the effect of hangover-induced tinnitus but the sound coming out of my phone.

'Can you hear me?' Mum shouts over the whoosh and swish of a gale, her hair plastered across her face and her waterproof jacket flapping violently. Behind her, purple heather as far as the eye can see blows this way and that. 'We've come all this way to Brinkley Edge, but we'll not be able to fly anytime soon, the wind being what it is,' she says between short gasps.

My parents have been obsessed with paragliding ever since they settled in Harrogate before I was born, and spend most weekends up on the moors, either waiting for enough of a light breeze to inflate the wing of the sail or killing time whilst a gale-force wind gradually subsides, and then when they do eventually chance upon ideal weather conditions, it's all over in a matter of minutes. A quick sled run from the top of the edge down to the fields below. I've never understood it.

'That's a shame,' I say, trying to mask my apathy. 'So I didn't get through. They didn't sign my collection.'

There. I've said it. Short. Sharp. Painless.

'Sorry?'

Maybe not that short. Not that sharp. And not that painless.

I take a deep breath. 'The pitch went badly and they gave it to someone else.'

'I'm not getting a word you're saying. Let me turn downwind.'

The image on my screen becomes a close-up of Mum's nostril before tilting this way and that to show a few members of the Mile High club sheltering in a narrow gulley between two huge gritstone boulders and then Mum comes back into the frame, her eyes streaming with wind-induced tears and her hair a tornado of salt-and-pepper flecked strands.

'The Horse wasn't that impressed.'

'They were or they weren't impressed?' she says, sticking her finger in her ear.

'They weren't!' I scream, my head now banging with pain.

She shoots me a look of confusion.

I reach for the tea Fabrice has brought me. 'They gave it to someone else.'

'Alan?' My mum hollers, her hand now over the camera. 'Ramona's on the phone!'

I hide my head beneath the pillow as the sound of Dad's heavy breathing starts up.

'Congratulations, love. That's brilliant news. We'll have to—'

'They said no, Dad.'

A beat.

'Sorry, love, the line's not great.'

'They said no.'

'Let me put you back on to your mother.'

'THEY SAID NO!' I scream, Fabrice's eyebrows shooting up as he scuttles out of the room.

Mum's face crumples. 'Hang on, love. They said no?'

'Yes!' I scream with infuriation.

'They said yes?'

'No! He said no.'

'Why?' She looks at me with incredulity.

'That's the thing, Mum.' My throat tightens. 'He thinks size-inclusive clothing is too exclusive.'

She wipes a tear from her eye with the sleeve of her jacket. 'Exclusive?'

'Because most people conform to the size 8 to size 16 bracket.' I tremble with rage. It doesn't matter how much thought I put into defining this collection. It doesn't matter what fabrics, colour schemes, textures and finishing techniques I choose. It doesn't matter what any of it looks like; it's just all about size. Size. That's the size of it.

'Your dad and I will be home in an hour or two. It's the weekend. Get on the train and come and stay the night. I'll make your favourite cauliflower cheese and you can sleep in your old bed.'

Thank God for Mum. She's always known how to cheer me up. Consolation hugs after sports day defeats. Volunteering to help on school trips I've hated just to cushion the blow. Serving up the most mouth-tinglingly creamy cauliflower cheese in the world that comforts, nourishes and nurtures. When the chips are down, I can always count on Mum.

And just like that, I am on my way to London King's Cross station with a marshmallow heart and a train ticket to Harrogate, wishing that my nerves would calm the fuck down. Only it turns out I'm not actually going to King's Cross after all and have autopiloted to work, getting off the bus at Shoreditch and tramping towards House of Dreams like I do every weekday. Gaaah. I glance at my watch. Luckily, I've still got plenty of time, so I may as well pop into the office, grab the jungle-print wrap jacket I really want to show Mum and then hotfoot it over to King's Cross.

The offices are always deserted on the weekend, those who choose to work extra hours generally preferring to craft from the comfort of their home, so it strikes me as odd that the lights are on and I can hear noises coming from The Horse's office. Wandering past three mannequins dressed in silk kimonos, I trudge through the open-plan shop floor, advancing towards the glass compartment The Horse has put his stamp on by means of a giant cactus, an abstract Picasso and a coat of Farrow & Ball kingfisher blue emulsion on the back wall, only to stop dead in my tracks. For there, draped over his desk, wearing nothing but the black tie he wore yesterday, lies Setayesh, legs akimbo, her long mane of black hair flowing over his paperwork, The Horse going at her hell for leather as though she's a piece of meat, his buttocks clenching and unclenching with each thrust. A house-plant tumbles to the ground, soil spoiling the carpet under his swivel chair, but still he goes on, eyes closed, face beetroot red, sweat dripping from his temples, shirt undone, trousers around his ankles as Setayesh is pushed back and forth across his table like a human windscreen wiper. And just like that, I know exactly why she has had her range of tiny clothes commissioned.

Slowly I transfer my weight to my back foot and tiptoe away, hoping that neither of them saw me. Then, crawling across the floor, I make a grab for the wrap jacket which hangs off one shoulder of the mannequin standing next to my sewing desk and once it's tucked beneath my arm I bolt out of the office as fast as I can.

Outside, I lean against the side of the building and catch my breath, my heart pounding. Really? Setayesh and The Horse? Eugh! I mean she's spectacularly vile, but she still could do better than him. However, that would explain . . . wait, she's shagging her way to her own clothing range? Wow, I never stood a chance. Although . . . fuck, she must be twenty years younger than him. Does that constitute being taken advantage of?

'Oh yes! Oh yes!' I hear her scream out of the window in what can only be faking it.

A whirl of emotions spin around inside me. Anger. Betrayal. Disgust. But the one that sticks is pity. How low must her self-esteem be to prostitute herself to The Horse? Then again, maybe they deserve each other. The Horse and The Devil in Lycra – it's got a certain ring to it.

And with a head full of images I wish I could unsee, this time I trudge along the pavements of Shoreditch in the direction of King's Cross station.

I glance around my parents' living room – a room in which I have spent the best part of two decades draped across the sofa watching everything from *Neighbours* to *RuPaul's Drag Race* – a sofa on which I have recovered from illnesses and tooth extractions, drunk the contents of my parents' drinks cabinet, been told my parents were getting a divorce and three years later subsequently told they were getting back together, and a sofa on which I have never felt so bad. I stare at the carpet, plucking bobbles of wool from the worn cushions and flicking them on the floor, my mum eyeing the small bits of fluff on her taupe shagpile as though they are naughty children that need to be dealt with later.

'They're fools.' Dad stretches his legs out onto the coffee table and rummages through the biscuit barrel for something chocolate-coated.

Mum rubs my knee in solidarity. 'At least you gave it your all, love.'

'Yes,' I say weakly, wondering whether I should divulge what I have since learned about Setayesh and The Horse and speculating over the language I would use to convey the act of shagging in the office to my parents. Doing the wild thing? Performing the horizontal cha-cha? Hiding the sausage? Bonking? Banging? Screwing? Or do I go full-out Bill Clinton and call it sexual relations? But before I can find the words, Mum is up out of her seat and delving through piles of recycled wrapping paper in the wooden bureau in the corner of the room.

'I've been thinking. Now might be the time to give you this.' She holds up a small box. 'It was your grandma's, and the idea was for you to have it on your wedding day – something old, something blue – but I'm sure she'd have agreed that it's probably best you have it now, what with you not being the marrying type.'

Not the marrying type? Is that even a thing? I mean, isn't marriage all about finding the right person, no matter how long it takes, rather than eligibility having some unspoken expiry date you're only made aware of once you've hit it? My head spins. Is this Mum's way of consoling me after my failed pitch? Picking me up, dusting me off and building me back up again with a family keepsake? Man, I love my parents, but shouldn't they be showering me with words of encouragement and life-affirming refrains like 'you can still do it,' rather than hijacking my all-time low and layering it with further perceived failings? Because that's what it feels like. Hapless Ramona. Hopeless Ramona. Let's give her a conciliatory prize to tide her over.

'Aren't you going to open it then?' Mum stands over me, beaming from ear to ear.

'Is this supposed to cheer me up?' I say sniffily.

Dad shoots me a stern look over his reading glasses. 'Don't be so rude to your mother!'

My cheeks flush with shame. Maybe I am being a spoilt cow after all. Slowly, I lift the lid. And there it is, a blue Wedgwood pendant featuring a plump white cupid with a bow and arrow set in a simple sterling silver circle. I recognise it immediately as the necklace my grandma – Dad's mum – wore to every celebration for as long as I can remember. Christenings. Birthdays. Weddings. Funerals. She'd always wear her Wedgwood.

'Aw, I remember this.' I run my finger over the porcelain cherub, swallowing the bittersweet taste of sentimentality and spinsterhood.

'She would've wanted you to be happy,' Dad says in a way that suggests I am not at all happy, which I guess right now, this second, is fair to say but is way off the mark in the grand scheme of things. Generally speaking, I'm perfectly happy. I have good friends, a good social life, a fulfilling career (well, nearly) and I don't need a boyfriend, fiancé or husband to make me feel complete, so why is my nose prickling with emotion? I don't know whether it's losing to Setayesh, having my relationship status officially acknowledged as spinster or the rush of pride that I feel knowing how much that pendant meant to my grandma, but a lump has formed in my throat and I've lost the ability to speak. The pendant is beautiful. Solid and intricate. Mum fastens it around my neck and the cold touch of the stone against my skin feels reassuring, in the same way as my grandma's home was a comfort to me, providing me with an outlet for knitting, sewing and all things handicraft, and I vow never to take it off.

'There you go!' Mum sits back down to admire the necklace from the comfort of the sofa. 'Suits you.'

'He's sleeping with the girl whose work he commissioned.' I blurt out at the carpet.

Mum straightens her back, runs her hands over her thighs and lets out a steady stream of breath through her nostrils as though preparing for a tough yoga pose, all without looking at me.

'He what?' Dad spits bourbon crumbs out of his mouth in horror.

Mum shakes her head furiously. 'That doesn't sound right, Ramona.'

'I know! I . . .'

She fixes me with the same look she gave my music teacher when he suggested that I wasn't gifted enough for the school choir. 'You know I got told the other day that I need three teeth taken out and an operation on my jaw.'

'Really?' I say, wondering what her dentistry has to do with Setayesh and The Horse doing the wild thing.

'I'm not going to have any of it done though!'

I hold her gaze, still unsure where she's going with all this.

'Your dad persuaded me to go to another dentist and seek a second opinion. And this second chap told me that I needed no such thing.'

'Riiiight.'

'Well, shouldn't you do the same?' She snatches the biscuit barrel from Dad and attaches the lid with unnecessary rigour.

I stare at her for a moment. 'What do you mean?'

'The Horse said no, but he was biased – not financially, as it turns out my dentist was, but emotionally. You need a second opinion. Someone else might say yes?'

'It doesn't really work like that with fashion, Mum. It was a panel interview. Three of them. I mean, The Horse's word would have been final, but he wasn't alone.' And yet, as the words are leaving my lips, I'm reminded of Donatella Ricci and her insistence that Giovanni would love my designs. Wasn't she over from Milan for a short stay before the Gala opens next week? Didn't she give me her business card? I spring out of my seat, an idea taking form.

'Where are you going?' Mum says as I walk out of the room.

I find Donatella's card in my jacket pocket. On one side it has her details in gold calligraphy and on the other is the logo of the Gala di Milano with this year's dates stamped beneath it. 10 Giugno – 14 Giugno – Hang on, isn't it 10th June on Monday?

'What are you doing?' Mum calls after me.

Gathering up my phone, I log onto the intranet at work and look up Donatella Ricci in the global directory and there she is, reporting to none other than our clean-cut, suited-and-booted CEO, Giovanni Columbo. A few more clicks through news stories and up-and-coming events, and I'm staring at a black-and-white image of a model wearing what looks to be one giant tulip flowering at her torso, advertising this year's Gala di Milano which, according to the intranet 'will be a bigger and brighter affair than ever this year' with Giovanni himself opening the event and Donatella listed as a creative director. The pair of them together at the same event? Surely that's an omen. Didn't The Horse say I needed to invest more time in seeing what's out there? Attend fashion shows? See the latest haute couture on the catwalks?

My pulse quickens, a frisson of excitement bubbling under my skin. I wouldn't even need to chase down any commissioning agents individually if they'll all be at the gala. If only I could . . .

I log into Skyscanner and see that there's a flight leaving Heathrow tomorrow which would get me in to Milan early evening. Opening Booking.com, it doesn't take too long to locate a small hotel just outside the fashion district within my price bracket from which I can easily walk to the Gala di Milano. Bingo, a plan is coming together! Goosebumps spring up all over my arms and a bolt of adrenaline shoots right through me. Isn't it time I was more Zhané? My stomach fizzes. She'd be so proud of me. Though I'd better get a move on if I'm to pack all the pieces I need, along with their accessories.

'Ramona?' Mum calls through from the kitchen.

'I'm afraid I can't stay the night,' I say, sticking my head around the door. 'Thanks for the necklace! And the thing about a second opinion! I'll text you when I land in Milan.'

'Milan? But what about your job?' Mum stands at Dad's side looking dazed and confused.

'It's a work trip. Kind of.' I slip on my coat and am halfway out of the door by the time they catch up, Dad asking if I want to take my old diaries he has gathered from the attic and Mum shouting something about me not forgetting to make Auntie Sue's outfit for an impending christening.

Running my fingers over my grandma's pendant, I feel a surge of strength – Grandma Matthews was certainly a force of nature and wouldn't have accepted anything less of me.

It's time for a trip to Milan.

CHAPTER FOUR

Raffa

The Girlz

Ramona

I think I might just be that sea anemone on my way to find my hermit crab 🦀🐚🌷

Flora

😴 Are you still drunk?

Ramona

Remember Giovanni Columbo, House of Dreams CEO that @Zhané thought was hot? I'm on my way to Milan to show him my work.

Zhané

Go, Roma!! Only as you're the one travelling, you're the hermit crab 🦀

Flora

Am I missing something?

Zhané

I need every last detail on Milan so I can live vicariously through you! Insta the hell out of it. But promise me you won't go full-on Setayesh with the CEO? Remember: 🚫🙈🚪

Flora

Can someone explain that last message?

Zhané

Keep up, Flor! Don't shit on your own doorstep. Gotta shoot to drop Leo at nursery. Good luck, Roma!!

Flora

Safe flight and wish me luck tonight – I've got a date with eyebrow boy.

Ramona

Eyebrow boy?

Flora

He was a 98 per cent cohabiting match, 95
per cent coparenting match. It hardly gets
better than that!

Zhané

Not the one who told you on your first date
that he donated his little toes to science?

Flora

Everyone has to compromise . . .

Four hours later and all passengers have boarded flight AZ249
to Milan Malpensa, the doors are closed, seat-belt signs illuminated, cabin crew at the ready for take-off and yet our plane has
been sitting on the tarmac of London Heathrow airport for a
good half hour now. Judging by the shuffling of bags and clicking of abandoned seat belts, passengers are getting pretty restless,
fingers pointing out of the windows to an engineer who appears
to be making his way towards one of the engines of our aircraft.
Reassuring. Not.

In an attempt to distract myself, I bury my head in the pages
of the brilliant Juliet Uzor's latest sewing book – she didn't win

The Great British Sewing Bee for nothing – and am trying to wrap my head around the idea of upcycling a vintage dressing gown into a party dress (the colours and cut are magnificent), but it's difficult to concentrate with such a distractingly handsome man occupying the seat next to me. It isn't just the cut of his suit against his athletic physique or his striking amber eyes and smooth olive skin that have caught my attention, but something else, too. An aroma of cedar and sandalwood is playing havoc with my pheromones and I can't for the life of me suppress the urge to sneak looks at his preposterously muscular thighs which are stirring up all sorts of feelings, none of which are cerebral, my stomach tightening and skin tingling with every micro move-ment he makes.

'Bloody Alitalia,' he says out of nowhere.

I freeze. I had him down as Italian but he has a definite antipo-dean twang to his accent. And is he talking to me? Or is he talking to the guy on the other side of him? Or maybe he's just talking to himself. Either way, shouldn't I say something? But what?

'Yeah.' I manage, too little too late for it to be interpreted as anything other than a half-hearted afterthought. For fuck's sake, what's the matter with me? Then just as I'm berating myself for being verbally constipated, one of his earbuds falls out, bounc-ing off his thigh (not that I'm still looking at them) and rolling between my feet.

He shuffles his foot this way and that. 'Sorry, do you mind if I . . .'

'Sure,' I say too quickly.

And just as I'm reaching down for it, so is he, my senses height-ening as the high notes of his aftershave tease my nostrils and the back of his hand brushes against my ankle, a delicious shudder running down my spine. Were it not for my unshaven legs and the blob of chewing gum balled in my fist, this could be considered a romantic meet-cute but rather than a coming together of fingers and a meeting of eyes, it's a messy, scrappy affair where his earbud rolls into the chair leg where someone else has only gone and stuck *their* discarded chewing gum, him recoiling in disgust and frowning as though it was me that planted it there. A rush of heat travels to my face and I don't need a mirror to know that my neck and shoulders have gone a red and blotchy shade of humiliation.

'Are you travelling for business or pleasure?' I blurt in a desperate attempt to restore normality, aware that my cheeks must be glowing with a lurid pink phosphorescence difficult to ignore. *Travelling for business or pleasure!* Could I really not have come up with anything better? What a dick.

'Neither.' His voice definitely has an Australian lilt to it.

'Oh, I . . .' My eyes flicker over his thighs.

'I'm travelling for a funeral.' He dusts his earbud against the lapel of his jacket and pops it into a plastic case. 'My grandmother's.'

'I'm sorry, I . . .' Now I feel like a super-dick.

'How about you?' His question is tinged with obligation and I wish I could retract this whole back and forth which is putting neither of us at ease.

'Business,' I say, my appetite for small talk somewhat depleted knowing that I've pushed goodwill to the absolute limit by jetting off to the Gala di Milano for a two-day work trip and thanking my lucky stars that Chinara, my line manager, was so accommodating with my last-minute request to bolt on three days of annual leave. It's nice that she feels disappointed and cheated on my behalf and will do anything to cushion the blow of losing out to Setayesh.

He casts me a fleeting glance. 'No disrespect, but you don't look like a businesswoman.' His vowels may be sprawling but his consonants are nearly as strong and well-defined as his thighs and each time he applies the Australian question inflection to the end of each sentence, I have the sensation of my insides turning to warm treacle. It's only when I take a moment to swallow my feelings, pushing them down into the pit of my stomach and hoping that they won't resurface, that I question whether his comment was an insult or a compliment. Scratching around the recesses of my brain for an appropriate response, I eventually settle on, 'You don't need to dress like a businesswoman to do business.'

'Touché!' He bursts into laughter, his amber eyes shining with delight and sending my stomach squirming with desire. 'What line of work are you in?'

'Fashion.' My chest tightens as soon as the word leaves my mouth. Coming out here to meet Giovanni Columbo felt like the right thing to do from the safe sanctuary of my mum and dad's house where the comfort of chocolate bourbons and hot tea took the edges off any hurdle life might throw my way, but now it seems foolish. Amateur. Uncomfortable. Disrespectful, even. Is it not a little arrogant to rock up at a fashion shoot, ambush the CEO and insist on a second chance? 'I'm sorry about your grandmother.'

'She was ninety-three.' He runs his hands up and down his thighs with resignation and reaches into his bag for a packet of Polos. 'She made hats until her eyes failed her at ninety.'

'She was a hatmaker?' I say, interest piqued.

'The Milliner of Milan.' He nods proudly.

'The Milliner of Milan.' I repeat, mesmerised.

'Mariela Marino. You may have heard of her?' he says, rolling back the sweet wrapper and offering me a mint.

'Sure. Yes. Of course.' I have never heard the name in my life but she obviously means something to a lot of people including her hot grandson, and I don't want to burst his bubble with my ignorance. And besides, what credible clothes designer wouldn't know of the Milliner of Milan? Mariela Marino. It has the ring of a superhero, rolling off the tongue like melted chocolate. Mariela Marino. Erudite. Luxurious. Beautiful. 'Amazing.' I add, realising that I am genuinely absorbed in conversation rather than making small talk for the lust-fuelled sake of it.

'Then you'll have heard of La Casa dei Cappelli?' he says, wrapping his tongue around Italian words with an effortlessness that suggests he's bilingual.

'No.' I study his face, trying to work out whether he's talking about a famous landmark or a pizza restaurant.

'La Casa dei Cappelli. The house of hats. It's quite famous. My grandma has most of her collection there.'

Images of row upon row of bespoke headpieces in all their finery fill my mind's eye, a smile creeping across my face at the thought of such a heavenly sanctuary of creativity and craft. 'Whereabouts in Italy is it?'

'Tuscany.' He lowers his voice until it hits a deep and husky tone synonymous with aftershave commercials and for a moment I wonder whether he's going to append, 'Pour homme.'

My skin tingles, my stomach fizzes and I swear my temperature has soared a few degrees and is still rising. 'I'll look it up,' I say, fanning myself with my laminated emergency landing card.

'It's in a small village called Altaterra – high ground – and it really is. The village is perched right on the top of a hill overlooking miles and miles of countryside. The sort of place you go to get away from it all. You should pay it a visit whilst you're over, especially if you're into fashion.'

'Yeah?' My voice comes out as a squeak.

He scratches at the stubble on his jaw and holds my gaze. 'Yeah. People come for miles to see my grandma's village.'

'I'll make sure I check it out,' I say, hoping that I'm coming across as casual.

'You should, definitely.' His eyes remain faithful to mine.

'Truth be told, I don't know Italy all that well,' I say, wishing I could be a bit more *Eat Pray Love*, when it comes round to travelling, taking time to discover the nuances of a country and its culture, adventuring beyond the confines of a city guide map and exploring the minutiae of a place. Who knows, I could even go full hog and research indigenous resources and go on to make sustainable clothes out of dried pineapple skin and olive pits. Or maybe that's a step too far. The seat-belt sign extinguishes, my daydream along with it.

'Looks like we're going to be stuck here a while.' My hot neighbour shoots his breath up at the overhead lockers.

'I'm Ramona,' I say, desperate to keep the conversation going and wondering whether I should accompany the words with a handshake but decide that my palms are way too sweaty and I still haven't found anywhere to stick my chewing gum.

His face lights up. 'Like the American novel?'

'Sorry?' I feel caught off guard. Usually, when my name gets a mention, it's met with the tuneless hum of a Ramones song.

'The 1884 novel written by Helen Hunt Jackson. You know, the one about the orphan who suffers at the hands of racism?'

A feeling of warmth permeates my every fibre, spreading from my stomach and extending through my limbs until it feels as though my whole body is aglow – it's impressive that anyone my age would know of my fictitious namesake, let alone remember the publication date and author, and yet here is a man who rolls it out like it's nothing. Intelligent. Cultured. And smoking hot to boot. Surely, this isn't just lust.

His smile broadens. 'Sometimes us Aussie-Italians aren't as uncouth as we look, eh? I think they made the novel into a play. Have you seen it?'

'No,' I say, feeling like a cultural heathen. 'I didn't even know it *was* a play.'

'I'm Raffa,' he says, bristling with impatience as people start to get out of their seats and luggage starts to fall out everywhere.

'Like the tennis player?' The words have left my lips before I can think them through.

'Ha, yeah. I get that all the time. Either the tennis player or the ninja turtle, but rarely the Italian renaissance painter and architect.'

And it strikes me that I have just done to him what everyone else does to me and have effectively just hummed a Ramones song back in his face. My skin prickles. 'Sorry. I . . . Is it short for Raphael?'

'Raffa to my friends. Raffaele if I want to sound cultured.'

My stomach liquefies at the Italian pronunciation of his name. 'Pleased to meet you.'

And although it's nice to learn of his name, the formal introduction seems to have been the kiss of death to our exchange, both of us stuck for conversation and the atmosphere in the cabin changing from a thrum of impatience to a hum of resigned chatter, everyone desperate for take-off.

We must have been parked up on the airport tarmac for the best part of an hour by now, but time has somehow chosen to run at triple speed and although I would ordinarily be feeling like a frustrated caged animal, I'd be lying if I said I wasn't enjoying the delay, now that conversation with Raffa has resumed. We've covered a lot of ground, Raffa and I. Everything from Michelangelo to Michael Jackson, swimming to rugby, the price of houses in Italy compared to the UK, the economy, the ever-changing government, the virtues of Limoncello – great for digestion and flushing out the liver – the taste of tea, the texture of leather – I've had more deep and meaningful conversation with a complete stranger than I've collectively had with my friends over the last month.

Eventually, the cabin crew get the all-clear and we are jetting through the air towards Milan. Raffa has fallen asleep in his spectral crime novel, *The Dying Squad*, which, judging by the cover looks as dark and mysterious as he is and I am left to my own thoughts, which ricochet between Setayesh gloating at my defeat, her saccharin smile glittering outside the meeting room and her butt naked body draped across The Horse's desk.

'Sorry, could I just trouble you to . . .' Raffa shuffles to the front of his seat and gestures to the overhead luggage compartment.

'Oh, sure,' I say, realising that I'm boxing him in to his seat. I get up just as the dude on the other side of the aisle gets up and I find myself stuck in some sort of half-upright, half-crouched position – a kind of crane-kick stance, had the Karate Kid been highly inflexible, overweight and prone to arthritis. My knees creak and I pray that Raffa doesn't hear, my mind running over-time and deciding that what is probably even more embarrassing is the camel toe that I am no doubt displaying, the creases of my cotton trousers embedded in my crotch.

Eventually the man moves along and I am able to manoeuvre myself into the aisle, allowing Raffa to reach into the overhead locker for a leather satchel that is wedged behind the love of my life: Hugo, my faithful Husqvarna sewing machine; a piece of vital equipment I have owned for seven years and is now a friend I cannot live without. New sewing machine models will come and go, their specifications incrementally superior, but nothing can match Hugo when it comes round to reliability. He may be unable to perform three hundred and five stitch types, but when am I ever going to need to embroider a winking cat, a saluting robot or any other iPhone emoji? No, Hugo is perfect, thank you very much. He has everything I need: an automatic double nee-dle threader, adjustable speed control, a built-in feed-dog mech-anism and the ability to form a buttonhole of any size in one simple step. What's more, in the seven years I have had him, he has never broken. Not once. And as our friendship has grown, it seemed only fair that I name him and being a Husqvarna U-stich Go, what better name than Hugo?

'Is this yours?' Raffa gestures to Hugo's shiny hard case, his biceps bulging with the full weight of the sewing machine as it plunges into his arms and I have to bite my lip and look away, my ovaries doing a flip-flop move, which leaves me feeling the sort of light-headed I associate with watching Bradley Cooper movies. When I turn back, he's looking down at the Husqvarna U-stich Go font etched into the case.

'Yes. I've got a couple of commissions I need to finish whilst I'm out here,' I say, remembering I've actually got four if I include Auntie Sue's christening outfit.

'So, you're travelling to Milan to become a fashion designer?' he says, in a way that suggests I am nothing short of a cliché, millions of British women and their sewing machines jetting off to Milan on a daily basis to wow the world as a seamstress. A dressmaking Dick Whittington in search of gold thread. Or simply a dressmaking dick.

'I *am* a fashion designer,' I say, perhaps a little too defensively.

It's weird. I've never before been so bold with the introduction of my profession, preferring instead to prevaricate with unnecessary detail. Textiles designer. Garment technologist. Visual merchandiser. My skin prickles with unease. Stella McCartney. Vivienne Westwood. Coco Chanel. *They* are fashion designers. Not me. Call it imposter syndrome, but I don't think I'll feel worthy of the title until someone has actually heard of me or my brand, so why am I suggesting that I am one now?

Raffa takes a leaflet out of his bag and sits back down in his seat. 'Look, I know this is going to sound a little odd, but . . .'

He hands me a glossy cream pamphlet with a photo of a beautiful woman wearing the most striking headdress I've ever seen – peacock feathers and netting attached to a bejewelled satin band – and it takes me a few moments to recognise it as an Order of Service for his grandmother's funeral, a feeling of awe and inspiration quickly replaced with one of discomfort.

'The last three pages summarise her eulogy. She was a truly remarkable woman.' He fiddles with this fingers, nodding solemnly at her photograph and his grief unsettles me. 'You should keep that. It's got the Casa dei Cappelli address on it and if you've time, you should definitely visit. You know what us Aussie-Italians are like. The more, the merrier.'

Twenty minutes later, I am still clutching Mariela Marino's Order of Service as we land in Milan with a rumble and a bounce, the plane doors opening to allow a cool breeze to blow through the cabin and a wild luggage reclaim frenzy ensuing people fighting to get their belongings out of the overhead lockers and taking each other out in the process. The baby on the row in front of us starts to cry, his mother trying to placate him with one soft toy after another.

I undo my seat belt and turn to Raffa. 'It was nice meeting you.'

'You too.' He holds my gaze and everything inside me melts. 'Oh and I meant what I said about visiting Altaterra. You'd be very welcome at my family's house, too. As we say in Italy, every bird finds his own nest beautiful, but I promise Altaterra is something spectacular.'

'Thanks. And good luck with the funeral.' I take Hugo's handle, which is still hot from Raffa's touch.

'Good luck with your fashion range. I'm sure you'll knock 'em dead!' He smiles and walks off, all tight hamstrings and clenched buttocks, leaving me to watch his retreating back head down the gangway and disembark the plane.

And just like that the scent of cedarwood evaporates; Raffa is gone and my heart is left jackhammering with a mixture of career-induced nervous tension and the gnawing disappointment that I will never see this bronzed god ever again.

Outside, my face tingles in the afternoon sun as I stride across the glittering tarmac towards Milan Malpensa's airport terminal, dragging Hugo on my wheelie case with one hand and reaching for my shades with the other. A cluster of cypress trees sway in the breeze and a house sparrow hops across a wooden board brandishing the slogan, 'Dare to dream'. If that isn't an omen, then I don't know what is. Who knows, the unclouded skies of Italy might just be the perfect backdrop for a Plus Size woman to bring her Plus Size dreams to life.

CHAPTER FIVE
Milano

Milan is buzzing – not the rat-race buzz of London and the collision of its bewildered commuters with their ill-fitting suits, hunched shoulders and stress-pinched faces, but a happy, sensory buzz. A warm blast of air hits my face as I exit the metro station at Montenapoleone to the welcoming smell of hot waffles and sunshine. The sultry sound of a saxophone wrestles with the whir of an engine, a red Ferrari revving on the pavement just outside Prada, and it feels good to be alive.

I take in the clean, cobbled streets and pivot my wheelie case over the lip of the last step, Hugo tilting to one side and threatening to fall into the gutter, sending me flying into a gaggle of girls clutching huge, shiny Valentino bags – all the girls identical with their long dark hair, oversized sunglasses, white vest tops, designer jeans and black patent heels. Who needs a catwalk runway when every pavement of Milan hosts a real-time fashion show? Gazelle-like businesswomen. Super-stylish shoppers. Designer belts hugging tiny waists. My stomach turns to stone. Is there really a gap in the market for people like me and the women I represent?

Further down the street, Versace's window display catches my eye. It's a veritable piece of art in its own right – four titanic arched windows illuminated in different colours, featuring displays representing le Quattro Stagioni. An icy-blue neon hue showcases winter's offering: a Polly belted brushed wool coat coupled with thigh-high suede boots and a cashmere turtleneck, whilst dazzling yellow lighting casts man-made rays of sunshine onto summer, a Trésor de la Mer bikini with matching handbag – because everyone takes their clutch bag to the beach! Autumn's leather trouser suit is at least a bit more practical but has clearly been designed for the 0.008 per cent of the population who are over six feet tall and under a size 8. Spring's chiffon minidress isn't much better, as unforgivingly transparent as it is colourful. Not a single one of their outfits is remotely flattering unless you're a single-digit size, in which case you'd look great in a freaking popsock (with matching handbag, of course).

I rebalance Hugo on my wheelie case and trundle past Gucci, Pucci and Prada, taking in their window displays – strapless swimming costumes with gold chain belts. Crocodile skin ankle boots. Ruched stretched-silk satin midi dresses. An off-the-shoulder ballgown with an emerald feathered trim. Haute couture at its finest. Mannequin after mannequin, some of them plastic, some of them cloth, some of them headless; all of them unrealistically slim. I carry on in search of my hotel, a small family-run establishment supposedly five minutes from here, but each time I take a side street, the blue dot on Google Maps seems to move further away.

The ratio of luxury labels to high street brands only increases as I head further across the Golden Triangle towards Via della Spiga, where elegance is a prerequisite and star people, with toy dogs peeping out of designer handbags, swagger aplenty. Three women step out of Dolce & Gabbana wearing red lipstick and tortoiseshell cat-eyed sunglasses, their sleek dark hair scraped back into statement ponytails. That heavy sensation in my stomach travels into my throat and it feels as though I have swallowed a pebble – the only thing oversized here is sunglasses. Why is everyone so intimidatingly . . . thin?

Flora

> Because they either have the metabolism of a hyperactive hyena or they don't eat.

Zhané

> Because there is nowhere for people over a size 16 to shop on the Monte-whatever-it's-called, which is why the world needs RAMONA AWESOME MATTHEWS and her FUCKING BRILLIANT BODY-INCLUSIVE CLOTHES!

My heart fills with hope. Everyone needs a Zhané in their life, and I'm lucky to have her in mine. Who knew that the girl I'd been partnered with in PE all those years ago and had a right go at me for not doing the requisite amount of sit-ups would go on to be one of my lifelong best friends. It may have taken a couple of awkward workout sessions at the beginning (with Zhané you do things properly or not at all) but I knew when she defended the small adjustments that I made to my PE kit (the insertion of an elasticated belt and a decision to drop the hem whilst most girls in my class insisted on taking theirs up), that she'd be in my life forever. And I guess the pair of us knew a year later when Flora started Meadowhead Comprehensive as the new girl in Year 8, and rolled up her sleeve to reveal a row of small daisies she'd inked around the cuff of her school shirt, that we'd found our tribe, the three of us moving to London as a trio to find fame and fortune (AKA a mouldy flat in the arse end of nowhere, waiting tables in Soho to make ends meet until we all got 'proper jobs').

Zhané

Are you manifesting?

Wandering further, I try to visualise Curvaliscious as my own brand wedged between Versace and Louis Vuitton – it's good to dream – bold prints on Plus Size mannequins and an array of accessories to boot, but no matter how hard I try, I can never see beyond big bubble font that would look more at home on a cheap birthday card than above the window of a high-end fashion boutique. Curvaliscious is fun. Non-threatening. Frivolous. It doesn't take itself seriously and isn't the sort of name you picture in sleek gold italic lettering.

I pass the entrance to the Brow Bar and stifle a laugh: a tall, elegant woman surrounded by Gucci bags reclines in the window seat as a younger woman tends to the tinting of her lashes – a far cry from my local brow bar at home where clients look like tired geography teachers and are surrounded by Iceland carrier bags bursting with frozen ready meals. Voyeurism is quite the sport here where la vita is indeed dolce and glamour reigns over domesticity, nobody queuing at the bus stop or arguing about the price of loo roll.

'. . . Lady Gucci imprisoned in the San Vittore jail for ordering the murder of her husband.' A well-dressed man in aviator sunglasses swaggers down the centre of the street with a group of tourists in tow, an Italian lilt to his accent, vowels drawn out as though they are whole words in their own right. 'And our next stop, Armani.'

He hovers just outside an impressive three-storey building bursting with elegant designs and accessories so delicately crafted they're as much art as they are apparel. Unable to tear myself away, I follow the tourist group through the big brass doors, catching sight of my reflection in a floor-to-ceiling mirror and I have to say that I'm pretty darned pleased with my outfit. Coupling leopard-skin print Converse with casual mid-length V-neck black cotton dungarees over a baggy white T-shirt and accessorising with a leopard-skin print hair tie was a bold look but I've just about pulled it off. The bright red lipstick, overlapping gold pendants and wire-thin bangles add a touch of casual-chic edge I'm quite proud of. Who needs to be a size zero to have style?

The tour group navigates its way through womenswear and beyond a display of Sesia bags I know to be made from dyed calf skin – something that makes me bristle with disgust every time I think about it. Moving swiftly on, I see a sign for the bamboo bar and roof terrace. A quick glance at the drinks menu – Negroni, Americano and Spritz – has my mouth watering.

'Aperitvo, Signorina?' A waiter greets me from the lift, a small round tray balanced above his head on the palm of his hand, and I'm reminded that, here in Italy, waiting tables is a profession that requires skill and commands respect unlike the spotty teenagers back home who are paid the minimum wage to cock up your drinks order and make it abundantly clear they'd rather be elsewhere.

Tastebuds piqued, I concede that an Aperol Spritz might be just the thing. 'Si. Grazie.'

With the grace of a swan, he takes hold of my case and with one sweeping movement wheels it to the cloakroom with a flourish, nestling it beneath a row of expensive-looking coats. I follow him over to the roof terrace, an immaculate structure of minimalist sophistication where huge arrangements of twisted bamboo stand in sparkling glass vases on low-set tables and cream leather seating is the order of the day. We pass tables of mothers and daughters, businessmen and models, and wind up at an empty table next to a woman with such a huge hat – Bombshell's saucer champagne wedding collection if I'm not mistaken – that I'm forced to reposition my chair.

Glancing beneath the tables as I tuck Hugo under my legs (there's no way I'm letting him out of my sight and handing him over to the cloakroom), I spy faux pearl-embellished leather Jimmy Choo sandals with an elegant five-inch trompe l'oeil heel. Next to them, on similarly slim ankles, a divine pair of butterfly-blue leopard-print slingbacks glitter with glass-beaded ankle straps. Incredible. I get a sudden urge to call Fabrice. He loves a good heel.

'Hey, it's me,' I say, watching a woman sashay out of the lift in a tailored trench coat and what I recognise as Valentino Garavani Rockstud Alcove ankle boots. Dreamy. 'I'm calling you from the Armani bar.'

'Bitch!' Fabrice spits playfully.

'Oh, 100 per cent.' I smile, wondering where her trench coat is from. 'So, I caught Setayesh shagging The Horse.'

'You caught Setayesh shagging a horse?' Fabrice says, horrified.

'Not *a* horse. *The* Horse.'

'Jesus, I don't know what's worse!'

'I wish you were here. You should see—'

'Oh, shit buckets!' Fabrice growls. 'This fucking thing . . .'

'Caught you at a bad time?' I say, drawn to another diner's acetate sunglasses and trying to work out whether they have a Roman or Venetian crystal finish.

'I'm on in an hour for a 5 p.m. aperitif performance and I've burst out of my dress. There's a big chuffing hole where the zip has come away and . . . fuck, I can't go on stage like this!'

'Can you put a Lycra vest top underneath?' I suggest.

'I can't fit *anything* underneath. It's already three sizes too small.'

'Wrap a shawl over the top?' I take a sip of the Aperol Spritz the waiter has placed before me.

'I'm supposed to be Dolly Parton, not Red Riding Hood's freaking grandmother!' he groans, the sound of splitting material audible.

'Style it out,' I say.

'What?'

'Think of all those improv courses you did. Build it into your act. Either you've just been ravaged and everything's ripped and askew from the rampant sex you've just had in the corridor or the other queens tore your dress to smithereens out of pure jealousy.'

'This is why I love you, Ramona Matthews. Them bitches have been roughing me up because everyone wants a piece of Polly Darton. Send my love to Rome!'

'Milan.'

'Gotta go. Ciao, darling!'

'Ciao.'

I lean back against the soft leather seat and think about Fabrice. He has always been there for me, driving me to hospital appointments the time I broke my leg, dedicating songs to me from his drag booth, telling me I can do things that I think I can't. Supporting me, bolstering me, accompanying me. It feels weird being without him now. He'd love it here – the style, the sophistication, the swagger. My attention drifts to an orange Lamborghini which has arrived on the street below, its engine throbbing with the subtlety of a Kardashian, and my glass is empty. It's time to find my hotel.

The Parrocchetto del Paradiso hotel is set in a labyrinth of side streets just off the fashion district's Golden Triangle, where pavements morph into terraces lined with al fresco diners and white starched tablecloths flap in the evening breeze. With its humbug carpets, softened edges, rounded lines, and exotic bird colour palette – parakeet greens, flamingo pinks, kingfisher blues – this guest house has all the trappings of a tropical retreat and I wish I could stay here forever. Sunlight streams in through my bedroom window, casting a rainbow spectrum across the shiny wooden floorboards and lighting up the Egyptian cotton bedspread.

The en-suite bathroom is white and airy and smells of Lily of the Valley, a claw-footed standalone bath angled diagonally across black and white marble floor tiles with a vase of snow-white gladioli as tall as me standing next to it. I feel very lucky that House of Dreams is paying for it and that Chinara, my boss, has been so supportive of me coming to Milan, sorting me out with an industry pass for the gala which is waiting at the box office for me and fast-tracking my annual leave through the system, all the while telling me she believes in me and that the whole thing is a 'fucking travesty'.

On the wall behind the bed, half a dozen life-size parakeet models hang in a haphazard arrangement, some painted gold, others lacquered in bold, tropical colours whilst one larger one is made of polished wood. I sit down on the bed and run my fingers over the sheets. They feel soft, strong and infinitely expensive. Throwing my head back on the pillow, I look up at the frescoed ceiling – plump cherubs floating around a night sky, brandishing brass instruments and bronze goblets – and I feel that I have stumbled across a small heaven. Good karma indeed. Tomorrow is going to be a good day; I can feel it in my bones.

I lie there for a moment listening to the hum of chatter and the chink of glasses that floats through the open sash window; a reminder that Happy Hour is underway and that here in Italy, two-for-one Aperitivo isn't restricted to the sixty minutes it is back home and whilst it's tempting to head back out and wile away the evening sipping cocktails, I need to keep a straight head for tomorrow. What's the point in coming all this way to piss an opportunity like this up the wall?

Just as I was beginning to think that things were going my way, my phone jingles with a text.

Setayesh

> Sorry, the gala is sold out tomorrow, so you won't be able to count your trip to Milan as work and will have to take the whole week off as leave.

I read the message three times, trying to digest the words. What about being able to expense my hotel? What about the cost of the flight? What about the industry pass that Chinara has waiting for me at the box office? At first, I think this is just some kind of bad joke, but then reality kicks in and I am forced to accept that this is exactly the sort of backstabbing, underhand behaviour typical of Setayesh, though how she has the authority to veto my trip and why she's choosing to target *me* given that she got the gig remains a mystery. My heart drops.

Of course. She'll have seen me when I caught her in action with The Horse and now that she's been promoted to senior whatever-it-is on account of having her collection commissioned (AKA shagging her way up the corporate ladder), I am going to pay for this big time!

Ramona

But I'm here already!! In Milan!!

Setayesh

Me too. Aart and I are staying at the Mandarin Oriental. Want to meet for coffee?

Do I want to meet for fucking coffee? Fire blazes across my breastbone.

Ramona

So, I've flown out here for nothing?

Setayesh

That's why you'll have to take the whole week off as leave, which means we also won't reimburse you for the hotel and flights.

Pumped with fury, I throw my head back on the bed and scream into the pillow. Fucking Setayesh. I picture her in halterneck silk pyjamas snuggled up next to The Horse on a cream leather sofa as she hand-feeds him oysters whilst he picks his teeth and watches golf on some enormous plasma television, his home the sort of ostentatious country house featured in *Hello!* magazine.

I was promised those tickets. All I had to do was pick them up on the door. Just how am I supposed to get into the fashion show and meet anyone of note now? My jaw tightens, acid rises in my throat and my adrenal glands are firing on so many cylinders it feels as though I could sprint a marathon and still have the energy to explode into a million tiny fragments.

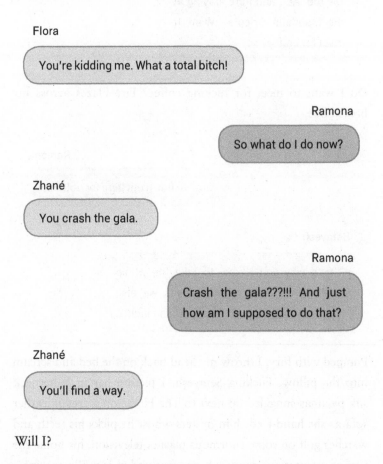

Flora

You're kidding me. What a total bitch!

Ramona

So what do I do now?

Zhané

You crash the gala.

Ramona

Crash the gala???!!! And just how am I supposed to do that?

Zhané

You'll find a way.

Will I?

CHAPTER SIX
Il Gala di Milano

Gatecrashing the Gala di Milano might have seemed like a viable option after emptying the contents of the mini bar last night, but it certainly doesn't sit right with me this morning. I leave Hugo locked up in the deposito bagagli in Milan train station, choosing to travel light with an armful of prototypes, my phone and a lipstick. Dressed in my asymmetrical, off-the-shoulder, polka-dot wrap midi dress, I hotfoot it through the Quadrilatero de la Moda, memorising the sob story I have created with input from both Zhané and Flora.

Zhané

And remember, when you become the lowly assistant who has been sent out to pick up three missing dresses, you're Finnish and don't speak a word of Italian or English.

Flora

> All Finnish people can speak
> English, Zee!

Zhané

> Whatever. Just don't get caught up
> in conversation. The fewer words,
> the better.

Flora

> I once went out with a guy from Helsinki.
> Gorgeous arms.

Horns beep and exhaust pipes rumble, rush hour true to its word, workers darting here, there and everywhere like clockwork, all of them dressed to impress. In Milan, the IT guy isn't some bloke with hairy toes who drags himself out of bed at midday, sees little daylight and stumbles to work in flip-flops and an unironed black T-shirt. Here, he is clean-shaven and well dressed – tailored trousers and polished leather shoes. No tie. No big clunky rucksack with water bottle attachment. And definitely no body odour. Just a man in an open collar shirt and trousers that fit. La semplicità è l'ultima sofisticazione. Perfect.

Pumped with adrenaline and knotted with nerves, I see the Palazzo Mezzanotte in the distance and a moment later am standing in the sun-streaked Piazza Affari face to face with a line-up of street performers – statue centurions, acrobats, flamethrowers, everything from Leonardo da Vinci posing with oil paints and an easel to a bearded, robed Galileo Galilei complete with tele-scope – all of them equally spaced against the backdrop of a huge, grandiose white building. Home to the Italian stock exchange, the Palazzo Mezzanotte has become home to some of the greatest fashion shows of all time and although I've seen it in so many photos, the sheer scale of its pillared frontage takes my breath away. However, it's Maurizio Cattelan's five-metre high sculpture of a veiny marble hand giving onlookers the middle finger that really catches my attention. How can it not? Sitting on a huge stone base, the fascist salute with its chopped-off fingers, apart from the middle one which is held upright in defiance, speaks a million words.

Repositioning the dresses over my arm, I get ready to reprise the role of lowly fashion assistant, yet looking at the queue which snakes down the side of the building and loops back on itself, I'm wondering whether I have the gall. My mouth dries and my legs tremble. Can I really do this?

Fabrice

Go, go, go! You'll regret it if you don't.

I take a deep breath and kick into gear, trotting as fast as I can across the piazza and over to the front of the queue, where I arrive flustered, out of breath and panicking that this might end up costing me an arm and a leg even if I do manage to blag my way in.

'Permisso. Please,' I say, barging my way through to the security guard, who has his nose in someone's bag that he is inspecting with a large torch. 'House of Dreams?' I flash my work ID card at him. A woman head to toe in feathers and her thigh-high booted sidekick shoot me a death stare, but there is no time for guilt here.

The security guard looks up from the bag. 'L'ingresso al pubblico è più avanti sulla destra.'

'Sorry, I'm Finnish and I don't speak any other language. None at all. Not even a single word of English. Not even the tiniest smidgeon,' I pant, out of breath and trying to ignore both the confused look travelling across his face and the acute stitch that is shooting short, sharp stabs of pain across my lower abdomen. 'Oh and non parlo Italiano either!'

He raises an eyebrow and nods over to a trade entrance further up the side of the building.

'Grazie,' I say, trying to catch my breath before gathering up the dresses again.

Poking my fingers into my ribcage to try to alleviate the cramp, I hurtle over the cobbles towards a small group of people clustered around a huge metal door through which a giant wooden horse flanked by scantily leather-clad gladiators is being wheeled. I'm about to launch into the role of lowly assistant again when a man wearing a bronze, double-breasted suit, the trousers cut off just above the knee and the sleeves of the jacket replaced with what look to be two giant gold concertinas pushes past me.

'Er, mi scusi,' I say, trying to work out who is in charge, a man with a clipboard turning around and looking me up and down.

'House of Dreams,' I plead, showing him my ID card.

He shakes his head with a solemnity that suggests someone has just died and points me back to the main front door, sweeping me out of the way to clear the path for three bare-chested men in tai chi trousers with Chinese writing stencilled across their foreheads in black ink. Shit. I lean against the handrail and bite my bottom lip in contemplation, watching as a giant sparkly human ladybird clips first the huge stone pillar and then a bewildered passer-by with her spotted wings before angling herself through the door. Bringing up the rear, a man in a green body stocking with a yellow painted face framed by large white felt petals roller-skates in, dragging behind him a knight in shining armour, no questions asked. An idea takes hold.

Peeling off my shoes and folding my Curvaliscious dresses over the handrail, I hop back across the cobbles, around the corner and over to the line-up of street performers. Deciding that the centurion costume is guaranteed to fit, I peel a crisp twenty-euro bill out of my pocket and hand it to the man in uniform.

'Per favori,' I say, desperately yanking at his leather tunic. 'Can I borrow?'

Fifty euros later and we have a deal, our exchange taking place in a subterranean public toilet from which I stride out in knee-high strappy leather sandals, metal-plated shoulder armour, a leather tunic and an ornate, red-plumed gold helmet. Everything is uncomfortable – the sandals, several sizes too big, make a loud slapping sound against the stone steps as I re-emerge outside, a shield in one hand and a spear in the other.

Striding across the piazza, the tunic slopping over one shoulder and the metal armour clanking against my spear, I do my best to remain upright, the edges of the sandals catching on the cobbles and the helmet falling further down over my eyes with every step. It feels as though I have conquered Rome by the time I arrive back at the trade exit. Picking up the dresses and draping them over the shield, I stride through the door behind a man in a leather kilt with a nonchalance I have never before mustered. This centurion lark suits me.

It takes my eyes a moment to adjust as I step into the main hall, a giant dome with paper arches overhead, creating the illusion that we are housed within a cardboard village. Electronic music echoes through the auditorium, the lighting alternating between pink neon and a yellow hue. A woman in a backless catsuit with Gucci embossed across her leather belt hands me a brochure which I instinctively hold to my nose, breathing in the scent of freshly printed gloss paper and exhaling with relief. I made it! Fizzing with excitement, I take in my surroundings. Two parallel runways have been set up, joined by a thrust stage, each with two rows of chairs lining the edge.

Mesmerised by the mishmash of fashion in the room – the audience seems every bit a part of the show as its hosts – my eye is drawn to a collection of vintage dresses by Stephane V, who has upcycled antique lace to incorporate glass into his designs in homage to his glazier friend in Nice. It shouldn't work but the intricate embroidery of glass droplets in the fabric are the work of a genius, rainbow spectrums of light bouncing off the delicate beads to dazzling effect, one of the models wearing a hooped dress with a ring of beautifully ornate shot glasses dangling from the hem. Amazing.

My eyes dart around the room in search of Giovanni Columbo, but it's almost impossible to pick out anyone with the amount of headwear going on, especially when I can barely see out of my own. Then, judging by the officious-looking man strutting around with an iPad who is rounding up a group of bare-chested gladiators and directing them backstage, I am about to get shunted into a catwalk line-up. Hastily, in spite of the too-big sandals, I dash to the bathroom.

A moment later and I am back in my polka-dot dress. I take a photo, determined to give Fabrice a flavour of flamboyance, but before I can properly capture the event on film, the lights dim and the music dips.

'Tre minuti. Three minutes, please.' A voice announces over the loudspeaker.

People take to their seats, the fashion hoi polloi heading to the first runway with enough six-inch gold ankle boots and handbags between them to open their own boutique whilst the second seems to be more heavily attended by the press. Without an allocated seat, I'm a little unsure what to do with myself and figure that maybe I'll hang at the bar. Is it too early for a G&T?

The lights fade and a spotlight appears on the stage. Into it steps Giovanni Columbo, a small, taut man in a crisp white shirt who wouldn't look out of place in a Gucci commercial. He runs his fingers over his designer stubble and launches into an introductory speech, though the only words I can pick out from his Italian spiel are Prada, Gucci and Pucci. I'll make sure to seek him out later.

A strobe starts to pump out jagged beams of light on the beat of a remastered version of New Order's 'Blue Monday' which fills the auditorium as a steady stream of tall, thin catwalk models strut their stuff down the runway, all equally spaced and paced.

The designs are unquestionably awe-inspiring, polished leather being the order of the day with leather miniskirts, oversized jackets, waistcoats, pinafores, all with tailored accessories. Maybe I should have kept my centurion tunic after all. The next collection is by Gucci and features every kind of feather imaginable – ostrich, flamingo, peacock, macaw.

More women swagger this way and that, all sashaying like clockwork and slowly I am lulled into a trance, outfits coming and going and all merging into one as each model ticks the ethnic diversity box – West African. East African. South East Asian. Native American. But all of them are as tall as they are thin and not one of them doesn't have the proportions of a rake. Within ten minutes, I've become so desensitised to it all that I can't see the satin from the silk, the crepe from the cotton and all I can think about is where are the bigger women?

Fendi bum bags. Louboutin heels. Gucci capes. Pucci culottes. Everything made for the tall and thin. Putting the haute in haute couture. Cameras whiz down the side of each catwalk on a wire rig, a collective 'wow' filling the auditorium when a girl modelling an embossed white lace ankle-length dress with three-dimensional flowers embroidered around the V-neck takes to the stage, her whole bodice made entirely from glass. Again, Stephane V Couture.

'What are you doing here?'

I feel the touch of someone's fingers on my arm and look up to see Setayesh glaring down on me like an eagle that hasn't eaten for a few days. My heart almost stops, my stomach freefalling and a loud ringing starting up in my ears. Holding onto the bar behind me, I lean back and take a deep breath. She wears diamanté ankle-strapped high heels and a transparent body stocking over garish red underwear, a huge fake jewel inhabiting her navel. Chin raised, hands on hips, she runs her tongue over her bottom lip as though working up an appetite. 'I thought I told you, you're not supposed to be here, Ramona.'

I feel the ground shift beneath me. 'Hi. I . . .'

'How did you get in?' she spits.

My stomach twists. 'I just wanted to meet Gio . . .'

'You gatecrashed?' Her eyebrows dance all over the place and, like a cat swatting at a toy mouse, it's clear she's having fun with me and I am nothing but her plaything.

I fix her with a grin. 'I like to think of it as taking initiative.'

The Horse plods over with my discarded centurion costume folded up in his arms, the red-plumed helmet sitting on top of the leather sandals. 'I believe this is yours?' he says, thrusting the pile into my hands.

'Yes. No. Look, I . . .'

But before I can come up with a plausible argument for being here, I am being bundled out by security.

Outside, the air feels oppressive and the sun's burning rays ravage the back of my neck until my skin stings. Belittled and rejected, I wander away from the Gala di Milano, my Curvaliscious dresses redundant in my arms. Returning the centurion costume to my performing friend, a numbness takes hold of my limbs. My head feels as though it is made of smashed glass that has been glued back together, some bits missing and some altogether in the wrong place and everything hurts. This was not how today was supposed to go.

My phone bleeps.

Flora

> Mr Salim has given us notice!!! He wants
> us out of the flat by the end of the month!

I look up. The giant statue of the fascist finger looms before me and I couldn't have put it better myself. The whole world has just given me the bird. Slumping against a bench, I reach into my bag for a packet of paper tissues, my fingers finding the pages of Mariela Marino's Order of Service. Wiping a crumb off her face with my elbow, I stare at the words printed below her picture:

Born in a small village outside Milan, the daughter of a farmer, Mariela Marino's unique and groundbreaking style saw the fashion designer put Italian hats on the world map. Leaving school at fifteen to work the land, Mariela fled her childhood home for Milan, where she landed an apprenticeship with well-known milliner, Alessandro Romano, whose clients included Sarah Jessica Parker and Queen Elizabeth II.

Mariela went on to design her own label after graduating from Milan's Marangoni Institute and quickly came to fame with her daring approach to fashion, persuading singer, Madonna, to wear a piece of headgear featuring a felt fried egg with golden thread yolk dripping down one side of her face. After decades of living in the spotlight, Mariela retired to her home in Altaterra, a small Tuscan village, for a quiet life. The future of her hat emporium, La Casa dei Cappelli,

remains under question, the local community campaigning
for its recognition as a national heritage site, affectionately
dubbing it the jewel of Altaterra.

I turn over the booklet, the glossy pages smooth against my fingertips, and here on the back page as though lit up in neon is the hat emporium's address: La Casa dei Cappelli, Via Martini 11, Altaterra, Toscana.

Running my fingers over my grandma's pendant and squeezing the cherub between my thumb and forefinger, I feel a burst of exhilaration as the answer stares me straight in the face. Don't I have everything I need here? Laptop, designs, Hugo? It's a no-brainer. Or is it? In such a small village, I'm bound to bump into Raffa, especially if he's part of some funeral procession, and wouldn't that look pretty bunny boilerish? Desperation personified? I chew my nails, a prickle of unease spreading across my skin.

Zhané

> But isn't the whole fucking point that you
> *do* bump into him?

Flora

> You HAVE to go, Mona!! I can move your stuff out
> to my dad's with mine — you've hardly got anything,
> other than clothes — and Mr Salim will reimburse us a
> month's rent if we're out by the weekend.

Life as I know it is crumbling around me and everything I know seems to be in freefall. I should feel panicked, but if I'm honest, I feel liberated. That flat in a Lewisham tower block never felt like home anyway.

Ramona

Thank you. You're a star xx

Inhaling deeply, I grab my belongings and set off for the train station. After all, what the hell have I got to lose?

CHAPTER SEVEN

Tuscany

Sun cascades over red slate roofs, an eternal golden tapestry stretching over the rolling hills, neat hedgerows replaced by meandering stone walls. The tick of a grasshopper. The hoot of a wood pigeon. Hay bales basking in the summer heat, neat and cylindrical, plump and proud. The taxi rumbles along the country lane, old stone buildings clinging to rocky edges as we climb towards the uneven rooftops of a perched village, a cluster of pastel-coloured houses tumbling down the hillside on my left. The hum of a distant tractor. The buzz of a nearby bee. A landscape of yellows, oranges and everything in between. Sandstone walls. Fox-red shutters.

The lane narrows the further we climb, Altaterra true to its name; a tiny stone village balanced atop a thick ledge of limestone.

We head for the summit where honey-coloured dwellings surround a medieval bell tower that juts into the skyline, reigning over the valleys below like a crumbling king. Cobblestones the shade of caramel. Heavy bronze doors. Apricot-coloured walls. Carpets of golden wheat, blowing in the breeze. An autumnal palette on a summer canvas.

I look out of the window and swallow hard. Spurning my return flight to the UK and embarking on a trip to Tuscany seemed like the right thing to do a few hours ago, but now I'm having second thoughts. What self-respecting woman allows herself to follow a man she met on the plane halfway across a country in the hope of their paths crossing again? I spend the next few minutes reinforcing my own narrative – I needed a getaway. Somewhere quiet and sleepy, sunny and peaceful that will allow me to lie low and lick my wounds. Somewhere I can relish in being anonymous. I've always wanted to go to Tuscany and now I really want to pick out a hat at La Casa dei Cappelli. It would surely be a travesty to learn about such a national treasure and not see her work. I'm neither lovestruck nor fickle and am simply looking to work on ~~his thighs~~ my size-inclusive clothes range from one of the most beautiful ~~men~~ places in the world. Jesus, what's the matter with me?

Pushing all thoughts of Raffa out of my head, I check the time on my phone. I'm a little early, but the Airbnb guy suggested the place will be ready from three o'clock and given that it's already six, it's not like the accommodation won't be ready. The taxi driver points out a gothic building, Palazzi di something or other, standing on the edge of a small village square set in the shade of a frescoed church. My mind boggles. How can such a remote village have its own palace? I sip my water and look out across hills blanketed with olive groves and am just romanticising about picnicking beneath the shade of an ancient oak tree with a man who looks like Ryan Gosling when the driver disturbs me from my reverie.

'You have correct address?' He pulls up outside a small alimentare and turns off the engine.

'Casa del Pittore, quindici, Piazza Berrettini. Yes.' Have I pronounced it correctly? Maybe quindici is fifty not fifteen. Maybe it's not a number at all. Maybe I'm mixing it up with Medici – whoever or whatever they were – the Medici code. No, I'm thinking of the *Da Vinci Code*. Gaah. I bring up Google Translate on my phone. 'Casa del Pittore, quindici, Piazza Berrettini. Yes.'

'There is no number fifteen.'

I look up at the small row of shops in the village square – il panificio, l'alimentari, la farmacia – and over to a small trattoria set back behind an ornamental fountain, a few circular tables laid out front where locals sip wine in the evening breeze and children play marbles in the dirt, a scraggy dog lying at their side.

The taxi driver consults his satnav and looks up at the 'Piazza Berrettini' sign hanging above the grocery store and gestures to each building in turn. 'Twelve. Thirteen. Fourteen. Yes. Fifteen?' He pulls his shoulders up around his ears. 'Poof!' He puffs open his hand like an explosion of octopus legs.

I train my eye along the ramshackle buildings, numbers neatly displayed on small white plaques. He's right; the sequence jumps from fourteen to sixteen.

'Maybe in between?' I say, pointing to a gap where the remnants of a rusty bicycle lie abandoned in a strip of long grass, a small brown sparrow standing on the exposed metal spring of the saddle. 'Let me at least take a look.'

I get out of the taxi, the evening heat coiling around my bare legs, and I'm ambling to the overgrown entrance when it dawns on me that I've made no arrangement whatsoever to pick up the key and have been given no entry code. I'd better investigate.

Brambles tear at my ankles as I trample through the undergrowth, and just as I'm contemplating what species of snake are native to Tuscany and if I should perhaps retreat, I see a sign for La Casa del Pittore through the gap of a broken wooden gate, a meadow of wildflowers stretched out before it. Returning to the taxi, I pay the driver and grab my belongings.

'Airbnb?' he says, giving an appreciative nod to my tip.

'Yes!' I say, realising I can't be the first guest at Marco & Maria's getaway.

'Buon soggiorno!' He tilts his cap in my direction, smiles and drives off.

Pushing open the wooden gate, I find myself in a tangle of goose grass, the garden overgrown and wild. Breathing in the sweet perfume of meadow flowers, I wade through wild poppies, cornflowers, red campion, buttercups and an electric pink flower I don't recognise, a small kitten bounding away from me and disappearing over the wall. Picking through nettles and sticky green leaves, I head for the front door, an uneven wooden structure set askew in a rotting frame, its turquoise paint peeling off in large strips. It turns out I needn't have worried about the key as the door is unlocked, dutifully creaking and juddering as I push it open, to the point where I worry it might come off its hinges.

The smell of garlic hits me as I stumble into the kitchen, its flagstone floor uneven beneath my feet. As my eyes become accustomed to the light, I make out a large rustic, country kitchen table and shelves cluttered with shell ornaments and china curios. The owner clearly has a penchant for hens – a hen teapot, hen oven gloves, hen salt and pepper pots, an apron with hens running horizontally around the border, a Welcome to Cluckingham Palace sign hanging above the doorway to the next room, a hen tea tray, a hen . . . I mean, a real hen! No, not just the one – three of them. Three real-life hens, strutting freely about the kitchen and pecking at the cracks between the flagstones only inches from my feet. Did I just let them in? I look up to see a fourth and a fifth hen strut in from an adjoining room. No, they were clearly here before I was. I lift my foot away from the largest of the brood, a dark ginger bird with large claws and fuller feathers, who stares me down with a look that threatens to eat my soul.

'Shoo!' I open the door and try to waft her out like a bad smell.

She blinks, cocks her head to one side and struts into the living area with an air of defiance, her claws kicking back the woollen rug as though to scatter seed. Her light brown friend follows her around the sofa, hotly pursued by a scraggly white hen with a mangy foot and a much smaller speckled brown one bringing up the rear. Talk about pecking order! I watch as they head through a doorway into the next room. Do they want me to follow them? Tentatively, I shadow them, my feathered friends leading me into a darkened room that smells of mothballs.

I turn on the light to reveal a huge silk rug laid out across the stone floor and a dark green velvet chaise longue tucked against the wall next to a grand piano. Dust dances in a shard of light that streams in through the small window, illuminating a large bookcase of leatherbound classics and a display cabinet full of porcelain dolls, their glass eyes all swivelled towards me. A shiver runs down my spine. On Airbnb this place was listed as a bright and spacious getaway retreat with all mod cons. Pah!

My eye is drawn to the line of books on the shelf in front of me, the words lupo and mannaro appearing in several titles and a crispy page yellowed by sunlight fluttering to the floor to reveal a sketch of a werewolf. My skin prickles. I tuck the page back into the book and return it to the shelf. An old-fashioned jack-in-the-box sits on the coffee table, Jack himself bent over in a U-turn on the end of his exposed concertina, and two chickens stare up at me, their beaks angled in exactly the same position, their expression mirrored – heads cocked to the right, wattles thrust forward, and I'm reminded of the twin girl ghosts in *The Shining*.

'Go!' I shoo them away, more hens appearing from nowhere. There must be seven of them. Eight. Nine?

Ducking my head beneath the low wooden beam, I walk out of the piano room and up the scuffed wooden staircase to the floor above. The stairs would be quite the centrepiece were they not scratched by claws and soiled with hen shit.

Upstairs is as creepy as downstairs, net curtains shimmying in the breeze, an embroidered poem mounted in a picture frame next to an oil painting of a swan hanging outside the bathroom and small cloth bags of lavender scattered in odd places, their scent more of a dry pot pourri. Mercifully, the doors to the rooms are shut and the hens have been confined to the dark corridor. I open the first door to reveal a small bedroom with floral wallpaper, dark mahogany furniture and a porcelain commode contained in a wooden chair set beneath the open window. The heavyset bed frame takes up most of the space in the room and reminds me of the bed Little Red Riding Hood's grandmother was confined to in the illustrated hardback my grandpa used to read to me when I was little. It is draped in a stiff, white throw that feels as though it has been washed a million times over, the cotton so paper-thin and crisp that it almost gives me a papercut when I lift it.

I dump my bags next to the bed, my eyes flickering from the hand-painted flowers on the porcelain commode to the pearly petals of an old-fashioned wall lamp and then down to the blob of hen shit that has taken up residence on the leather toe strap of my LK Bennett nude suede sandal. Gross! I march on the heel of my foot to the bathroom, trying to discourage the green gunk from sliding between my toes. The bathroom is at least clean, modern and has a reassuring smell of citrus bleach – a power shower poised over the bathtub and a row of cleaning products on the windowsill. I grab a bottle of bathroom cleaner and the cloth next to it and set about running my sandal under the cold tap when the door clicks open.

'Ciao!' A voice chimes out from the landing.

I drop my sandal into the wash basin.

'Signorina Martina?' A young man in baggy harem pants and a tie-dye T-shirt (has there ever been such a crime against fashion?) looks over at me, his strong arms decorated with tattered friendship bracelets. He must be my age – maybe a couple of years older – but it's difficult to tell, the gentle laughter lines around his eyes belying the soft skin of his cheeks and a light beard running over his jaw. He holds a chicken under one arm and a bag of shopping in the other, the expression on his face a muddle of confusion, his ice-blue eyes running first over my sandal and then the bottle of bathroom cleaner I am holding.

'Signorina Matthews,' I correct him, praying he won't put the hen down. I need at least one chicken-free zone.

He runs his fingers through a mop of blond, curly hair. 'You're late.'

I drop my sandal to the floor with a clunk. 'If anything, I'm early.'

'You're three hours too late now so that doesn't work.' He sets the bag of shopping down on the floor and stares at me. His crystal-clear eyes have a depth I could get lost in, were it not for the circumstances. Transfering the bundle of feathers from one arm to the other, he pads to the bathroom, his bare feet sticking to the wooden floorboards and making a squelching sound as he goes.

'I gave you my train times. I said early evening . . .' I splutter with indignance.

He shakes his head, muttering Italian expletives under his breath and dismissing me with a floaty hand that suggests my opinion is neither relevant nor valid. His arrogance sends a chill through my bones. I am paying good money to stay in his weird, old shit-caked house, and he has neither the decency to clean it before I arrive nor apologise for the state of the place. The hens. The bedlinen. The commode. The werewolves. The possessed porcelain dolls. This was supposed to be a clean and airy apartment, not the inside of a chuffing chicken coop, and to boot he's being out-and-out rude. Seriously, who the hell posts photos of pristine white surfaces, Egyptian cotton bed linen and staged vases of daffodils only to lure customers into a dirty, dark cesspit of hen shit? I'll be writing to Airbnb about this.

'Please can you clean under the bath, under the beds and also the ceilings?' He thrusts a feather duster into my hand which I mistake for the chicken he is clutching and let out a screech as it clatters to the floor. A look of mischief flashes across his face. 'You don't like chickens?'

The hen under his arm flaps her wings and I'm not sure whether it's the fluttering of feathers or the frenzied clucking sound, but a pathological revulsion of chicken squawking sends me stepping backwards. The backs of my knees catch on the top of the bathtub, sending me sprawling into a line-up of toiletries and taking the shower curtain down with me, bottles of shampoo tumbling into and around the bath, the shower head letting out a few drops of water that hit the top of my head and cascade slowly down my face. 'Sorry.' I haul myself up onto my elbows. 'Chickens are not really my thing.'

'I will take the chickens.' He laughs, brushing a ringlet of blond hair out of his face.

'Thank you,' I say, peeling myself out of the bathtub.

True to his word, he takes the hen downstairs and rounds up the others, ushering them into the garden, where they squawk and peck at each other before separating out into the tall grass.

'And please bleach the toilet downstairs!' he shouts up the stairs and slams the door shut, the whole house rattling.

I stick my head out of the window and see the top of his head, a mass of unruly, blond curls appearing in the garden. 'I'm not the cleaner, you know!'

He looks up at the window. 'And remove all chicken poop!'

It feels as though I have been sucker punched in the chest. What an arrogant shit. And even if he has mistaken me for the cleaner, he can go fuck himself. If that's the way he treats his domestic staff, no wonder whoever was meant to come and clean hasn't showed up. Tosser. I sit back on the bed, throw my arms behind my head and exhale sharply at the ceiling, trying to clear the negative energy that now lingers in the room and replace it with happy thoughts. Deciding that a wander around the village will get rid of any ill-feeling, I'm about to lock up when there's a rap at the door.

'Signorina Ramona?'

I stick my head out of the window and see that the mop of curly blond hair has reappeared at the door below.

'Yes?' I reply from the window.

'A thousand apologies. I have been thinking you are the cleaner for the lady who lives here. The agency is always charging her so much money and doing nothing, so I try to manage them for her. And now I realise you are my guest because I see their message to say they cancelled again.'

'Yes.' I fold my arms beneath my chest and lean on the windowsill until he comes into full view.

'Are you here for the funeral?' he says.

'No.'

'You play a musical instrument?'

I frown. 'No.'

'Then what is this?' He gestures to something I can't see as it's obstructed by the lip of the porch roof.

Reluctantly, I trudge down the stairs to the front door to find him standing next to Hugo.

'Ah, I didn't realise I'd left it outside. Thank you. It's a sewing machine,' I say, unsettled by the penetrating gaze of his blue eyes that burn with such an intensity I find myself nervously fingering the stud in my left ear and wishing he'd go away. 'A machine for sewing clothes.' I expand, miming the feeding of fabric beneath an imaginary bobbing needle which only looks like a shit dance move.

'Ah. Una macchina da cucire?' he says, enthusiastically. 'You're a . . .' He clicks his fingers at me. 'The tailor of Panama! Piers Brosnan.'

'Kind of.' God, he's a cheeseball.

'I am Marco, your host, and you are Ramona.' Another finger click, this time followed by the point of an index finger. 'Like the Ramones!' He belly laughs.

There we go. Every time. Give him a few more seconds and he'll be singing:

'Bye bye baby!' he yells tunelessly, his fingers strumming an air guitar.

I hold onto my bag and force a smile.

'I'm sorry we don't start so well.' He shakes my hand then picks up Hugo by his leather strap. 'Let me take you to your true accommodation. At the moment, you are in my neighbour's house.'

'Oh!' I say, watching as an elderly woman saddled with shopping makes her way through the long grass and feeling a tiny bit guilty for snooping in her commode.

'Signora Abbadelli!' Marco nods over to her.

Acknowledging him with a nod of the head, she continues about her business.

'Come this way,' Marco says, leading me down a set of stone steps and over to another door hidden around the side of an extension, this one firmly on its hinges.

'For you.' He dangles a key in front of my nose.

'Thanks.' I take it and go to use it when he dissolves into laughter.

'It is only a principle!' He chuckles. 'Nobody locks their doors in Altaterra . . . but just in cases.'

I flash a withering smile as we step into a small apartment that looks a whole lot more like the photos on Airbnb. A small kitchenette with a folding table next to a window looking out onto the valley below. A modest living area with a sofa and television. A spiral staircase up to a mezzanine bedroom with a small en-suite shower room. It's tiny but perfect.

'You will be happy here,' he says, and I'm not sure whether it's a fact or a command.

'Very.' I glance at the coffee machine and wonder how to use it.

He plonks Hugo down on the kitchen floor. 'You have fabric?'

'Not yet.'

'Tomorrow is the market in the village. There is lots of fabric. Lots of colours. Lots of . . .' He rubs his fingers together as though trying to coax a rabbit into a hutch as he searches for the word in English.

'Different material?' I suggest.

'Yes. Different material. Bene.' He looks around the room and, satisfied that everything is as it should be, steps back towards the door. 'And once again, I'm sorry for breaking your boxes.'

I look around in search of something smashed but can see nothing broken.

'It's an expression.' He shakes his head. 'Ciao.'

'Ciao,' I say, only realising when he's halfway down the garden that I haven't asked all the basics – like where to buy milk and whereabouts this market is. 'Scusi!' I shout at his retreating back. 'Where's the market?'

He turns around and frowns.

'Il mercato? La mercata?' I say, wondering whether markets are masculine or feminine in these parts.

'Ah,' he says, a glimmer of recognition flashing across his face. 'Meet me at the market at nine o'clock tomorrow and I will show you.'

'But I don't know . . .'

'On the paper.' He raises his hand to me and waves goodbye.

I leave the door open, the glow of the evening sun spreading over the tiled floor and infusing the room with long shadows and big promises. I wander around the room, inspecting all the mod cons – a four-slice toaster, a set of sparkling ramekins and a whole host of kitchen utensils but nothing as homely as Cluckingham Palace next door. Over on the table next to the window, I discover a handwritten note next to a glass cake dome sheltering a variety of pastries:

Dear Mr Ramona,

Welcome to La Casa del Pittore. We hope you enjoy your stay in Tuscany. Please to let us know if you are needing plates of interest. La Cattedrale Santa Lucia is only five minutes by quick feet and you can buy fresh bread, milk and toilets from the village shop. Our market takes place every Sunday in the village square. The Wi-Fi code is on the router behind the armadillo. The sofa is for decoration only and just to touch *the piano next door if you are a player. Also, you must read all of the books during your stay.*

To greet you, some pasticcini in the glass tunnel.

Buon Appetito e Benvenuti in Italia!

Maria y Marco

Below the signature is a printed photo of my hosts, Maria and Marco, sharing a giant cocktail bedecked with fresh mint and strawberries, their heads pressed together affectionately and their eyes shiny with elation. Let's hope that she's easier to deal with than he is!

Lifting the glass lid and helping myself to a croissant, my mouth infuses with the taste of icing sugar and flaked almond, just as my phone jingles with an incoming email that turns my blood to ice.

From: Setayesh.Akhtar@houseofdreams.com

Cc: Chinara.Musa@houseofdreams.com

Subject: Termination of Contract

Ramona,

It has come to our attention that you have taken unauthorised leave.

As is company policy in any business, you are required to raise a holiday request via the HR portal and gain line manager approval before you are permitted to take time off.

In addition to the above act of non-compliance, you have damaged the company's reputation by breaking into the Gala di Milano without a ticket in order to pitch your clothing range that has already been rejected. This not only undermines Aart's decision-making, but also shows a blatant disrespect for company time.

You have therefore left us with no choice but to terminate your contract.

Yours regretfully,

Setayesh

Setayesh Akhtar
Senior Design Lead, House of Dreams

A feeling of vertigo plummets through me. How could any human being be so perfidious, so underhand, so two-faced? Not content with winning the commission, the Devil in Lycra is also hell-bent on crushing my career. Lost and confused, shocked and stunned, a feeling of betrayal sloshes around my gut like toxic sludge. With shaking hands, I pour myself a glass of water and take it out to the terrace, allowing my shoulders to heave with a few sobs of self-pity. I mean what the actual fuck?

Outside, everything slows. My skin tingles with the heat of the evening sun, the leaves of the higgledy-piggledy fruit trees in the next field rustling and shimmying in the light breeze as though chatting to one another in fervent agreement. The tinkle of glass beads from the dreamcatcher above. The distant cry of a shepherd rounding up his goats, their bleats and bells chiming in response. My shoulders relax a notch. I look up at the expanse of blue sky, the tiniest wisps of cloud vapour streaming out like cotton wool and for the first time in a long time, feel true perspective; the world is a much bigger place than House of Dreams and it's about time I started living a little. The feeling of betrayal slowly dissipates and the bitter taste in the back of my throat gives way to something sweet. Is this the taste of freedom?

A yellow-billed cuckoo hops from branch to branch on the lower bough of a fig tree laden with fruit. It's a far cry from the sound of police sirens, car alarms and rattling exhaust pipes back home in Lewisham – the swish of grass in the evening breeze, the buzz of a bee, the chirp of a lark, the cluck of hens and the distant ring of church bells. Lost in the fragrant scent of the Italian scrub, I am filled with the distinct feeling that losing my job might just be a blessing in disguise. Screw Setayesh. Screw The Horse. Let the two of them screw each other. Life's too short. I look down at my phone and revel in blocking The Devil in Lycra's number.

Goodbye to bad rubbish. Tuscany awaits.

CHAPTER EIGHT

Altaterra

The village square looks nothing like it did yesterday, the gentle rustle of trees and tinkle of piano music steamrolled by the hustle and bustle of a vibrant food market, the smell of pan-fried chorizo, the squealing of children, the hollering of merchants and the clanking of pans an assault on the senses. Slow-roasted garlic porchetta. Deep fried arancini. Calzone al ricotta. Tray after tray of warm Tuscan focaccia drizzled with olive oil, sprinkled with salt and topped with rosemary. Buonissimo.

Market traders tout their wares, shouting from the backs of parked vehicles packed with products. Skipping ropes. Watering cans. Dog harnesses. Polyester Minecraft onesies. Anything and everything the village is deprived of on a day-to-day basis and is all the better for not having. Over on the far side of the piazza, children crowd around a game of table football whilst parents

107

haggle over Italian pastries – deep-fried dough balls filled with custard and topped with powdered sugar, almond and pistachio biscotti, white chocolate cannoli and jam-oozing heart-shaped cookies served by a mother, daughter duo dressed in gingham blouses. A group of middle-aged men in circulation-stopping Lycra rest their bicycles against the wall of the pharmacy to flock around a bargain bin of seamless socks whilst a stray dog slaloms between them, its tail standing erect like a radio antenna as it sniffs its way through cabbage leaves and squashed tomatoes in pursuit of dropped sausage.

Marco is nowhere to be seen so I browse the stalls, making my way over to the most enormous olives I've ever laid eyes on: Leccino olives, Frantoio olives, Moraiolo, Nocellara, Coratina olives – I feel like a culinary heathen for thinking olives were simply either green, black or purple and resolve that I will come back from this trip a better, more cultured person. Refine, genteel and civilised. The sort of woman who attends poetry recitals, speaks Latin and can identify bird breeds from their song alone, and not the biscuit dunking, tea swilling philistine that I am.

I amble through the crowd, intrigued by the notion that locals seem to favour items they can't grow themselves – kitchenware, crockery, cheap electronics, garden furniture, gaudy battery-operated plastic toys – whilst visitors to the village descend upon the local produce. Leather goods are flying off the back of a van – handbags, money belts, purses and wallets, a woman surrounded by cheap sandals propped up on cardboard shoe boxes is doing a roaring trade.

'Qualsiasi paio di scarpe, venti euro!' she bellows over the hullabaloo.

I make my way past the shoe display and over to a large transit van parked up in the far corner of the square, where huge rolls of fabric hang from a metal frame installed next to the stone wall. With the dress I need to make for my godmother in mind, my eye is drawn to a roll of shimmery blue fabric which is far more what she's after than the one I've bought and Sue should really have the best for her grandson's christening. Who knows, creating a dress for Sue might be just what I need to get back on the (clothes) horse and provide inspiration for a brand-new Curvaliscious collection.

'Buon giorno!' The stall owner looks over, sweat trickling from his brow.

'Ciao,' I reply, inwardly congratulating myself on my longest exchange in Italian to date.

'Inglese?' he says, bursting my bubble.

'Si,' I say in defeat.

'Many, many fabric. Brushed cotton. Dyed cotton. Chambray. Cotton lace. Cotton trill. Gabardine Jacquard . . .' He goes on, a swell of nausea building inside me: I may well be able to identify every single fabric he has on display, but I could never reel them off in a second language. How did I delude myself into thinking I could ever get by without even the most basic Italian? Buongiorno. Ciao, Bella. Mamma Mia. Arrivederci. Dov'è il teatro dell'opera per favore? If I'm to stay for a while, I'd better get learning fast.

The shimmery blue fabric looks even more beautiful closer up, intricate squiggles of silk threaded into the weave. I run my fingers over the material. It feels thick and soft, its fibres tightly woven together – unexpectedly high-quality produce considering this is a random village market in the middle of nowhere – and I can't help but think it would make a great Plus Size evening gown if paired with the right accessories. But no sooner has the thought entered my head than a deep wave of nausea filters through me. Have I really got enough resilience in the tank to create a new collection and have it rejected all over again?

'Try before you buy!' The stall owner winks, and I let out a nervous laugh, worrying that my fingering of his fabric is an etiquette no-no here in Italy.

'I can make for you a special price,' he says, clicking the heels of his heavy black boots together in the dirt. My eyes run over his attire. Like a hairdresser with an overgrown mullet, he's an unusual advocate of his profession, shunning clothes made from high-end fabric and choosing instead to dress like stage crew, head to toe in black.

I'm mentally stringing together enough Italian words to ask how much a ten-metre length costs, mixing up my quanto costa with my per favore, when a hand appears on my arm.

'Ciao, Ramona!' I turn around to see Marco, who looks totally different without those dreadful ballooning harem pants and a hen tucked under each arm. He's dressed for the beach – surfer shorts, flip-flops and a faded green T-shirt – his mass of blond curls tied back in a piece of elastic, a few errant spirals framing his face, and is about to launch into conversation when a woman around my mum's age strong-arms him into a heated exchange about artisan bread.

'One moment,' Marco says, just as a delicatessen stall owner thrusts a spatula of soft cheese into my hand. He holds his index finger up at me and I'm not sure whether he is gesturing for me to wait or whether he too would like to sample the Gorgonzola, but before I can fathom his intent, he turns his back on me to talk to his friends.

I lick the spatula, a salty, earthy taste infusing my mouth that makes me all of a sudden nostalgic for sleeping on hay bales in a rustic barnyard surrounded by a picnic of bread and cheese laid out on gingham tablecloths – not that I have ever slept on hay bales in a rustic barnyard but there we go – the flavour just has that feel about it. Savouring the creamy aftertaste, I turn back to the fabric stall owner. 'I'll take ten metres of the blue cotton,' I say, chickening out of trying to speak Italian and resorting to finger jabbing.

I hand over a wad of euro bills, suddenly bemused by the idea that it is somebody's job to design the look and feel of new banknotes, and I'm wondering who gets the final say as to which image is featured on it when Marco turns back to me. 'Come, Ramona. I introduce you to Maria.' He walks me over to a burger van selling gourmet Italian sausage, the scent of roast pork and herbs carrying on the air, and leans on a narrow wooden counter so high up, I have to stand on tiptoes to peer over it. A moment later, Maria's head pops up on the other side. She has big, dark inky eyes that sparkle with a smile that comes from deep within, and she has the longest lashes I've ever seen. Flicking her mane of long black hair to one side, she offers me her hand.

'Ciao,' I say, beguiled by her beauty.

'This is Signorina Ramona, our new tenant for the week,' Marco says, helping himself to a sausage sample and dropping it into his mouth.

'Pleased to meet you,' she says, wafting smoke away from the pan behind, her heart-shaped face lighting up to reveal a perfect set of pearly white teeth.

'You too,' I say, trying not to stare at her eyelashes.

'Please help yourself.' She gestures to a saucer of salsiccia Toscana on cocktail sticks and plucks the next order from a row of tickets behind her.

'She is always very busy on the day of the market,' Marco says apologetically, stepping aside to allow a group of people to place their order.

'How long have you guys had the apartment for?' I say, trying not to burn my mouth on Tuscan sausage.

'Two years. This will be our third summer.'

'Nice.' I watch as an enormous man in sunglasses advances towards us, his thick moustache framing a wide grin.

Marco beams as the man envelopes him in a hug. 'Ramona, I introduce to you, Signor Zaccardi.'

The man lowers his sunglasses onto the bridge of his nose and shakes my hand. He has a full head of white hair, and his linen suit is more crinkled and creased than age itself.

'Signor Zaccardi makes the most beautiful shoes in the world,' Marco explains.

My eyes travel to Signor Zaccardi's feet and are met with the most gargantuan pair of polished chestnut brown brogues I have ever seen – to say they look like boats is an understatement. These shoes are full-on *Titanic*. Cursing myself for being sizeist – I'm supposed to be an ambassador for Plus Size apparel and here I am, jaw hanging open at a pair of larger-than-average feet – what a fucking hypocrite! I rearrange the expression on my face into one of serenity, an ill-practiced look Fabrice often tells me looks more like constipation, and am about to comment on the quality of his craftmanship when he beats me to it.

'I make good shoes.' He twiddles his moustache. 'Not cheap ones, like those.' He gestures to the shoebox towers of cheap sandals in the corner of the square.

Marco pats him on the back as you might a faithful dog and looks across at me. 'You need shoes? Signor Zaccardi is your man. There is no inhabitant of Altaterra without a pair of Zaccardi shoes.'

Signor Zaccardi ruffles Marco's hair with fondness. 'I am making shoes for Marco and Maria for the wedding of the century.'

I turn to Marco. 'Congratulations.'

A look of confusion flashes across his face. 'Ah, no, it is the wedding of Valentina and Flavio. Maria and I are only guests.' He looks across at the middle-aged woman who leans into our conversation, her sun-streaked hair protruding from an ink-black, beret-style hat finished off with a flurry of feathers. 'And I present to you, Mrs Bergamaschi,' Marco adds just as a gust of wind threatens to swipe the magnificent masterpiece from her head.

'Ciao.' She holds onto her hat as she leans over to kiss me on each cheek. Upon closer inspection, it is even more spectacular, hand-sculpted pleats of satin concertinaing back to give the shape of a turban and an explosion of wispy, soft black feathers bursting from a crease in the back like a flurry of black confetti. Nothing short of art.

'I love your hat.' I circle the top of my head with my finger.

She looks at me as though I have grown feathers.

'Amo . . .' I continue, trying to remember the Italian for hat. 'Cappella?'

'You love the chapel?' Marco frowns.

'Her hat!' I sigh with frustration. 'I love her hat.'

'Cappello,' Marco says with a bite of exasperation, Signor Zaccardi slapping his thigh and chuckling in delight.

'Is it Elsa Schiaparelli?' I say, studying the feathery detail. 'The label, I mean.'

The three of them meet my gaze with narrowed eyes and I feel like a small shrew amongst a flock of eagles. I haven't felt this much outsider angst since I tried to join Flora's book club, who dispatched me from their Zoom call for recommending *You Had Me at Halloumi* as the next read, a volume apparently not quite highbrow enough for their literary tastes. I scrunch up my feet inside my trainers with discomfort and wonder what I said that was so wrong.

'My mother made it,' Mrs Bergamaschi says, an Aussie twang to her voice. 'It's Mariela Marino.'

'The most beautiful hats you will ever see.' A solemn look spreads across Signor Zaccardi's face as he looks up to the heavens and takes an enormous white handkerchief out of his pocket to dab the corners of his eyes.

The penny drops. 'You must be Raffa's mum?' I say, taking in her fresh-from-a-funeral fitted black dress and statement black earrings, my motormouth running away with words I haven't yet thought through.

A huge smile breaks out across her face as she opens her arms to me. 'Yes, and you must be . . .' She clutches onto her hat as it nearly takes off again. 'It's so lovely to meet you.' She hugs me to her chest like a long-lost friend.

I feel my skin flush around my neck. Who does she think I am and why the hell have I mentioned Raffa as though we are good friends? A shudder of discomfort runs down my spine as she squeezes me into her collarbone until the only thing I can smell is her perfume. I feel like a fraudster – or at least an intruder. This poor woman has just buried her mother and here I am, opportunistically shaking her down for information on her hot son who I've met for all of a few hours on a plane. For fuck's sake, what's the matter with me?

'I'm so sorry you missed the service. Bloody British Airways, eh?' she says, blotting a tear away with a paper tissue. 'Sorry, I know I didn't get to see my mother that often but I'm going to miss her terribly.' Her voice cracks and she starts to sob into her hanky. 'You'll miss her, too, eh? I know how close you were, Italy being a whole heap easier to get to from the UK than Oz. Thanks so much for making all those trips over. She appreciated it, you know. She thought very highly of you.' Through teary eyes she looks at me with a fondness I don't understand and it's only when I see the startled expression on Marco's face that I realise I am nodding. Slowly, but nodding, nonetheless.

'I'm sure she . . .' The words get caught in my throat as her tears trickle down my neck. 'I mean I've never—'

'She was always talking about you,' she goes on. 'All those triathlons. All those – what are they called again? – Tough . . .' She searches for the word.

'Tough Mudders?' I suggest without thinking.

'That's it. A go-getting girl after my own heart.' She grasps me by the shoulders and holds me away from her so that she can study my face. 'I don't know how you do it, getting electrocuted under all those layers of ice, jumping through fire and scaling those climbing walls without so much as a rope. So brave. Honestly, I'm in awe.' She looks me up and down and grins. 'Raffa said you wouldn't have thought it to look at you.'

115

I feel my cheeks flush further. 'I'm not sure—'

'Still, you should never judge a book by its covers . . . but you can judge a woman by her hat, as my mother used to say. Didn't she have some wonderful sayings? *As mad as a hat with wings. The guinea pig never lies. How many beans make five?* She was one of a kind, eh?'

'Urm,' I muster as she thrusts my head back into her collarbone.

'I'm so sorry we never got to meet until now. I kept saying to Raffa that you should come over to Melbourne but I know it's difficult to get time out of training. He showed me your schedule. Very rigorous. Honestly, it's so impressive. All those medals. And beating the Russians in the semi-finals like that last month. I mean . . . mind-blowing. I just wish it was all on the television. You'd think it would be an Olympic sport by now, wouldn't you? That's what I said to Derek.' She nods over to an older, larger version of Raffa, who is fending off a group of children with a handful of euros.

My skin bristles. 'Listen, I think you might have got me mixed—'

'Derek?' She calls him over.

'I think there might have been a misunderstanding,' I say, catching Marco's eye and gearing up to an explanation of the truth. 'I can't even run one hundred metres without—'

'So modest.' She taps the back of my hand affectionately. 'Raffa always said you were very self-effacing, shunning the limelight and not wanting to make a fuss. And giving away your medals to under-privileged children? That was such a sweet gesture. And donating your prize money to that village in Africa? So lovely of you.'

Marco clears his throat loudly.

'Derek, come and meet Raffa's girlfriend.' She beckons over her husband and to my horror I find myself wedged between Raffa's parents just as Raffa himself comes strolling across the village square in a blue shirt and cotton shorts, an Order of Service in one hand and a beer in the other.

Marco catches my eye and raises an eyebrow.

'Very nice to meet you,' Derek says, shaking my hand.

I notice the stoic expression on Raffa's face morphing into one of alarm as he draws nearer, slowing his steps and eyeing me with distrust, and I wish more than anything that teleportation was a viable option and that I could just magically disappear with my dignity intact. My heart starts to pound inside my chest like a prisoner desperate to escape. It's not his confident stride, his dazzling amber eyes or his strapping frame. It's not even the citrus musk that fills the air as he wraps his arms around his mother and squeezes her to his chest, the muscles around his shoulders dancing under his shirt, but there is something about Raffaele Bergamaschi that makes my lungs feel so tight they might just burst.

Sofia holds onto her hat as another gust of wind threatens to knock it off her head. She looks over to Raffa. 'Darling, we've just met—'

'Ramona?' He frowns.

A look of horror travels across his mother's face. 'This isn't Oona?' she says, taking a step away from me and looking me up and down as though I have just committed a crime. 'I thought she was a bit . . .' She puffs out her chest, her body inflating like a territorial pigeon.

'I'm not who you think I am!' I hold my hands up.

'Actually . . .' Raffa turns towards me and to my utter astonishment, slings an arm around my waist and plants a kiss on my cheek. 'Yes, you are.'

'I can explain,' I say to anyone who will listen.

Raffa looks straight into my eyes. 'Let me explain, darling.' He takes my hand with such an assurance it feels like he is reclaiming what is rightfully his and turns back to his parents. 'Oona is short for Ramona. Kind of. It's just that Ona sounds weird so we stuck another "o" in there and . . . yeah, Ramona. Ramoona. Oona. That's kind of how it happened, isn't it?' He looks at me with puppy-dog eyes, and I find myself unable to speak. A maelstrom of tiny fireworks pop and fizz throughout my body as he envelopes my hand in his before my senses return, and I momentarily worry that he might be some kind of body-under-the-floorboards guy with whatever he is plotting. Checking that he hasn't pickpocketed my phone and keys (still in my jacket pocket), I make a mental note not to eat or drink anything that may be offered to me.

'I'll explain later,' Raffa says, to my hair more than to me. 'But you'd be doing me a huge favour if you just went along with it.'

Out of my peripheral vision I see Marco shaking his head and leaving and although I know this is fifty shades of weird, I figure this could be a whole heap of fun, too. As long as Raffa is not a psychopath, this could be a welcome diversion from what has been a pretty bleak state of affairs. An oasis of unbridled fun in a desert of depressing gloom. Seriously, hanging off the arm of one of the world's most eligible bachelors is hardly a chore, is it? Worse case they figure it out and we look stupid – something I've grown accustomed to over the past few days.

I glance around the huddle of Raffa's relatives who have formed a circle around us. 'Pleased to meet you all.'

CHAPTER NINE
La Casa dei Cappelli

'La Casa what?' Fabrice says. At least I think that's what he says, but the signal is pretty shocking. It doesn't help that his office is situated in the basement of a converted Victorian house with double stud walls. Only the best for Pomfrey & Wibble, Highgate's longest established corporate accountancy practice.

'Cappelli. It means hats.'

'Get you!' he says.

'Judging by all the hype, Mariela Marino was a pretty big deal over here. She has her own Wikipedia page and everything,' I say, scanning the Mistress of Millinery's early history.

Fabrice lets out a snort. '*I've* got my own Wikipedia page!'

' . . . blah blah. "Fled the glitz and glamour of Milan in the nineties to live a peripatetic existence for twenty years before

119

settling in rural Tuscany. Marino is famous for a wide range of hats, including the cartwheel, the dragonfly, il serpente il seno."' I read as much as I can before my laptop screen goes blank and the battery dies.

'And Hot Grandson has inherited the lot?' Fabrice says.

'Yep. We're going up there today. He wants to pick my brain about all things fashion and then tonight I'm his girlfriend at this big evening meal they're having.'

'Remind me why you're having to pretend to be his girlfriend. Only that to me has red flag written all over it.'

'Because his girlfriend heartlessly dumped him shortly before the funeral and his relatives have been desperate to meet her – they live in Australia and Raffa has lived with this girl in the UK for two years – and now his mum is terminally ill and just wants to see him settled down with the right girl and—'

'That's you?'

'I bloody wish I *was* the right girl, Fabrice. You should see him. He's ridiculously hot and is a really sweet guy at the same time. Honestly, he just wants to make his mum happy.'

'Riiight,' he says after a long pause. 'Well, if you find anything suitably ostentatious at her hat shop, let me know as I need something classy to wear when I'm on the float at DragFest. Something that sets me apart from the rest. Something so eye-catching that I end up winning the whole damned thing and can hand in my notice at Pomfrey & Wibble to travel the world.'

'I'll keep an eye out.'

'I mean it, Vivienne. Mr Wibble has brought in new accounting software that none of us knows how to use and I need to get out of here as it's crushing my soul. Did I tell you Queen Bea and I have commandeered an open-top bus for the occasion? A double-decker. Something feathery wouldn't go amiss.'

'Sure,' I say, plonking fresh bread down on the chopping board and hunting around the kitchen for a bread knife. 'How did your gig go the other night?'

'Gig?'

'Your dress had ripped and—'

'Oh, I thought you meant the threesome Rico and I got embroiled in last night . . .'

'Whaaaat?' I screech, discovering that the life-sized wooden hen next to the toaster is actually a knife block (something no doubt inherited from next door) and dragging out a serrated blade.

'. . . is what my drag queen next-door-neighbour was saying the other night.' He adopts his corporate telephone voice and I instantly know that Mr Pomfrey, his boss and co-owner of Pomfrey & Wibble Corporate Accountants, has returned to his desk.

'Right,' I say, chuckling. Mr Pomfrey has no idea that the mild-mannered, clean-cut, suited-and-booted man he hired eighteen months ago and sits opposite almost everyday moonlights in six-inch diamanté heels and sequined evening gowns as Polly Darton come eight o'clock in the evening. 'And when do you need this particular set of accounts by, sir?' He goes on in the posh voice he reserves for bookkeeping clients, a clipped enunciation to his vowels that wouldn't go amiss alongside home-made ginger beer and tomato sandwiches in an Enid Blyton voiceover.

I stifle a laugh with a slice of bread. 'How was the threesome then?'

He clears his throat. 'Well, Mr Maguire made his deposit a little earlier than planned, but other than that, tickety-boo.'

'Ha!' I bang my knee on the table, iced water going up my nose and dripping down my top.

'I won't lie, Mr Ainsbury-Saxton, I've never seen someone who can deplete his reserves twice in a matter of hours, but you live and learn . . . You live and learn.' He snorts with laughter, all those years at drama school coming into fruition – you honestly wouldn't think he was anything other than a privileged, pompous twerp. 'And although these were physically verified assets, I'm not sure they realised their holding gain.'

I laugh, plugging my mouth with more bread.

'That said, I did look at Mr Maguire's projection and although his growth rate was impressive, it just didn't sustain.'

'Is he looking at you?' I say, between giggles. 'Mr Pomfrey?'

'Absolutely,' he chimes.

'Have you not invited him to one of your drag nights yet?' I chuckle.

'Mr Pomfrey has his own extension.'

I nearly choke on my bread.

'Would you like me to put you through?'

'No!' I howl.

'Jolly good. Well, I can only apologise on his behalf for the double entry and I look forward to speaking to you soon, sir.'

'Righto, sir,' I say, wiping tears of laughter from my face.

'Goodbye, Mr Ainsbury-Saxton.' He hangs up.

My stomach aches from giggling and then, just like that, the sense of deep joy and exhilaration that has set me aglow evaporates into something heavy and distasteful. Shouldn't Fabrice be able to openly talk about his extracurricular activities without fear of judgement?

Fabrice

> You're overthinking it! I actually quite enjoy leading a double life! I wouldn't get that schoolboy-behind-the-bike-shed rush of adrenaline if everyone was au fait and accepting.

Assured, I finish my mozzarella and tomato sandwich and set to work on creating a spreadsheet listing all the major Italian fashion houses and the name of their senior commissioning agents, which isn't as easy as you'd think, their names mainly unpublished. I manage to identify six and spend the next hour customising design submission emails to them all and then realise that time has evaporated. I'm supposed to be leading my own double life at La Casa dei Cappelli in only a matter of minutes and whilst I'm pretty certain that strict punctuality is not high on the agenda of Italian consciousness, a promise is a promise, and I don't want to renege on a plan that's only just been made.

Zhané

> Hang on a minute, I didn't understand that last bit. He wants you to pretend to be his girlfriend because ????

Flora

> Because he wants to stick his tongue down her throat!

Ramona

> Because he wants to show his dying mother that he's happy and settled.

Zhané

> And he can't be happy and settled if he's single??? This is EXACTLY what is wrong with society! Romes, you realise you're effectively pimping yourself out as a mail-order girlfriend?

Flora

> It's romantic!

Zhané

> It's insane.

Ramona

> It's for one night only.

Flora

> My friend's friend had an arranged marriage
> and fell hook, line and sinker for the guy they
> set her up with. It can happen, you know . . .

Zhané

> That's fucked up and most definitely didn't
> happen. It's just the sort of shit devout parents
> tell their terrified daughters before they force
> them into an arranged marriage to make them
> feel like there is hope. Fairy-tale endings cannot
> happen when a relationship is based on a pack
> of lies. Look at Tom Cruise!

Flora

> Some things are just meant to be x

My head is a jumble of thoughts as I apply more mascara than is necessary and ditch my trainers in favour of high-heeled wedges. There's no denying that pretending to be Raffa's girlfriend can only be a recipe for disaster for him, the truth bound to come out at some point, but from my side of things, as long as I don't get too carried away with the notion that we are in an amorous relationship and continue to remind myself that this conscious coupling is a sham, it should be a good laugh. Just what the doctor ordered. So why am I feeling first-date nervous about meeting him today?

Fuck it. I grab my bag and head out.

The village itself is a labyrinth of tight-knit cobblestone alleys, its rough-hewn stone buildings and grassy banks encircled by a sandstone wall. From the top of the path, I look out across the valley of rolling cypress groves and saffron-hued fields, a sweeping panorama of greens and golds. A crumbling archway leads me into an alleyway draped with washing lines, table-cloths, bedlinen and a row of Y-fronts fluttering in the breeze.

I wander past small stone houses, baskets of roses and sage hanging next to painted wooden doors. A tortoiseshell cat sprawls out on the step of a wine cellar dappled in sunlight, La Cantina signposted on a small wooden panel and I make a mental note of which path I've taken, in the hope of picking up a bottle of vino rosso later on. Next to it, an abandoned shop front with tiny bay windows either side of the door, so thick with dust and woolly with cobwebs that it's impossible to see inside. Higher up, two women sit side by side on a wooden bench, their fingers methodically twisting and turning around crochet hooks, the cotton yarn in their lap bobbing this way and that. It's not until I look closely that I see they're working together to craft a single garment, each of them crocheting outwards from the middle. True sisterhood.

'Buongiorno!' One of them raises a crochet hook and gives me a toothless smile.

'Buongiorno!' I return the sentiment.

The alley winds around a small bakery, butchers and a gela-teria boasting a whole spectrum of ice-cream flavours. Ciocco-lato. Pistacchio. Stracciatella. Mandorla. Limone. Fragola. My mouth waters. I vow to come back here, too. Up the hill I climb, perspiration bubbling on my brow, and I can't help but feel that my wedge heels are turning out to be a bad choice, what with all the uneven cobble stones. As smooth as seashells, they may look pretty and date back to medieval times but they're an ankle-twisting safety hazard. Next time, it's trainers all the way.

La Casa dei Cappelli may be the only hat shop in this tiny village and indeed within a fifty-mile radius, but that doesn't make it any easier to locate. Conceding that I'm a little lost, I gather up my phone to open Google Maps, my chest fluttering with hope when I see an email reply from Valentino:

From: Viktor.Kuznetsov@Valentino.com
Subject: Curvaliscious: a brand new high-end fashion range

Dear Sir/Madam,

Thank you for your designs. You will appreciate that we get a high volume of submissions and are unable to assess each one fully. We do, however, note that this is a Plus Size collection, which is not something that Valentino get involved with.

Thank you and best of luck elsewhere.

Best regards,
V.K

My heart sinks and my limbs fill with lead-heavy despair. With all the strength I can muster, I put one foot in front of the other and stride up the hill. It's only when I look up that I realise I have hurdled walls, jumped over stiles, climbed over railings, squeezed through gaps and negotiated fig trees, lemon trees, pear trees, only to find myself back where I started.

'Scusi,' I say to the crocheting women, who nod with amusement as I embark upon my second lap. If I can ask the way to the theatre, surely I can ask for directions to the hat shop? 'Dov'è il . . . Mariela Marino?'

Crochet hooks suspended mid-air, the pair of them share a look of concern. 'Mariela Marino?' one of them says, her brow furrowing with deep sorrow. 'Mariela Marino è morta. Mariela Marino is dead.' She looks up at the heavens and prods the four corners of a crucifix into her chest with the dramatic tension of a wronged nun.

'Oh, sorry, no,' I say, flustered. 'I meant her shop. Urm. Dov'è il . . . urm, er, La Casa dei Cappelli, por favor, I mean per favore?' Surely, they'll get the gist this time.

Both of them stare at me with a blank expression. Maybe not.

'Erm. Cappello?' I say, miming a very tall, top hat and instantly regretting it.

They look at me as though I am an alien, which I am. In a fashion.

I scratch my head. 'La Casa dei Cappelli?

'Aaah.' The woman on the left sits upright, the creases of her old-fashioned pink housecoat unfolding beneath her bosom. 'Alla fine della strada, gira a sinistrsa, a destra del panificio è il palazzo con la porta rossa.'

I watch as her arm snakes here and there, lefts and rights accentuated with a flurry of the fingers. I understand left, bakery, palace and then something about a red door, which I guess is better than a kick up the arse, so I say grazie and wander back up the hill but would be lying if I said I understood where I was heading.

After a third lap of the village and a quick Google Translate, affirmation that 'palazzo' does not necessarily mean palace and can just as easily be an edifice or building, I eventually locate a red door next to a small shop doubling as La Posta. There's no sign of any hats but short of spotting any other red door, I give it a knock.

A moment later, a man in huge underpants and an oil-stained vest appears on the step. 'Salve.' He strokes his moustache.

'Mariela Marino? La Casa dei Cappelli?' I say hopefully.

'Ah, la porta rossa!' He chuckles, the sound of phlegm rattling in his chest. 'Su per la collina, poi giu per il vicolo a sinistra, poi prendere il secondo sentiero a destra vicino al sicomoro.'

'Grazie,' I say, wondering if I'll ever be able to decipher the Italian language and am just about to give up and go back to the house when I see one of the crochet ladies panting up the hill towards me.

'Aspettare!' she says, waving. 'I'll show you.'

'Thank you!'

With bowed legs and creaking hips, she leads me down Via Martini, a narrow, unassuming alley to a red door that juts out from a small porch, shaded by a stone cottage on either side. There is no sign for the Casa dei Cappelli just as there is no sign of any actual hats nor of a window in which to display them. How the hell did Mariela Marino ever get any business if nobody could find her?

'Here?' I say tentatively.

'Si,' the woman says, encouraging me to knock.

The door is ajar. Warily, I hammer my knuckles against the painted timber and once it's clear that nobody is going to answer and that both the woman and her knitting have gone, gingerly I push it open.

The room lying before me is spacious and echoey. Its contents have been cleared out, the bookcases empty, the walls devoid of pictures and the entirety of Mariela Marino's life possessions stacked into sad little piles, a stark reminder that our time on earth is fleeting and transitory. The curtain flutters in the breeze and I stand there for a while, affected by the loss of someone I never knew and tinged with a sorrow I don't quite understand.

'Ramona!' Raffa appears at the bottom of the stairs at the back of the room. His olive skin glows against his white T-shirt and he makes me feel a little short on oxygen. My eyes travel to his feet. He's about the only man I know that can pull off flip-flops. 'Thank God you're here.'

For a brief moment I delude myself into thinking that I actually *am* his girlfriend and am about to run into his arms and kiss him on the lips when reality forms a tight grip around my throat, and I wonder why I've come here.

'Can I take you upstairs?' he says, my heart skipping a beat and my ovaries performing some sort of fallopian Mexican wave in reaction to his words. It's all I can do not to ask him to say it again so that I can get out my phone, hit record and play it back when I'm alone.

'Sure,' I say.

I follow him up the stairs, his preposterously tight bottom directly at my eye level, and I wonder if I could get away with taking a bite out of it. Undisturbed by the movement of his athletic frame, the staircase has an altogether different reaction to my heavy footing, emitting the sort of creaks and groans that accompany arthritis. I shuffle over to the wall in the hope of silencing the sigh of each step as I follow him, only to lose my balance, face planting straight into his buttocks.

Mortified, I pull myself up. 'Sorry, I . . .'

'It's these stairs. They're ridiculously steep,' he says, reaching out to give me a hand.

'Thanks.' I smile deliriously. He really is lovely.

At the top of the staircase, a mannequin's head sculpted from smooth, black marble sits on an antique dresser. It is crowned with the most awe-inspiring, retro tulle fascinator I've ever set eyes on – layer upon layer of black net and black polka-dot voile, angled horizontally like millefeuilles stacked one on top of the other. I feel giddy with excitement.

Raffa turns to me. 'Ready to have your mind blown?'

I try to erase the fantasy that is building in my head, pushing away images of Raffa and I rolling around on a four-poster bed, Egyptian cotton sheets discarded along with all inhibitions. His hands gliding over my skin. My fingers finding the small of his back. And I have to get a grip of myself. This is about hot hats, not hot sex.

He pushes open the door to reveal a spacious room with a smell that reminds me of the workshop room back at House of Dreams. Breathing in the scent of creativity, I look around at hats of all shapes and sizes displayed around the room on shelves, in cabinets, on hooks. Hundreds of them all in one space.

'Come on in,' Raffa says with a twinkle in his eye.

I have a feeling this is going to be good.

CHAPTER TEN
Hats, hats, hats

The hat emporium, as Raffa likes to call it, is a bright, airy room that would make a great space to host a teashop. Its floorboards painted white, its walls papered with a pretty pink, floral print and a huge glass chandelier hanging from an ornate ceiling rose, it is nothing short of shabby chic. If downstairs there wasn't a single hat in sight, here you can't move for them; every wall dotted with headgear of all shapes and sizes. Straw boaters. Felted cloche hats. Brushed cotton berets. Beautiful pillbox hats with a ribbon trim. Wide-brimmed hats. Delicate lace headpieces. Turbans. Elaborate pieces you might wear to Ascot. Ornate creations designed for parties and weddings. Swimming caps adorned with rubber flowers. Haute-couture hats showcasing household objects on their summit. A bottle of Veuve Clicquot champagne sprouting from the top of one whilst another boasts pasta in all its forms – farfalle, macaroni, rigatoni, paccheri – prolapsing from a felt bowl, its chinstrap dangling down from the windowsill upon which it is perched. It's as much an art exhibition as it is millinery.

'It's like a treasure trove.' I look around in wide-eyed wonder.

'Yeah, well, enjoy it while you can!' Raffa throws his keys down on a velvet upholstered chair and flicks through a pile of papers.

'Sorry?'

'It won't be around for much longer if the villagers get their way. They want us to sell up and turn it into holiday apartments.'

'But that would be sacrilege!'

'Tell me about it. Ma's really upset about it and my grandma would be turning in her grave if she knew,' he says, picking up a ribbon-edged trilby and putting it back down again.

'But I thought . . .' I stall, trying to recall what was written about the Casa dei Cappelli in the memorial leaflet Raffa gave me on the plane. 'I thought the villagers were campaigning for it to become a national heritage site?'

'That's what they tell the Press, but trust me, they have ulterior motives.'

'I'm sure they'll see sense,' I say, my eye drawn to a framed photograph of a young woman with high cheekbones and cupid's bow lips, posing with a shoe strapped to her head. Homage to Dalí? My head spins. Thank God I took a punt on getting on that train to Altaterra.

'The men's selection isn't quite as exciting.' He waves his hand in the direction of an alcove of men's hats taking up at least six shelves. Fedoras. Panamas. Trilbies. Peaked caps. Homburgs. Cowboy hats. Bowlers. Campaigns. Pork pies. 'But still pretty cool, huh?' he says, perching a trilby hat on his head and winking.

I can't help thinking that if Fabrice were here, he'd point out that gender is a construct, but instead I chuckle. 'Very Humphrey Bogart.'

My eyes skim the top row of women's hats next to the window. A swimming cap adorned with feathers. Another which appears to have felt leaves stuck all over it in a flower fairy-meets-acorn type of arrangement. A polystyrene hat moulded into a swirl of Mr Whippy ice cream. A hat in the shape of a teapot, its spout and handle counterbalancing the weight of what looks like hand-painted porcelain. Another one depicting a skyscraper built from grey felt, its windows embroidered in a silver weave.

'Do you want to try one on?' he says, dragging out a stool upholstered in pink velvet and reaching for the ladder.

'Thanks.' I take a seat, dropping my bag between my feet and gazing around the room at masterpiece after masterpiece and wishing that I could somehow bring Mariela Marino back from the dead and tell her how extraordinary her work is – not that she won't have heard it a million times before, but it feels wrong that she's not here to see the impact her creations have on people and reap the rewards of the legacy she has left behind. The fact that she has gifted something so special to the human race blows my mind. To think that generation after generation will marvel at her work. It's incredible and makes my own endeavour to launch a size-inclusive clothes range feel small and insignificant, and yet inspires me to think big and do better.

'Which one do you fancy?' Raffa breaks my daydream by unclipping the stepladder from the shelf, shifting it along the floor and parking it below a row of 1950s-style hats. He reaches for a crimson brushed cotton cloche number with a black velvet trim. 'I think this one's very you.'

I pull a face. 'Because you know me so well, you mean?'

He laughs. 'Fair point!'

I twizzle the hat between my fingers, the fabric soft yet solid, and I can feel from the texture and shape that it's of the highest quality. Taking it back out of my hands, he rotates it one hundred and eighty degrees and places it onto my head, pulling it down over my ears and fluffing out my hair below. A bolt of electricity shoots down my spine as his fingers brush against my bare shoulders.

'Thank you,' I whisper, trying to act normal in spite of the chemical reaction that is going on inside my knickers.

He holds up a baroque-rose hand mirror inches away from my face and invites me to gaze at my reflection. 'Just doing what I've seen my grandma do!'

I study the woman staring back at me and would love to say that I look chic and sophisticated, but truth told, I look not too dissimilar from the woman who runs the sorting office in *Postman Pat*: austere, frumpy and a little bit simple. 'Not sure it's quite me,' I say, laughing.

'Only eight thousand euros, that one,' he says, looking at the piece of card in his hand.

I try not to choke, whipping it off my head with maybe a little too much haste. 'You know, I should probably learn a bit about Oona and about you, too, if I'm to come out with you guys this evening,' I say, stroking the brushed cotton in an anticlockwise direction.

'What do you want to know?' he says with a disarming shrug.

I rack my brains. 'How long have we been in a relationship?'

'Two years, three months and nine days.'

'Riiight,' I say. 'And how did we meet?'

'At my friend's art gallery. It was the grand opening and you outbid me in an auction for a watercolour I had my eye on.'

'Did I?'

'You did . . . which is why I was forced to make a move on you so that we would end up moving in together and I could share the hare.'

'Share the hare? Is that prison lingo?'

'It's the name of the painting. A bright-eyed March hare hidden in long grass. Awesome piece. We would have saved a lot of money if we'd have joined forces earlier and bid together.'

'OK, so you guys are like the Romeo and Juliet of the art world?'

'Not really. I mean we both love Joseph Raffael's paintings – the flowers he paints are unbelievable. Have you seen them?' An expression of dreaminess overcomes him. 'His work is a master-class in texture. He painted this owl and, just by looking at its feathers, you can see how soft and layered they are.'

I make a mental note to Google Joseph Raffael's artwork when I get back. 'And how old is Oona?'

'Twenty-nine.'

'OK. And you share an apartment in Hackney?'

'Yeah, one of the new builds next to the canal.' He sets about bubble wrapping a brushed cotton bowler hat and packing it into a cardboard box. 'This one is promised to Signor Zaccardi.'

'OK. And does Oona have a job on top of the sports stuff?'

'*The sports stuff?* She's a professional sportswoman, it's not just some casual hobby!' He frowns and I feel suitably chastised, the glow of embarrassment permeating my cheeks. 'But yeah, she works part-time in my friend's art gallery – the place we met – and does the odd weekend when I play rugby.'

'Rugby, of course.' My eyes fall to his thighs and a feeling of vertigo sets in. 'Are you a sports professional, too?'

'Nah. I play rugby at county level but I'm a project manager in a bank.'

'OK,' I say, committing this to memory. 'Favourite food?'

'Cheesy chips. Steak. Anything you can chuck on the barbie, typical Aussie that I am.'

'Right.' I watch him slide the hat box into a large cloth bag. 'Favourite song?'

'Bruce Springsteen. "Dancing in the Dark".'

'Good choice. Favourite drink?'

'Pale ale. Or a good craft beer.'

'Favourite film?'

'*Three Men and a Little Lady.*'

I let go of the hat in my lap. 'No.'

'Huh?'

'I feel sure that Oona wouldn't go out with you if she knew that!' I say, knowing this would be true of any twenty-nine-year-old, self-respecting woman.

'She did know.'

'And she didn't mind?' I say aghast.

'It's a great film, Ramona.'

'Oona.'

137

'Oona.' He chuckles. 'It was my dad's favourite and I used to like watching it with him.'

'OK, I'll let you off. Favourite book?'

He scratches his chin. 'I don't really read books.'

'How can you not read books?'

'I read a lot of papers for my job so the last thing I want to do is more reading in my spare time. I'm more into sports.' He looks across at me. 'I guess I'm more into the physical stuff.'

'Okaaay,' I say, reddening as he holds my gaze, my stomach flip-flopping in delight.

'I like reading sports magazines if that counts?' he says after a pause in which I blush further, my whole chest feeling hot and prickly.

Getting a grip, I digest his words. What he's saying is entirely unattractive and yet the way he delivers it is anything but. I feel discombobulated. Based on my string of interview questions, we are totally incompatible and Flora's internet dating algorithm would never deem us a match, but does any of that really matter? This isn't real after all. This is just one friend helping out another in the hope of getting laid.

'I'm a decent cook if that makes up for it?' he says, sensing my disapproval. 'I bake bread every day back home and make a pretty bonza paella.'

'In that case, I'll let you off,' I say, wondering what it would feel like to be presented with freshly baked bread every morning.

Spellbound by the way he moves like liquid over to a basket of fascinators on the dresser, the muscles in his legs flickering as he goes, I decide that if I was Oona, I too would have overlooked his appalling taste in movies and his lack of interest in books to focus on the physical aspects of the relationship. But on thinking about it, he surely knows something of literature given that he recognised Ramona as a novel back when I met him on the plane?

'If you don't read books, how did you know about Ramona?'

'We studied it at school. My English teacher was a bit of a thespian so gave us a pretty good grounding.' He looks into the basket and plucks out a classic headband silhouette accented with a fabric flower and coral-hued feathers which sweep from left to right in a grand display of opulence. 'What about this bad boy?' he says, pulling out the price tag. 'Retailing at only two thousand euros.'

'It's gorgeous,' I say, admiring the detail as he wanders back over and, sweeping my hair over my shoulders with the back of his hands – there it is again, that shiver down my spine and that flutter in my knickers – attaches it to my head, which spins uncontrollably now that his crotch is right at my eye level and is having such a peculiar effect on me that I can't quite find my words.

'There we go.' He lets go of the fascinator, the price tag fluttering down into my lap.

I try not to flinch at the pinching pain. 'I think this might be designed for a smaller head,' I say eventually, prising it away from my throbbing temples.

After trying a third hat – if you can call attaching a Rubik's cube to an elasticated band a hat – I sense by Raffa's increasing glances at his wristwatch that my allotted dressing-up time is fast running out and that he has places to be. Still, it was fun whilst it lasted.

'Look, thanks for bailing me out.' He places the Rubik's headband back on the shelf. 'You have no idea what Mum's like once she gets her mind set on something.'

I look up at him, a million plot holes dancing around my head. 'Are you sure it wouldn't be easier to tell her the truth?'

He scrunches up his face. 'If she wasn't terminally ill with only a matter of weeks left, then maybe, but this is a woman who struggles to get out of bed most days – I know she looks all chipper, but trust me, she's faking it – and has written a bucket list with "See Raffaele settled with a nice girl" on it.'

'Right,' I say, making eye contact with the floor, a lump forming in my throat at the thought of my own mother being terminally ill and all the things I'd want to experience with her, knowing that it may be for the last time. It must be heartbreaking seeing someone that you love slowly deteriorate in front of your eyes until there's nothing left. Poor guy.

He wanders over to the window and stares out at the rolling hills spread out below and leans his hands against the folded shutters. 'Most of the stuff she has on the list I have no control over whatsoever, but this one I do . . . I have to do this for her.'

'Sure,' I say quietly, thinking of Mum in her paragliding gear about to take one final leap off a cliff, tears springing up in my eyes.

'It'll be OK.' He picks at his fingernails.

'She must have seen plenty of photos of Oona and know that I look nothing like her, though!' I say, pushing all thoughts of my not-dying mother out of my mind and thinking about the six-pack stomach Oona must have developed as a professional triathlete.

'You have similar hair,' he offers. 'And Mum's memory's not great.'

'But she's still got her eyesight, right?'

'Look, she didn't bat an eyelid yesterday, did she?' he says. 'That's how the whole thing started, after all. She was the one that jumped to conclusions.'

I chuckle at the memory. 'I can't believe your dad didn't say anything.'

'Dad's too busy mending cars to notice what's right under his nose, let alone ten thousand miles away. If it's not part of an engine, it's not worth looking at. No offence but I could turn up with a chimp and he wouldn't notice.'

'None taken.' I get up and browse the hats on the other side of the room whilst he locks the drawer beneath the desk in the corner. 'Still, selling me as an Olympic triathlete is a bit of a stretch. I don't think I've been able to touch my toes for about a decade.'

'Do you need to?' he says with sparkling eyes and I feel my insides go soft and gooey, the pull of attraction getting the better of me.

'Can I see a picture of her?' I say, needing to anchor myself in reality and sabotage my fantasies which are running away with me right now, my mind a carousel of happy-ever-after moments of Raffa and I – in bed, on a private yacht, on our wedding day.

'Of Oona?'

'Yes.'

He takes his phone out of his pocket and flicks through his images, holding up his screen to show a portrait shot of her holding up a bronze medal, her face plastered in mud and pride. A sweatband holds back her hair which is matted with dirt and the grin on her face appears to be genuine. She's half the size of me.

'She looks lovely,' I say, wondering why I even asked to look.

'Yes.' He sighs.

'So what happened? I mean why did you guys split up?'

'She ran off with my best friend.'

'Noooo. I'm sorry. When did you find out?'

'Last week. As it happens, she was still going to come to the funeral as a gesture of goodwill – you know, for exactly the same reason that you're stepping in now, but . . . well, I'm not sure what went on yesterday, but she clearly didn't board the plane.'

'I'm sorry. That's totally shit,' I say.

'Yeah, but thanks to you, the day is saved.'

'Dial-a-girlfriend at your service,' I say in a voice that I have never spoken in before, giving a quick salute.

Fortunately, he laughs but I have now become conscious that I am acting like a total cheeseball, my mind looping back to a montage of cringeworthy moments – me stripping off in that meeting room and struggling to get the watermelon backless sundress on fast enough for my pitch. Setayesh glowering at me in the corridor. The Horse telling me my collection is too big (yet not big enough). Seeing the pair of them going hell for leather over his desk at work, Post-it notes fluttering onto the office floor with each thrust. Setayesh pulling one over on me and doing me out of the gala tickets. Getting sacked from House of Dreams. Surely I'm due an upward spiral?

'You OK?' Raffa looks up with concern.

'Yeah,' I say, trying to push my thoughts away. 'I just . . . I kind of lost my job and have no reason to go home so I thought I'd check out your grandma's legacy. I hope you don't think—'

'I was just ribbing you!' He squeezes my arm.

'As long as you . . .'

His hand moves to my shoulder. 'I'm very glad you came,' he says softly.

My skin tingles in response. 'Me too.'

'And it would mean the world to me if you'd come out for dinner tonight,' he says, his amber eyes connecting with mine and a rush of desire flooding through me.

'I . . .'

'Please.' He holds my gaze. 'It's just one night.'

Sparks fizz and fly inside me like tiny firecrackers, my stomach flutters and the ground shifts beneath my feet. Could this be the beginning of something great?

CHAPTER ELEVEN
Just one night

From: Irene.Moretti@Versace.com
Subject: Curvaliscious: a brand new high-end fashion range

Signorina Ramona,
Many thanks for your submission. I found your designs innovative and fun but am unable to take things further with Curvaliscious as we do not represent Plus Size apparel.

Cordial salutations
Irene Moretti

Fighting the downward tug of despair, I try to put the email out of my mind. Hanging out with Raffa at one of Tuscany's finest restaurants should be a joyous experience and not one tarnished with a lingering feeling of despondence. Onwards and upwards. After all, just because two fashion houses have rejected my work, it doesn't mean that the others will.

From: P.Barone@Pucci.com
Subject: Curvaliscious: a brand new high-end fashion range

Mr Ramona,
We do not represent Plus Size apparel so it's a 'no' from us.

Distinti Saluti,
P. Barone

Make that three! I take a deep breath, apply lip gloss and head out. Why can't the fashion greats recognise my Plus Size genius? Why can't anyone see the potential? Am I totally delusional in my quest for putting Plus Size clothing on the Haute Couture circuit? Thank God I have Raffa to distract me and a fun night out ahead. An evening of escapism and a couple of glasses of vino rosso will be just the thing.

It's four hours later. Slathered in factor fifty and dressed in my best cotton floaty kaftan, I weave my way through the chicken grain that Signora Abbadelli is scattering out in the garden and head down to the village square. A shiny minibus waits under the shade of a plane tree as the sound of Aussie-Italian chatter interspersed with raucous laughter resonates over the hillside. Pollen spores drift lazily in the evening haze and the air smells of summer – a potpourri of jasmine, tarragon and rosemary mingling with the scent of sun cream, perspiration and hot tarmac. I'm sweating; the sun still blisteringly hot even though it's six in the evening and I've already finished the two bottles of water I've brought for the journey, what with the restaurant being a good ten kilometres away.

A quick pit stop at Ciccone's, a shrine to Madonna and one of only two bars in the village suggests I'm not the only dehydrated tourist in town, the burly man behind the bar (Enzo, according to his name badge) declaring that he is out of 'acqua' and pointing at the empty coolers behind him. He looks at me unblinkingly and makes a pumping motion with his fist, an action I'm not sure whether to interpret as an insult or the suggestion that I go milk a cow. It's only when he points outside that I clock the drinking fountain at the other side of the village square, surrounded by a huddle of hot and bothered people clutching various-sized vessels. I go to join them, Raffa appearing by my side, a look of relief plastered across his face.

'I was beginning to think you wouldn't show up,' he says. 'I tried to swing by the address you gave me to pick you up so that we could arrive together, but I couldn't find a number fifteen.'

'It's not the easiest to—'

'I told Mum you were on the phone to your parents – if she asks,' he says with an air of impatience.

'OK.'

'Sorry.' His face softens. 'I'm just really worried about her. She vomited before we left, and I don't know how she's going to get through this evening.'

146

I shouldn't stand there studying him, but I can't help it. He wears a plain pale-yellow T-shirt and khaki shorts which accentuate his dark olive skin and his stubble is clipped around his jawline. 'Sorry,' I say, wiping my damp upper lip with my sleeve – attractive – and trying to smile without showing my wonky front teeth. 'I had to chase a couple of chickens out of the house before I could lock up.'

'I'm trying to work out if that's a quirky British metaphor.' He raises an eyebrow.

'No. Just factual.'

He lowers his voice. 'Where are you staying?'

'La Casa d'Oro, 5, Piazza Leonardo da Vinci,' I say with a proud flourish, reciting the address from 'Fifty facts about Raffa' – a three-page document he emailed over this afternoon.

His face glows with amusement. 'Well done, but really, where are you staying?' His voice is low and husky, and my imagination is running wild at the thought of him inviting himself around after dark and doing me in every which way possible.

'La Casa del Pittore, quindici, Piazza Berrettini,' a voice interjects before I can reply.

I turn around to see Marco, a 'Tuscany Adventures' name badge pinned above the front pocket of his cotton shirt. Jangling a bunch of Linea Azulla keys in his hand, their logo matching that of the bus, he avoids eye contact, choosing instead to focus on the horizon, a look of concentration etched on his face. I study his outline like a spot-the-difference puzzle, trying to work out what has changed since I last saw him and it's only when he twists his head back towards us that I notice his beard has

147

vanished. He looks infinitely better, his near clean-shaven look revealing a dimple in his chin that would be endearing if it didn't also accentuate the deep groove in his forehead – a serious furrow that could only come about from decades of frowning.

'You've met my old friend, Marco, I see.' Raffa pats Marco on the back, a gesture that Marco is clearly not anticipating, judging by the way he only just recovers his footing, stumbling forward on the cobbles and casting Raffa a thinly veiled passive aggressive sneer, styling it out as a running walk towards the bus.

Raffa thrusts his hands into his pockets and shakes his head. 'He's been arsy with me ever since I beat him in the village chess tournament fifteen years ago.'

'Fifteen years ago? That would make you what, eighteen?'

'Seventeen.'

'But that's ridiculous,' I say, glancing at Marco, who catches my eye and looks away.

Raffa shuffles his feet around in the gravel with unease. 'Tell me about it . . . but then again, Marco is a bit ridiculous. I went out with his sister when I moved into the village aged nineteen – trust me, Altaterra is not where you want to live when you're a teenager – and he was a proper douche about it. Following us everywhere. Grassing us up to his parents for smoking weed. Typical small man syndrome.'

I steal another glimpse at Marco, who is now boarding the bus, clipboard under one arm and a whistle hanging from a ribbon in the other, and although he doesn't look that small, I can see where Raffa's coming from in terms of his desperate need to assert authority.

'Apparently his sister hardly speaks to him these days,' Raffa goes on. 'Last I heard she was living in America and wouldn't return his calls. I mean who can blame her? He's a total control freak. "Don't do this. Don't do that." Seriously, he's a tyrant in the making.'

I raise an eyebrow, looking again at Marco, who is lining people up and checking them off his list with a headmasterly precision.

We make our way over. His family are gathered in wide-brimmed straw hats (functional, certainly nothing that Mariela Marino would put her name to), sunblock smeared across their faces, water bottles topped up, sunbreaks and parasols making their way into the luggage hold. That's one thing to be said for the Aussies; they certainly know how to deal with hot weather.

'Done the old slip, slop, slap, Oona?' Raffa's mum plants a kiss on my cheek and I feel my skin ignite with shame. Am I really going to go through with this charade and respond to another girl's name all evening? 'You know, you've made a sick woman very happy,' she says, passing me a stack of blue, disposable vomit bags and grabbing my arm. Yes, that's what I'm doing. 'It's so lovely to see Raffa truly content, it really is. I know I sound a few stubbies short of a six-pack but just you wait until the pair of you have a couple of ankle-biters of your own and you'll see where I'm coming from. Motherhood takes nerves of steel, you know. You never stop worrying about them, even when they're grown-up, and especially when they live so far away. It's just such a relief that he's found someone special. And such a lovely, sensible girl like you!'

I offer up a withering smile, guilt corroding my insides and wonder if I will ever be described as a lovely, sensible girl again and, based on the fact that I am about to go through with this hare-brained idea, decide that the answer is firmly no.

'Come and sit next to me on the bus, won't you, love? Be nice to get to know you a little better.' She loops her arm through mine, the lip liner around her mouth stretching into the broadest of smiles, and before I have time to protest, I am being strongarmed onto the front row of the bus, boxed into the window seat by Mrs Bergamaschi and her enormous straw hat, a heavy feeling of unease loitering in my gut and the total and utter inability to swallow settling in.

'You're not travel sick, are you?' She looks at me with concern as the bus snakes around the bend, the lane ahead narrowing. 'You look awful pale, love.'

'I'm fine,' I say, feeling a sudden fondness for this woman I've known for only a matter of minutes and then an overwhelming surge of sadness that she'll have met her maker by the end of the year – it's always the best people that go first – and resolve to make this night special for her.

She puts her hand on mine and looks at me earnestly. 'How's Patsy?'

I try to recall the details of Raffa's set-up in Hackney, but mentally cycling through the list of rugby friends, work colleagues and neighbours, I can't remember there being a Patsy. 'Good,' I say, glancing out of the window and wondering how I can jump out of it.

'Only Raffa said she was finding it awful difficult to walk. Has she had the op now?'

My eyes flicker to Raffa, who is mid-conversation with an uncle on the row behind, oblivious to the interrogation I am being put through. 'I'm not sure,' I say, which is at least truthful but judging by the perplexed look that has fallen across her face, it is not the response she is looking for. Flustered, I rearrange my fringe and stare at my hands. 'There's a long waiting list, what with the NHS backlog,' I append, sucking air through my teeth and nodding earnestly in an attempt to add gravitas.

Her face becomes an unconscious frown. 'Dogs are being treated through the NHS now?'

'Dogs?' Heat rushes to my face, my heartbeat quickens, and my brain switches into overdrive as I scrabble around for a plausible way out of the conversational cul-de-sac I've found myself in. 'Yes. All part of the latest government restructure . . . The minister of health is a great lover of animals, you see. Ever since he got a rescue puppy. A German Shepherd from Greece.' I watch as her eyes widen in surprise. 'Honestly, you'd be amazed. "Pets are part of the family" has become a strapline in the Party's manifesto and dogs are pretty much included on every health plan, so Poppy should be treated any time soon,' I conclude, aware that I'm maybe overdoing it now.

'Poppy?' She frowns. 'Raffa always calls her Patsy.'

'Poppy. Poppadom. Popsicles. Patsicles. Pats. Cow Pats. Patsy. We've a ton of nicknames for her,' I say, pulling the cuffs of my kaftan down over my mosquito-bitten wrists and wishing I could disappear into thin air. 'Dear little thing, I really miss her.'

'Little?' She pulls her handbag into her stomach and grasps it tightly. 'I've never heard a St Bernard referred to as "little" before.'

I bite my lip. 'I guess I still think of her as a puppy.'

Along with coming on my period for the first time whilst on a foreign exchange trip in Paris and not having the French vocabulary to acquire sanitary products, this has to be one of the most stressful conversations of all time. How the hell has Raffa not told me about the dog? This is definitely not worth the stress. I could be strolling around the village streets in happy, solitary peace right now. Or sipping a cold beer out on the taverna terrace in the evening sun. Or making Sue's dress, which I now have the right thread and material for and should be working on right now if she's to have it in time for the christening. I swallow hard. It doesn't feel right, duping Raffa's family like this. It was a ridiculous idea, and heaven knows why I ever agreed to go through with it but it's too late to back out now – I am on the bus, part of a funeral procession on its way to celebrate the life of a much-loved lady and this is a straight-through journey with no stops for the faint-hearted to alight at.

'How are the veggies coming along?' she says, her eyes pin sharp with intrigue. 'Raffa tells me you're a keen gardener.'

'They're good,' I say, remembering that Raffa and I are supposed to live in a third-floor, one-bedroom flat with a small balcony overlooking the canal, and wondering if maybe I have an allotment somewhere to grow this litany of legumes she is referring to or whether I make do with a window box of edible plants and an indoor herb garden.

'Tomatoes, wasn't it?' she says.

'Uh-huh.' I nod, every muscle in my body tensing with anticipation.

'You know a tomato is actually fruit, not a vegetable. Isn't that right, Derek?' She looks over at Raffa's dad, who is fast asleep, raises a despairing eyebrow and turns back to me. 'Does Raffa have any interest in gardening? Derek's flaming useless. Not interested in anything unless it's got a motor.'

'Don't listen to her,' his dad grunts, eyes shut. 'Lies and more lies.'

An inquisitive look spreads across her face and, sensing that I'm about to be further bombarded with questions, I know I need to change tactics and become the interviewer rather than the interviewee.

'How are the cats?' I switch into Oprah mode. 'Flopsy and Mopsy, isn't it?'

'Well-remembered,' she says, patting my arm and glowing with pride. 'Flopsy brought in a bird the other day, which wasn't as bad as the frog the week before, but still not nice and of course Tia wasn't too happy about it.'

Tia? Tia? I rack my brains, visualising the family tree that Raffa drew as part of the introduction to his family section but draw a blank, unable to recall a Tia in any of the boxes.

'I can imagine.' I stare vacantly out of the window and wonder whether I can press the emergency stop button.

'And what about the poetry, how's that going?' She catches me off guard.

I shoot Raffa a look, annoyed at myself for taking my finger off the pulse and not being quick enough to stave off her interrogations with questions of my own. 'Your mum was just asking me about my poetry,' I say in a please-bail-me-out-quick tone that seems to cause him a great deal of amusement, his eyes gleaming with mischief. Is he actually getting off on this?

'Yeah, I was telling Ma about all those open mic nights you do back home.' A sardonic smile stretches across his face like plasticine until his whole expression becomes a giant Cheshire cat grin. Open mic nights? What the fuck is he playing at?

'Okaaay,' I say slowly, clocking the look on Marco's face through the rear-view mirror and wishing the small, stabbing feeling in my chest would disappear. Marco's eyes are narrow with disdain and his jawbone is clenched so tightly that it protrudes from his skin, neat little knots forming below his ears. A cold shiver runs down my spine as I avert my gaze, the bus swinging around a blind bend and a shimmering green lake coming into view, Lago Smeraldo just as breathtakingly beautiful in real life as it is on the postcards. Enough is enough. As we grind to a halt on the gravel, I resolve that this is as far as my journey goes.

'Sofia, I think there's something you should know,' I say, gathering my belongings into my lap and glancing at Raffa for long enough to see a look of panic dart across his face.

'Look at the lake, Ma!' Raffa says, avoiding my gaze.

The whir of the bus engine cuts out and all heads turn towards the glittering emerald pool of water before us. I inhale sharply, but before I can so much as string a sentence together, Marco has jumped into the aisle and is clapping his hands together to summon our attention.

'Benvenuti al Lago Smeraldo,' he says, gesturing to the expansive lagoon behind us. 'Non abbiamo tempo per nuotare ora, ma forse sulla via del ritorno . . .'

Raffa's dad stands up. 'Didn't understand a flaming word of that, mate. Can you repeat it in English for the dumb Aussie over here?' He belly laughs, and I'm reminded of Alf Stewart from *Home and Away*, what with his no-nonsense Australianisms, and find myself half-hoping that for entertainment's sake he at some point rolls out, 'Stone the crows, you flaming galah!'

Marco fixes him with a grin. 'Certo. Certainly. Welcome to the Emerald Lake. We don't have time to swim now but maybe after. If you haven't eaten too much.'

'Don't quit on me,' Raffa whispers through the gap between my headrest and the window, squeezing my shoulder with assurance. 'I promise I won't set you up again like that. It just kind of turned me on, watching you get all het up about it.'

An unexpected tingle starts up in my groin.

'Sorry, I know I shouldn't have said that,' he adds.

I try to digest what he's just said, but it's difficult. Guys like Raffa generally don't get turned on by girls like me but I have to admit there is something exhilarating about the uncertainty of the evening and the twists and turns it is taking. My breath thins and a delicious ripple of desire runs over my skin as I look out at the emerald lake. His hand lingers on my shoulder, and I don't want him to move it.

'You can't stitch me up like that though,' I say in a low voice, determined not to drop my guard entirely. 'I'm doing you a favour here.'

'Did you not find it even the slightest bit funny?' he whispers.

'No!' I supress a smile, aware that we are fast becoming a bickering couple.

Marco shoots me a dirty look and, as everyone is ushered off the bus, all I can think about is having a real lover's tiff with Raffa and the make-up sex that would inevitably follow.

Outside, on the white sandy shore, Raffa drapes an arm around me as my eyes skim the shimmering lake that stretches out towards huge limestone cliffs on the other side. Children play at the water's edge, flicking sand in each other's eyes and running off squealing. The smell of salty air hits my nostrils and I wonder what it would feel like to wade into the water, the cool brine gliding over my body and seeping into my hair. Further along the shore, a cluster of rowing boats are moored next to a small wooden jetty and behind it, a larger motorboat branded with 'Bergamaschi' in swirly blue italic font. It seems the Bergamaschi family have quite a presence out here.

Sofia turns towards me. 'What was it you were needing to tell me, love?'

'Ramona's just nervous that we're going to a fish restaurant and she's recently turned veggie, haven't you, Oona?' Raffa interjects, smooth as you like.

'Urm.' I stifle a laugh. There's something about being both Ramona and Oona in the same sentence that sums up the situation perfectly.

'She ate a dodgy octopus when we were in Santorini last summer and it's turned her completely off seafood,' he goes on.

Sofia turns back to me. 'Oh, you should have said, love. We could have picked another restaurant.'

'No, honestly . . .' I glare at Raffa, whose eyes are gleaming with mischief.

He puts his hand inside mine and gives it a squeeze and I feel the gentle tug of yearning as he leads me to the water's edge. 'Thank you for doing this,' he says, brushing my jawline with the back of his hand. 'I promise it'll be fun.'

'This way!' Marco blows three sharp blasts on his whistle, lining us up in single file along the shoreline like an overzealous teacher on a school trip.

All fifteen of us follow him along the rocky shore, one in front of the other, which at least means we're off the hook for small talk. Seagulls squawk from a huge nest of twigs precariously balanced on a raft suspended in the lake, birds circling and flapping above, but it's the silhouette of something else soaring through the sky that catches my eye. In the distance two paragliders sail across the endless blue horizon, dipping and gliding on the wings of the evening breeze, one slightly higher than the other. I squint into the sun, making out a man with a red helmet, legs held out perfectly straight behind him as he floats away from the white limestone cliffs and over the lake towards us. My mum and dad would love it here.

'You OK?' Raffa jolts me back into the here and now, his eyes following my gaze as we stand side by side on the terrace directly below the restaurant. His arm is slung around my shoulder and I consider for a moment whether his thumb really is caressing the top of my arm in a smooth, rotational movement or whether I'm just getting carried away in another daydream, but when I turn to look, there it is – an undeniable public display of affection.

'Too much?' He dips his head to my ear.

'It's actually quite nice,' I say, cursing myself for being so British about the whole thing and not suggesting that he goes a little further with his role play. His fingers sliding under my bra strap and slipping down my top might be quite nice, for example. 'Have you ever paraglided?'

'Sky dived. Bungee jumped. Abseiled Sydney Harbour Bridge but never paraglided. Doesn't appeal to me, to be honest.'

'My parents love it,' I say, wondering what Mum and Dad are up to right now and deciding they're probably floating somewhere below the clouds as we speak. 'They say it's the best feeling in the world.'

He looks me straight in the eye. 'Better than sex?'

Counting everyone two at a time with outstretched fingers, Marco sneaks a glance at Raffa and looks away again.

'Surely nothing feels better than sex?' Raffa's eyes twinkle.

'Chocolate milkshake with Oreo biscuits?' Marco chimes without even looking at us.

I let out a snort of laughter, his delivery so mechanical and dry, it takes me by surprise.

'He obviously hasn't had great sex,' Raffa whispers, his eyes lingering on mine until my whole body squirms with delight.

Marco guides us up to the restaurant terrace, Raffa's parents flanked by a huddle of Italian aunties leading the charge and Raffa and I bringing up the rear, my eye fixed on the man in the sky.

'You want to go paragliding?' Marco says as I reach the top of the steps.

'Urm.' I stall, remembering everything Raffa said about Marco earlier and realise I'm probably about to be lectured on the perils of adrenaline sports and letting myself in for a full risk assessment and health and safety brief.

'Nah, we're good thanks, mate,' Raffa says, brushing an insect off my shoulder with the back of his hand and my whole body simmering with desire.

'I know the man who makes this paragliding if you want to go,' Marco carries on and it strikes me that this isn't about policing my safety, rather a kick-back commission he is clearly in line for.

Raffa grabs my hand and turns to Marco. 'Honestly, we're good thanks, mate.'

We make our way over to a table set for fifteen, silver cutlery glinting under the sun and the corners of the white, starched tablecloth fluttering in the breeze. I'm ushered to a chair between Raffa and his father – welcome respite from the one-woman hurricane that is his mother. Rather than have half of the party with their backs to the lake, the table has been set up so that all fifteen of us are horizontally aligned and have a perfect view. Piano music tinkles in the background. The sun is slowly starting its descent, casting an orange glow over the water, gulls and paragliders silhouetted by its yolky blush.

'You're doing great,' Raffa whispers in my ear, his hand simultaneously squeezing my thigh and setting off a chemical reaction so strong I feel that I could single-handedly power the electricity of a small village.

The menu arrives, my mouth watering at the prospect of sea bass, and then I remember my recently acquired vegetarianism and flip to the vegan section. But fuck it. Why should I be put in a box? It's me doing Raffa the favour so surely, I should be the one calling the shots. I order sea bass on a bed of fresh vegetables, Sofia far too engrossed in conversation with one of Raffa's aunts to bat an eyelid and Raffa choosing to bite his tongue rather than say anything. Wise.

Twenty minutes later, after only one fuck-up (a conversation about horoscopes leading me to divulge I'm a Virgo when apparently, I'm a Libra) and a long exchange about the gotchas of a Virgo-Libra cusp, the food arrives.

I'm unfolding the expensive napkin set out on my dinner plate and spreading it across my lap when the chink of cutlery against glass rings out and Sofia announces a toast.

'To Mum.' She holds up her flute of prosecco. 'Who lived life to the full and was afraid of nothing. To Mariela Marino, the milliner of Milan.'

'To Mariela.' A chorus of voices accompanies the clinking of glasses.

'To Mariela,' I whisper, thinking about all those hats and resolving to get back to my own designs first thing tomorrow. If Mariela Marino didn't give up, then neither will I.

'Now I've never been good at speeches, but Raffa tells me we've got a lot of talent sitting around the table. Would Oona like to read us one of her poems, maybe?' Sofia's voice chimes out loudly.

Raffa pushes his thigh into mine under the table and everything slows as the realisation that I am Oona, an urban poet and veritable vixen at open mic nights, takes hold. Heads turn in my direction, drinking momentarily paused in expectation of the lyrical elegy that is about to burst forth from my lips.

'I couldn't.' Heat rushes to my face. 'Nobody could do her justice.'

'Don't be shy, love.' Sofia goes on. 'Raffa said you'd prepared something.'

Fire rises through my throat, torching the back of my mouth and fizzing up through my ears. Is he for fucking real? I'm about to fling my napkin on the table, stand up and walk out when Raffa snatches my hand.

'I didn't mean to stitch you up.' He looks at me imploringly. 'I just mentioned it to Mum a couple of months ago, when you wrote it as Gran was getting admitted to hospital. I didn't—'

Slowly the rage inside me dissipates as Raffa's face twists in grief, his eyes pooling with tears and his bottom lip quivering and it's clear that he's actually telling the truth and hasn't strung me up and laid me out to dry. A surge of sympathy overcomes me. Here is a man who has lost his beloved grandmother and long-term girlfriend all within a week and is about to lose his mother, too. And rather than seeing him for the jaw-droppingly handsome sex god that I have been lucky enough to hang out with today, it strikes me that he is, at heart, a vulnerable human being struggling to hold back an avalanche of hurt, powerless at the hands of a Mother Nature insistent on his nearest and dearest slip-sliding away. And as I watch him bite his bottom lip, it occurs to me that he doesn't want to be at this table any more than I do, especially now that his dad has got to his feet at the end of the table.

'Don't come the raw prawn with us, love. Everyone would love to hear it.' His father raises a glass in my direction.

Poetry has never been my forte, my English teacher once describing a ditty I wrote about my cat as 'an assault on the senses and not in a good way'. I stare at the tablecloth and almost stop breathing when, out of the corner of my eye, I see that Raffa is getting out of his chair.

He puffs out his chest. 'Can you not give her a break? She's only just met you guys.'

His father eyeballs him down the table. 'Strike me pink, Raffa. The girl's no shrinking violet. You know I threw your mother in

161

at the deep end when I first met her. Literally. We were at an out-door pool, and I didn't know she couldn't swim. Give her a fair suck of the sauce bottle and she'll be right!'

Raffa grits his teeth. 'I'm not sure she—'

I don't know whether it's the look of loss stamped all over Raffa's face or the two glasses of prosecco that I have already knocked back, but for some unknown reason, I am rising to my feet.

'It's OK.' I grab hold of Raffa's arm, partly to offer moral support and partly because I've underestimated the heel of my shoe and am about to fall into his tagliatelle.

'Hats.' I announce with alcohol-induced confidence. 'Raffa's grandma made lots of hats.' I glance up the table on one side and then turn to the other and try not to think too much. 'Nothing was old hat. Everything was new. She'd throw her hat in the ring for almost anything.' I lose concentration, realising that what I've just said rhymes and trying to work out whether the next line also needs to rhyme when Raffa takes hold of my hand and squeezes it, the row of heads twisted in anticipation fading into the distance.

'Thank you,' he whispers under his breath.

Buoyed by his affection I launch into a new ramble though it's difficult knowing where to direct the speech, what with us all sit-ting in a long line facing the lake. 'With a feather in her cap and a bee in her bonnet, she was the maddest of hatters. Completely hatstand.'

'Completely hatstand! She'd have loved that, wouldn't she, Sofia!' Raffa's dad looks at his wife and erupts into laughter.

'She would!' Sofia nods, her face brimming with affection.

'What a ripsnorter!' his dad continues. 'Once a cane toad, always a cane toad.'

'Come on, Pa. Time and a place.' Raffa digs his hands into his pockets.

I have no idea what he's talking about but judging by Raffa's reaction and the strained grimace lodged upon Sofia's face, it is not complimentary. Still, whatever the subtext, it allows me more time to think up a few more cheesy hat sayings.

'Carry on, dear.' Sofia turns to me stoically.

'For at the drop of a hat, she'd make many more. And many more after that, too. She never ate her hat. And she never talked through her hat. She had many skills and wore many hats. Yes, hats off to the lady that gave us all hats. The marvellous milliner of Milan.'

Thankfully, there is much applause from the Australian contingent although the native Italians are looking bemused.

Sofia rises to her feet. 'Thank you,' she says, positively aglow with joy.

Raffa rubs the small of my back and looks at me with tears in his eyes and I know, right there at that moment, that it is the gaze of grateful man. A gesture of appreciation. One human being rescuing another, a problem shared and halved.

'Thank you.' He squeezes my knee as we sit, and I know he means it.

The meal continues in harmony, conversation centring on Mariela and what a wonderful woman she was. Newspaper articles proclaiming her work as genius, obituaries from fellow fashion designers – one from Giovanni himself, declaring her a shimmering pearl in an ocean full of sharks – and countless letters between her and a mystery lover known as 'X', though these are all in Italian and I only understand the odd word here and there. The atmosphere is celebratory over sad, happy over harrowing and although I am effectively gatecrashing the memorial service of a woman I never knew, it feels as though I understand the very essence of Mariela Marino and feel lucky to have learned about such a remarkable tour de force. And even luckier to be in the company of Raffa, who is now leaning into me, his elbow on the table, his hand on my thigh and a twinkle in his eye.

Who knows where tonight might take us?

CHAPTER TWELVE
Under the moonlight

Four glasses of wine, three hours and two more design rejections (Gucci and Prada did at least manage to address me by my name) and I'm awash with emotion. Moonlight streams across the village square, silver shards throwing distorted shadows over the cobblestones. The bus has long disappeared along with Raffa's relatives and now it's just the two of us and an orchestra of ticking crickets that fills the silence that grows between us. We've been making small talk about big things – his sporting career, his job, his ailing mother and the pressure that puts on his whole family – and now we are all talked out, standing in front of each other as the clock in the stone tower chimes midnight, shuffling about uncomfortably and not knowing what to do with our hands.

'That was pretty nice of you, doing what you did back there,' he says eventually, our eyes sharing a conversation of their own. 'It was a pretty big ask and . . . that thing with the poem. That took serious guts.'

I try to suppress the deep yearning in my groin. 'Sorry it was just a load of random shit. Poetry and I are not natural bedfellows.'

'Trust me, it was a whole lot better than one of the sombre, political ones Oona used to write. Seriously, they loved it.' He takes my hand in his. 'And they loved you, too.'

Butterflies start up in my stomach, my insides dissolving into liquid and every coherent thought leaves my brain as the touch of his palm against mine sends a small bolt of electricity sizzling through my body.

He looks at my lips, a rush of wanton lust bursting through my every fibre, then lowers his voice to a husky whisper which sends the tingling feeling in my groin into overdrive. 'Look, I really want to kiss you, but I feel like that would be totally abusing the situation given that I've already taken advantage of your super humanly good nature.'

And that's when I take destiny into my own hands and make the move that he respectfully won't make. I kiss him softly on the lips. Right there in the village square. I kiss him softly and in return his lips press hard against mine, his arms engulfing me, cradling me to his chest, holding me against his stomach and pressing my groin into something hard. I break away to smile, but he has no interest in slowing to savour the moment, his kisses urgent and unstoppable, his tongue pushing hard against mine as he walks me backwards across the square, his hands massaging my back, my shoulders, my collarbone and greedily grabbing at my chest.

'Hey,' I say, lifting his head in an attempt to slow things down.

'Hey.' He meets my eye for a split second and then pushes me against the side of the farmacia, lifting the edges of my kaftan, his hands everywhere. My thighs. My neck. My butt. My breasts. I feel like I'm losing control.

'Stop a sec!' I say, but he either doesn't hear me or decides not to, anchoring me to the stone wall with his groin and the twists and turns of his persistent tongue. 'Stop!' I tense up, my body turning brittle as I try to shut down each kiss and give myself a chance to take hold of the moment.

'What's the matter? I thought you wanted this,' he whispers.

Not *this*, 'Raffa, stop!' I say, panicking that I'm way in over my head when, out of nowhere, the shrill sound of a loud whistle pierces the midnight air, Raffa stopping in his tracks.

'You heard her!' A voice comes out of the dark. 'She said stop.'

Raffa shields his eyes from the moonlight with the palm of his hand. 'Marco?'

'Leave her alone.' Marco appears in the village square, swathed in moonlight, his movements tired and sober. He jangles the keys to the coach in his pocket and advances across the cobbles, a look of disgust imprinted on his face.

'Can't you give a guy some privacy?' Raffa holds me to his chest, my grandma's pendant getting caught over the button on his shirt as I rearrange my dress to protect my modesty.

Marco frowns, making no sign of going anywhere.

'No disrespect, mate, but this is none of your business.' Raffa pulls away from me, the chain of my necklace snapping and the Wedgwood cherub sliding down my top.

I scoop the porcelain cherub out of my bra and squeeze it in my hand, holding my breath as Marco thrusts his hands into his pockets, looks up at the moon and returns his gaze to Raffa. 'I see a woman asking a man to stop and he is not stopping. How is this not my business?'

Raffa lowers his voice and takes a step away from me, doing up the fly of his trousers with one swift movement. 'Vaffancullo, Marco.'

Marco lets out a huff of air in a kind of strangled laugh. Slowly he stalks towards Raffa, staring him down like a wild animal ready to pounce. 'Turning blind is too easy. Five years my father beats my mother and five years the neighbours hear everything and say nothing because it's none of their business. If they had chosen for it to be their business, maybe she would be able to see out of both eyes. So, I think actually this is very much my business.'

'I'm not hurting her, you know.' Raffa holds up his hands in surrender.

Marco shakes his head. 'Maybe not on the outside.'

'I'd never hit a woman.' The colour is now draining away from Raffa's cheeks, and he looks more agitated than ever.

'It is not always hitting,' Marco says slowly and clearly, as though talking to someone armed and dangerous.

'Did I scare you?' Raffa turns to me. 'Only that would be a bit rich saying I scared you when you were the one who started this. You were the one who kissed me.'

My heart is pounding, and I've somehow lost the ability to speak.

'I thought we were having fun. We'd had such a great night and . . . I just felt there was a chemistry between you and I. A connection. And . . . I dunno, you were kind of giving me all the signs that we were going to get it on tonight and so when you kissed me, I just went with it. You can't blame a man for acting on impulse.'

'I . . .' I can't articulate what I want to say, because I have no idea what I'm even thinking, emotions gurgling and rushing in a whirlpool of confusion and shame. It was indeed me that instigated this. It was me that has spent the last twenty-four hours fantasising about this exact moment and yet it's me putting on the stoppers now that it's finally happened, and I don't really understand why. Sixth sense? My mind spins and my legs tremble. I feel so, so stupid. The insanity of pretending to be his girl-friend because I wanted to be and then doing a complete U-turn once I had the chance. What a mess.

'Leave her now, please.' Marco stands his ground, tucking an errant blond curl behind his ear, which immediately springs free again. 'Signorina Ramona, I will take you back to the house.'

On shaky legs, I stumble towards Marco's outstretched hand. I want to say thank you, and sorry, and thank you again, but the words stick in my throat and I can't seem to put one in front of another let alone say them aloud. Like a Dickensian gentleman, he offers his elbow in an act of chivalry, and as I loop my arm through his, it feels as though I have finally reached dry land after being lost at sea. He may be a control freak, but who cares? I turn back to see Raffa skulking in the shadows, his shape shifting as he straightens himself out, shakes his head with incredulity and disappears off into the night.

'It's a good thing I always take my dog's whistle with me,' Marco says brightly as we amble up the hill.

'You have a dog?' I say, grateful for a reassuringly pedestrian conversation I can anchor myself to, and desperate for my heartbeat to calm the fuck down.

'I *had* a dog. Until recently.' His voice becomes a whisper, words drying on his tongue and although he turns his face away from me, I feel his sadness.

'I'm sorry.' I squeeze his arm, my mind a flicker board of flashbacks to only a moment ago when Raffa was grabbing at me greedily, his hands everywhere.

'Are you OK?' Marco says as he leads me up the hill.

I feel like such an idiot, Marco knowing everything. The charlatan girlfriend thing. The getting it on with the village playboy up against the wall of the pharmacy thing. The crying out for Raffa to stop thing. I only checked into his place two days ago. What the hell must he think? Back home, I am a respectable woman with a head for business and an eye for design who makes good choices and doesn't drop her guard purely because her head has been turned by a good-looking guy. Here though, I am a shallow, pathetic fool. My cheeks burn with humiliation and every step back towards the Casa del Pittore feels like ten.

Finally, we reach the tumbledown wall and overgrown garden of the place I am currently calling home. A wave of calm sweeps over me as the long grass swishes reassuringly against my legs as I head towards the front door and I feel my shoulders relax though my hand still jitters when I put my key towards the lock and miss the keyhole entirely.

'You want me to stay?' Marco says, taking the key and opening the door for me.

'No,' I say quickly, almost falling into the kitchen with the relief of reaching safety.

'Madonna Santa! I didn't mean . . .' He screws up his eyes with self-awareness. 'Just to guard the place. You know, like a dog, in case Raffaele returns. I can sleep on the couch downstairs.'

'I'm all right. Thank you,' I say, desperate for him to leave so that I can have a shower and wash away the whole incident.

He looks at me earnestly. 'Raffaele is not a good man. He did a similar thing to my sister when she was only eighteen, and I still cannot forgive him.'

'I'm sorry,' I say, recalling Raffa telling me he'd dated Marco's sister rather than forcefully groping her late at night in a car park. What an asshole.

'I wanted to explain to you earlier, but it was difficult and . . .'

'It's OK. It was my fault.'

'No, Signorina Ramona. It was not your fault.' He shakes his head with agitation. 'You should never say these words.'

'Look, thanks for getting me home,' I say, wrapping my fingers around the door frame.

'Good night, Signorina Ramona.' He turns away and closes the door behind him, and I am finally left with my own self-loathing.

I look down at my grandma's keepsake, the chain broken in not just one place but two, and it almost feels as though she too got caught up in the altercation and is watching what I'll do next. Slipping the Wedgwood pendant off the chain, I squeeze it tightly in my balled fist as though to protect her. How could I have been so careless? My skin starts to itch. My grandma would have been appalled. I can picture her now, rolling her eyes and shaking her head the way she did whenever my dad told a bad joke. Running my fingers over the cold, hard porcelain cherub, I close my eyes and thank my lucky stars for Marco turning up when he did. Heaven knows what would have happened if he hadn't appeared.

CHAPTER THIRTEEN

Cracking on with cracking on

The Girlz

Flora

How did it go with hot grandson?

Zhané

Did he throw his metaphorical shrimp on your red-hot, sizzling barbie?

Flora

Was he up for your bush-tucker trial or did he keep his Joey in his pouch? ;-)

Zhané

> Did he get out his didgeridoo?

Zhané

> Please tell us you're too busy having Aussie-Italiano rampant sex to reply to these messages.

It's 6.00 a.m. and the bedroom is bathed in sunlight, the first rays of the morning streaming through the curtains and illuminating the room as though willing it awake. I try to roll over and go back to sleep, but my brain has other plans, flashbacks of last night springing up in my mind's eye and refusing to be squashed back down. Fabrice's voice rings in my ear: 'Remind me why you're having to pretend to be his girlfriend? Only that, to me, has red flag written all over it.' Why didn't I listen? I throw my phone down onto the bed and pad over to the window, the tiled floor reassuringly cool against the soles of my feet. The distant crow of a cockerel sends the hens into a clucking, squawking frenzy outside, feathers flapping and claws scuffling on the gravel path. I pull back the curtains to see what's going on when my eye is drawn to a large, purple tent that has been pitched alongside the stone wall, blocking the gateway entirely.

Upon closer inspection, I see the outline of a figure moving around inside, its mass ballooning and then shrinking until it becomes the silhouette of a fully formed body with arms and legs. Eyes fixed firmly on the shifting shape, I reach for the broom propped down the side of the wardrobe and try to slow my rapid-fire heartbeat. Quite how clutching a brush is going to help, I'm not sure, but the weight of it in my hands makes me feel slightly more armed and allows me to do what any self-respecting alpha female would do and hide behind the curtain, holding my breath as I peep through a narrow gap. Surely this is private land and people can't just pitch a tent willy-nilly wherever they feel like it?

The canvas bulges on one side as the body of a man bends over and a sleeping bag gets tossed out into the tall grass, shortly followed by a pillow, a small duffle bag and a set of metal poles, the tent collapsing in the middle and a man appearing out in the garden. Squinting behind the curtain, I try to get a better look at him but although it's broad daylight, his head is cocooned in a hood and I can't see his face. Paranoid that he's seen me, I turn away, listening to the sound of tent poles clanking as they are gathered together, the creak of the gate, the click of the latch as it swings shut, the fading crunch of footsteps through gravel and finally the growl of an engine and the clink of small stones against the metal undercarriage of a car as whoever it was disappears.

My heart beats like the clappers, and when I do finally allow myself a glimpse out of the window, I'm left staring at a rectangular area of slightly discoloured flattened grass wondering who the mystery man was and making a mental note never to walk barefoot through the garden given that it obviously doubles up as a nomadic toilet. I may have only got this place as a holiday let, but I'm not entirely convinced that I like the idea of a strange man sleeping in the garden. Especially after what happened last night. In need of a friendly face, I pick up my phone and am about to call the girls when I realise it is only 5.00 a.m. back home.

Ramona

Let me know when you're up. It'd be good to talk x

Zhané

Been up since 4.30 with Leo. Call me x

Flora

Been pity club! it. Defo bitstream x

Flora

Sorry, worse for wear. Been clicking at La Rumba.

Flora

CLUBBING, not clicking! Let's Skype x

I grab my laptop, jump back onto the bed and fire up Skype, arranging last night's events into chronological order as the call connects and my gal pals come into focus, Zhané dishevelled

176

in her pyjamas and Flora all smudged lipstick and silver sequined jacket.

'When you say handsy, what do you mean?' Zhané's eyes narrow in the top window of my screen.

I chew the piece of raggedy skin under my thumbnail and reach for my grandma's pendant, its absence painfully present. 'I just felt out of my depth. He didn't do anything wrong but . . .'

A flash of anger flickers over Zhané's face. 'Romes, he did *everything* wrong. You asked him to stop, and he didn't. That is fundamentally wrong.'

'Exactly.' Flora nods furiously in agreement.

The back of my neck prickles with discomfort as I stare at the cactus-print cotton eiderdown and wonder whether the designer's intention was to make it look like a repeated phallus. I'm not actually sure what happened last night, my emotions shifting like the flick of a switch. One minute I was feeling so flattered that a guy like him could be interested in a girl like me, and the next minute feeling that I had no control whatsoever over what was happening. I pick at my fingernails.

'He became so forceful so fast,' I say, tears springing to my eyes.

'This is what happens!' Zhané spits. 'So many victims don't speak out because they consented at the start.'

My throat dries. 'He didn't assault me. He didn't actually *do* anything to me!'

Zhané shakes her head with exasperation. 'Forcing his hands all over you even when you asked him to stop doesn't sound like he didn't do anything to you, Romes.'

'She's right,' Flora says, sobering up. 'What would have happened if Pablo hadn't shown up?'

'Marco!' I correct her, aware that my friends are conducting one of their emergency interventions and that unless I surrender to their way of thinking, our three-way friendship will no longer take on the form of the equilateral triangle it has been to date and will be bent into that of an isosceles in which Zhané and Flora have equal lateral power and I have considerably less.

'I dunno . . .' My voice peters out as I start reliving the whole thing for the millionth time, Raffa's hands coming at me like a colony of bat wings fluttering through the night sky and no matter how many times I try to peel them away from my body, they just come back again and again. Who knows what he'd have done if Marco hadn't showed up. Would he have stopped? Would he have carried on despite my pleas, leaving me to recount an entirely different version of events from the bowels of a provincial Italian police station, him in the cell next door? Hot tears spring to my eyes and the screen blurs, the outline of my friends bleeding into one other and my skin feels tight.

'This is where the patriarchal system lets us down,' Zhané shouts over Leo's screaming. 'When will men understand that "no" means "no" even when it doesn't align to their desires?'

'Not all men,' Flora says sheepishly as the figure of a man crosses behind her, his fingers massaging her shoulder as he goes.

Zhané claps her hand over her mouth. 'Eyebrow boy?'

'No.' Flora buries her blushing face in her hands and then types a message into the chat.

Flora

Buns of steel boy. He's a keeper!

'Flor!' Zhané squeals.

'I'll tell you all about it another time.'

Zhané turns her attention back to me. 'Roma, first things first, you need to get out of that village. If it's as tiny as you say it is, you'll bump into him all the time.'

'It's OK – he's leaving today along with the whole Aussie contingent. Trust me, I won't leave these four walls until I know the coast is clear,' I say, trying to take back control.

'Good,' she says with an air of approval.

'And then what?' Flora adds.

I inhale slowly, threading the Wedgwood pendant onto a thick piece of cotton and tying it around my neck with a double knot – so what, if I can never get it off? 'I was thinking I might hang around here for a while and catch up with Curvaliscious stuff.'

'Maybe work on a new collection?' Zhané's eyes light up.

'I don't know. I might play around a bit. I've got my sewing machine here with me and a batch of decent fabric so . . .'

'Yes! Get back on the horse, well not *The* Horse per se.' Flora giggles.

'Glad you're talking sense, Roma. He was a dick. You weren't. End of,' Zhané says before muting herself and shouting something to someone off-screen. 'Listen, I'm going to have to go. Leo's just pulled the curtain rail down and is about to jab it through the window. Stay bold and brave.'

179

The call ends and I am left with a whirlwind of thoughts. How my friends are right – I said 'no' and did not consent, but Raffa forced himself upon me anyway, so it's no wonder that my very foundations feel rocked. Yes, I was stupid and will never again allow lust to overrule common sense, but a brief lapse in good judgement doesn't give a man carte blanche to grab and grope you against your will, does it? And then I think about how I really loved Flora's silver sequined jacket – call it a coping mechanism, my brain needing to detach from the cortisol overload, but I loved the zipper-cuff detail and the way the shoulder pads added shape without overpowering her. Yet the one thought that settles is how Bold & Brave would make a brilliant name for a new Curvaliscious collection. Instead, I shall channel all this negative energy into something positive, and what better outlet for releasing my rage than creating a brand-new clothing collection? Fauna & Flora may not have cut it, but nobody can dismiss a Bold & Beautiful collection that is as unashamedly vibrant as it is unapologetic. Bold cuts. Daring hemlines. Dazzling detail. If there is one thing that com-ing out here to Tuscany has taught me, it's to take a chance, so why wouldn't I with my clothing range?

I set to work immediately. Taking the roll of shimmery blue fabric I bought from the market, I unravel it across the table, relishing the softness of the material in contrast to its strength. A frisson of excitement runs down my spine as I hold the fabric up to the light. Sorry, Auntie Sue, but either you're brave and bold, or this dress isn't for you.

I concentrate first on the bodice and then on the cut around the waist and hips, deciding an off-the-shoulder vintage fifties style dress might be just the thing. A bit of a Brigitte Bardot meets *Breakfast at Tiffany's* vibe going on. Granted, I'll need some more fabric for a fluffy petticoat to give the skirt a bit of a lift and a brass-buckled belt would be perfect, but I can always improvise.

A couple of hours in and I feel like a new woman. That's the thing about sewing; it's such great therapy and will never let you down. Consistent, methodical and sensual, the meditative act of committing needle to fabric has been a friend to me for years now, providing distraction from exam results, escapism from my parents' divorce and the trauma of them getting back together again. Immersing myself in my creative work always leaves me feeling calmer, happier and more at one with the world, anchoring all spiralling thoughts and giving them a place to rest. Sitting at the kitchen table, I feed Hugo a length of the shimmery blue fabric, tucking the cotton fabric over at the seam and watching as it glides below the bobbing needle. Out of the kitchen window, I see Signora Abbadelli tending to her beloved hens and behind her a backdrop of blood-orange poppies that sway in the breeze, the sun-dappled Tuscan wheatfields rolling out like golden carpet. I breathe in the smell of fresh coffee. It feels good to be sewing again. Sketching designs can be liberating and frustrating in equal measure; like creating anything afresh – committing those first words to a blank page or that first brush stroke to a clean canvas – it's exhilarating to see where the seed of an idea takes you, the pencil lines either becoming a big tangled mess of nonsense, or metamorphosing into something with potential.

Sewing, though, is a completely different craft. It's a full-on sensory experience. The texture of the fabric against your fingers, the gentle buzz of the sewing machine, the hypnotic wobble of the reel of cotton thread as it unwinds, the way a stitch can look so different in one light to another. The soft, strong touch of cotton. The tough, rough feeling of tweed. The smooth, almost waxy, feel of silk. There is nothing more gratifying than caressing the yarn of a high-quality fabric and shaping it into a living, breathing article of clothing. At last, I feel at one with myself.

Once I've finished the dress, I step back to admire my handiwork – it's not exactly what Auntie Sue asked for and I've no idea whether she'll like it or not, but it's definitely bold and brave. The sequined embroidery around the bust and the attention to detail around the neckline sets off the piece nicely but it's the sequined lightning bolt that shimmies up the bodice of the dress that really catches the eye and it will take a confident woman to pull this off. I swallow hard. Although Auntie Sue is a confident Plus Size woman (people say I get my curves from her), I'm not sure the dress is entirely appropriate for a christening, but before I can video call her, there's a knock at the window. Removing the pin balanced between my lips and jabbing it into my collar, I pad over to the door with my cup of coffee, hoping that a quick blast of fresh air might cool it down a notch.

'Buongiorno.' Marco stands there, smelling of sunshine and fresh croissants. He is dressed for the beach in flip-flops, faded denim shorts and a pale-blue T-shirt that brings out the colour of his eyes, a bicycle propped up against the wall behind him. 'For you,' he says, thrusting a paper bag of patisserie into my hand. 'It's still warm.'

'Grazie. Thank you.' I peer down at a plump almond croissant, but instead of my mouth watering, I can only feel the hot fizz of my cheeks flushing and shame seizing my whole body at the thought of everything that Marco witnessed last night.

'I just want to check that you're OK,' he says. 'And also to reassure you that the Bergamaschi family have left Altaterra. I drove them to the airport earlier in the bus so you will have no worry with this . . .' He hops from one foot to the other. 'This situation with Raffaele.'

'Thank you. And thanks for helping me last night.'

'You are making clothes?' His eyes flicker over my shoulder towards the dress hanging from the lamp.

'Just a dress for my auntie.'

He looks impressed. 'May I look?'

'Come in,' I say, feeling a tiny bit like damaged goods as he goes out of his way to make me feel at ease, tiptoeing around the table (not just metaphorically), keeping his distance and travelling fluidly around the kitchen with no sudden movements, just as a zookeeper might tread softly around the enclosure of a frightened bird. And whilst I appreciate the gesture, it's also a little bit creepy. 'Would you like a coffee?'

'Sure,' he says, circling the dress to admire it from all angles. 'You know, Maria has travelled everywhere to find a dress like this for the wedding but . . . I don't suppose . . .'

'You think Maria might like something similar?' I say, excited at the prospect of creating another outfit with sequins.

'I'm sure she would, if you have the time,' he says, studying the detail of the embroidered neckline and blowing out his lips in wide-eyed admiration, and I allow myself a private smile of fulfilment at the way the sequins catch the light, a sunbeam bouncing off the tiny silver-blue reflectors to give a captivating sparkle effect set off against the stylish yet simple skirt.

'Time is something I have lots of at the moment, though I imagine you've got new guests that will be wanting the apartment come Saturday, haven't you?' I let out a nervous laugh and then become self-conscious, realising I sound just like my mother before she's had a drink at a dinner party which, trust me, is not a good thing.

'We actually had a cancellation ...' His eyes shift around the kitchen, making an inventory of the subtle changes I have made to his home – the glass jar next to the toaster now full of pyramid PG Tips teabags, the white lace tablecloth replaced by a strawberry-print length of cotton left over from a tote bag I made this morning and the traditional cafetiere replaced with the plug-in coffee maker I picked up at the market. 'If you want to stay another week?'

'Great, and yes, please. If you tell her to come over, I'll measure her up,' I say, my eyes faithful to the pen I am rolling over and over between my fingers, a shudder of unease running over my skin when I realise he is *still* looking at me. What's going on here? One minute he's commissioning a dress for his partner and the next he's giving me lingering looks. This is so not cool.

He clears his throat. 'It's just it's not so easy to know the size when the baby is still growing.'

'Oh!' I say, feeling foolish for misinterpreting his awkwardness as interest in me and then overcompensating with wild hand gestures and a huge grin, all the while blushing like a lobster. 'Ah, she's pregnant?'

Marco bites his bottom lip. 'Yes. You didn't notice?'

'No, but then again I only saw her from the shoulders upwards when she was in the burger van.' I busy myself with my tape measure, unsure why I am so surprised. It's not as though having a baby is that shocking for a couple in their thirties, it's just . . . I don't know.

The silence between us ballooning, I rummage through the drawer in the kitchen table and present him with my business card. 'Just get her to email me her measurements – bust, hips, shoulders, inside arm, outside arm, and I'll see what I can do.'

'So, you're a fashion designer?' He turns the card over and over in his hand.

'An unemployed fashion designer at the moment,' I say, running my old faithful measuring tape between my fingers and enjoying the way its soft leather feels against my skin. 'They didn't really like my latest collection.'

'It is their loss,' he says with an earnestness that not only makes me feel good about my work but also makes me feel valid, which couldn't come at a better time because lately I've been feeling as though the whole world is caving in on me and I'll never get anywhere with my designs. In fact, sometimes I have these awful recurring nightmares where Setayesh and The Horse list all of my faults, one after the other, on national TV and I wake up in cold sweat. But most of the time, I feel unremarkable, invalid and redundant so a bit of praise every now and again is very welcome. 'I think maybe Raffaele already showed you his grandmother's Casa dei Cappelli.'

'Yes! Such an amazing place and such a shame the whole thing will probably get knocked down to make holiday apartments!'

He looks down at the floor with regret. 'Some people only ever think of money.'

'Yup.' I turn away to alleviate the awkwardness that is growing between us, my eye catching the trampled rectangular patch outside where the tent was. 'Oh, I should probably tell you that there was a man here last night,' I say, pointing out of the window in the direction of the flattened, faded grass, but Marco is too absorbed in photographing the dress to take notice of my outstretched finger.

'Okaaay.' His eyes widen with surprise.

'I don't know who it was, but he had a really big, purple—'

'Sorry, did we agree a price?' His eyebrows shoot towards the ceiling and I can only imagine that he has never seen a micro-sequined starlight bodice on stretch mesh before but know I shouldn't judge.

I shake my head. 'He was medium build, medium height and had this absolutely enormous—'

'OK!' He holds up his hand as though to stop traffic.

'I mean I only got to see it properly in the morning when it was on its way down, but—'

He clears his throat loudly and reaches for the coffee I have poured him. 'Maybe I give you some extra nights in the apartment in place of paying cash!' he says, and judging by the urgent way in which he brings the cup to his mouth, it's clear that he's more interested in a caffeine fix than my sighting of an intruder on his land.

'I'm not sure about hair or eye colour as he had his hood up the entire time,' I go on.

'The entire time?' Colour drains from his face.

'Yeah. If you come over here, I'll show you where he erected his—'

'Please!' he splutters and I can't work out whether it's the intensity of the coffee or the scalding temperature that is making him choke, his eyeballs bulging cartoonlike while hot, brown liquid splashes against the floor tiles as he reaches for the table to steady himself.

I pass him a sheet of kitchen roll and remove the cup from his hand. 'I just wondered if he was a friend of yours?' I say, taking care not to launch straight into wild accusations.

He mops at his coffee-stained T-shirt with the paper towel and frowns. 'What is his name?'

'I don't know. We didn't actually speak, we just . . .' The words die on my tongue as he bites his lip with agitation. 'Are you OK?'

'I guess you are on holiday,' he says hurriedly, throwing the soiled kitchen towel in the bin and picking up his bag. 'I need to go. Thanks for the dress information. And if you want to try to save La Casa dei Cappelli, you can find the petition against its destruction at the Post Office. Good day.'

Unable to leave fast enough, he collides first with the table and then into the door frame before breaking into a run through the garden without giving so much as a second glance at the discoloured grass beneath his feet. Strange man. And if he is actively suggesting that I petition against the Casa's destruction, does that mean he's pro its preservation as a national heritage site or is he just calling my bluff?

Once it's clear he's not coming back, I settle down to sketch a few ideas for maternity dresses that Maria might like – a one-shoulder, empire chiffon gown with flower ruffle, a plunge-neck ivory eye-lash lace maxi dress, an A-line tea-dress-length vintage dress with a sash tie waist – and just like that I feel at one with the world: screw Raffa. I have tea, I have Hugo and I have the Tuscan sun streaming through the back door.

And it's only when I've been outlining and contouring, delineating and shading for an hour or so that my heart drops into my feet and it dawns on me that Marco must have thought *I* had a man here last night. Oh. My. Godfathers. What the fuck must he think? First Raffa and then a stranger all on the same night? Jesus.

I feed an edge of silk beneath the bobbing needle and prick my finger, a small bead of blood appearing on my skin. Damn! I suck my finger, replaying the whole conversation in my mind's eye. 'I guess you are on holiday.' Oh, the excruciating shame of it all. What must he think of me?

Zhané

Relax, Roma. Who gives a damn what he thinks of you?

And that's the weird thing – I shouldn't give a damn, but for some unfathomable reason, I do.

CHAPTER FOURTEEN
Wedding apparel

Three weeks later, freckles have sprung up all over my arms and face, my hair is sun-streaked and my skin has taken on the complexion of a ripe apricot. My few worldly possessions are sitting in one of Flora's dad's many spare rooms and life here in Altaterra has moved on, the villagers I have so far got to know dubbing me lo stilista inglese. Even Signora Abbadelli seems to have accepted me as her neighbour, greeting me with a nod of acknowledgement each time our paths cross rather than the look of disgruntlement she previously reserved for me.

Tuscany has certainly taken my mind off The Horse and Setayesh, my Bold & Brave collection extending to three dresses, a sequined jacket inspired by Flora's and a glittery jumpsuit I'm dying to wear, should I have an occasion to dress up. The village rumour mill seems to be in full flow with all sorts of contradictory stories concerning the status of La Casa dei Cappelli – the baker claiming that the building has already been sold to property developers whilst the woman from the Post Office suggests that there's still hope in saving it. Whatever the truth, I signed the petition. It can't hurt to go belt and braces with something so important. Whoever it is that's looking to cash in on the jewel of Altaterra should be ashamed of themselves. Making wedding costumes needs to take priority now, though, what with Valentina and Flavio's big day only two weeks away – nine outfits down, seven to go!

With the imminent village wedding, I have a captive market here and it's proving more lucrative than I'd imagined and the only way I can deliver the orders on time is to adopt a strict routine. Mornings comprise three hours and several coffees at the sewing machine before a leisurely stroll around the village in search of breakfast, then another shift of pinning and stitching before a late lunch out on the terrace in the shade of Marco and Maria's fig tree. Afternoons are strictly reserved for fittings and adjustments, which have become quite a lengthy affair, what with each villager using the session as some sort of priest's confessional, offloading all sorts of gripes, groans and petty jealousies. Then I treat myself to a much-needed cool down under the outside hosepipe in the early evening.

'Ramona?' Marco's head pops around the door.

'Si?' I muster. Surely three alterations in one day are beyond the call of duty? But then again, I can't complain – he's almost bent over backwards to accommodate me, offering me another month's rental on a quid quo pro basis that works out in my favour and is nothing short of a miracle considering it is peak holiday season and everything gets booked up so fast around here.

'We need your urgent help,' he says, out of breath.

'Riiiight,' I say, glancing at the pile of half-made clothes on the sofa and wondering where in my backlog I can squeeze in 'urgent help'.

'Francesca, the Mother of the Bride. She needs a new dress.'

I drop my needle and look up. 'What's the matter with—'

'Ramona?' A bewildered middle-aged woman with a streak of electric blue in her white grey hair pushes past him, leaving him all but splayed up the wall. She wears a long trench coat and a look of concern, the corners of her mouth drooping in defeat. 'My dress, it is ruined!' She unbuttons her coat to reveal a silk evening gown which is both too small and too big; practically gaping at the shoulders yet so tight at the waist that it is bulging at the seams, but it's not until she turns around to show the enormous tear down the back of the dress that I realise what a write-off it really is, the rip running through the fabric rather than along a salvageable seam.

'This is how the model wears it.' She thrusts her phone at my face, showing a young woman with the proportions of Setayesh posing in the same evening gown. 'How am I supposed to look like this when she is celery and I am a watermelon?' she explodes. 'She is fine vermicelli and I am plump conchiglie?'

I throw her a sympathetic smile, leaning in to inspect the gown more closely. 'May I suggest a different outfit?'

'Different?'

'Something stronger. Something more flattering. Something more modern.' I grab my phone and scroll through my back catalogue of Curvaliscious sketches until I find the one that I'm looking for – a design I have long dreamed of making. 'Maybe something like this?'

She looks at my screen, her face filling with horror as her eyes connect with the pencil marks depicting a tailored high-waisted trouser suit and fitted satin corset. 'Really?'

'Really.' I nod.

Her expression softens, a chuckle escaping her lips. 'Signorina Ramona, I think I might be a few decades too old for a corset.'

'Nobody's too old for a corset,' I reason. 'Not if it's made correctly.'

'Ma che guai!' She looks at Marco and shakes her head in a way that suggests I have told her to attend the wedding butt naked. 'Lei è fuori di testa! Un corsetto? È pazza!'

Marco glances at me and then turns back to Francesca, his hands clasped together almost in prayer. 'Maybe you should try?'

'Dai! I am the village pharmacist, not the village whore!' She runs her fingers through the electric blue streak in her hair and exhales through both nostrils with fierce indignation, her eyes darting around the room, resting first on the fabric stacked up on the kitchen table, then moving to the dress hanging in the window and finally settling on the calendar hanging next to the wall clock, at which point her expression changes to that of a startled deer.

I turn to see what she is looking at and then notice the date marked up in red ink:

il matrimonio dei Flavio e Valentina.

Blowing out her cheeks and ejecting a steady stream of breath, she turns back to me. 'I guess, with such little time, I have no alternative . . . In any case, if I go to the shops, there is never anything stylish for celebrations. Either I buy something that looks like a tent or the design is entirely black to make slim the larger women. Always black.' She shakes her head. 'I am the Mother of the Bride, not a new widow. But seriously, why is there nothing for the larger woman for celebrations?'

'A lady after my own heart.' I gather up my tape measure and lead her to the changing cubicle. 'Don't worry, you're in safe hands. I know this is very different from what you see in the shops for larger women, but that's a good thing. I'm here to make you look and feel beautiful but comfortable on this special day.'

Half an hour later and I have all the measurements I need to make Francesca the corset I have in mind using leftover coutil from Auntie Sue's dress, however Marco is still loitering, which is eating into precious sewing time.

'Thank you for signing the petition.' He brushes down the sleeves of his Best Man's jacket and stares at his reflection in the bedroom mirror that I've wrestled downstairs and into the kitchen – the only full-length one in the house. His hair is shaggy and unkempt, and the rest of the outfit he's wearing is at odds with the blazer he has just slipped on – flip-flops, board shorts and a scruffy 'Born to Surf' garish yellow T-shirt jarring with the clean lines of the fitted jacket.

'No problem. Although I don't understand what's happening half the time! I mean, just who are these villagers that want it demolished?' I stab a needle into my wrist-band pincushion with unnecessary force.

'These villagers?'

'Who want to sell La Casa and replace it with holiday apartments?' I probe.

Marco throws back his head and laughs. 'Let me guess . . . Raffaele told you this?'

'Yes,' I say, submerged by the slow dawn of realisation that this was total BS.

'It is Raffaele who wants to sell. We, the villagers, are trying to save it.' He smooths the brushed cotton down over his chest and angles himself this way and that, tugging gently on the lapel whilst rolling his skateboard back and forth over the stone floor with one foot. 'You don't think . . .'

'It looks great,' I say, running my hands over his shoulders to accentuate the cut, a slight frisson running over my skin at the touch of his neck, which disappears as quickly as it started up with the clunkety-clunk of skateboard wheels against the stone floor.

He twists his mouth to one side. 'You don't think it's too . . .'

'Too what?' I say, trying to swallow my frustration.

Too small? Too big? Too long? Too short? Too dressy? Too casual? Too simple? Too complicated? I hold my breath in my cheeks. This is the third time in three days that Marco has come in for alterations and I don't have time for this. Delivering Maria's dress to spec seems to have put me firmly on the map as Tailor of Altaterra, which is fantastic for business but a little daunting now that I have the responsibility of creating a whole wedding wardrobe for three Best Men, two Maids of Honour, Mother of the Bride, Mother of the Groom, and one of the bridesmaids who has become so disillusioned by the progress of her current seamstress that she's cancelled her order and commissioned me to deliver a floor-length, off-the-shoulder, mauve mermaid trumpet gown with built-in bra and boning. The design itself is not as complicated as it sounds but sourcing enough satin in the right shade of mauve (not too purply and not too grey) is proving to be problematic, the guy from the fabric market stall explaining that it would be quicker for me to travel to Florence myself than for him to source it.

Marco wrinkles up his nose. 'Too different?'

I clamp my jaw shut and bite the inside of my cheek. My backlog of wedding apparel orders is increasing by the hour and yet he seems hell-bent on taking me down with one bloody jacket which, in my humble opinion, is an absolute triumph, the made-to-measure dark navy fabric gliding over his chest and the felted aquamarine chest pocket trim offsetting the colour of his ice-blue eyes. Can't he see that this high-end cotton blend blazer is nothing short of a smart-chic masterpiece and that the only reason it looks so ridiculous is because he's coupled it with the gaudy look of a teenage skateboarder? The jacket has so much potential, for fuck's sake, and yet here he is pissing it up the wall. By all means, layer it over a sky-blue Oxford slim-fit for a classic look, pair it with a crisp, white T-shirt for a contemporary twist or go all-out David Beckham and wear it over a bare chest for all I care, but since when has shoving it over the lurid wardrobe of a skateboarding manchild worked for anyone?

He looks at me in the way my parents' aged King Charles Spaniel eyes pigeons who have dared to enter his garden, his neck twisted to one side with curiosity. 'You don't think it's a little different from the other Best Man jackets?'

'It's only the cut that's different.' I exhale sharply. 'You're all different shapes and sizes so you all needed a slightly different cut, but once you've all got the same flower arrangement, nobody will notice,' I say, bundling him out of the jacket and slipping it back onto the hanger. He may have time to ponder and procrastinate but I certainly don't.

He grabs my arm, a small jolt of electricity taking me by surprise as I spin round and look into his glacial blue eyes. 'I'm sorry,' he says, 'this arrangement with best men and bridesmaids is not an Italian tradition so I am not familiar with the etiquette. It's just something Flavio does to keep his mother quiet as she has American heritage. I actually love this jacket more than the other Best Men jackets. You are a superstar, Ramona. Thank you.'

'See you tomorrow, then!' I say, almost too quickly. Did we just share a moment back then?

'A domani!' He picks up his skateboard, tucks it under his arm and disappears through the long grass.

As soon as he's gone, I stand with my back against the door and tell myself I'm losing it. Good old Ramona, letting her overactive imagination run riot. But then again, wasn't there an urgency to the way in which he grasped my arm? A spontaneity that took us both by surprise? A fleeting look of longing in his ice-blue eyes? I shake my head in an attempt to dispel my ridiculous fantasies. Of course I'm being stupid. He is betrothed to one of the most beautiful women in the world, so why the hell would he give me a second glance?

Pacing around the kitchen and trying to regain some sort of status quo, my chest tightens at the sight of all the fabric heaped up on the sofa. Knocking up a few bohemian wedding outfits within the idyllic setting of the Tuscan hills felt like a fairy tale a couple of days ago, but things are getting somewhat out of control now everyone wants additional extras thrown in. Matching garters. Matching scarves. Matching God knows what.

The main challenge is working here at the house. For starters, the kitchen table is too high and without an adjustable chair its positioning is giving me backache, a knot forming below my left shoulder that I can't seem to get rid of, no matter how much I poke and prod at it. This morning when I woke, it felt as though my shoulders had seized up entirely. The light isn't crazy brilliant either. Daytime is obviously fine, what with enough sunshine to power a small country, but it's difficult to see properly once the sun has gone down; only the other night I wasted three hours using the wrong colour thread and had to unpick it all.

What really isn't conducive, though, is trying to use the bathroom for fittings. I hadn't realised that the left-hand side of the building is overlooked and poor Signor Zaccardi got the shock of his life the other day when the Auntie of the Bride, a kind, voluptuous lady, low in body confidence, was standing in her underwear beneath his kitchen window. Three days later and neither the voyeur nor the vu are quite recovered but on the upside Signor Zaccardi has a den available to rent, something that apparently needs a bit of a declutter but has inbuilt ceiling strip lights and great potential.

Zhané

A den?

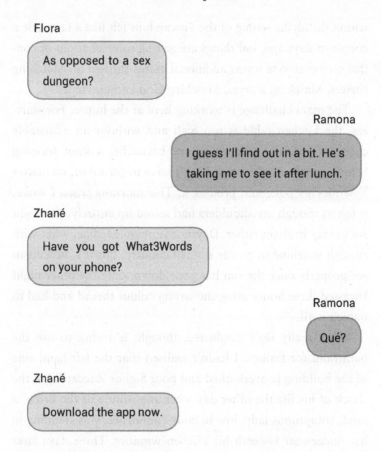

Flora

As opposed to a sex dungeon?

Ramona

I guess I'll find out in a bit. He's taking me to see it after lunch.

Zhané

Have you got What3Words on your phone?

Ramona

Qué?

Zhané

Download the app now.

I do as she says, marvelling at how brilliant a concept it is that a unique combination of three words has been assigned to every three square metres of the world in order that the exact where-abouts of somebody can be pinpointed in the event of an emergency. Mum could have done with something like this when she paraglided further than planned and ended up with her wing impaled in a pine tree deep in a forest on the other side of the moors and could only describe her location as 'woody'. It took five hours, a sniffer dog and a search party of nine to find her. It's mind-boggling to think what inventions people come up with.

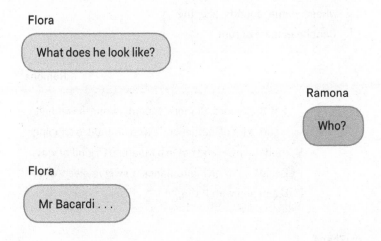

Flora

What does he look like?

Ramona

Who?

Flora

Mr Bacardi . . .

That's the thing about Flora – she's always on the lookout for love and has some kind of inbuilt matchmaking gene that means that everyone she meets is a romantic prospect and she automatically assumes that everyone else is programmed this way, too. Still, sometimes it provides a bit of fun . . .

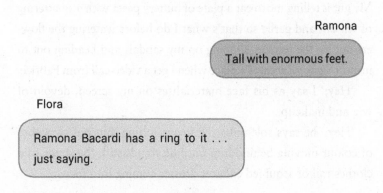

Ramona

Tall with enormous feet.

Flora

Ramona Bacardi has a ring to it . . . just saying.

Zhané

> You cannot go out with a man whose name sounds like the Caribbean taste of rum.

Ramona

> For the record, Signor Zaccardi is mid-seventies, wears a lot of leather and has a draught-excluding moustache — and not in a Magnum PI kind of way. Besides, I'm giving romance a swerve given what happened with Raffa.

Zhané

> Good plan and good luck with the 'den'! And remember … the moment you feel like it could be dodgy, it is! Trust your gut.

My gut is telling me to eat a plate of buttery pasta with a smattering of sea salt and garlic so that's what I do before watering the flowers out on the terrace, slipping on my sandals and heading out to inspect Signor Zaccardi's place when I get a video call from Fabrice.

'Hey,' I say as his face materialises on my screen, devoid of wig and makeup.

'Hey,' he says solemnly, the image jolting, blurred swooshes of colour moving behind him until he stands still, the shape of a clothes rail of sequined cabaret dresses coming into focus.

'What's up?' I say, sensing that something serious has happened. 'Are you in a shop?'

He nods. 'Barbarella's. I need you to make me a dress. The one I bought won't cut it.'

'I knew it was serious. Are you OK?'

'It's DragFest in three weeks and Cinderella has nothing to wear to the ball! Do I sound OK?' he says theatrically, plucking a rainbow scooped-back, block-sequined fishtail dress off the rail and holding it in front of him.

'Mr Pommes Frites granted you annual leave, then?'

'Kind of. He thinks I'm attending an accountancy conference in Milton Keynes. Look, I need you to make me something like this . . . mixed with this.' He grabs a feathered ballgown with slutty fishnet-cum-bondage bodice from an outstretched hand and holds it up over the top of the dress. 'Only with bigger shoulder pads, more décolletage and less material. I need to show my legs off. Less frou-frou and more you-you.'

'Me-me?' I say mockingly, locking up the house and heading out through the meadow, the sunshine so bright that I have to shade my phone with my hand to see Fabrice at all.

'Sorry, I've just been watching *RuPaul's Drag Race* for a bit of inspiration and it's got the better of me. You know what I mean, though. I need something Princess Diana meets Beyoncé. Snow White meets Katie Price. Bambi meets Jessica Rabbit. Sassy but stylish. Slutty but sophisticated. Something Drunk Ramona. Feel-good Ramona. Fun Ramona.'

I feel dizzy as he carries the phone through the shop and over to the fitting room, where a brightly lit cubicle with an angled mirror awaits. Propping up the phone up on what must be a stool, he treats me to a full frontal as he takes off his trousers and shimmies into the sequined rainbow fishtail dress. I look away, letting myself through the gate. 'You could always wear the white feathered catsuit that you wore last year. You looked fabulous in that.'

A look of disdain flickers across his face as he pulls the dress up over his torso, the fabric stretching at the seams as he tries to ease his arms into the ruched sleeves. 'The same outfit I wore last year? Vivienne, I'll be singing from the top of a glittery Union Jack double-decker bus – Queen Bea has done such an amazing job with it – and if I turn up in last year's togs, I'll never live it down! DragFest to me is what Curvaliscious is to you. It's not just child's play, you know. My whole future depends on this. You know they're offering a million euros to the winner? Just think what we could do with a million, Vivienne! I could quit my job for starters!'

As I head down the alley towards the village square, Fabrice chuntering away about what he'd spend his winnings on and the sun tickling the back of my neck, I spot an electric-blue flash and Francesca, Mother of the soon-to-be village Bride, comes into view. She wears a white lab coat and clutches a paper bag with a green cross on it. Flickering her fingers at me through the branches of a bush bursting with hot-pink flowers, she beckons me over. I wave back, jabbing my finger at the phone apologetically and look away before she can chase after me for an update on her made-to-measure corset, which I would have finished by now, had I not got the order in for the Best Men's suits. 'Fabrice, I'd love to make you a dress but I wouldn't be able to start it for two weeks as I'm up to my ears with wedding orders and—'

'Wedding orders? I thought you were working on a new collection for Curvaliscious?'

My mouth dries.

'Sassy frocks for Plus Size women!'

'The money from the wedding orders is funding my Curvaliscious designs. It's win-win,' I say, indignance rising in my chest though I feel like a fraud because, let's be honest, it's not as if I've been busting a gut to get my new collection off the ground. In fact, if someone had told me a couple of months ago that I would put Curvaliscious on the back burner to make mainstream wedding outfits, I wouldn't have believed them – and yet here I am, selling my soul purely because The Horse dented my confidence and said 'no'.

Didn't a newspaper editor say 'no' to Walt Disney, firing him because he lacked vision? Didn't Steve Jobs get fired from Apple in the early days? Wasn't Harrison Ford told by a whole heap of film executives that he didn't have what it took to be a star? And would Martin Luther King have been the US civil rights trailblazer he was had he just stated that he had a dream but chose to do nothing about it? God, I'm pathetic.

'So, there's no chance of a Plus Size frock for a sassy woman in three weeks then?'

'DragFest is three weeks away?' I say, chewing the inside of my cheek and wondering just how I can prioritise this without letting any of my Italian customers down.

'Gah, this fucking sleeve!' He rotates his arm backwards and tries to twist his shoulder into the gap. 'You're the only one who can save me from humiliation, Vivienne. There are hundreds of dresses that would be perfect but none of them are big enough for a burly man of six-foot two and a half. I broke the zipper on the last bodice I tried on and ended up buying it just because I felt bad. Please, Vivienne! You're the only one who will understand what I'm looking for.'

'Bambi meets Slutzilla?' I muse.

'Exactly!' he says, giving up on the dress and letting the sleeve fall at his side. 'I could mail you my measurements . . . ?'

A feeling of unease curdles in my gut. Fabrice has been there for me through thick and thin. Looking after me when my parents split up and again when they got back together, picking me up after my failed pitch and rescuing me with an emergency hair salon appointment when I dyed my locks a misjudged wishy-washy blue. How could I possibly turn my back on him now?

'I'm not sure whether I trust the post for sending you the finished thing, though. I made an outfit for my Auntie Sue and despite sending it special delivery, it only just made it in time.'

'Well, "blimey O'Reilly" as my mother would have said, we can't risk that, can we? I'll mail you my measurements pronto. Oh, and just one thing: regardless of the dress, promise me you will not give up on your dreams?'

'I promise,' I say quietly.

And with that he disappears, and I am left staring at my phone screen which flashes up the time (12.14) in big digits with a hollow feeling in my stomach. Is it true that I have neglected Curvaliscious and given up on my dreams, putting my designs on so much of a back burner that they'll probably never make it to the forefront? Whatever happened to striking whilst the iron was hot, having gained the ear and the eye of Donatella Ricci? Will she remember me in a year's time? Two? Just when exactly am I going to come up with these new designs?

Reeling with self-doubt and full of imposter syndrome, I gather up my phone and pull on my trainers to meet Signor Zaccardi.

CHAPTER FIFTEEN
Signor Zaccardi's place

I spot Signor Zaccardi sitting on a bench next to the ornate fountain in the village piazza, a small scruffy dog sitting at his heel. He wears the same creased linen suit and shiny leather shoes he has worn on each occasion that we've met and dabs at his forehead with an enormous cotton handkerchief. A band of cloud has formed above the medieval bell tower that marks the central and highest point of the village and an easterly wind has swept in, rustling the leaves of the ancient olive trees lining the hillside walkway like royal guards and blowing dirt over the cobbles.

'Salve!' I call over, wondering whether I should have gone for a simple 'ciao' when he doesn't look up and then notice that he's adjusting his hearing aid.

'Piacere,' he says, once I'm standing right next to him and thrusts his enormous slab of a hand into mine to deliver the firmest of handshakes. Looking up at the moving pale grey clouds, he shrugs his shoulders in a way that suggests the sky has let us both down with its refusal to go all-out-blue and shakes his head apologetically.

'Is it your dog?' I watch as the wiry-haired mutt at his heel shuffles its bottom in the dry dirt and looks up in the hope of food.

'This is Pepé, the village dog.' He bends down and reaches for Pepé's paw. 'When my son lived here, he had a small shop in the village where he sold Italian meats. Salami. Prosciutto, Soppressata, Pepperoni. Pepé was always there, waiting for the small pieces of meat to fall to the floor, and now he expects the same from me even though I am no butcher.'

'He's lovely,' I say, tickling Pepé's chin.

'Come, let me show you the room.' Signor Zaccardi heaves himself up to standing – I'd forgotten how tall he is – and sets off across the cobbled square. 'I'm not so sure you will want it because it has been neglected, but I can offer you very cheap rent.'

'I'm sure it'll be great.'

Pepé trots alongside us as we venture down a small alley I've not seen before, the keys clanking together in Signor Zaccardi's hand as he slowly negotiates the winding stone steps down to the lower path, steadying himself on a metal handrail that has been fitted to the side of a sandstone building – a small library (Biblioteca), it turns out. We round the corner into a small courtyard, where a woman sits beneath the shade of a lemon tree, her nose in a paperback novel. I've a mind to squeeze in alongside her and pour myself a tall drink of iced water from the glass jug on the bistro table next to her but Signor Zaccardi has quickened his stride over to a bronze door carved into a stone archway and I figure that if I don't keep pace, I could get lost in this warren of hidden gardens. A patch of wild strawberries grows next to the stone steps he is marching towards and he bends down to pick the ripest, feeding a plump, red berry to Pepé, who devours it instantly, and handing the other one to me.

'Grazie,' I say, popping it into my mouth and relishing the explosion of flavour on my tongue. 'Delizioso!'

With strawberry-stained hands, he inserts a variety of different-shaped keys into the lock, the door finally springing open to reveal a much smaller courtyard overgrown with brambles and nettles. He tramples down a path towards a stone outhouse whose doorstep boasts a basket of eggs, feathers stuck to their shells in places.

'Here.' He stops before a ramshackle building which looks not altogether unfamiliar but I can't quite place. Maybe I'm just thinking of a horror movie. The spooky haunted house from *Hotel Transylvania* or the crumbling cottage in *The Quiet Man* maybe. Pepé folds his ears back and barks as Signor Zaccardi brushes away layer upon layer of thick, dusty cobwebs to run his fingers over the peeling paintwork of rotten shutters, a strip of dried paint splintering off and falling into the overgrown grass below. Signor Zaccardi inspects his jailor's keyring whilst Pepé's bark becomes a high-pitched whine. The smell of rotting flesh hits my nostrils, the stench growing stronger as we draw nearer and a bodies-under-the-floorboards surge of fear takes hold of me as he fumbles for the lock. Is this legit? I may have What3Words on my phone but other than my friends two thousand kilometres away, who would decipher Planet.Cup.Table?

'This is it?' I say, glancing at what looks like the sort of dilapidated, windowless stone building a shepherd of yesteryear might have hunkered down in to protect his flock from perilous weather – not an obvious choice of headquarters for a high-end bridal boutique.

'This is the back. You will prefer the front.'

Tail between his legs, Pepé slinks off and I'm tempted to join him, the pungent smell intensifying further as we near the door. With shaky hands, Signor Zaccardi selects the largest key from the jailor's ring and jabs it into the lock, the door bursting open as though it has been forced shut against its will for centuries. The stench of rotting fish hits us immediately. I pinch my nose and splutter on the fumes, the taste of decay permeating the back of my throat, Signor Zaccardi squeezing his face into his elbow and wheezing. It takes a moment for my eyes to adjust from blazing sunshine to the darkness that shrouds the space before the area in front of me slowly morphs into the shape of a workshop both wider and longer than I'd expected. Signor Zaccardi steps into the room and reaches for the light switch.

'Welcome,' he says, pulling an enormous pair of Marigold gloves out of his pocket and squeezing his giant spaded hands into each one.

The clunk and whir of overhead strip lights kicks in and the room is illuminated in all its glory. A mountain of empty sardine cans, fishbones and discarded tins of cat food lies before us, making it impossible to go any further, pilchard heads dangling out of metal dishes, sour milk turned to yoghurt thick with mould in others. A table has been dismantled and is folded up against the wall to make way for whatever feeding frenzy went on in here.

'So?' Signor Zaccardi looks to me expectantly.

I clear my throat, trying not to choke on the rancid air. 'It's . . . I mean . . . I suppose . . .'

'Don't worry, I know it is no place to work. I told Marco you would not want to make clothes here, but he insisted.' He shields his mouth with his handkerchief. 'Mariela loved cats. She had hundreds of cats. Too many to keep in her house so they lived all over the village and here, where she would feed them.'

I open my mouth to reply and wish I hadn't, closing it immediately.

'The smell is so bad,' he says apologetically. 'I thought maybe it needs a clean but there is too much decay here – maybe a decade of meat and fish tins. I'm sorry to waste your time.'

I'm about to agree with him when my eye is drawn to the two small bay windows at the front of the room. They may not be huge, but they're big enough to feature a mannequin's bust and if the glass front door was clear of cobwebs, it could showcase a studio very nicely. I study the windows and have the sense that I've been here before. Déjà vu? I try to get my bearings. Hang on a minute, are we in the derelict building next to the wine cellar that sits beneath the Casa dei Cappelli? Thoughts ricochet around my head. He did just mention Mariela's cats. Have we really just done a full circle outside?

'Is this part of Mariela Marino's hat shop?' I ask, confused.

'The hat shop is above.' He points up at the ceiling. 'If you look on the right, there is a staircase which joins my place with hers.' He gestures to an unremarkable door in the wall and my mind fills with images of Tim Burton and Helena Bonham Carter's passageway between their neighbouring houses. 'We were very close,' he says, clutching his chest and wheezing. 'Perhaps too close.'

'Are you OK?' I say, worrying that he's about to keel over and realising that it may not be my dead body that gets pulled out of here.

'I need . . .' he splutters.

'You need air!' I say, bundling him into the great outdoors, where we both take enormous gulps of oxygen. Never has it felt like such a luxury to be able to breathe.

He sits down on the stone step and inhales the fresh Tuscan air as I run back through the courtyard and grab the library's jug of ice water, shouting 'Scusi' at a couple of al fresco readers.

Signor Zaccardi clutches the jug to his chest and takes a giant glug. 'Sorry,' he says, wiping droplets of water off his thick moustache with his huge handkerchief. 'I did not know there was so – so much smell!'

'Were you together? You and Mariela?' I say somewhat clumsily, but he doesn't look fazed and I'm momentarily grateful that international conversation can be so direct and definitely more forgiving. Things are less complicated when words are a means of getting from A to B, rather than journeying through the ambiguity of suggestion. Ordinarily, I would never be so bold.

He mops his brow with his handkerchief. 'We were in love for fifty years but sadly, we could not be together.'

'Why ever not?' I say, gesturing for the jug.

'Because I was too Jewish and she was too Catholic. My parents disapproved of her. Her parents disapproved of me, and we didn't want to upset anyone and—'

'So you missed out on loving each other your whole life?' I say, horrified.

He chuckles, which only starts up another coughing fit. 'We loved each other a lot. Just not for the world to see.'

'That's a shame,' I say, picturing the two of them caught in a clandestine embrace in the shadowy corners of her hat emporium, all closet kisses and backstreet encounters.

'Many times, I asked her to marry me. Many times she said no because it would break the heart of her mother and father. And so I stopped asking.'

'That's sad,' I say, recalling Mariela's eulogy and the mention of her marriage to someone with whom she had children and whose surname was not Zaccardi. 'It must have been very hurtful.'

'We were in love before she got married. We were in love throughout her marriage. And we were in love when her marriage broke down . . . A little like your king!' he adds with a chuckle.

'My king?' I say, confused, wondering if he's referring to Raffa.

'King Charles III and Camilla Parker Bowles,' he says, reminding me how much more clued-up the non-British are about our Royal family than we are and wondering who the Princess Diana of this situation was.

'Did her family know? Mariela's, I mean. Not Camilla Parker Bowles.'

He clears his throat with a gravelly cough. 'It was no big secret here in Altaterra. Almost everybody knew that her husband was in love with the mayor many years before they ran away together, and that she and I were in love, too.' His eyes look misty with melancholy. 'We made shoes together. We made hats together. We made love together. Everything here was ours.' He gestures at the building behind us. 'And so it fills my heart with sadness that it will be gone.'

'Gone where?' I say, confused.

'When Mariela died, she gave La Casa dei Cappelli to her grandson, Raffaele.'

I shudder, making eye contact with the ground. Just the very mention of Raffa's name makes me feel soiled and humiliated.

'He has decided to have . . . how do you say this when you sell things to a big room of people? The man with the hammer. The person who offers the most—'

'An auction?'

He clicks his fingers in affirmation. 'An auction.'

'He's auctioning off all of the hats?'

He nods. 'And also the building.'

'Is that what Mariela wanted?' I ask, horrified.

'No! Her wish was to keep the hats together as a collection. She told Raffaele many, many times that the hats should stay together but he has decided to ignore her wishes. Instead, he will auction everything.'

My throat tightens. 'He can't!' I drop my head into my hands, remembering the conversation Raffa and I had about the value of each hat when we were trying them on and feeling a wave of guilt. Hadn't I commented on the worth of each one, declaring the pillbox hat to be worth over ten thousand pounds alone? Have I in some way enabled his grand plan?

'Unfortunately, he can. As the only grandson, he inherits everything.'

'But Raffa loved his grandma. Why would he want to . . .' My words peter out. Maybe all that stuff about idolising his grandmother was part of the 'nice boy' act, too.

Signor Zaccardi gazes at the stone building behind us, dabbing at the corners of his eyes with a large handkerchief. 'He wants to buy my studio so that he can sell it with her hat shop above and make real money.'

A bitter taste forms on my tongue. 'You're not going to sell it to him, are you?'

Taking a step backwards and looking up at the building, Signor Zaccardi takes his handkerchief and waves it in the air as though surrendering. 'Although I have a passion for making shoes, shoes do not make money for retirement.'

'But you can't! If he gets your studio, La Casa dei Cappelli doesn't stand a chance!'

A feeling of nausea overcomes me as I look up at the row of small, intricately sculpted statues of Italian saints, running around the periphery of the building, each corner featuring a miniature gargoyle doubling as a waterspout. The external architecture alone is magnificent but that's nothing compared to the inner sanctuary of Mariela's hat shop upstairs, and yet all of this is going to be sold at the drop of a hat (maker)? The baroque hand mirrors. The glass chandeliers. The antique walnut dressers. I feel lightheaded just thinking about it. It's almost inconceivable that La Casa dei Cappelli will cease to exist in a matter of months and all the hats gone. I may have only been inside once, but it was an experience of a lifetime and one I'll never forget.

Signor Zaccardi looks at me with hangdog eyes. 'I have phoned Raffaele. I have written to him, but nothing. He ignores everything from me and every day that goes by, the auction gets closer.'

My mouth dries. All of those hats. That whole collection. They belong together. The work of a genius – or rather, the entire works of a genius. Of course, it goes without saying that auctioning off each piece will raise a small fortune fast but isn't this about playing the long game? Fashionistas and hat lovers from all over the world would pay money just to ooh and aah over Mariela Marino's assortment of headgear for years to come without needing to sell a single piece and the family could maintain the building with the proceeds. What on earth is Raffa thinking? A collection is a collection. It's not meant to be broken up.

'I'll take the room!' I blurt out, before I've had chance to think it through.

'Are you sure?'

'First week free of charge whilst I clean it out and do it up, and then I'll pay you rent.'

'Signorina Ramona—'

An energy takes hold of me. 'Anything to stop Raffaele Bergamaschi getting his hands on anything else that doesn't belong to him!'

I'm not quite sure how I'm going to pull this off, but if it means saving the hat emporium from extinction, honouring Mariela Marino's dying wishes and putting Raffa's nose out of joint in the process, ignoring this opportunity is not an option.

And besides, this place oozes so much creative karma, maybe a studio within the confines of the Casa dei Cappelli will be just the place to finish my Bold & Beautiful collection.

'Only if you're sure?' he says, plucking a sardine skeleton off the sole of his shoe.

'I am, 100 per cent. *Cento per cento.*' I nod, trying to convince myself as much as anyone else.

He goes to shake my hand and then thinks better of it, a soiled Marigold glove not entirely an attractive prospect to touch, so he then tries to hug me without making any actual body contact, which ends up looking like some sort of Teletubbies greeting, the pair of us dissolving into laughter.

The sound of footsteps on gravel disturbs the moment and our heads twist to see Maria waddling through the courtyard in a long floral dress, cradling her eight-month bump with the weariness of a woman who is ready to give birth. At her side is a petite woman with electric blue mascara and a bleached-blonde cropped pixie haircut, dressed entirely in white. White jeans. White crochet top over white vest top. Even her cork-heeled sandals are white, yet somehow it works.

Marco appears with a bucket of cleaning equipment, pushing his way urgently past both of them to greet me. 'You saw the place already?' he says, alarmed.

'Yes.'

'With all the cat food tins and— ' The look of horror on his face intensifies.

'Yes.'

'I'm so sorry, Ramona. We wanted to clean it first. To show you how good it can be.' He casts a look of disappointment in

Signor Zaccardi's direction before turning back to me. 'I know it smells. I know it's dirty. I know you won't like it, but trust me, it has so much potential! If nobody takes it, Signor Zaccardi will sell it to Raffaele and that's why—'

'I said yes,' I say, supressing a smile.

'I brought a team of people to help clean the place so that you can see it when it looks better.' He goes on, gesturing to the woman in white next to him before turning back to me. 'Wait. What? You said yes?'

'Yes!'

His face is an explosion of happiness as he takes my hands in his and squeezes them tightly. 'Mamma Mia, you don't know the relief this gives me. You and the goat man who lives in a stable with his herd were our last chance.'

'Riiiight.'

'Pleased to meet you. I am Valentina.' The woman in white steps forward and offers me her hand, which wrongfoots me entirely as all this time I have imagined the bride-to-be as a tall brunette.

'Piacere. Nice to meet you!' I shake her hand, which feels doll-like in mine. 'I've heard so much about you! I'm making your mother's outfit for the wedding.'

She looks at me with big brown eyes and smiles. 'Lo stilista inglese!'

'Si,' I nod, resolving that I must learn some Italian.

'Thank you so much for making my mother's wedding out-fit,' she says in perfect English. 'You have no idea how stressed she was until you came along and convinced her to go for something different. My future mother-in-law, however . . .' She pulls a face.

'Oh dear,' I chuckle. 'They always say that planning a wedding is up there with moving house in terms of stress.'

She grabs hold of my arm. 'You've not met my mother-in-law. Trust me, I would prefer to move house any day!'

Marco pulls out a roll of bin bags from his bucket. 'We will start with the cat food tins.'

'We?' I look up as the thrum of voices and the crunch of approaching footsteps gets louder, a group of twenty or so villagers arriving en masse, all of them wearing old clothes and carrying buckets of cleaning products. 'Why does everyone care so much?'

'Ramona, the people of this village have all grown up with La Casa dei Cappelli at the heart of this village. It is as important to them as their own homes are and an Altaterra without La Casa would be like the Italian renaissance without Michelangelo. La Casa is the jewel in the crown of the village and we do not want to lose it and it will help the economy of our village if tourists come to see her collection.'

'You have another bag for the garbage?' Valentina pulls on a set of overalls.

'Sure.' I reach for the roll Marco has propped up on the stone wall. 'But . . .'

'We must work together if we are to save La Casa.' Valentina pulls on her overalls and buttons up the front of her boiler suit with gusto. 'You've met my fiancé, Flavio?' She looks up at a tall, dark man with a military haircut who has arrived at her side and I recognise him immediately as the local petrol attendant who spends most of his time on the garage forecourt filling up a steady stream of mopeds, Vespas being all the rage out here.

'Piacere di conoscerti.' He offers me his hand as though I am his sergeant major.

I return his smile with one of my own. 'Ramona.'

'Ah, lo stilista Inglese.' His face softens and his shoulders relax. 'Ho sentito molto su di te. Stai cucendo la maggior parte degli abiti per il matrimonio.'

Unable to understand a word, I look to Valentina for help, but she is too busy handing out bin bags to a steady stream of villagers, so I reply with a simple 'Si' and hope that I haven't committed to producing yet more outfits for the wedding.

'We cannot let Raffaele Bergamaschi win.' Valentina pinches her nose and steps into the pit of rotting fish, a rubble sack in one hand and a bottle of Odour-Eater in the other.

As I stand and stare, more villagers arrive – the stern lady from the Post Office who always struggles to peel out stamps, the portly barman from Ciccone's, the florist's daughter who helps out with some of arrangements on a Saturday, the baker from Pasticceria d'Oro and his children, the man with the thin moustache who drives the school bus, the teenage twins who run the launderette – and it becomes clear that some greater plan has been masterminded and I have somehow become a pivotal part in village life, although what exactly is expected of me remains a mystery.

CHAPTER SIXTEEN
Mummification

A day later and the villagers of Altaterra have managed to evacuate the entire contents of Signor Zaccardi's place and by slipping cash to a team of builders working on a nearby house renovation, the debris has been moved out of the village. It took sixty-four rubble bags, an old pair of curtains and a broken wheelie bin to get rid of the mountain of discarded cat tins but finally I am left staring at the space where Signor Zaccardi and Mariela Marino shared their most intimate moments. If only the walls could talk.

The room looks at least three times bigger than it did yesterday now that the rubbish has gone and the glass panels of the door have been freed of cobwebs and given a clean. Sunshine pours into the room, casting beams of light across the oak floor like a generous wizard, and for the first time I see the true potential of the place. The first port of call is to keep the windows open and get rid of the smell. The second is to bleach and scrub the living shit out of everything – Marco has organised a hit squad for later today – and the third is to give the walls and ceiling a fresh lick of paint, which Marco assures me Flavio will start this evening. Once that's all done, I'll set to work on Fabrice's DragFest dress – an extravagant design I came up with when I was looking back at pictures of Mariela Marino's hats and had the good fortune to stumble across a photo of a model wearing an exotic Caribbean carnival outfit which was technically more bikini than dress but with a little customisation could be just the thing.

In the meantime, I've agreed to meet Marco at the village bar regarding 'something urgent'. My mind boggles.

'I need you.' Marco looks into my eyes with urgency.

'Sorry, I . . .'

'Because you're English and because you now have the secret staircase.'

'Riiiight,' I say, trying to shake the feeling of arousal that is short-circuiting around my groin and replace it with one of deep concentration.

'The hat auction will be held in English for all the tourists, and we need to borrow the secret staircase from you.' He grasps my hand excitedly and then, seeing the look of surprise on my face, lets go of it as quickly as he took it.

'Why do you need the staircase?' I say, enjoying the sensation of his warm hand against mine.

He scratches his chin in thought. 'I can't see that Raffaele will leave peacefully so we may need an emergency exit.'

'Raffa will be there?' A surge of horror rushes through me, adrenaline coursing through my veins, and I am suddenly overcome with a violent urge for the bathroom. It never crossed my mind that Raffa himself would be there – isn't he the sort of person who would send someone else to do his dirty work? Hire some poor unsuspecting woman to fix his problem and then molest her as his way of thanks? I take a deep breath, but no matter how much I try to push down the feeling of vertigo that rises in my stomach, it just won't go away.

Marco looks at me, kindness pooling in his eyes. 'We don't know, but maybe. Don't worry, we will look after you, Ramona.'

'Thanks,' I say, realising that he has dropped both the prefix and formality of Signorina, our relationship shifting up a gear into first-name friendship territory, and then wondering whether I need looking after. Isn't it more about Raffa needing to meet his comeuppance?

'It will be OK.' He takes my hand, and this time doesn't let go, a tornado of feelings spinning inside me. Gratitude. Faith. Uneasiness. Anxiety. Hope. Revenge. But overall the overwhelming sense of solidarity that comes from another human being gripping my hand. An oasis of dry land in a choppy sea and, for some reason, I don't want him to let go. His hand feels warm, solid and reassuring in a way that suggests I have known him for years, but there's also a hint of something else that raises my pulse and sees me nervously fiddling with my hair and checking over my shoulder. It's inappropriate really, I tell myself, thinking of Maria and pulling my hand away with self-chastisement, but whatever *is* or *isn't* going on, it's certainly nice to have a real friend out here.

'So do you accept your mission to take Raffa down, 007?' He looks at me and grins.

Just Raffa's name alone is toxic enough to leave a metallic taste in my mouth, every fibre of my body reeling from the memory of that night. There is no way I am going to miss out on being a part of his collapse.

I sit on my hands so as not to instinctively reach for him again. 'Yes, but how?'

He looks at me with a goofy smile. 'All will be revealed.'

The next day I make my way down to the studio with Hugo, stopping every hundred yards or so along the cobbled path to transfer his weight to my other arm. It's only eight o'clock in the morning but the sun already has a kick to it, the skin on the back of my neck prickling with heat. As I open the door, the smell of fresh paint hits my nostrils, light streaming in through the windows and reflecting in the glass door panels. The brilliant white walls make the space look twice as big as it did yesterday, an expanse of polished wooden flooring gleaming in the morning sun. Inside, the space is shady and cool, its robust stone walls keeping out the heat and the only sound I can hear is that of birdsong and the trickle of water from the courtyard fountain outside. I'll be happy here.

Unfolding the portable table propped against the wall, I wheel it into the end of the room and angle it so that the light catches its centre. Just as Signor Zaccardi suggested, the tabletop is waist-level – the perfect height to work at. The smell of fresh croissants drifts in from the Pasticceria d'Oro and I feel at one with the world. I even have a changing room, courtesy of a curtain Marco has hung around a small alcove at the back of the room. This is going to be perfect, and nothing can burst my bubble.

My phone jingles with the arrival of an email.

From: N.Oman@Armani.com
Subject: Curvaliscious: a brand new high-end fashion range

Dear **XXX,**

Thank you for your design submission. Armani are always on the lookout for fresh, new designs.

We greatly valued your **XXX *(list at least two personal qualities here) e.g. attention to detail/ inventive flair/ innovative eye*.** However, after careful consideration, we regret that **XXX (INSERT COLLECTION NAME)** does not align to our brand.

I'm sure this will be a disappointment, but I would like to say that we wholeheartedly enjoyed your **XXX (INSERT one of the following: experience and insights/ enthusiasm and creativity/ tenacity and drive.** It was a very tough decision for us.

Distinti Saluti,
N. Oman

Could they seriously not have found the time to fill in the blanks?

I will NOT let this get me down. I will NOT let this get me down. I bite the inside of my cheek until I can taste blood. That was the final rejection from the emails I sent out, and I don't know whether I've got the strength to go through it all again. Time for some play therapy.

I set to work on Fabrice's dress, pinning, stitching, folding, snipping and styling, hours slipping by so quickly that when I look at the clock, a minimalist digital flicker board that Valentina donated, I can't quite believe that it's midday already. Holding up the sequined bodice, I go to attach a net skirt but the fabric that I've chosen for the gown that sits over the top isn't quite right and lacks that pizazz needed for DragFest.

Putting the dress to one side, I apply the finishing touches to the lace-beaded crystal rhinestone bustier I have promised the Mother of the Bride, a sense of satisfaction overcoming me, knowing that I have created something worthy of a Bold & Brave design. I hold it up to admire the detail around the edges of the corset – Signora Francesca may be a large lady and this may well be the first time she has dared to wear something so figure-hugging, but I know she can pull it off. Body contouring is all about accentuating curves rather than hiding them and every mother deserves to feel amazing on their daughter's wedding day. If you've got it, flaunt it.

It's at that point that it strikes me that I should be displaying this very outfit in one of the bay windows at the front of the studio but draping it over a hanger and dangling it from a hook does not do it justice. It would be so much easier if I had a mannequin. Something well-proportioned and reflective of a real woman, the shoulders adequately broad and the chest sufficiently robust to carry a plunging neckline. Even if it doesn't have a head or legs, a three-dimensional bust torso would at least bring the piece to life. Flicking through YouTube videos I am surprised to discover that making your own model isn't that difficult. All I need is a bucket, some bandages, Vaseline and a tub of liquid plaster. How hard can it be?

The staff at the Farmacia are keen to help, selling me a whopping tub of Vaseline and enough bandages to mummify the population of the village. It turns out that this isn't the first time the pharmacist has been approached for plaster in this regard – Mariela herself was a fan of creating plaster head mannequins. He points me in the direction of a huge tin of powdered plaster and I part with a bundle of cash for the privilege, a sense of pride setting in later as I plonk my newly acquired items on the kitchen table – my conversational Italian skills are coming along nicely – let's hope that my DIY ones are not too far behind.

Deciding that the studio is too overlooked, I get to work in the apartment. After wiping down the kitchen surface, I drag out my laptop, but it's difficult to see the screen, what with the sun's glare and when I draw the blackout blind, the only lightbulb in the kitchen only goes and pings. I send Marco a text, asking if there are any spare lightbulbs hiding in the apartment, and set about watching videos in the dark. The best making-a-mannequin clip I can find demonstrates the process in six simple stages, the first being all about covering yourself in plaster, which may sound daunting but doesn't actually take that long.

Snip. The bandage.

Dip. In the liquid plaster.

Strip. And place on your body.

Got it. I should be able to manage this solo.

Opening the packet of bandages, I set about cutting them into strips no longer than the width of my body and stack them in front of me on the table. It's too hot to wear leggings and a skinny long-sleeved top like the model in the video, so instead I opt for my nude, seamless pants and faithful sports bra, which gives enough support to feel like I'm not going to trip over my nipples but equally doesn't hoist my chest into an unnaturally scaffolded position beneath my chin. Perfect. Then, taking the roll of cellophane, I set about cling-wrapping my body like it's just your average day in a meat packing factory. Cocooning my girth in layer upon layer of see-through film, I begin to take on the resemblance of a giant slab of pork and it's only when I try to bend over that I realise I can barely breathe. Man, it's hot.

Sweat trickles down my spine and my underarm feels like a damp sponge when I touch it. I'm starting to regret this but no pain, no gain and to coin a *Mastermind* phrase, 'I've started, so I'll finish.' I look down at the laptop screen. The next stage is about smothering yourself in Vaseline – something that reminds me of my Great-Auntie Maude's final days in hospital and makes me shudder with discomfort – but getting lubed up is apparently an integral part of the process which can't be bypassed as it allows the cast to slip away from the skin seamlessly later on. My back itches, but I can't get to it – at least not without ripping the cellophane. I look around the kitchen for something that might double up as a scratching stick. Fish slice? Wooden spoon? Settling for a pair of bacon tongs, sweet relief fills my whole body as the plastic pincers reach places my fingers can't. Now for the Vaseline.

Coconut Oil plays in the background of the video and I smile to myself. What better way to get lubricated than to the immortal tunes of Lizzo? Of course, the whole thing would be a hell of a lot easier if I had someone to help me, but other than the girls and Fabrice, who are hundreds of miles away, there is no one I would entrust to see me in this state, my sweaty bare flesh trapped in a skin-hugging, translucent jacket like processed sausage. Oh well, here goes . . . I slap a Vaseline palm against my waist and set about greasing myself up. It's like basting a turkey. Stomach. Back. Chest. And . . .

'Hello?' a voice calls from outside.

Shit.

'Ramona?'

I look down at my greasy palms. I am something out of a pornographic horror movie.

'Ramona, are you there?'

Marco's distinct voice makes me want to die.

'Can I come in?' He taps at the window.

Fuuuuuuuck. Tiptoeing across the stone floor, I go to crouch behind the table but the cellophane doesn't allow me to bend and I can feel it stretching in places it shouldn't, my heartbeat ringing in my ears and rivulets of sweat running into my crevices.

'Ramona?' He raps on the door.

My face starts to feel clammy. I close my eyes and hold my breath, praying he'll go away, the room swirling around me and my mouth filling with saliva. It feels as though parts of my cheeks are missing, my skin disappearing in patches and reappearing in the wrong places, my nose on my mouth, my mouth in my ears, my chin in my chest – my face an absurdist Picasso jumble of body parts and the stone floor looming towards me.

'I'm coming in to change the light bulb.'

Before I can call out to stop him, the door opens. When I open my eyes, the flagstone floor threatens to engulf me, my senses sloshing around, and it feels as though I am being sucked up and thrashed around in a stormy sea beneath the pull of a wave I have no control over and no idea anymore which way is up. I'm both hot and cold. Sweaty and clammy. Light and heavy. A dichotomy of extremes. My legs buckle. The room rushes towards me and sweet relief takes over as my head clunks against the cold stone and I pass out on the kitchen floor.

I come round under the glare of the new one-hundred-watt lightbulb Marco has suspended from the ceiling, and oh my God, am I really lying on the kitchen table mummified in cling film and Vaseline under the watchful gaze of my holiday-let landlord? I look down at my chest and see, to my horror, that the cellophane has been cut open in places.

Marco peers down at me, a look of concern in his ice-blue eyes. Tucking a spiral of blond hair behind his ear, he reaches for my hand. Instinctively, I try to cover my chest with my arms but that only draws attention to my waist or lack of, so I shift them down a little and drop them over my stomach.

'I know I look like a madwoman,' I say, swinging my legs over the side of the table and reaching for a tea towel to protect my modesty. 'But I was just trying to make a mannequin. Un manichino? And . . . I don't know . . . It got a bit hot and . . .'

He peers into the pot of gloopy white mulch sitting next to me. 'Un manichino?'

'A mannequin, yes.' I quiver under a novelty Christmas tea towel, small robins in Santa hats dancing across my crotch, and accept the glass of water he is thrusting into my hands.

'Do you feel better now?' he says.

'Yes. Thanks. Totally fine. Thanks.' I back away until the knobs of the oven press into my partially bare backside.

He picks up the paintbrush. 'Do you need help?'

My chest tightens and my mouth dries. It feels as though I've entered some mad Korean reality TV game where life imitates art, art imitates life, surrealism is real and I have absolutely no fucking clue what is happening as he rolls up his sleeve, dips the brush into the pot of plaster, and with the carefree abandon of someone about to creosote a fence on a sunny afternoon, looks over at me as though it is totally normal to stand practically naked, wrapped in cling film in front of your landlord whilst he coats you in wet plaster in his kitchen.

I glance around for a defence weapon. Should I fend him off with a cheese grater? Bat him away with the fish slice? Jab him in the nuts with . . . where are those bacon tongs? Though when I stop to look at him, his hands hanging limply at his sides and a look of kindness etched on his face, it dawns on me that the problem isn't that I feel threatened. Moreover, a persistent tingling feeling has started up in my groin.

'No. I'm OK, thanks.'

The whole purpose of DIY is that you actually do it yourself, right?

'OK, sorry.' He retires the brush into the pot of plaster.

'Sorry, I'm . . .' I want to say that I'm truly mortified and can only apologise profusely for bringing wet plaster into his kitchen, but the words get stuck in my throat and all I want to do is dig a hole and die in it.

'I made you a tea with sugar to combat the shock.' He nods to a mug of steaming tea on the kitchen worktop.

'Thank you.'

'Well, if you're sure you're OK?' He picks up his jacket and slings it over his shoulder.

'Yes. Thank you. Perfect. Well, not perfect but . . .'

He flashes a sympathetic smile and leaves.

Frozen in panic, I wait until his footsteps are out of earshot and then scream as loudly as I can and run my head under the cold tap in a bid to wash away the sting of humiliation, but it's no use – that has to be up there with the toilet door swinging open on the train from Lewisham to London Bridge to reveal me, knickers around my ankles, taking a dump in front of a carriage full of commuters as one of the most embarrassing moments of my life.

Flora

> Noooooooooooooo! 🧟‍♀️🧟‍♀️🧟‍♀️

Zhané

> Wait, wait, wait . . . He offered to paint your naked body in plaster?

Ramona

He was trying to be helpful.

Zhané

Hmmmmmm.

One thing's for sure: I can never see Marco ever again. It would just be far too excruciating for both of us.

CHAPTER SEVENTEEN
Giuseppina Sicilliano

The next day, I'm beavering away at the mermaid trumpet gown in my new studio when a woman's face peers in at me from the other side of the glass. Her raven-black hair has been combed up into a beehive and her skin is crinkled like crêpe paper, white powdered cheeks tinted with garish red blusher cream. Like a fox peering into a rabbit warren, her eyes dart around the room as though searching for clues, her ring-adorned fingers working nine to the dozen, fiddling with large porcelain beads that dangle around her neck like polished marbles. I smile at her, hoping that the scowl etched into the grooves of her face will soften but she only stiffens further, her eyes narrowing and her lips disappearing into a thin streak of lip liner. I'm about to pop my head out and welcome her in with a 'Prego' when she bustles in through the door, the letterbox coming loose and hanging by a thread. Another thing to fix later.

Dressed in a floral print raincoat, beige patent heels and carrying a leather handbag in the crevice of her inner elbow, she looks me up and down without apology, her gaze meeting the cheap flip-flops attached to my feet.

'Devi essere la nuova donna inglese?' she says.

I catch 'donna' and 'inglese' and am happy to concede that I am undeniably an English woman but then she's removing the sunglasses propped up on her head and jabbing them aggressively in my direction, eyes ablaze, spouting forth with a tirade of Italian that I can't make head nor tail of. I retreat with each syllable until I'm backed up against the wall, face to face with a seemingly very angry woman.

'Scusi.' I hold my hands up in surrender. 'Parlo solo un po' di Italiano.'

'Pah!' She marches past me, her eyes darting between the brilliant white walls to the freshly painted ceiling and over to the rolls of material stacked up on my work bench. She runs her hand over the length of tufted gold silk I have been asked to make a waistcoat from – which would be better served to uphol- ster a chair – and turns back to me. 'You're here for holidays or for a long time?'

'A month or so? I'm not quite sure yet.' I try to relax, though it's difficult when you're a rabbit cornered by a fox who has just broken into your warren and is staring right at you. 'It's lovely, though. The village. I love Tuscany. It's . . . Are you interested in having something made?' I ask, shifting my attention to business as she starts rifling through the patterns on my table and helping herself to my peppermints. 'I'm taking quite a lot of orders at the moment for Flavio and Valentina's wedding. Dresses. Suits. Skirts . . .'

'Why are you here?' Her eyes remain faithful to a pattern for a two-piece cotton skirt suit she is holding.

'Me?' I say shell-shocked. 'I was just visiting and—'

She looks up at me with a steely glare. 'Visitors do not open shops.'

'Oh, it's not a shop,' I say. 'It's just a studio. I couldn't work back in Marco's apartment so—'

'So, the clothes are not for sale?' Her beaklike mouth twists into the shape of a walnut.

'The clothes I have here are pre-orders. People have requested them and I'm making them on demand, but I'm not opening a shop. I don't want to take—'

'Take trade away from local people?' Her head swivels round like a tawny owl. 'You know business is like friendship. It takes a long time to build and only a short time to destroy.' Her glassy eyes look straight through me. 'What is your name?'

'Ramona.'

'I don't like it.'

I feel like the stuffing has been knocked out of me and for a moment, delude myself into thinking that she's going to append, 'I love it' in a Simon Cowell on a reality TV show panel kind of way, foxing the audience with a false start, but she stops there.

I take a deep breath. 'Well, there's not a lot I can do about my name, I'm afraid. I was given it at birth. I like it, and it doesn't normally cause offence.'

She puts down the pattern and looks at me. 'I don't talk about your name. I'm talking about you opening a shop and taking over the village. I don't like it at all.'

Flustered, I edge towards her. 'Look, I'm not trying to take over. I just needed more space. Somewhere bigger to work.' I look around for something to offer her. 'Would you like a cup of tea?'

She frowns. 'Tea? At this time?'

'Coffee?'

'It's too hot for tea or for coffee. Limoncello on the rocks, yes.'

I laugh and then realise she's not joking. 'What business are you in?'

'Leather goods,' she says, picking up my design of the corset I've just made.

My eyes automatically shift to her handbag – a scaly orange thing that wouldn't look amiss in a reptile house.

'Handbags, belts, wallets, laptop cases, phone cases . . . My husband has this business for forty years and will continue until the day he dies, so please . . . if you could at least leave leather goods to us.'

'Of course, I . . .' I feel every bit like an intruder. A foreign object that has invaded a peaceful little village and taken advantage of it. A bulldozer. A trespasser. An interloper. 'I'm not here to steal your business, I'm just . . .'

'Business is difficult in Altaterra. Before the virus and Brexit, we had international tourists for the summer, the spring, even the winter for skiing in the mountains but now . . . the shops are shutting, the bars and restaurants close their doors . . .'

I find myself shadowing her as she spins around and clip-clops towards the door, my jaw hanging open as she pauses in front of the corset in the window to examine the detail. 'That one is for Valentina's mother,' I say proudly.

She turns around slowly, her white complexion taking on a purple hue.

'I'm quite proud of the boning – probably the neatest one I've ever done.' I laugh nervously.

'It's for Francesca?' Her eyes widen.

'You know her? She's lovely, isn't she? So fun, so—' I garble nervously.

'La Mama Mia!' She shoots air out of her nostrils and picks up the hanger, her nose scrunched up as she studies the corset from all angles. 'Francesca Bianchi is wearing this?'

'Yes,' I say, wondering what on earth is the matter with it. It's one of my best pieces, the delicate beading around the crystal rhinestones catching the light and sparkling from all angles.

She holds it up to her chest and then thrusts it away from her body, examining it at arm's length, a look of revulsion travelling across her face. 'Madonna Santa!'

'Is there a prob—'

'You know who I am?' She pulls at the corset, yanking it this way and that, and I want to tell her to stop it, only she is having the same effect on me as Gillian Harvey, the school bully, had on me when she locked me in the biology lab and tried to set fire to my hair with a Bunsen burner, and for some reason I can't tell her off.

'Urm.'

'I am the Mother of the Groom. I am Flavio's mother.'

'Oh—'

She drums her fingers on her hip, her eyes darting across the row of dresses hung on a pole away from the wall. 'Do you know what I'm wearing to the wedding?'

I figure the question is rhetorical and I shouldn't jump in with some random guess. A straitjacket? A pantomime horse outfit?

'A long dress that hides the neck, the legs, the arms, all of my skin because I am now sixty-six years old and it is not good for a woman of my age to wear something like this, no?' She slams the hanger back onto the hook I have erected in the window. 'Francesca, the Mother of the Bride. You know how old she is?'

I frown. 'Her age is of no—'

'Seventy-three!' she spits. 'Seventy-three years old and she is choosing to wear something that is made for a teenager.'

An overwhelming urge to defend Francesca, who has been nothing but kind each time I've met her, takes hold of me. 'She looks *great* in it,' I say, remembering how the twinkling brown sequins had brought out her twinkly brown eyes, the shape of the corset accentuating her waist and propping up her chest in a way that was sophisticated over slutty, classy over crass, and coupled with her blazer, looked nothing short of fan-fucking-tastic. 'I don't think anyone should be confined by their age.'

'Dignity!' She straightens herself out and brushes up the collar of her raincoat. 'Age with dignity!' And with that, she flounces out of the shop, chest puffed out and raincoat billowing, turning back only to shout, 'And you should really get a mannequin!' through the closing door.

It's only when she's out of sight that I realise I've been holding my breath, my lungs burning as I release a stream of air out through my nostrils. What a woman. I'm helping myself to a peppermint when the door swings open and the one-woman tornado that has just turned me upside down and inside out reappears.

Twisting her face into a crooked smile, she lowers her voice. 'How much does it cost?'

'Sorry?' I splutter.

'The bustier.' Her eyes narrow until they are nothing but slits of shiny black. 'How much does it cost?'

I take out my phone to remind myself how much I've charged the Mother of the Bride and show her the figure on my screen.

'Bene.' She nods. 'I'll take one.'

'For you?' I say, trying to control my surprise.

'Yes. Only tighter. I need it to be tighter than that of Francesca.'

'You're not bothered about dignity or me taking business away from the locals?'

'Business?' She scrunches up her face. 'There is no time for business when there is a war.' She offers me her hand. 'Giuseppina.'

For a moment I think she's tasked me with a command but then I realise she's merely introducing herself.

'Nice to meet you, Giuseppina. I'd love to help, but I'm really sorry – I don't have the time to make another one,' I say.

'The morning has gold in his mouth.' She looks at me with a stony stare.

'Sorry?'

'I am here now. The first in the shop.'

'It's not a shop.'

'You can take my measurements now. I can choose the style now. I can pay you now.' She opens the clasp of her reptilian handbag and drags out her leather purse. 'How much do you want? Five hundred? Six hundred?'

'I can't . . .'

She advances towards me, her face full of authority. 'There is no such word in Italian. I have the money. You have the skills. Let's go!'

I'm not sure I've quite understood what gives her the right to be so pushy and make a mental note to be more assertive myself.

She plucks Francesca's corset off the hook again. 'What size is this?'

'It's made to measure so it's not a particular size.' I feel my hackles rise.

'Approximately?'

I swallow hard. 'A woman's measurements remain between her and her seamstress.'

'I like you,' she says, her face relaxing and her eagle-like stare giving way to that of an inquisitive pigeon. 'I will pay you eight hundred euro but no more because I need the rest to buy a hat at the auction.'

'You're going?'

'Everybody's going. Francesca and I will both be bidding for the Columba Bianca.'

'The Colum . . . sorry?'

'The Columba Bianca. The White Dove. You must know it?'

I think back to the afternoon I spent at the Casa dei Cappelli, but I have no recollection of any kind of hat featuring a white dove. 'I don't think I've seen that one.'

'Nobody's seen that one. That's the point. It has been held under lock and key for fifty years now. Mariela wore it at her own wedding, and it's so sacred that nobody has seen it since, but next week we will see it at the auction in all its glory.'

'I see,' I say, thinking back to what Signor Zaccardi told me about Mariela's marriage and wondering whether the disappearance of the White Dove hat is more down to her burning it than keeping it sacred but before I can give it too much thought, Giuseppina is plucking my tape measure from around my neck and marching into the cubicle.

Then, in only a matter of minutes, she is handing me her measurements written in ink on a scented paper handkerchief and pressing sixteen crisp fifty-euro bills into my hand.

'You need a mannequin in the window by the way. It doesn't work like this.' She scoffs once more for extra effect.

'Uh-huh,' I say, the memory of mummification-gate haunting me.

'And maybe you will show my corset in the window instead of Francesca's?'

I hold the door open for her, imagining what drama may unfold at the thought of both Mothers of the Soon-to-be-weds bidding against each other for the Columba Bianca and wondering whether this in itself should become a ticketed event – I personally would pay money to see this in action – Mother of the Bride versus Mother of the Groom in the battle of all battles – and then an idea starts to take shape in my head. What better double act to headline the disruption of a hat auction than these two formidable alpha females? Aren't they just the thing to upset the apple cart?

'And it must be gold.' Giuseppina shoots me the look of a disgruntled pigeon and struts out of the shop. 'You'll need to go to Florence to find gold.'

I watch through the window as she straightens herself out, slings her scarf around her neck in an act of defiance and then,

241

chest puffed out like a robin in winter, strolls across the court-yard with purpose and precision until she's eventually out of sight. I'm not sure where I'm going to find gold taffeta at such short notice, but I'd better find out fast because Giuseppina Siciliano is clearly the sort of flame-breathing dragon you do not want to disappoint.

'Florence?'

'She's not the sort of woman you say "no" to!'

'Ah, you mean Firenze!' Marco pops his head out of the kitchen sink cupboard, an effervescent glow of enthusiasm and sweat to his face.

It's early evening and we are back at the apartment, my plan to never ever see Marco again somewhat thwarted when the kitchen tap developed a leak, water spraying everywhere and, unable to find the stopcock to avoid total flooding of the apart-ment, I had no choice but to phone him.

Spanner in one hand and a tea towel in the other, Marco lies sprawled across the kitchen floor on his back. He mops up another puddle of water and casts the tea towel to one side, then sticks his head back into the cupboard under the sink, his hand outstretched in anticipation of the washer I have been clutching for the last ten minutes. The good news is that Marco is acting as though the man-nequin incident never happened, focussed on the job at hand. The bad news is that although he's totally zen about it, I am plagued by the most excruciating flashbacks and can't look him in the eye.

'Apparently, it's only an hour away so I could do a bit of a hit-and-run.' I drop the small metal ring into his hand with a flourish.

'Hit-and-run?' He grimaces as a drop of water escapes the U-bend and lands on his nose and rolls down his cheek.

'You know, head straight to the fabric shop, grab the stuff for Giuseppina's outfit and come straight back. Who knows, I could be back within three hours.'

'Are you insane?' His head reappears from under the sink, bearing an expression of abject horror, deep furrows etched into his brow and the small dimple in his chin disappearing entirely. 'Firenze is not a supermarket or a place you go because you have to. Only a blind man can arrive in Firenze and leave ten minutes later.'

'Oh.' I reach for my grandma's pendant, the cotton repair job I did on the chain cutting into my fingers, and start to worry that I've really offended him.

He slides out of the cupboard on his back, face smeared in grease and hair damp with sweat around his temples, my eyes drawn to a small triangle of his T-shirt several shades darker than the rest, which rises and falls against his chest. Tucking a blond curl behind his ear only for it to spring back out immediately, he sits up. 'Firenze, or Florence as you like to call her, is one of the most beautiful places in the world. To Firenze, you make a pilgrimage. To Firenze, you go for your honeymoon. To Firenze, you travel for a trip of a lifetime. You do not go there for a "hit-and-run!"' He throws down his spanner with an angry clatter. 'There. All done.'

'Thank you,' I say sheepishly. 'I'm sorry if I caused offence.'

Getting to his feet, he pours himself a glass of water from the kitchen tap, ducking his head back under the sink and standing back to admire his handiwork. 'No more leaky tap.'

'So you think I'd need longer then?' I drum my fingers on the kitchen worktop behind me and try to work out what amuse-bouche I could rustle up as a peace offering but a bowl of cornflakes or a slice of dry rye bread clearly isn't going to cut it.

'Three days is perfect. Two days is OK. One day, too rushed but at least you see all the sights. One hour, impossible.'

A rap on the window has us twisting our heads like startled meerkats. Outside, Maria fiddles with her car keys, propping a box on the windowsill and twisting her arms this way and that. I go to let her in.

'Ciao, Ramona!' she says in that sing-song voice of hers.

'Ciao.' I take the box off her and wander back inside. It contains a Peppa Pig baby bouncer, which I carefully place on the kitchen table.

'How's your vacation going?' She follows me in.

'Great, thanks. I'm just planning a trip to Florence tomorrow, although getting there looks quite complicated with it being two buses and a train.'

'Marco?' Maria calls over to him. 'Why are you not taking Ramona on your Vespa?'

'Sorry?' He turns off the tap.

'To Florence, it's either two buses and a train or a simple journey on your Vespa.'

'No, no, don't worry,' I say, sensing Marco's reluctance.

'Of course, Marco will take you.' She helps herself to a grape from the fruit bowl and sits down. 'Won't you, Marco?'

He scratches his head and tries to mask a look of frustration. 'Of course.'

'No, no, seriously, you don't need to do that for me,' I say, a sudden flashback of mummification in cling film flickering through my mind and a fresh wave of humiliation crashing over me.

Marco places his hands on Maria's shoulders. 'Although tomorrow you have the doctor's appointment.'

'Valentina can come with me. Seriously, it's no problem. Go!' she says, playfully. 'Have fun and eat lots of ice cream!'

Marco throws his hands up, a grin spreading across his face. 'Then I will take you to Florence, Ramona.'

Repressing my excitement, I turn to Maria. 'Well, as long as you're OK with it.'

'Why would I not be OK with it? You are our guest and to come to Tuscany without seeing Firenze would be a crime,' she says.

Crouching at Maria's side, Marco rubs his hands over her stomach, pressing his ear against her bump and mutters gobbledygook to his unborn child. Watching him goof around with Maria is heartwarming. He'll make a brilliant dad.

'That'd be great. Thank you.'

And just like that, I'm popping off to Florence.

CHAPTER EIGHTEEN

Florence

Fambo

Mum

> How lovely. Florence is where your
> dad and I went on our honeymoon!

Ramona

> Your first or your second?

It's hard not to be cynical.

Mum

> I'll choose to ignore that. Make sure you check out the Galleria della . . . God, my brain's not been the same since the menopause. Alan – what was the name of the gallery in Florence where Michelangelo's David is?

Dad

> Didn't Michelangelo's David run off to Spain?'

Mum

> You're thinking about Michel-André's David who followed that young man out to the Costa del Sol. I'm talking about the statue.

Dad

> You mean the Galleria dell'Accademia where Rambo was conceived?

A feeling of unease travels to my stomach. Was I seriously conceived in an art gallery?

Mum

> That's it! Lovely cloakroom ;-)

Ramona

Eugh. I was conceived in the cloakroom of a Florentine art gallery?

Mum

It was either there or a shady corner of the Boboli Gardens. Have fun, Rambo. It's the kind of city you fall in love in.

I take an extra sip of strong coffee, shuddering at the thought of Mum and Dad going at it al fresco in such a public place.

Ramona

Let's hope not as I'm going with my soon-to-be father landlord!

Mum

Typo sorry. It's the kind of city you fall in love *with*. Have fun!

As the birthplace of the Italian Renaissance and one of the most historic cities of the world, Florence should be a celebration of art, culture and a small but exuberant window into la dolce vita, so why do I have a feeling of unease building in the pit of my stomach? Gripping onto Marco's waist as we snake through a labyrinth of narrow cobbled alleys on his little red Vespa, my conscience gets the better of me. For here I am, being driven around the Tuscan capital in all its glory, about to go shopping for gold coutil to appease a woman I only met yesterday, whilst I should really be finishing off Fabrice's dress for DragFest, which is all he ever texts about at the moment. The problem is hitting the seamstress's equivalent of writer's block. No matter how much I style and shape the fabric I have back at the studio, it's never going to have that wow factor, but I don't have time to start all over again.

The surrounding architecture is breathtaking. Piazza after piazza hosting elaborate basilicas, ornate chapels and gargantuan museums with terracotta domes, but nothing can prepare me for Il Duomo – a gothic-inspired cathedral complex with huge polychrome marble panels in varying shades of green and pink standing in a huge, cobbled square boasting cafés, gelaterias, restaurants and shops. Street merchants sell battery-operated flying toys – luminous helicopters and spiralling wheels hovering above the heads of a crowd of tourists who huddle around the bell tower with cameras and maps.

Marco pulls up outside a tobacconist and removes his helmet. 'You cannot come to Florence and not see Il Duomo.'

I take off my helmet, a rush of endorphins flooding through me, and I'm not sure whether it's the adrenaline-induced ride on his Vespa and feeling like I might just fall off with every twist and turn, or the jaw-dropping beauty of this place, but Mum was right: there is no way that you cannot fall in love with this city. Spellbound by the craftsmanship that has gone into Il Duomo, I can't take my eyes off it. We circle the cathedral just so that I can marvel at it from every angle possible, and explore the piazza, the gentle tinkle of piano music carrying on the air from an open window of the opera house, and it feels as though I've been transported to another world.

'One hundred and forty-two years, it took to build.' Marco gazes up at the architectural wonder before us. 'You know the dome is like a Russian doll? There is a dome inside the dome to keep it stable.'

'It's unbelievable,' I say, almost speechless.

'Come on, let's go see the Porcellino,' he says, leading me through a maze of alleyways to Via Roma, where Prada hugs the sweet spot of a handsome piazza dotted with restaurants boasting al fresco dining and framed by all the Haute Couture giants: Gucci, Pucci, Armani, Fendi, Dolce & Gabbana. Full of envy, I scan their window displays, trying to imagine what it might feel like to open my own store alongside them, a cocktail of hope and longing causing me a dizzying sensation, but before I can become too emersed in my daydream, Marco is whisking me over to the Uffizi, where a small market has been set up behind huge stone columns of a grand, stone edifice obscured by an enormous Gucci banner, and over to a bronze statue of a wild boar.

'Il Porcellino.' Marco rubs his hands on the pig's head. 'He's famous in Italy. Originally from Rome, we call him, "The Piglet".'

'Look at his teeth!' I say, gesturing to the boar's gaping jaws.

'Here you put money to make a wish.' He points to a small hole in the bronze statue. 'If the coin falls, your wish will come true.'

'Right,' I say, dragging a shiny coin out of my pocket and feeding it to the pig in the hope that I find enough gold coutil to make both the bodice for Giuseppina Sicilliana and a dress for Fabrice within the next hour so that I can spend the remaining two hours sightseeing guilt-free. The coin drops into what sounds like water but I'm too busy unhooking my pendant from the pig's snout to give it too much thought.

'Porca miseria!' he says. 'Now rub the nose!'

'Sorry?'

He sets about polishing the pig's face with the palm of his hand. 'If you want to guarantee that you will come back to Florence, you need to rub the nose.'

I laugh at his solid-gold bullshit but give the pig's snout a gentle polish anyway, not wanting to cause offence.

'OK.' He gathers his hands together excitedly. 'First, La Casa dei Tessuti di Firenze. Florence's fabric house.'

'Let's do it,' I say, my mouth watering at the sweet smell of crespelle wafting over from a pancake hut, but resolving to save my appetite for ice cream.

Within the space of ten minutes, we have crossed piazza after piazza, my heart singing as we walk past ornate fountains, baroque facades, bronze spray-painted street performers posing as statues and a wealth of renaissance architecture until we reach an unassuming building with a window display featuring three headless gold mannequins draped with the most incredible silks I have ever seen. A finely woven off-the-shoulder sari in a rich coral colour with golden thread lovingly laced evenly throughout. An elegant floral silk featuring cascading roses neatly pinned above the central mannequin's bosom and a striking, ruched length of cyan fabric draped over an ornamental antique chair.

'Prego.' Marco gestures to the entrance.

A man in top hat and tails opens the heavy brass-handled door for us and I think of Mariela, wondering if the magnificent black silk creation atop the doorman's head is one of hers, my heart filling with fresh dread at the thought of the Bergamaschi family auctioning off her collection, one by one, and hoping that Marco's plan comes good.

'Wow!' I say, taking in the vast space that lies before us, fabrics neatly stacked on dark wooden shelves running from floor to ceiling and glass cabinets stocked with layer upon layer of colourful weaves. Looking around the shop, it feels like going back in time, oil paintings of Florence hanging in heavy gold gilded frames on the few spaces of wall available and a marble chequerboard floor giving way to robust teak counters where smartly dressed staff measure lengths of fabric with old-fashioned wooden metre rulers.

'Versace, Prada, Armani, Bulgari . . . they all start here.' Marco says proudly. 'You know haute couture originated in Florence?'

'Really?' I say, surprised. 'I'd always assumed it was Milan.'

'Milano took over in the 1970s, but Florence is the original home of made-to-measure clothes.'

I stifle a chuckle at his two-syllable pronunciation of the word 'clothes' and recall the way he previously referred to 'i-roning his clow-thes,' a feeling of warmth spreading through my chest. 'La Casa dei Tisuri designs the fabric.' He goes on. 'You know, of course, the Strada della Lana?'

'Urm.' I feel all of a sudden a little bit like Eliza Doolittle at Ascot in *My Fair Lady*.

'Wool Street, I think you say in English.' He studies my blank expression. 'In North West Italy, between Milan and Turin. Here you find the fabric mills that make the finest tissues. And then they come here.'

'Amazing,' I say, eyeing roll upon roll of luxurious fabric.

We wander over to an area with a table stacked with piles of glossy fashion magazines featuring iconic models in eye-catching poses. A vintage cash register sits atop a wooden block, its shiny brass buttons and levers begging to be pushed, and I try to imagine this place a century ago, women in long floaty dresses pointing out high-quality fabric with frilly umbrellas in the hope of making extravagant petticoats.

'Posso aiutarla?' A man with ruddy cheeks and small ringlets of dark hair cascading from each side of his top hat approaches us, the tails of his dress jacket following neatly behind.

Marco turns to me. 'What would you like to see?'

'Grazie.' I smile graciously at Mr Top Hat before turning back to Marco. 'Can you ask him if he has any gold coutil?'

'Coutil?' Marco frowns.

'Tightly woven, strong cotton, to make corsets,' I explain.

Mr Top Hat looks at me with beady eyes. 'Certo, Signorina. Da questa parte per favore.' He leads us over to the far corner of the room, where he takes a tall ladder, clips it onto a brass rail and slides it in the direction of a tall cupboard. Climbing each rung with the precision of a seasoned circus performer, he balances halfway up and reaches over to a pile of neatly folded fabric to carefully deliver a cellophaned parcel into the palm of my hands.

I look at Marco. 'Can I open it?'

'What is the point of having the cake if you cannot eat it?' His face brightens.

I feel the corners of my mouth turn up in amusement. His quirky expressions may catch me off guard, but they also have a way of making me feel at ease – he can be endearingly goofy at times and I like it. Reaching over to touch the fabric, its weight takes me by surprise – for such a tight weave, I'm amazed at just how soft, smooth and reassuringly heavy it is. The only problem is that it's silver.

'Do you have gold?' I say. 'Oro?'

Within seconds, Mr Top Hat has shimmied back up to the top of the ladder. He shakes his head. 'Sorry. Only silver.'

Ramona

How about silver?

Giuseppina Siciliano

I would rather die.

Marco reads the text over my shoulder and bursts into laughter. 'She has this reputation! She breaks the boxes for everyone.'

'Breaks boxes?' I say, confused.

'*Annoys*. She annoys everyone.'

I turn to Mr Top Hat. 'I'm afraid it has to be gold.'

'Mi dispiace.' Mr Top Hat says, shaking his head. 'We do not have gold.'

A moment later we are reunited with the streets of Florence. The city is a lot calmer than the hectic hullabaloo of Milan, its red roof-tops basking in the morning sun and its cobbled roads quieter and less frenetic, the pace of life clearly slower here in Tuscany's capital.

I take a moment to drink it all in, the imposing Gothic architecture of the red-domed Cattedrale di Santa Maria del Fiore reigning supreme at one end of the street and the Palazzo Strozzi, a free-standing building made of rusticated stone standing at the other. Through an ancient archway stands another church of majestic beauty, its pillars decorated with crowned serpents and floating angels, and it feels a little as though the city itself is a museum of Renaissance art.

'Next stop, the Emporio della Seta,' Marco announces.

'The silk emporium?'

He nods. 'You learn fast.'

Marco is turning out to be good company – easy-going, laid-back, interesting and thoughtful, his anecdotes about the city both funny and engaging. At times, it's like having my own tour guide and I don't think I've had this much fun since I've been out here in Italy – I just worry that he's finding the trip too arduous.

'But first, ice cream,' Marco announces, steering me towards a gelateria cart. Maybe he's not finding it too arduous after all.

We take our ice creams, Marco plumping for cherry whilst I devour pistachio, and wander slowly across the square.

'I hate my glasses, but really needed them just then to read the ice cream flavours,' he says, peeling them off his nose and propping them on top of his head. 'Three months ago, I could read a little but now everything is . . .' He waves his hand in front of his face in a fast motion.

'Blurred?'

'Yes, blurred. This is why I cannot be a pilot.'

'You wanted to be a pilot?' Intrigue suddenly has a hold over me.

'I *was* a pilot.' The weight of his words hangs in the air. 'I was a pilot for ten years before my eyesight is not good enough. Now, I no longer have a licence.'

'That must be tough.'

'Yes.' He looks to the horizon and says nothing further.

We stroll alongside each other in silence, licking our ice creams, the tingle of the morning sun on our faces and the chatter of people filling the air around us.

He clears his throat and puts on his sunglasses. 'There is no better feeling than flying. It's difficult to explain. It's like . . .'

I gaze up at the sky and think of my dad waxing lyrical on the beauty of flight. 'Floating like a bird on a wing, not a care in the world, at one with Mother Nature, just you on the skies and—'

'Like driving a car only faster, I was going to say.'

'Oh. Sorry.' I let out a nervous giggle. 'My parents paraglide.'

'Like this?' Marco says, holding his arms out in the air and running down the street with his jaw hanging wide open. 'Or like this?' He mimes standing on a surfboard.

I laugh. 'The first one.'

'In the air? Not on the water?'

'In the air,' I concur.

'I understand.' He nods. 'Flying a plane is like flying a kite, bringing it fast up, up into the air, and then when you reach the wind, there you cruise. You see first birds, then clouds, then just blue.'

Before I know it, we've walked another mile sharing stories as we go, and have reached the bank of the River Arno, a vast expanse of fast-flowing water. In front of us stands the most amazing bridge I've ever seen, its majestic arches topped by a jumble of multi-coloured buildings, all different shapes, sizes and colours that look as though they've been cut out of a magazine and stuck to a canvas in an abstract collage.

'Il Ponte Vecchio,' Marco announces proudly. 'You want to go and explore?'

We round the corner onto the bridge, a row of evenly spaced flags flying above the shops lining each side of the walkway. Three jewellery boutiques sit side by side, their wooden shutters propped open to reveal window displays showing off a dazzling array of gold with everything from watches to wedding rings.

'I would love to live in Florence,' he says, peering into a shop and out of its back window at the river. 'For me, it's paradise. Especially if I could drive a boat and get paid for it.'

'Marco's River Cruises. It has a ring to it.'

'You know the Medici built this bridge because they had their homes on one side of the river in the Pitti Palace and their offices were on the other side in the Palazzo Vecchio, so they needed to cross all the time. The man who builds this is Vasari and so they name this il corridoio Vasariano.'

'The Vasari Corridor?' I hazard a guess.

'She is getting good with her Italian!' Marco laughs. 'You see the line of windows up there?' He gestures above the row of shops with an outstretched finger. 'This is the corridor, but it is also an art gallery.'

'Can we get up there?'

Marco looks at his watch. 'It depends if you want to look at the paintings of Rembrandt or Leonardo da Vinci, Raphael and Michelangelo or look for Signora Siciliano's fabric.'

'Of course,' I say, feeling rebuked and instinctively reach for my pendant, my go-to comfort blanket, but it's not there. 'Oh shit!'

'Oh shit?' Marco looks at me earnestly.

'My necklace. It was a present from my grandmother and . . .'

'It's gone?' His eyes travel over my neck.

'Yes,' I say, searching the pavement for a small lump of blue porcelain.

'Oh, shit the bed!' he exclaims.

I laugh. 'Where did you learn that?'

'My English friends . . . Shit the bed. Shitstick. Shituation.'

'It's certainly a shituation.' I concede. 'My parents will kill me.'

Marco turns on his heel. 'If we go back the way we came, we will find it.'

My chest feels stringy and tight. This is a family heirloom. An antique that has been passed from generation to generation, a consolation prize for not getting married and something I can't just lose like this. 'If I return home without it, I'll never—'

'You're returning home?' he says, a look of concern rippling across his face. 'You know I don't need to rent the apartment to anyone else for the rest of the summer.'

'Really?' I brighten.

'Really.' He smiles. 'Now come on.' And with that, he takes my arm and pulls me back along the bridge and down towards the riverbank, a topsy-turvy feeling creeping up on me. Are we becoming a little *too* close?

His eyes skim the pavement as we retrace our footsteps and settle into a slow gait that allows us to comb every inch of the ground as we go and, lost in the mundanity, I decide that I made up the whole growing close thing and I've been too heavily influenced by Flora's propensity to read romance into everything. Platonic relationships do exist and this is one of them.

Two things strike me about the walkways of Florence. Firstly, that there is no litter – like none whatsoever – and also, there is no dog poo. The streets are so clean you could almost eat your dinner off them, pigeons flocking merely to socialise rather than to scavenge. We head towards the piazza where we bought ice creams earlier, Mario asking the girl behind the counter if she's had anything handed in, but there is no sign of my pendant. My heart sinks. Isn't this needle-in-a-haystack madness? I retrace my steps in my mind's eye, remembering holding up various lengths of fabric beneath my chin at the fabric shop. 'La Casa dei Tisuri,' I say. 'I've a feeling it's there.'

'Hey!' Mario runs over to a cycle rickshaw driver who is dropping a couple of tourists at the fountain. He negotiates a deal, jumps up into the carriage and looks at me. 'Come on!'

I climb up next to him, our shoulders squished so tightly together that I can feel the muscles of his upper arm against mine. The rickshaw driver cycles through the cobbled backstreets of Florence, firing up his stereo and shuffling through his playlist until 'Crazy in Love' blasts out of his speakers, Marco flashing me a wide-eyed smile, his eyebrows wriggling with discomfort. We wind our way beneath balconies and begonias, Marco, Beyoncé and I, turning heads as we trundle down a narrow lane, where a cluster of people gather beneath a window.

'Il Museo Casa di Dante,' Mario explains.

I get that it's a museum and that it's the house of Dante, but I have no clue who Dante actually is, feeling both ignorant and uncultured. All I remember is that film, *Dante's Peak*, about a volcanologist with a raging eruption on his hands and my mum quite enjoying Pierce Brosnan's performance. She's always liked a bit of Pierce, especially as Bond. Though now I'm thinking Dante might be a ballet dancer. Or am I confusing her with Darcy? Dante, Darcy?

'You know all about Dante, of course?'

'Of course,' I say, trying to sound all-knowing.

'This is the family home where Dante wrote *la Divina Commedia*,' he says proudly. 'You know it?'

'Yes, it's hilarious,' I say, figuring it's a comedy everyone should have heard of.

'Hilarious?' He frowns.

'Hilariously ironic, I mean. The irony. The subtlety. It's very clever,' I say, digging myself a hole. 'She's very clever.'

Mario turns towards me and gives me a knowing look. 'Dante was a philosopher, a poet and a writer of medieval times. When *he* was only twelve years old, he was promised in marriage to a family friend but really, he was in love with another girl: Beatrice. He wrote all about searching for her, yearning for her, admiring her. His words are beautiful. Apparently. I don't understand a fucking word of it myself.'

I let out a snort of relief. 'Oh God, I'm so glad you said that. I'm the same with Shakespeare. So, which girl did Dante marry, the family friend or the beautiful Beatrice?'

'The family friend. I can't remember her name, but he wrote so many declarations of love to Beatrice, his true sweetheart, although she was married to someone else.'

'That's tragic,' I say, watching as the tour guide leads them into the house.

'I know. His life was very tragic.'

A feeling of contempt rises up inside me. 'I mean for the girl he married! The girl whose name nobody can remember. The poor girl who had to marry him whilst the whole world hero-worshipped him for writing a poem about another woman he was not-so-secretly in love with? Imagine how humiliated, unappreciated and undermined she must have felt. Surely that's worse than poor Princess Di had to put up with? Seriously, it sucks.'

Marco pulls a face. 'I've never thought of it that way before.'

'Well, maybe you should.' My lungs fill with fire. 'And if Beatrice married someone else anyway, maybe she didn't feel the same way about him. Maybe he was like some weird stalker she couldn't get rid of. Maybe he was just some sleazy married man harassing her.'

'Maybe,' Marco says softly with a shrug of the shoulders and I know by the way that he disengages and stares off into the distance with a faraway look in his eye that I've overstepped the mark with my outspokenness. I should really learn to be more zen about these preposterous patriarchal predicaments and bite my tongue if I want to spend longer in his company, but just when I'm working up to an apology, he turns around to look at me. 'You know, I like the way you bring a different point of view. I like the way you challenge life.'

'Phew!' I laugh. 'I thought I'd upset you!'

'Never!' He shakes his head and chuckles.

Our journey continues, zigging and zagging through the streets of Florence until we slow on the approach to another ornate chapel.

'La Chiesa di Santa Margherita,' Marco announces. 'This is where Beatrice is buried.'

My eye is drawn to a wicker basket set on a table in the entrance to the graveyard beside the church, a group of teenage girls dropping scraps of paper into it.

'People write their hopes and prayers and then drop them into the box for them to come true. Sometimes they leave stories of love that is not returned.'

'Unrequited love?'

He turns towards me and nods gravely, his ice-blue eyes connecting with mine. 'Unrequited love.'

A bolt of electricity jolts through me quickly followed by wave of sadness at the sight of one scrap of paper blowing away in the breeze, its author's hopes and dreams with it.

'Can we stop here a second?' I blurt out.

Jumping from the rickshaw before it's even come to a halt, I run back to the church and up the side towards the graveyard. Then, helping myself to a piece of paper from the pile held down by a stone on the table, and one of the pencils next to it, I write:

Please help me find my grandma's pendant.

Done. I chuck it in the box and run back to the rickshaw and it's only when we're on our way again that I realise I didn't make a wish about Curvaliscious and feel racked with guilt. Didn't I make a promise to both Fabrice and, more importantly, to myself that I'd prioritise it above all else? How will I ever achieve my dreams if I don't put them first?

Ten minutes later, we're pulling up outside La Casa dei Tessuri behind a taxi with its hazard lights flashing as a whole host of people shunter roll upon roll of fabric into the boot. Marco glances at his wristwatch.

'I should really go back to be with Maria for her doctor's appointment,' he says.

'Oh. Right. Of course.' I turn to look at him, deciding that he smells nice. Nothing too perfumed or specific, but the faint fragrance of good old-fashioned soap and sunshine.

His face crumples with frustration. 'I'm sorry we didn't find your necklace.'

'Yeah, well,' I say, touching my chest and feeling myself flush a little as his ice-blue eyes connect with mine. 'Thanks for helping me look for it. And for the guided tour, and the ice cream, and . . .' It strikes me that I want to thank him for so many things – for helping me translate in the fabric shop, for commandeering the rickshaw, for showing me the Ponte Vecchio, but ultimately for his company.

'I can wait ten minutes if you want a ride home?' he says, jangling the key to his Vespa in front of my nose.

A pull-push of emotion starts up inside me. On the one hand, I want nothing more than to jump on the back of his bike, completing the day trip together and sharing a laugh and a joke on the return leg, but on the other, I feel that we are teetering on the edge of what is appropriate and what is not. Our time together has been great, but at the end of the day, he is in a relationship with a baby on the way and although sharing ice cream, anecdotes and rickshaws is just about morally acceptable, it's important to keep boundaries, especially as he's my landlord.

'Thank you, but I'll get the bus back.' I smile, keeping a lid on my emotions.

'Are you sure?' he says with . . . is that a flicker of disappointment in his eyes?

'Yeah. I need to look for my pendant and sort the fabric out, so . . .'

'OK,' he says, kissing me on each cheek without a moment's hesitation. 'Good luck.'

And as he walks off, whistling as he goes, I am left feeling upside down, inside out, and bereft in a way I've never felt before and it's almost as though he has accidentally taken something of mine with him. I exhale with frustration. This excursion may have been nothing more than a platonic interlude to everyday life to Marco, but if I'm honest, it has meant more than that to me and although I didn't go looking for it, my feelings have somewhat crept up on me and are now leading me a merry dance. Is it all in my head or did he enjoy it as much as I did? Either way it needs to be nipped in the bud right now. He is spoken for. Off limits. Off the market. And I should definitely not be thinking of him like this. In fact, I should not be thinking of him at all.

CHAPTER NINETEEN
Maria

The journey back to Altaterra is long and winding, the bus calling at several villages down in the valley before it makes its slow ascent towards the cluster of terracotta buildings perched on the hill I call home. Pressed up against the roll of garish yellow fabric Fabrice has chosen for his DragFest dress and the silver coutil Giuseppina eventually settled upon, there is little in the way of leg room. It's a shame I didn't find my grandma's necklace, but I did at least gain intrinsic knowledge of Renaissance Italy and feel infinitely richer for having sampled the gems and gelati of Florence, so why the cavernous void?

I cast my mind back to my second visit to the fabric shop, La Casa dei Tessuri somehow not quite as awe-inspiring as it was this morning, the room smaller and darker, the fabrics not quite as vibrant and the wooden cabinets less polished than I remember them to be when I was with Marco. My eyes traced the marbled floor over to the corner where we'd looked at the silver coutil earlier, but there was no sign of my necklace.

'Signorina.' The man with the top hat recognised me instantly. 'Posso aiutarla?'

'Si. Urm. Per favore. Urm. Necklace,' I said, miming threading a chain around my neck with both hands. 'I don't suppose you've found a necklace.'

'Un momento,' he said, half bowing as he backed away towards the cabinet, returning a moment later with a wooden tray of beautifully presented silk cravats.

'Oh, er, thanks, but . . .' I took out my phone and showed him a photo of me at Pandora's Box with Fabrice only four weeks ago, zooming in on the pendant hanging around my neck. 'Have you seen this?'

Judging by the baffled look on his face, he had not.

'OK.' As I blew air through my lips with frustration, a wrap of satin caught my eye. It may not have been coutil, but it was gold and, coupled with mesh of some kind, it could definitely work for both Fabrice's gown and Giuseppina's bodice, so I video-called Fabrice straight away.

He answered, fanning himself with a Pomfrey & Wibble pamphlet from the office. 'Vivienne, so nice of you to drop by!'

'Sorry I've been off-grid, but I've not forgotten about DragFest and think I might just have found something perfect to make your dress,' I said, trying to brush aside the disappointment of Marco having to leave. 'Do you want to see it?'

'You've got a face like a slapped arse,' he said with a frown. 'What's the matter with you?'

'Me? Nothing! I'm having the time of my life in Florence!'

'Well, if that's what you look like when you're having the time of your life, I'd hate to see you on a bad day,' he said, picking up a snow globe from his desk and giving it a shake, small pieces of glitter raining down on a two-dimensional cutout of me, him and a reindeer taken last Christmas. 'Is it Setayesh? Has she been up to her shenanigans again?'

'No. It's all gone quiet on that front since I got the sack. I guess that's one—'

'Is it Curvaliscious?' he said, shaking his head with exasperation. 'Did you get another rejection?'

'No!'

'Is it a man?

'Of course it's not a man!'

'A woman?'

'It isn't . . .' I said, trying to shake the emptiness swelling inside me. 'It isn't anything. Look, do you like this?'

Holding up the roll of gold satin and pulling out a length of fabric for him to see the ripple effect of the light hitting the material, I looked to him for affirmation but the expression on his face only reminded me of the time he stood barefoot on a slug in my mum's kitchen last Christmas.

'No offence but gold is so passé,' he said, dismissing it with a flick of his hand. 'It needs to be something more exotic. More vibrant. More me!'

'More *you*?'

267

'It's a carnival, not a cabaret, Vivienne. It needs to be something fun, fabulous and feathery.'

'What about this?' I held up a wrap of silk the colour of a setting sun.

His face brightened. 'Do they have that in more of a *yellow* yellow?'

Picking the nearest shade to yellow I could find, a watery lemon that would look great in summer on dark skin, I held it up to my phone camera.

'More yellow than that,' he said, lifting his legs onto the desk in front of him and crossing one foot over the other – Mr Pomfrey must have been out for lunch.

I reached for another wrap of silk with a golden hue. 'This?'

He shook his head. 'More yellow. You know, yellow-yellow. Canary yellow.'

I reached for the brightest yellow in the shop – a length of silk so garish it was like being screamed at – think Tweetie Pie meets a psychedelic bumblebee and you're halfway there.

Clapping his hands together with glee, he beamed from ear to ear. 'Perfect.'

'Seriously? It hurts my eyes,' I said, holding the material at arm's length.

'Dead serious. It'll need a bit of Ramona magic, of course.'

'Of course.'

Scrambling to peel his feet off the desk with an urgency that suggested Mr Pomfrey was back from his lunch break, Fabrice adopted the tone of voice he reserves for clients. 'A great choice of colour, Mr Ainsbury-Saxton. I'm sure your curtains will look marvellous.'

Our call reverted to voice only and judging by the crispness of his vowels, I was no longer on loudspeaker.

'I'll need to know your exact measurements. Chest. Waist. Arm length. Leg length.'

He went on. 'I'll send you the figures close of play. You'll notice, of course, that some of the assets have depreciated over time, so don't be too alarmed if they're not quite what they were last year.'

'And if you can let me know nape to waist, too,' I said, stifling a laugh.

'Of course, sir. Although there won't be too much waste, that I can guarantee!'

'Is he looking at you?' I giggled. 'Mr Pommes Frites?'

'Super. I'll get a breakdown of those assets as quickly as I can, Mr Ainsbury-Saxton, I promise . . . Very well then, goodbye.'

'Goodbye.'

And with that, I was left standing smirking for a good few minutes. I do miss Fabrice.

My phone call to Giuseppina took twice as long and was half as fruitful, culminating in me holding up half the fabric in the shop for her to scrutinise and reject, finally settling for the silver coutil that the shop assistant showed me this morning. God only knows what Valentina is letting herself in for – it must be true love if she's willing to inherit such a flame-breathing dragon as a mother-in-law.

After a convoluted train journey and two interconnected bus trips with an hour's wait between, the Altaterra shuttle bus pulls into the village square and turns off its engine. The warm feeling of familiarity engulfs me as I climb the hill in the late afternoon sunshine, breathing in the scent of honeysuckle and summer. A great spotted woodpecker stands on the gatepost as though keeping watch over the apartment, its pied black-and white plumage setting off the red marking on the crown of its head. He dips his bill as I approach, taking flight as though his shift here as watchman is over. I open the gate, the long grass swishing between my legs and tickling my feet as I stride towards what has become home.

'Ciao!' A voice calls over from the kitchen window.

I look up to see Maria and instinctively wonder if Marco got back in time for their appointment and whether this is some sort of intervention, but there is a singsong quality to her voice that feels warm and welcoming.

'You had fun in Firenze?' She opens the door and lets me in. 'I hope you don't mind – I am a little early for the dress fitting, so I make coffee.'

Of course, the dress fitting! It's been booked in for a while now. I'm clearly not thinking straight. 'Sure.'

'Valentina is also here.' She smooths down the fabric of her emerald-green maternity dress over her bump and looks to Valentina, who appears at her side wearing a baby pink jumpsuit with small white stallions rearing up all over it. 'She wanted to ask some questions about il vestito da damigella d'onore.'

'The bridesmaid dresses.' Valentina hops from one foot to the other excitedly. 'I just had a few questions.'

Inside, Maria has cleared all my crap on the table into a neat pile and set out a plate of chocolate marzipans and three cups of coffee. Perching on one of the kitchen chairs, she tucks her long silky hair behind her ears and offers me the seat opposite whilst Valentina springs around with restless energy.

'I hope you didn't mind me taking Marco away from you for the day,' I say, looking at Maria, eager to let the elephant out of the room.

'Of course.' She draws her hand to her throat. 'He is not my property, and in any case, I think he had a lot of fun.' Her twinkling eyes shift to meet Valentina's gaze before travelling back to me. 'Did you?'

So zen is she about Marco and I parading around Florence that I wonder whether this is a trap and that maybe she has brought Valentina round to help lynch me. 'It was great,' I say tentatively. 'Florence is amazing.'

'Did you see Il Duomo?' Valentina's eyes light up like sparklers.

'Yes,' I say, reeling off all the landmarks we saw earlier, the goldsmith boutiques on the Ponte Vecchio, the forgotten statues of the Boboli Gardens, the Palazzo Strozzi, the Uffizi Gallery, the Brancacci Chapel, Piazza Santa Croce, the smile on Maria's face only widening further. 'Thanks so much for agreeing to it all. Did Marco make it back on time?'

Her eyes narrow with confusion.

'Didn't you have a doctor's appointment?'

'Ah, yes,' she says, as though she has just been plucked from a deep reverie. 'The scan for the baby. It's all good. He moves around to the correct position now. Before he was backwards. You want to see a picture?'

'Sure.'

She drags her wallet out of her pocket and peels a black-and-white glossy ultrasound screen-print from it, showing a grainy picture of her unborn child all curled up in a ball, Valentina and I leaning in to get a closer look.

'Aw, bellissimo!' Valentina's face softens.

'Wow,' I say, studying a pair of tiny feet. 'You must be so excited.'

'Yes.' Her liquid eyes fill with love.

'Not long now,' I say, gathering up my tape measure.

'Four weeks.' She gets up, allowing me to take first her inner and then her outer arm measurement, which I save in my phone – thank God for Notes – swiftly followed by bust, hips and I am just about to circle her baby bump with the tape measure when she grabs hold of my hand.

'There is something I wanted to say to you.' Her face hardens and her expression changes from one of unbridled joy to one of deep concern.

I look over to Valentina, who drops her gaze to the floor and a bolt of horror jolts through me. Is this about me spending time with Marco?

'Raffa will be back in Altaterra for the auction,' Maria says.

A feeling of unease stirs in my gut. 'He's definitely coming, is he?' I say, wondering whether the whole village is aware of what went down with me and Raffa that night. My face flushes with heat. What on earth must they think? Some crazy English girl pretending to be his girlfriend for the night, getting wined and dined in one of Tuscany's best restaurants and then complaining when it all moved too fast? I shudder just thinking about it.

'You need to stay strong and keep your distance from him.' Valentina comes over and, placing her hands on my shoulders, looks at me square on. 'Signora Ramona, he is not a good man.'

'Don't worry, I worked that one out for myself.' I offer up a half-smile.

Valentina nods to Maria. 'Tell her.'

Maria bites her bottom lip and fiddles with the hem of her dress, her expression changing to one of deep regret. 'The reason Marco hates him so much is because he made me pregnant when I was very young, and then just disappeared.'

'You too?' I say, remembering that Marco said Raffa had dated his sister and treated her appallingly, too. It seems like Raffa is quite the village playboy.

She nods. 'As soon as he realised I was pregnant with his baby, he ran away and left me. I had an abortion, and everybody knew about it. The people in the shops. My friends from college. That is what it's like living in a village. He goes back to Australia, and I had to deal with everything alone.'

'I'm really sorry.' I watch as tears spring up in her eyes.

'Che cazzo.' Valentina paces around the kitchen, arms folded under her chest.

'I still feel guilty now about that baby, but I did not want to be a single mother at such a young age, and I did not want Raffa in my life, so . . .' Maria shuffles the salt and pepper pots back and forth across the table. 'So I terminated.'

'I'm sorry.' I get up to rub her back whilst Valentina offers her a sheet of kitchen roll to dry her eyes on.

'Promise us you will not leave the village because of him?' Maria takes my hands in hers. 'He will try to make you feel sorry for him, but it is only bullshit. Solid gold bullshit.'

'It's good advice.' Valentina nods in agreement.

'Honestly, you're speaking to the converted.' I can't get the words out fast enough. 'I'm not planning on talking to him let alone spending any time with him.'

273

'But not every man is bad, Signor Ramona.' Maria gives my fingers a squeeze. 'My brother is a good example of a very kind man. Straightforward. Honest.'

'Her brother is the best.' Valentina colludes.

'OK,' I say, wondering what Maria's brother has got to do with all of this. I could really do without people forcing their family members on me right now, especially as the Raffa incident is still pretty raw. 'You know it is possible to be happy without a man at all?' I say.

'Of course, of course,' she says apologetically. 'I'm sorry, no pressure. No pressure at all. Just promise me you will not leave because of Raffa.'

'I promise,' I say, my mind looping back to the conversation with my parents where I was branded 'not the marrying type' and presented me with Grandma's Wedgwood pendant as a consolation prize, and feeling guilty all over again for firstly having it mangled during the exchange with Raffa and then losing it altogether.

Scribbling Maria's measurements down on the back of an envelope and sliding them under the toaster, I arrange my expression into that of someone calm and capable. 'The dress will be ready next week with a little extra room in case the baby has a big growth spurt.'

'Thanks.' Maria gathers up her belongings. 'And thank you for entertaining Marco today. Sometimes he's like a puppy that needs to be exercised.'

Valentina picks up her handbag. 'Thank you for the coffee. I'll email you about the bridesmaids' dresses.'

And with that, they are gone, my thoughts returning to Raffa and a restlessness starting up inside me, a foreboding energy lingering in the room.

The Girlz

Ramona

Raffa is coming back to the village next week to auction off his grandmother's hats 💀 💀

Flora

Time for you to come home?

Ramona

I can't. Apparently it's IMPERATIVE I stay for the auction.

Flora

Why?

Ramona

Dunno. Apparently 'all will be revealed'.

Zhané

> The dude is coming back. Forget all this bullshit with the auction and get the hell out of there!

But that's the thing; I can't just forget about the auction as I have a stake in this just as much as everyone else has, and over the last few weeks have become part of the Altaterra community. I can't just up and leave, especially with all the wedding apparel orders I am responsible for delivering. Besides, Maria and I have made a pact to give Raffa his comeuppance and I can't let her down.

Zhané

> OK, listen. I know it means a lot to you, but if you're going to stay there whilst he comes back, PLEASE promise to be careful xx

Flora

> *Forwarded*: Make your own Pepper Spray

> Put 2 tbsp (30 g) of cayenne pepper in a bowl and cover it with rubbing alcohol. Add 1 tbsp (15 g) of vegetable oil and let it steep overnight.

Fuelled by anxiety, I head to the studio. There's only one way to let off steam and burn off all this negative energy and that's by sewing. I turn on the radio, tune in to Toscana FM, and settle down to create a dress worthy of DragFest. What I wouldn't do to spend an evening with Fabrice right now, gossiping and laughing, teasing and joshing. Life is lighter with Fabrice in it and isn't that just the tonic I need, rather than lectures about dangerous men and the perils of being single?

Stitching and beading, ruching and gathering, twisting and shaping, pinning and pleating, I set about creating the bumblebee evening gown-cum-cabaret costume I have designed: a dazzling daffodil-yellow feathered affair with a plunging, ruffled neckline with a built-in black sequined bikini offset by capped sunflower sleeves and layers of bright bumblebee-yellow net flowing from the back in a detachable tutu train. Hidden press studs mean that Polly can shimmy out of the gown and reattach the feathered wings and yellow net tutu train to the bikini, giving that wow factor. If parading something as attention-grabbing as this along the open top deck of a glittery Union Jack flag double-decker bus around Europe doesn't get you noticed, then I don't know what will.

'It's great that you feel so passionately about this, Ramona, but I need to be honest with you; the designs are a little too . . . big.'

I stitch and stitch. Isn't it about time I shoved The Horse back in his (horse) box?

'The thing is, Ramona. There's no room for you.'

I gather and fold. Isn't it about time I proved to Setayesh that there *is* room for me?

'Whilst we strongly support body inclusivity, Plus Size apparel is too niche for our brand.'

I twist and turn the fabric before me. Isn't it about time I put myself out there?

Cross-stitches, backstitches, chain stitches, French knots.

Shell sequins, leaf sequins, reversible sequins, flower-head finishes.

Glass beads. Bugle beads. Gold chatons.

Hotfix crystals, Swarovski crystals, twisted raffia ribbon and crochet thread rings.

Hour upon hour I sit at the sewing machine, Hugo working overtime, crafting throughout the night, the dress growing in size and features until, finally, I am spent. Cramp seizes my fingers, my back aches and my eyesight is blurred. I look at the clock over the door to the secret staircase and see that it is four in the morning, but the dress is ready.

Exhausted, I drag myself back down the hill in the still of the night and am pretty much asleep as soon as my head hits the pillow.

The next day, I surface at around 11.00 a.m., my fingers set like claws. It feels as though my hands have been trapped in a vice overnight and arthritis has set in, but the moment I reach the studio and see Fabrice's dress in the sober light of day, a strong sense of pride kicks in. Looking at the bright, vibrant bumblebee gown in all its glory – the capped sleeves, the sequined bikini, the feathered wings, the headdress – it was worth every bit of back ache. Warm with pride, I take the dress to one side and hang it on the other side of the door to the secret staircase to keep it safe before I can arrange its transportation. I can't afford for it to go missing.

Fabrice

Guess who was amongst my audience last night?

Ramona

The Devil in Lycra? 😈

Fabrice

Mr Pommes Frites and Mr Wibble!! They're only a couple!!!

Ramona

Shut the front door!!!!!

Fabrice

I'm still in shock 😱

Ramona

Did he know it was you?

Fabrice

No idea. You'd think so though . . .

Ramona

I don't know. You and Polly are very different people.

Chuckling away to myself at the thought of Fabrice performing his drag set in front of his bosses, I pour myself a strong coffee. With Mr Pommes Frites and Mr Wibble finally in the know about Polly Darton's nocturnal goings on and a costume to die for, it feels as though Fabrice is having a Renaissance all of his own. I just wish he wasn't thousands of miles away.

Still, there's no time for sentimentality with the hat auction all set for tomorrow and Marco insisting that I have a 'compulsory invitation'. I wonder what lies in store . . .

CHAPTER TWENTY

Surprise

'Let me help.' Marco eyes me hungrily, paintbrush poised mid-air. 'It would allow my inner artist to come to life.

Aware of my near-naked body, I try to lie as seductively as possible. 'If you're sure you don't mind?'

Splat. The cold bandage hits my cellophaned skin, a shiver jolting down my spine as the cool liquid oozes through the cling film and trickles down my chest.

Snip. I close my eyes and listen to the slicing of scissors.

Drip. Liquid plaster hits my skin, the sensation cooling, sensuous and highly erotic.

He would only have to move his head a couple of inches and his lips would be brushing my breast.

Tinged by guilt, I pull away, plaster dripping onto the flagstone floor. 'Are you sure we should be doing this?'

He looks down at the spots of plaster on the flagstone floor. 'Don't worry. I will mop before it becomes solid.'

'I didn't mean . . .' I whisper, my whole body alive with electricity.

'Stay still.' He moves around my back and for a moment I am Demi Moore in *Ghost*, at the helm of a pottery wheel and he is a shirtless Patrick Swayze, engulfing me in his bare arms and sculpting my plaster cast with tenderness and precision. Abandoning the pot of wet plaster, he kisses me lovingly on the lips, our clay-smeared bodies becoming a writhing mess of breathlessness and the sound of clucking becoming louder and louder, until . . .

Wah! I startle awake only to find that I am not tangled up in a naked embrace with Marco but am actually being watched by a hen, her beady eyes darting this way and that as she claws her way along the headboard.

'Shoo! Shoo!' I chase her out of the room and down the stairs, clocking Signora Abbadelli out front with a bucket of chicken feed.

Locking myself in the bathroom, it takes several splashes of cold water on my face to distance myself from what just happened and realise it was only a dream. Still, it felt real. Mopping my face with a bath towel and pushing away all thoughts of Marco, I try to get a grip. After all, it's not every day that you sabotage the world's largest hat auction. And then it hits me. Today is the day I will see Raffa again. A feeling of dread plummets through my veins. Who knows, he may already be here in the village.

I'm taking a hot shower, running through all the insults I want to hit Raffa with but knowing that I won't when there's a knock on the door. Shoving on my kaftan, I rush downstairs. If it's Giuseppina or Francesca wanting to make any more last-minute adjustments to their corsets, I'm seriously going to lose it. With an air of exasperation, I open the door, but there, standing before me in the morning sunshine, is neither Giuseppina, Francesca nor Signor Zaccardi.

'Surprise!' Zhané thrusts a bottle of prosecco into my hand, her bag falling off her shoulder and swinging into the door frame.

'Buongiorno!' Flora's head pops up behind her.

It feels as though every particle of oxygen has been knocked out of me, my words lost somewhere down my windpipe. 'You – you came out all this way?' I say eventually.

'We knew today was important to you and we didn't want you to face Raffa alone.' Flora hugs me to her chest as she drags her wheelie case over the threshold and into the kitchen.

Zhané checks her step count on her Apple watch, waiting her turn to give me a squeeze. 'And also, we just fancied a trip to Tuscany. Three glorious days away in the sun without any child responsibilities. It's the dream.'

I squeeze her into my collarbone, her soft hair tickling my chin. 'It's so good to see you.' And it really is, my whole body tingling with happiness.

Pulling her inside, I take Zhané's bag and put the kettle on.

'How the hell did you find me?' I say, remembering how difficult it had been to locate the flat when I'd first arrived and that was when I'd had detailed instructions.

'Airbnb.' Zhané holds up her phone and reads: '*Hosts Marco and Maria welcome you to their big one-bedroom apartment with all mod-cons set back in the small village of Altaterra.* The taxi took a while to get up the hill, what with the huge traffic jam, but . . .'

'Traffic jam?' I frown.

'Yeah, it's carnage out there. Cars backed up all the way down to the valley and nowhere to park at all.'

A feeling of intimidation overcomes me. I must be able to count on one hand how many vehicles I've seen come up the road each day since I've been living out here, so this is headline news and surely means that the auction is going to be a pretty big deal and therefore its sabotage an even bigger one.

'And then the driver couldn't find number fifteen, so we had to fight through crowds of people to ask the lady in the bakery.' Flora adds.

Crowds? A lump forms in my throat as I watch Zhané take in the apartment, her eyes scanning everything from the kitchen appliances to the buckets of dried plaster under the chair. 'What's been going on in here?'

'Ha! It's a shame you weren't around. You could have helped mummify me in plaster and then Marco wouldn't have had to do it. I mean not that he did it, not really. Not in real life.'

Zhané's eyes narrow with confusion.

'Who is Marco?' Flora flicks through my fabric samples.

'My Airbnb landlord.'

'Riiight.' She shares a look with Zhané. 'Where's all your stuff? All your fabric? Where's Hugo?'

A rush of pride fills me as I realise how much I've achieved since I got here and how much life has moved on since we last spoke. 'Remember Signor Zaccardi's den? I'll take you down to my studio in a sec. Coffee?'

A few moments later, we are drinking coffee out on the terrace, the scent of the Italian scrub teasing our nostrils. The panoramic view of undulating Tuscan hills, lemon orchards and striped vineyards laid out before us feels new all over again; as though I have unwrapped a precious gift and am seeing it for the first time in all its glory; its greens, its grains, its golds. Breathing it all in – the terracotta roofs, the cobbled alleys, the stone bell tower of the church – I smile proudly as though it belongs to me. If only I could stay out here forever . . .

'Well, I must say, this is all a bit of a relief. We weren't sure what state we were going to find you in.' Zhané throws her head back and closes her eyes, enjoying the touch of the sun's heat on her face. 'What time is fuck-face due to arrive?'

'Raffa,' Flora explains.

'That's the thing. I have absolutely no idea.' I look to the horizon, where a tractor shifts hay bales around in the distance.

Zhané and Flora share a look of muted concern.

'What?' I say, fidgeting in my seat and struggling to get comfortable.

Flora drains her coffee cup and looks up. 'You don't need to put on a brave face with us. We know exactly what you're like.'

It feels as though I've been slapped across the face. 'What *am* I like?' I say, wholly unaware that I am *like* anything.

Zhané places her hand on my knee in the way a vicar might console someone who's just lost a loved one. 'A rock. A beacon of strength. A strong, independent woman.'

'But you're allowed to crumble.' Flora adds. 'This is a safe space. You know that, right? You can tell us anything.'

And then the tears come; slowly at first, a prickling sensation starting up in my nose and then building in momentum, my throat tightening and before I know it, the floodgates have opened, and I am nothing short of a snivelling mess of snot and tears. Maybe I haven't been doing so well after all. Maybe the auction, the wedding outfits, the panoramic Tuscan view and the plaster-cast modelling are all just an escape from the brutal truth: Curvaliscious has not sold. 'It's not anything to do with the Raffa incident, it's just . . . Fabrice said I've sold out. And he's right, I have. Making all these wedding outfits . . . it's just been . . .'

'Stressful?' Flora offers.

'Joyful?' Zhané suggests.

'It's been stressful and joyful, but more importantly, it's been a comfort blanket.' I whimper, realising that the last month out here has been pure escapism, the creation of wedding apparel providing a therapeutic soft cushioning from the brutal slaying I got at both the Curvaliscious pitch and losing my job at House of Dreams.

At some point I'm going to have to go back and face the music. I feel the ground below me shift as my world comes crashing down around my ears. What the fuck will I *do* when I return to London? A feeling of wretchedness overcomes me and all I want to do is dig a hole and lie in it. I reach for my grandma's pendant and feel the weight of its absence.

'Let's go out,' I say, brushing it aside and determined to get on with the day. 'I've got to go to the Post Office to send Fabrice's DragFest dress to him, unless one of you could take it back with you?'

'Sure!' Zhané and Flora reply in enthusiastic unison.

'Thank you. Now let me show you the studio.'

'Wait!' Flora waves my phone in front of me. 'I promised your mum you'd give her a call. She's worried about you.'

'Maybe later?' I say dismissively.

'No. Now.' Flora insists, looking to Zhané for affirmation. 'Your mum said it was vital now.'

Vital? Reluctantly, I video call Mum's number.

'Hi, Mum!' I wave as a close-up of Dad's nostril (I can tell by the hair) appears on the screen in front of me. 'Dad!' I extend the salutation as the pair of them appear side by side at the kitchen table, a cake tin positioned between them.

'Hi, love, we're just about to head out so I don't suppose we could give you a call later?'

It doesn't seem very vital.

Dad's face comes into the foreground. 'How are you getting on?'

'I'm fine,' I say. 'Especially now the girls are with me.'

'Good.' He nods reassuringly.

'Not wearing the necklace anymore?' Mum peers into the screen.

'I . . . Yes . . . It just doesn't really go with today's outfit.'

Mum chuckles. 'You know it has a habit of coming back.'

'Sorry?'

'Your grandmother lost that pendant about five times and it always came back. The boomerang, she used to call it.'

'Really?' I say, superstition clouding my thoughts. 'I'm sorry, I lost it in Florence and didn't want to tell you. I retraced my steps and looked everywhere, but we couldn't find it. I even made a wish at this really romantic church Marco took me to, la Chiesa

287

di Santa Margherita, where Dante was buried and . . . I dunno, if you drop your wish into this coffin, it's supposed to come true.'

Mum's ears prick up. 'Who's Marco?'

'My landlord.'

Zhané raises an eyebrow from the balcony.

'It's not like that!' I protest.

'Sure.' Mum's eyes sparkle. 'Well, I'm glad the girls are with you and I'm glad you called, but we're about to go flying.'

'OK,' I say, feeling all of a sudden nostalgic for standing on the moors with a flask of tea, waiting for my parents to take off and then seeing them float overhead, weightless in the cloudy sky, and I'm still thinking about it when the conversation has dried up and my dad has reverted to listing the ailments of people I have never heard of whilst my mum stuffs a freezer bag of flapjack into the pocket of the backpack.

A moment later, the call has concluded, and I am back on the terrace with Flora and Zhané, who are both staring at me in a way that suggests I am harbouring a secret from them.

'What?' I say, confused.

Flora looks at me with narrowed eyes. 'Was all that stuff about the necklace true?'

'Of course.' I look over to Zhané, who eyes me with distrust.

'You told us your landlord took you to Florence as part of a business trip to look for fabric, but from what you just described, it all sounded a bit romantic,' Flora says.

That's the thing about Flora, she's always looking at the world through love-tinted spectacles.

'It wasn't romantic,' I say maybe too defensively, checking myself and making an effort to take the sting out of my voice.

'We just did a few touristy things – you know, got gelato, walked along the river, checked out the sights and—'

'Hang on, hang on,' Zhané interrupts me. 'Your Airbnb landlord took you to Florence to get some fabric and you got gelato, went sightseeing, walked up the river and made sacred wishes at Dante's church and this is somehow *not* romantic? Roma, he has just Mr Darcyed the fuck out of you before your very own eyes, and you can't see it!'

'The same landlord that keeps shuffling reservations around to keep you accommodated in spite of it being peak summer season. Think of all the bookings he must have turned away!' Flora squeezes my knee with giddiness.

'It's not like that. He's in a relationship and expecting a baby.'

'Gotcha.' Zhané exchanges a look of resignation with Flora. 'We stand corrected.'

'Let's get lunch.' Flora grabs her bag. 'There's this place I really want to check out.'

Curious, I raise my eyebrows. There are only three establishments within walking distance where lunch is an option – la Parmigiana, the village taverna, Ciccone's, the bar next to it, and a small delicatessen-cum-café called la Salumeria off the main square and I've yet to see any of them referenced on TripAdvisor – but before she can elaborate, I clock the time, my stomach fluttering with unease.

'I should really be on my way to the auction.'

'No!' Zhané shouts, and then realising it came out a little too aggressively, softens her tone. 'I'm sure we've got time for a quick bite to eat first.'

'We could always eat here,' Flora says with a shrug of the shoulders. 'Saves us bumping into Raffa!'

And before I can object, the girls set to work, pulling out the contents of my fridge and rustling up a cold veggie platter. Ciabatta. Mozzarella. Basil. Tomatoes so plump and flavoursome they taste like a delicacy, but I'm way too anxious to eat. I may have played down the Raffa thing, but just the thought of being in the same room as him fills my chest with nervous tension so I leave the girls to it, investing the time in a Trinny London makeup video showing how to camouflage hooded eyes whilst they get changed downstairs.

Half an hour later the three of us set off up the hill for Operation Sabotage like something out of *Sex and the City*, Zhané in five-inch heels and a ruched cream silk dress, Flora in an emerald green suit and chunky gold jewellery and me in my glittery jumpsuit.

Several rows of chairs have been set up in an auditorium-style seating arrangement in the Casa dei Cappelli, a raised block with a lectern assembled opposite as part of a makeshift stage set at the front of the room. The space is awash with people, most of them villagers curious to see Mariela Marino's lifeworks rather than being here as serious buyers if hearsay is anything to go by, although the auction has clearly attracted the interest of some seasoned connoisseurs – a woman with crystal-framed reading glasses hanging around her neck on a thread of pearls was deposited just outside the front door by taxi and judging by the way she is flicking through the catalogue of items and punching guide prices into a pocket calculator, she means serious business, but maybe not nearly as serious as the smartly dressed man in a turban who stands amongst a team of professionals at the back of the room, scrutinising each piece like a magpie picking through treasure.

'Cinque minuti,' a voice booms over the speaker.

People take to their seats, the butcher, the baker and Francesca's assistant from the village pharmacy heading to the front row, where they sit fanning themselves with the auction catalogue. Valentina is nuzzled up against Flavio, her hands all over his torso as he helps himself to a steady stream of sugared almonds. Behind them, sit their mothers – Giuseppina separated from Francesca by the two bartenders, Enzo and Riccardo from Ciccone's and the village priest, who wears not one, but two strings of rosary beads today.

Maria occupies the seat at the end of my row. She wears a sleeveless navy-blue shift dress, showing off slender, toned arms and effervescent skin.

'How can someone so pregnant look so effortlessly stylish?' Zhané whispers to me. 'Honestly, when I was eight months gone with Leo, I just looked like a giant beachball.'

'She's nothing short of an Italian goddess,' Flora agrees.

Maria sees the three of us and waves.

'And she's really nice,' I concede.

Zhané lets out a sigh deep from within her lungs. 'Some women just have it all.'

As the room fills further, Zhané and Flora busy themselves handing out leaflets Signor Zaccardi has had printed about the history of the building, whilst Marco records the arrival of guests with a handheld tally counter. I am, meanwhile, too nervous to talk and sit in the front row in a cold sweat, wondering how all of this is going to pan out. It doesn't help that my friends keep sneaking little looks at each other and behaving peculiarly – they were clearly up to something earlier when they nipped off to buy stamps and didn't come back until half an hour later, the Post Office only a stone's throw away. I'm not sure what they're scheming, but it's certainly not putting me at ease.

It's several degrees hotter up here than it is down in my studio below and the standing fan that has been plugged in next to the stage area is doing nothing but circulate warm air. I watch as the room fills further, people snaking up the stairs and packing in tightly against the wall at the back, hundreds of pairs of eyes ready to marvel over the Mistress of Millinery's finest creations. Goosebumps spring up over my skin as a woman dressed in clinical white mounts the dusky pink pillbox hat that was designed for the late Princess of Monaco atop the auctioneer's cushioned stand, angling it in a way that shows off the oversized taffeta silk bow, its silver lining catching the light. My heart races. Mariela Marino's collection may be about to go under the hammer but it feels as though it is going under the knife.

I search the room for Signor Zaccardi but can't see him anywhere. He looked pale and withdrawn when I saw him earlier, his eyes red and puffy and the large handkerchief he carries around in his pocket tightly balled in his fist. Maybe the whole thing is too much for him. A trickle of sweat runs down my spine and the underwires of my bra start to itch.

'Signorella e signori, la vostra attenzione per favore. Posso presentarti Signor Bergamaschi.'

The energy in the room changes, an aroma of cedar and sandalwood filling the air, and adrenaline shoots through me as Raffa prances up the makeshift aisle in a crisp white shirt tucked into tight-fitted indigo jeans, one of his grandmother's pinstriped trilby hats perched on his head. His amber eyes lighting up the room, there's no denying that he possesses achingly good looks and is in peak physique – it's no wonder I took a shine to him.

Taking to the stage with an athletic leap, he clutches a pack of coloured cue cards in one hand and takes the microphone in the other. My throat tightens and the back of my neck starts to feel clammy, the churning of my stomach only settling when Zhané and Flora appear either side of me like protective bodyguards.

'Is that him?' Zhané whisper-hisses.

I nod, speechless.

'He's super confident,' Flora says with a look of disdain.

'He's super twatty,' Zhané adds.

I fidget in my seat, wondering whether he has spotted me.

'Signore e signori, benvenuti nella Casa dei Cappelli. Ladies and Gentlemen, welcome to the House of Hats. My grandmother, Mariela Marino, better known as the Milliner of Milan, would be thrilled that so many of you are here today.' Raffa clears his throat, his amber eyes darting around the room as he runs his tongue over his bottom lip and drinks in his audience. 'The pieces that you're about to see are some of the most beautifully made hats in the world, so no fighting!' He looks straight at me and flashes a smile, a burst of nervous energy short-circuiting my system and my legs turning all jittery.

'He's seen her!' Flora whispers across me to Zhané as if I'm not there.

Zhané folds her arms over her chest. 'What a creep!'

'Right, let's get this party started and open the auction,' he says, snatching the dusky-pink pillbox hat off its cushion and thrusting it into the air before there's any chance of Signor Zaccardi making an entrance. Fuckety fuck. This wasn't supposed to happen. The telephone hat was supposed to be first up, our whole script based on the impracticalities of having an electronic device strapped to your head.

'Let's kick off with one hundred euros.' Raffa's eyes size up the room like those of a greedy lizard.

The lady with the crystal reading glasses a few seats along from me nods, Raffa muttering a string of incoherent words before glancing at the back of the room, where the man with the turban discretely raises a bidding card, his hands clasped tightly together in front of him.

'Two hundred.' Raffa nods, his eyes shifting back to the woman with the crystal framed glasses. 'Five hundred?'

The woman nods, the bidding accelerating at pace the higher the stakes are raised, and before you know it, it's like listening to a verbal game of ping-pong, prices ricocheting back and forth across the room, the volley of numbers finally slowing and the hammer slamming down on three thousand three hundred euros, Raffa's face lit up like a Christmas tree.

'What's happening?' Flora whispers. 'I thought Marco said he'd make sure nothing got sold.'

'No idea!' I hiss, my eyes flicking over to the door to the secret staircase. Didn't Marco say he needed access to it today?

This is all too painful to sit back and watch, but for some reason, I am glued to my seat, mesmerised by Raffa's hand movements and before I have a chance to will my body into action, the woman in clinical white is handing over the crimson brushed cotton cloche hat with the black velvet trim I tried on when I was with Raffa, an excited murmur spreading across the room.

A shiver runs down my spine. It feels surreal that an item whose bid is opening at one thousand euros and is now being paraded in front of hundreds of people has taken pride of place on my head. I turn to Giuseppina, who sits up straight, her attention piqued whilst her husband busies himself with his phone, and I wonder for a moment just whose side she is on and whether she might just double-cross us all when push comes to shove. Whatever is going on in her head, she refuses to make eye contact with me, choosing instead to stare at the hat with the same intensity as Luke Skywalker did when he used the force.

To my horror, the door remains closed as Raffa opens the second bid, my heart dropping into the pit of my stomach as Giuseppina raises her hand, bidding again and again until the lot reaches four thousand euros and she is outbid first by the man with the turban and then by a friend of the woman with the crystal framed glasses who, between them, drive the price up to somewhere in the region of twenty thousand, although I've lost track. Indignance rises in my chest as Raffa licks his lips greedily, dollar signs almost visible in his shiny eyes. Why does he always get what he wants?

It looks like the whole sabotage is off, Giuseppina sharing a look of despair with her husband and reaching for the brochure to identify her next potential purchase – she clearly has no desire to help us here – whilst Francesca does little to suppress the smile of satisfaction that plays on her lips.

Raffa rubs his thighs with delight as the auction contin-ues at pace, three further haute-couture creations going for over five thousand euros – the shoe perched atop a gold beret once worn by Whoopi Goldberg to the Oscars, totalling fifty-two thousand – and the money keeps on rolling in, the smug expression on Raffa's face intensifying with each lot.

When Raffa holds up a white feathered wedding hat, Giuseppina tries her luck again, only for Francesca to outbid her almost immediately, the pair of them driving up the price tit for tat until Mr Turban outbids them both, closing the deal at eight thousand euros. Raffa's eyes sparkle with delight and it's all I can do not to leap out of my chair and punch him. Has he no shame? I start to sweat, the room spiralling and spinning, all the hats with it. That's the thing about Raffa: he oozes charm and confidence, the audience clearly enamoured by his smooth but casual delivery, and nobody is prepared to take him to task. My top lip feels clammy as I go to shuffle out of my seat.

'Roma!' Zhané yanks me back down into my chair.

'We can't let this happen!' I hiss.

'It's OK.' Flora takes hold of my arm.

But it's clearly not OK. Raffa is going to make a fortune and get away with it, brushing his late grandmother's dying wishes under the carpet for his own personal gratification and denying these villagers what should rightfully be theirs. If nobody is prepared to do something about it, then shouldn't I at least try? Then, just as I'm about to shake off Zhané and Flora, who have become attached to my arms like human shackles, the door to the secret staircase bursts open, an explosion of colour erupting before us all and the whole room takes a collective intake of breath.

'Scusi, scusi.' A larger-than-life figure takes to the stage, pushing Raffa aside and reaching for the anvil, the atmosphere in the room shifting from one of casual intrigue to full-on back-straightening, neck-craning, attention-grabbing curiosity. 'Move over, darling. You've had your fun and now it's time I had mine!'

Bewildered, Raffa flattens himself against the back wall and looks on, speechless. With sparkly black six-inch platform heels, platinum blonde nylon curls gathered up in a bee-hive, diamanté chandelier earrings, breasts like bowling balls, buttocks like soccer balls, draught-excluding eyelashes and a cinched waistline Beyoncé would kill for, Polly Darton is in the house. A sequined siren, she towers over the microphone, layers and layers of white net flowing from the back of the gown. It must have been a two-man job to get it on! I stifle a chuckle. No wonder Signor Zaccardi is a no-show and looked so pale earlier when I turned up at the studio.

My heart swells with happiness. I turn to look at Zhané, whose face is alight with rapture, and then at Flora, who giggles at my side as she records the whole thing on her phone. So, this is what they were plotting? Fabrice flew out with them and has been here all morning? A warm glow spreads through my body at the thought of them smuggling him into my studio and contriving reasons to keep me at the apartment just to keep me at bay from seeing him. That vital call with my parents! Grinning from ear to ear, I clap my hands together, a warm glow of pride rising within me as I watch in delight.

'They're fake!' Polly brushes a strand of nylon hair out of her enormous eyelashes and rearranges her chest as she takes in the sea of people before her, throwing a flamboyant ripple of her fingers in my direction. 'I'm not talking about my breasts; I'm talking about the hats. Do not be fooled, ladies and gentlemen.

The originals are *not* being auctioned because it was Mariela's dying wish that her collection remains a collection and the hats all stay together as an exhibition.'

'Whoa, whoa, whoa!' Raffa barges his way back onto the stage. 'They are very much the real article, and all final bids will be honoured.'

'Honoured?' Polly chews over the word in front of her audience. 'Honour is such a loose term as far as you're concerned, isn't it, Mr Bergamaschi?'

The sound of chair legs scraping across the floor sends a shiver down my spine like nails down a blackboard. Out of the corner of my eye, I can see Maria rising from her seat. 'It's time for you to leave, Raffaele! You're not welcome here,' she shouts.

Raffa's face becomes an unconscious frown.

'You heard her.' Marco leaps to his feet. 'You're a bully and we don't want you here.'

'Maybe we should put it to the audience vote.' Polly flutters her eyelashes. 'Do we want him in? Or do we want him out?'

There are front men and there are front ladies, and then there's Polly Darton, who is in a league of her own: serene like a queen but with all the swagger of Mick Jagger, she has a retort for everything and is not the sort of lady you go head-to-head with. I bite my bottom lip and give myself a good pinch, checking that it's all real, and grin like the Cheshire cat when I don't wake up.

'Out!' Maria screams.

A murmur of discontent ripples across the room, the smartly dressed man in the turban shaking his head in dismay and storming out of the room.

'God, this is like a soap opera!' Flora pulls at my sleeve, squealing with delight.

'I knew Fabrice would take him down,' Zhané sneers.

My eyes flicker between Fabrice's alter ego and Raffa, who is making an urgent phone call, his finger pressed into his ear.

Heads swivel as Polly Darton holds up the next piece of headgear to go under the hammer – a black velvet beret with an old-fashioned telephone embedded in the summit – not *the* telephone hat, but a telephone hat, nonetheless. 'Who amongst us would wear this?' she chides.

Nobody answers the question, the crowd still up in arms at the suggestion that the entire collection today is a bunch of replicas, coats snatched up and belongings gathered as people leave, a steady mass blocking the top of the stairs.

'Would you wear it?' Polly Darton holds up the hat and looks straight at me.

I raise my voice over the humdrum of the room. 'As clever and as beautiful as it is, I'm not sure I'd have an occasion to wear a hat like that.'

'You!' Polly Darton clicks her fingers at Giuseppina, people stopping in their tracks and the chatter in the room thinning to a silence. 'Would you wear this hat?'

Commanding the attention of the room, Giuseppina purses her lips and frowns. '*Nobody* would wear this hat. It is not designed to be worn. It is designed to be admired.'

'Exactly!' Polly Darton breaks out her award-winning smile, addressing the audience with a silk-gloved finger adorned with a huge crystal ring. 'If you bought this hat, you would keep it in your house, knowing its value, but you wouldn't wear it. I mean,

299

I might . . .' She brings her hand to her chest theatrically. 'But *you'd* probably lock it up only for it to gather dust and be seen by nobody. And that's not what Mariela Marino created it for, is it? She wanted her work to be seen.'

'We *all* want to be seen.' Giuseppina fans herself with the auction catalogue and looks over at Francesca.

'Some more than others!' Francesca folds one leg over the other and stares out of the window.

'Seen and admired.' Polly performs another twirl, much to the delight of the butcher on the front row, whose cheeks glow a pale pink, a dirty little chuckle erupting from his mouth as the split in her skirt parts to reveal an extra inch of leg. 'How much would you pay to see this hat and read about its creation? Who it was made for and for what occasion, the inspiration behind it, the reaction it got from people around the world? How long it took to make from what materials? Did you know for example that Silvio Berlusconi wore this telephone hat at a charity gala, where a property tycoon bid one million dollars to make a prime ministerial call from it to the White House?'

I have no idea whether this is God's honest truth or solid gold bullshit, but judging by the gasps that are filling the room, it is clearly having a mesmeric effect on our would-be bidders.

'These hats all have their own story, which will get lost if they are sold off individually but would live on if they were curated as a collection at a museum, each having their own backstory showcased. I was just messing with you about them being fake. They're actually 100 per cent authentic.' She massages her chest and looks over at the door. 'Signor Zaccardi?'

The door swings open to reveal Signor Zaccardi dressed in a navy-blue suit coupled with freshly polished chestnut shoes. His moustache has had a judicious pruning and a small spotted handkerchief sits in his breast pocket. People clear a path for him as he advances towards the stage, Polly Darton stepping down to accommodate him at the microphone.

'The Casa dei Cappelli will open as a Hat Emporium, inviting visitors from around the world to come and admire Mariela's work. These hats are for celebrating. These hats are for appreciating. They should not belong to one person, never to be seen again. Rest in peace, Mariela. And now Marco has something to say . . .'

Heads turn towards the back of the room, where Marco stands amongst a huddle of villagers. 'I would be happy to give a guided tour of the building which holds so much history. When it was built. How many people it took to construct the ornamental facade. How many hats it holds. Did you know, for example, that there is a secret staircase?'

Unable to contain myself, I jump up. 'I'd gladly pay ten euros for the privilege of entering this building, wouldn't you?'

'Eleven!' Zhané jeers from the back of the room.

'Twelve!' Maria follows.

'Fifteen!' Flora yells.

'Twenty?' Signor Zaccardi pipes up.

'Who would like to join me?' Marco walks over to the stage. 'I could give—'

Before Marco can finish his sentence, people are charging towards him, all wanting a little bit of history about the Casa dei Cappelli. As the crowd swells, I take a moment to savour our success but judging by the look of menace in Raffa's eyes as he charges back into the room and heads straight for Marco, I may be a little premature in my celebrations.

'If this is about what happened all those years ago, it's a pretty childish way of showing it.' Raffa fronts up to Marco, all chin and clamped jaw.

Marco throws his hands up in surrender. 'This is actually about Mariela's hats.'

'Which are absolutely none of your business!' Raffa snarls.

Tension mounts as a crowd forms around the two of them, people jostling to get a better view before Polly Darton bursts through them, pulling the pair apart as though they are nothing more than duelling schoolboys. 'Raffa, your mother should have thrown you away and kept the stork. Now go home!'

An eruption of laughter spreads across the room, which only angers Raffa further.

'Who are you anyway?' He glares at Polly. 'I don't even know you!'

'Polly Darton, sir.'

'Well, fuck you.' Raffa turns on his heel and storms towards the stage. 'I'm not taking all this shit from some washed-up drag queen.'

'Raffa, if you listen carefully, you will hear me not giving the slightest shit what you say about me. Now go home.'

'Seriously, who hired you?'

'I see you have van Gogh's ear for listening. The auction is over. Nobody wants to buy the hats.'

Bristling with anger, Raffa shakes his head this way and that, his jaw clenched so tightly that his face is slowly turning purple.

Then, shooting his breath at the ceiling at the realisation that he's never going to win an argument with a loose-lipped, six-foot drag queen, he storms out of the building.

Francesca stands up. 'Mi scusi, where is la Columba Bianca?'

Polly sneers. 'La Columba Bianca? Is that a type of pudding?'

'The White Dove hat,' Giuseppina shouts. 'We're here for the White Dove.'

Polly turns to Signor Zaccardi, the net train of her dress getting caught on the microphone stand and the squeal of feedback filling the room, everyone bringing their hands over their ears as she clambers back up on stage. 'The White Dove, Signor Zaccardi?'

Signor Zaccardi looks up with the solemnness of a bloodhound. 'I have searched everywhere but the Columba Bianca has gone.'

Gasps fill the room, Francesca eyeing Giuseppina with suspicion and Giuseppina returning her accusatory gaze with one of her own, rumours spreading like wildfire in Italian and English. *Mariela e stata sepolta con il cappello da Columba Bianca.* Mariela was buried wearing the White Dove hat. *Sofia Bergamaschi ha rubato la Columba Bianca.* Sofia Bergamaschi stole the White Dove.

I look out of the window to see Raffa running down the road with a baby-pink hat box wedged under one arm. He may have run off with his grandmother's most prized piece, but at the end of the day, isn't that a small sacrifice in the grand scheme of things?

'Mission accomplished.' Zhané nudges my arm and smiles.

'He's literally running out of the village!' Flora claps her hands together in delight.

Marco and Maria make their way towards us, wrapping their arms around us as we rejoice in a celebrative huddle, Signor Zaccardi joining us and dancing in delight.

Polly Darton sashays over to the window. 'You know he reminds me of a penny. Two-faced and worth very little.'

And as I watch Raffa's retreating back, I'm reminded of the story of the 'Three Little Pigs'. The wolf may have swept through the village and taken advantage of me and certainly of Maria, but he has clearly underestimated the strength of this third house. He can huff and he can puff all he likes, but he will not blow down the House of Hats.

Thank God for Polly Darton.

CHAPTER TWENTY-ONE
Polly Darton

I watch as first the wig, then its stocking and finally the dress comes off; Polly Darton is retired to a small wheelie case and Fabrice is laid bare before me, his face paler than I remember and his shoulders rounded with a despondency I don't recognise. Slowly, he peels off a row of feathered eyelashes and sticks them back in their wallet, then taking a damp ball of cotton wool to his eyelids, he wipes away the bold lines and swooshes of colour with rigorous, purposeful strokes I associate with peeling vegetables. As the glittered cheeks and pencilled-on eyebrows slowly disappear along with his alter ego, so does our conversation, the downward pull of his facial expression and body language unnerving me. I've never seen Fabrice like this before. He looks small and vulnerable, deflated and depressed – neither in keeping with his larger-than-life personality.

'You were amazing!' I go to hug him properly once he's got his T-shirt on but it's difficult, what with his body taking on the elasticity of a corpse with deep-set rigor mortis. I pretend not to notice, topping up his flute with prosecco courtesy of Signor Zaccardi and telling myself that he'll soon snap back into the familiar shape of the Fabrice we all know and love.

'I'm glad you enjoyed it as that was actually my last fandango.' He zips up his makeup bag with finality. 'Polly Darton is officially hanging up her wig.'

Struggling for words and feeling a little dizzy, I watch him toss the nylon blonde beehive into my bin, its mesh lining getting caught on the lid. 'Sorry?' I turn to him in astonishment.

'DragFest is off.'

'What?'

'I'm so sorry, I know you made a dress and—'

'What do you mean, it's off?'

'They lost their sponsor and it's too last-minute to find a new one.'

My stomach drops on his behalf. DragFest means everything to Fabrice and cancelling it will be like losing a limb to him. Not to mention the dress I have spent hours labouring over. How can such a feat of engineering go to waste?

'And then there's the small matter of me getting fired.' He slips on his trainers and glances around the studio.

'From Pomfrey & Wibble?'

'On the contrary. Mr Pommes Frites has taken rather a shine to me since seeing Polly in action and I ended up getting a rather substantial pay rise. No, I got fired from Pandora's Box,' he says mournfully.

'Why?' I say, aghast. 'You were raking it in for them!'

'The new manager didn't like my act. He said the only people who have heard of Dolly Parton are over fifty years of age and are not our target audience.'

'But Dolly Parton is timeless!' I say, plucking his wig out of the bin and shoving it in my bag for want of a better place to put it. 'She's iconic. She's international. She transcends all ages, all religions . . . all cultures, all classes . . . She's a revolutionary. A world phenomenon. A—'

'Tell that to Mr Verulkar.' He chews at his fingernails, his face tightening and the tiny muscles beneath his eyes twitching with harboured stress.

'Congratulations!' Signor Zaccardi pops his head around the door to the staircase.

'Complimenti!' Giuseppina's head follows.

'Brava! Brava!' Francesca appears somewhere between the two of them.

'Congratulations to you, too!' I raise my glass in their direction as they shuffle through the studio and disappear out of the front door.

Fabrice stands up and sinks his hands into the pockets of his jeans. 'Can we go somewhere a man can have his midlife crisis in private?'

'Sure,' I say, grabbing my keys.

Smiling wearily, he places his rough hands on my shoulders. 'Buckle up, buttercup. Get ready to see a grown man cry.'

Outside, I explain to the girls that Fabrice needs a moment, though they are far too deep in conversation with Marco and the soon-to-be Best Men to take much notice – and we head out to the hillside.

The sun has lost its kick and the smell of jasmine carries on a gentle breeze, bringing sweet relief to a hot, heady day. As the chiming of church bells become more distant and the evening sky morphs into a streaky swirl of pink and orange, we trudge towards a small path that dips behind a fig tree and snakes down the valley alongside a trickling stream. My bag is laden with fresh focaccia and half a bottle of prosecco which chinks against the two champagne flutes I thought I'd protected with a picnic blanket but seem intent on clinking together.

Following the stream further, iridescent butterflies dancing over a cluster of irises, their lilac petals fluttering at the water's edge, we reach the outskirts of a vineyard where the land opens up to reveal a panoramic view of the surrounding fields and valley below. A patchwork of yellow, greens and golds cascade down the hill like velvet blankets, stretching out towards a small terracotta-roofed village sitting at the foot of a shimmering emerald lake.

A scuffle. A snuffle. The sound of tiny hooves on gravel.

'What was that?' Fabrice looks over to the vineyard.

And there, between the twisted gnarly vines, a wild boar leads her piglets across dry soil to feast on grapes. With coarse hair, long narrow snouts and a mane of bristles, they shouldn't look cute, but they do, the babies a light ginger brown with cream stripes running across their coats. Standing stock-still, the mother swings her snout around and assesses us through beady eyes. Flight or fight? Satisfied that we pose no threat, she goes back to her business of foraging grapes, her piglets scurrying through her legs. The smallest one turns to look at me. *Il Porcellino*, I grin.

Fabrice turns to me, his eyes shining with intrigue. 'So, who is he?'

'Who's who?' I say, taking the picnic blanket out of my bag and flapping it in the air with a flourish.

He takes the opposite corners. 'I recognise that look, Vivienne.'

'What look?' I say, taken aback.

'That look of love.'

A nervous laugh escapes me. 'Trust me, that was not a look of love. Trapped wind, maybe, but definitely not love.'

'Riiight,' he says slowly, spreading the picnic blanket across the ground and helping himself to prosecco. 'Not ready to share yet?'

His jumping to conclusions riles me and I feel my cheeks flush with annoyance. How the hell is he reading romance into all this? It's infuriating. Fabrice can usually read me like a book – he knows everything about me – when I'm genuinely enthused or politely faking it, when I'm inwardly flustered, nervous or intimi-dated, when I'm tired and withdrawn, relaxed or so angry I'm about to explode; everything. Having hung out together for the best part of a decade, he knows me inside out, so how has he got this so wrong?

'It's more of a friendship thing.' I sit down beside him, taking the glass of bubbles being handed to me.

'What is?'

'The thing with Marco.'

'Ah, he has a name!' Fabrice flashes me a wry grin. 'So, there is a thing with Marco?'

'It's honestly not what you think. He owns the flat I rented here and he's just a lovely guy. Really helpful. Kind. Friendly. If it wasn't for him shuffling bookings around, I wouldn't have a roof over my head. Honestly, he's a lovely guy. He drove me to Florence on his Vespa and showed me all these wonderful places and—' The words tumble out of my mouth and I can't seem to stop them.

'Hmm.' Fabrice muses, a smile flickering across his lips.

'It's really not like that! He's just a genuinely nice human being!' I bat his arm away playfully.

Fabrice shakes his head. 'You're so shallow, Vivienne. Did anyone ever tell you that?'

'And he's about to become a father,' I blurt out, a feeling of wretchedness taking hold of me.

'Oh.' He holds his glass mid-air.

'Yeah, his partner is eight months pregnant.' A sigh finds its way out of my chest.

'There's nothing for you there, girl. Detach and move on!'

'Yeah,' I say, wondering why I feel a tiny bit envious of Maria every time the imminent birth of their baby is mentioned. It's not like I'm broody. I mean, I'm nowhere near ready for a baby, and yet it now feels as though I'm missing out. Though I'm not sure on what. I reach for the focaccia, breaking off a chunk of the soft, oily bread and popping it into my mouth, the taste of crushed rosemary and garlic lingering on my tongue. Isn't this what Italy is all about: fun, focaccia and friendship? I turn my attention back to Fabrice. 'How about you? What's really going on?'

He looks up at a flock of geese flying across the evening sky, their necks extended out in front of their bodies like a homing device. 'It's a long story.'

'I'm in no rush.'

'OK.' He reaches for the focaccia and clears his throat. 'Anil, the owner's son, has taken over the club and is having a bit of a shake-up. The other girls have been let go, too. He says drag is passé and that nobody wants to listen to a bunch of queens lip-synching.'

I inhale sharply, feeling as though I have just swallowed broken glass. 'Is he aware of the millions of people that tune into *RuPaul's Drag Race* every week?'

'Anil and awareness are not natural bedfellows. One day he'll choke on the shit he talks but for now, I guess he's got his own way.' He swills down the focaccia with prosecco.

'Well, that's surely his loss and some place else's gain,' I say, stretching my skirt over my legs in a bid to protect my shins from the early evening mosquitoes.

'No,' he says, emptying the bottle of prosecco into my glass. 'I'm done with it.'

'*Done*, done?' My skin tightens.

'Uh-uh. Polly Darton is goner than *Gone Girl*.'

'But . . .' My insides feel all stringy and everything seems out of place. An acidic taste forms in my mouth as I sit staring at him in disbelief. It's all too much; the moment too big. Fabrice quitting drag is like resigning part of himself. Handing over a large chunk of his personality and declaring it null and void. How will things ever be the same? Fabrice without Polly is like Ben without Jerry, Barrack without Michele, *Hello!* magazine without the celebrities.

I think about the hundreds of times I have watched him perform over the years and the places we have travelled to together, him attending all my fashion shows in return for me going along to all his gigs. Watching from the wings and bolstering each other. Supporting each other through thick and thin. I must have seen him perform at least a hundred times – everywhere from DragFest Romania to London Pride. And so it stands to reason that I'm not only friends with Fabrice, but I'm friends with Polly, too. Allowing her to be laid to rest would be like watching my friend euthanise himself. I can't let this happen.

I transfer half of the prosecco from my glass into his. 'But you're the best queen out there. Polly puts the pop in popular, remember!'

He leans forward, elbows propped up on his knees. 'You know I used to think it would all be worth it? I'd compartmentalised everything in my head. All the hours working at the accountancy were to put a roof over my head, pay the bills and keep me in frocks until I made the Big Time as a performer and could afford to jack it all in. Bookkeeping was always supposed to be a means to an end; the tedious nine 'til five grind enabling the bright future I was working towards on stage. I'd figured it all out. The costumes I'd wear. The persona I'd adopt. The songs I'd sing with parodied lyrics I'd crafted in a single cell of an Excel spreadsheet when I was supposed to be balancing books for clients. I'd written my leaving speech ten times over and could recite to you any version word for word. Sad, isn't it?'

'No,' I say, bursting with desperation and yet 'sad' is exactly how I feel.

'You know I must have daydreamed a thousand times over about what it would feel like to march into Mr Pomfrey's office with my resignation, a broad smile plastered across my face as I told him I was quitting my job to be a full-time performer. That I'd had this double life all along and that I was finally free to follow my dream. It would all have meant something then. The spreadsheets. The VAT calculations. The tedious conversations with Mr Wibble about his golfing holidays. All those last-minute tax returns. It would have all been worth it to get me to where I was finally going. And yet it's got me nowhere.' He throws his head back and exhales at the sky.

'Of course it—'

He holds up his hand in protest. 'You know, I really, honestly thought I could do it. Win DragFest. Pocket the prize money. Quit my job. Travel around the world as Polly, making enough money to live off without needing a day job. Nothing rich or fancy but enough to live off.' He bursts into maniacal laughter. 'What a fool I've been.'

'No.' I rise to my feet, hurt building full throttle inside me. 'No, you haven't!'

'Working a job I don't like. Wearing clothes that don't fit. Frittering my life away on a dream that won't ever come true and not having the self-awareness to get off the train, look myself in the mirror and realise that I'm past it.'

'That's enough now.' I reach for his hand, feeling as though someone is trying to rip my heart out.

'I'm fifty-nine, Vivienne. Too old to start anew with *anything*.'

'Stop it!' I whimper, tears now streaming down my face. 'Stop being so melodramatic! This is a temporary blip. You can't just give up.'

'Why can't I?'

'Because I'm not ready yet!' I yell angrily. 'I'm not ready to say goodbye to Polly yet!' And then I collapse into him, laughing and sobbing. 'Because obviously this is all about me really!'

He laughs, holding me in his arms and laughs some more, his whole body corpsing violently and I realise that I, too, am in fits of uncontrollable, maniacal laughter and that neither of us knows how to handle this. It feels as though someone has pulled the plug on the earth's gravity and we are floating around in the atmosphere, rudderless and unanchored.

'Polly isn't real, you know,' Fabrice says after an enormous silence.

'She bloody well is.'

'You know there is a smattering of truth to what Anil says.'

'How is there?' I squeeze him tightly to my chest.

'Drag queens were a novelty when the world was heteronormative, gender was binary, and sexuality wasn't so goddamned complicated. But now a cock in a frock is nothing out of the ordinary. There's no mystery. No intrigue. Je ne sais quoi has gone je ne sais ou! And it's getting harder to write comedy.'

'How do you mean?'

'You need to be media trained to put yourself out there these days. I used to think that by indiscriminately offending everyone, my material was inoffensive, but apparently not! How can I be 100 per cent bitch if I'm not allowed to bitch about anyone?'

'You're overthinking it. You're still amazing. Your act is funny, clever and relevant. Your voice is magnificent. You've still got so much more to give . . . You can't just go back to working for Pomfrey & Wibble without an outlet and badminton, walking cricket or collecting snow globes will never fill your inner

void. You'll be all yin and no yang. Come on, don't be a coward!'
I thump him gently on the chest and spring to my feet.

'How do you mean?' He looks taken aback.

'Giving up on your dream just because you hit a hurdle.
Letting go because you're frightened of being let go,' I say,
pacing up and down the picnic blanket.

'I *have* been let go!'

'By one person who knows fuck all! That doesn't mean you
have to give up on your dreams entirely.'

His face becomes a contortion of multiple expressions. 'Pot.
Kettle. Black.'

'What's that supposed to mean?' I say.

'You came out here to launch a Plus Size clothes range and
you've totally sold out!'

Shock hits me in the windpipe.

'Don't get me wrong, your wedding outfits are beautiful, but
that's not *you*. That's not your dream. Just because The Horse
told you that he didn't like your designs, you gave up.'

'No, I didn't,' I say indignantly.

His eyes narrow. 'Didn't you?'

'No. I've just been taking a little time out, that's all.' I bite my
bottom lip so hard I can taste blood.

His eyes narrow. 'Are you sure? Only I haven't heard you talk
about Curvaliscious all day.'

'What?' Tiny stabs of hurt fire up in my chest, a metallic taste
forming in my mouth.

'I've seen Best Men's jackets, bridal corsets, skirts, trousers
and dresses, but no sign of anything Ramona. At least *I* admit
defeat.' He gathers our belongings, the picnic apparently over.

I stand there on the hillside, the sun's final rays streaming across the Tuscan valley, the vineyard aglow in that magic-hour light, feeling rotten to the core. He's right, of course. I sold out. Fear of failure and lost confidence are a heady cocktail of negativity and I am under the influence of them both. How could I have allowed this to happen? What a hypocrite I am, suggesting he's a coward when that is exactly what I have become. I look across at him and see a broken man, and have never felt so unsettled in my life. Fabrice has always been so resilient, so imperviable, so unbreakable, and seeing him like this makes me feel as though life itself is coming undone. I need to fix this for both of us.

CHAPTER TWENTY-TWO
Pre-wedding Jitters

Two days later and I have seen more of Tuscany than I have the whole time I've been out here, the girls hiring a car from the town down in the valley and taking Fabrice and I across country, first to the sun-soaked streets of Sienna and then to Pisa. It's been so much fun travelling around with friends – an impromptu holiday I would never have experienced had I not decided to jump on a plane to Italy and pitch my clothing range. Holding up three fingers and pointing to a tub of pistachio ice cream whilst arguing over the pound to euro exchange rate isn't exactly the culturally enriching experience I had with Marco in Florence, but hey ho.

White ribbons have been twisted around the iron door knockers of the church in preparation for the wedding tomorrow and crate after crate of beer is being lugged off the back of a lorry and lowered into the Ciccones' underground cellar. Rumour has it Italian weddings are a grand affair. Wishing that I'd stuck to my guns and given the pre-wedding drinks a swerve (something Francesca insisted I attend in a fashion advisory capacity), I reach for my Aperol. With the wedding only twenty-four hours away, there's not an awful lot I can do about a lost bead or an errant sequin and it's uncomfortably hot here in Ciccone's, the aircon having packed up and the temperature soaring along with the heated conversation about Fabrice's performance at the auction that is unfolding in front of me.

'A man dressed like that brings a bad reputation to the village.' Giuseppina hugs her handbag close to her chest and refuses to make eye contact with anyone. 'We are supposed to be a village of historic beauty. A jewel in the Tuscan crown. But to have a man dressed as a woman—'

'That was no man.' Valentina swings her stiletto-heeled, ankle-booted foot over her knee, readjusts her bride-to-be hen party tiara and laughs. 'She was 100 per cent woman and 200 per cent wonderful.'

'She was great.' Maria sips at her orange juice and waves back and forth the small, plastic Italian flag she's been given as part of the hen party pack that was handed out earlier.

'She was colourful. She was entertaining. She was perfect!' Valentina slurs, her Sicilian lemon print silk sash slopping off her diminutive frame.

'*He* was . . .' Giuseppina rotates her fingers whilst searching for a word in English.

'Beautiful?' Maria suggests.

'Vibrant?' I add.

'Enchanting?' Valentina throws in for good measure.

Giuseppina shakes her head, batting our words away with the back of her hand. 'Uncouth! Just like this American bachelorette garbage.' She raises her glass of sparkling water at Valentina's sash. '*He* was loud and uncouth.'

'*She* was nothing of the sort.' Valentina runs her finger over the temporary tattoo she and each of her hens have stamped on their inner wrist of Flavio's face, all high cheekbones and steely resolve, framed by red love hearts, then looks over at me. 'You didn't get a Flavio tattoo?'

'Why would she want a tattoo of my son on her arm? Bachelorette parties are an American tradition that should stay in America.' Giuseppina rolls her eyes and looks over to her husband, who sits between Francesca's husband and Flavio on high stools, sipping beer beneath a montage of framed black-and-white Madonna posters, laughing and joking as the football scores flash up on the television screen next to them – at least, they haven't got embroiled in wedding politics.

I cast a sympathetic look in Valentina's direction as Giuseppina holds court, discounting Francesca's every word with a 'Pah!' and tutting superciliously at everything.

Valentina leans into me and whispers, 'I told you she was a piece of work. First the caterers quit and now the band because she is too difficult to work with.'

With the hearing of a hawk, Giuseppina jumps on us. 'We *have* a band. Flavio's cousin is the finest rock singer in Tuscany.'

Valentina lets out a sigh. 'I'm just not sure I'm a rock chick.'

Taking his bride-to-be's hand in his, Flavio kisses her fingers. 'They can do Blues, too.'

Valentina peers into her drink. 'I'm not sure I'm a Blues girl either.'

'A band is a band.' Giuseppina sighs with exasperation.

'You see what she's like?' Valentina whispers. 'The caterers quit, too, so Ciccone's is now making all the food.' She nods over at Enzo, who polishes glasses behind the bar with a whiter-than-white tea towel, a cigarette propped up behind his ear. 'But we still need three or four people to help bring food to the table and serve drinks.'

Feeling for her, I rack my brains. 'If it doesn't matter that our Italian is bad, me and my friends can help.'

'You can?' She looks at me imploringly.

'If you don't mind one of the waiters being Polly Darton? I mean, obviously he wouldn't look like Polly Darton, he'd look like himself, you know, unrecognisable . . .' I glance in Giuseppina's direction. 'And then Zhané and Flora are fabulous. Zhané is great with people and Flora's ridiculously well organised. There you go, you have a team of four at your service.'

'If you're sure!' Valentina takes hold of my hand and squeezes it.

'She doesn't like Rock. She doesn't like Blues. She doesn't like anything!' Giuseppina carries on, tilting her coffee cup aggressively at Valentina.

'She liked the original band we paid for.' Francesca defends her daughter, blocking Giuseppina's coffee cup with her own and I wonder for a moment whether they're going to battle it out with mochaccinos, the conversation plummeting into a tirade of lightning-speed Italian and flamboyant hand movements. I catch the odd word, making a mental note to look up *cazzo* and *coglione* when I get a moment, I can only assume they're types of pasta. The atmosphere further intensifies as they reach loggerheads about everything from music to menu choice, apparel to accessories, and judging by the speed at which printouts are pulled out of their pockets, the content of their speeches is also cause for argument.

I push my chair back, the legs scraping against the tiled floor. 'I should probably—'

'Sit!' Giuseppina thrusts me back down into my seat.

Doing as she says, I sit back and watch as the exchange enlivens, words accelerating, voices rising and arms flapping further and wider, and am just starting to conspire ways of gathering my belongings to join my friends for a picnic down by the river when Francesca grabs my arm.

'Ramona, do you have any colourful fabric remaining?' she says, but before I can answer, she turns to Giuseppina, her lip curling into a sardonic snarl. 'It would add a bit of colour to the evening. After all, we don't want everything to be white, do we?'

'What's that supposed to mean?' Giuseppina says snippily.

'We all know you've taken it.' Francesca's eyes narrow. 'La Columba Bianca. We all know it will suddenly turn up – Paff, what a coincidence! – right on top of the head of the Mother of the Groom just in time for the wedding. Isn't that what this is all about? Taking the attention away from my daughter and having it for yourself?'

Giuseppina tightens her grip on her handbag. 'Mama mia! I am many things but not a thief, and just for the record, I have never seen la Columba Bianca in my entire life.'

'Didn't Raffa take it?' I blurt out. 'We saw him run out of the auction with a hat box under his arm and assumed—'

'It was fake!' Valentina slurs.

'What?'

'He took what he *thought* was la Columba Bianca, but when he tried to sell it, he was told it was a replica and worth nothing, which means that the real White Dove is yet to be found,' Valentina explains.

Giuseppina grinds her teeth. 'Maybe we should start a search in your house, Francesca.'

Francesca's eyes narrow, her fingers reaching for the fork on the table and just when I think she's going to stab her adversary in the windpipe with Ciccone's fresh-out-of-the-dishwasher silverware, she sets down her cutlery and turns to me. 'On this note, I wanted to discuss wedding costumes with you.'

'OK,' I say tentatively, wondering what last-minute requests are about to come my way.

Her eyes wander over to Giuseppina and then back to me. 'We cannot wear the same clothes. You designed the corset for me and then she copies, but we are different. Different personalities. Different women. Different taste. I am the Mother of the Bride, Giuseppina is the Mother of the Groom. Different roles entirely and therefore . . .'

I feel my face tighten. 'I didn't think you were wearing the same outfit?'

Her eyes reduce to slits. 'We both have the same silver coutil corset, no?'

'Same fabric, different style. You have a tailored trouser suit and Giuseppina has the pleated skirt and jacket she requested,' I say, trying to keep my tone neutral and emotionless.

'Different style?' Giuseppina looks down her nose at Francesca and then back at me. 'What do you mean, different style?'

I sit back in my chair, the wooden backrest digging into my shoulders as Giuseppina and Francesca erupt into another verbal spat and Valentina casts me a sympathetic look.

'It's not your fault,' she says, shaking her head despairingly. 'It's—'

But before she can finish her sentence, coffee cups and spittle are flying at a rate of knots and the increasing petty protestations of both parties have reached a cataclysmic crescendo of shouting and finger jabbing. A plate has smashed, plump olives rolling all over the floor, water has spilt across the table and Giuseppina and Francesca are fronting up to each other like two male peacocks battling it out for a mate. Trying his best to break up the fight, Flavio stands between the two of them, sacrificing himself as a human shield and just when it looks like things are about to settle down, neither of the women wanting to take a direct swing at the groom-to-be, Giuseppina's husband joins in with a few choice expletives of his own which see Francesca's husband roll up his sleeves and join in the fray.

'Maybe you should leave,' Valentina whispers at me behind the palm of her hand.

Poor Valentina. You always hear about Bridezillas and their outrageous wedding demands, but she has been nothing of the sort and it's the mothers and their obsessive rivalry who are the divas in all of this. Seizing the opportunity, I grab my bag and rush out, leaving behind the sound of clashing voices and smashing crockery, grateful to gulp in the fresh Tuscan air.

'How did it go?' Zhané looks up from her paperback and withdraws her feet from the rails of the balcony.

'Spicy,' I say, clearing a space on the table and plonking down the bag of pastries.

'Marco came round looking for you earlier. He said Raffa has agreed to rent Mariela's hats out for the wedding – he's been liaising with Signor Zaccardi, apparently. Then he said there was another matter, too, so I asked if I could pass on a message, but he looked all flustered and said it was about the wedding and he'd find you later because he needed to say it in person,' Zhané says.

'Right, well, speaking of the wedding, I've got you all an invite if you don't mind helping out!'

'How?' Flora crinkles up her nose and examines her freshly painted nails.

'I've nothing to wear for a wedding.' Fabrice helps himself to chocolate cannoli.

'We're waiting staff,' I say. 'Enzo is going to kit us out with Ciccone's uniforms apparently.'

'Great!' Flora laughs as Fabrice swaggers across the terrace, holding an imaginary tray of drinks.

And although I'd love to join in the laughter, a rush of humiliation overcomes me because, of course, there won't be a uniform that fits me and like all those times before – my weekend job waitressing at a local café, paintballing at a friend's hen party, wearing that man-sized boiler suit to clear out all of those cat food tins – I will be singled out for being 'larger than life'. Pushing down the feeling of degradation that rises inside me and biting my bottom lip until it bleeds, I resolve that tomorrow I will get back on the Curvaliscious horse.

Enough of being made to feel small for being large.

CHAPTER TWENTY-THREE
The Wedding

Altaterra certainly knows how to host a wedding. Bells ring, bunting flutters and the turrets of the sandstone clock tower are decorated with gold ribbons and white roses. A pale-blue vintage Alfa Romeo polished to within an inch of its life has pulled up outside the taverna with its hood down, beeping its horn in jubilation as a procession of cars adorned with small white flags files behind. The village square is teeming with aunties and uncles, parents and grandparents, children and grandchildren, all dressed in their wedding finery as they stream out of the church. And hats. So many hats.

In fact, I don't think I've ever seen so many hats. Feathered hats. Multi-layered hats. Mesh cocktail fascinators. Understated, small, neat hats. Big, showy, floppy hats. A pink flamingo turban

(Francesca's assistant at the Farmacia), a tower of waxwork fruit (the lady from the bakery) and a Kate Middleton-style pink flower halo crown (Valentina's sister). With such an eclectic mix of headgear on display, the Casa dei Cappelli must have made a fortune in rentals over the last twenty-four hours.

'Still no sign of the Columba Bianca but Mariela would have been happy, hey?' Signor Zaccardi throws his arm around my shoulder.

Like a proud mother, I step back and survey the scene, taking a moment to drink it all in and allowing myself a private moment of reflection. 'Very proud.'

'You've seen Giuseppina?' he says, and I can't work out whether he is legitimately trying to locate her or wants to alert my attention to her outfit, but before I can ask, Fabrice is at my side offering thinly sliced bruschetta alla Romana on a small silver tray and suggesting, with pursed lips and a tilt of the head, that I am slacking from my duties.

Smoothing down the man-sized polo shirt Enzo took off his own back to give to me and tucking it into my Ciccone's apron, I pick up the tray of aperitivi parked on the table behind and resume my waitressing responsibilities, but it's difficult to ignore the clanking and banging coming from the stage, where a motley crew of friends and relatives scraped together by Flavio are setting up a drum kit, studying each component as though they've never seen it before, which in fairness to them, they probably haven't.

Circulating with a tray of drinks, my interest is piqued by the rumours that are flying around about the Columba Bianca – that it's on its way to Meghan Markle for her to wear at a Royal Wedding, that it's locked in the cellar of Ciccone's amongst the finest champagne, that Raffa's fake was a double bluff and that he did steal it after all. The different theories are fascinating. I look around for Giuseppina but it's Francesca that I spot first. Dressed in the silver corset and sparkly trouser suit I made her, she is rocking a pair of heels so vertiginous I would struggle to stand up in and yet here she is, gliding across the uneven cobbled stones, as though it's nothing. Hair teased into soft curls crowned by Mariela's silver hummingbird pillbox hat, a thin layer of silver net shielding her eyes whilst showing off the infamous blue streak in her hair, she looks every bit the Mother of the Bride and star of the show as she converses with Flavio's friend in the shade of the church. I watch as Maria joins them in the dress I made, which camouflages her baby bump and shows off her long, toned legs.

'Ciao!'

I turn to see Marco, flanked by the other Best Men, and a peculiar feeling comes over me as my eyes travel over the contours of his suit jacket and more specifically his chest. Aware of my indiscretion, I look away and then become aware of the oversized burgundy polo-shirt monstrosity I am wearing and feel my face flush with humiliation.

'You've met Gabriele and Eduardo?' He draws my attention back to the band of brothers in front of me.

'Hi!' I nod to the men alongside him, breathing in the citrus scent of his aftershave. 'All rocking your suits, I see!' I say, realising that's the sort of thing my grandmother might have said in this situation and trying to prise my eyes away from Marco's chest, which I really shouldn't be looking at. 'Aperitivo?'

'Grazie.' His friends help themselves to drinks.

'Ramona?' Marco beckons.

Heart fluttering, I look up to meet his gaze, his ice-blue eyes more turquoise than ever against the blue shirt he is wearing.

'I have something to ask you.' He looks me straight in the eye and butterflies dance in my stomach.

'Ramona?' Giuseppina appears at my side, looking nothing short of magnificent in her silver corset and pleated skirt, the tailored jacket ditched to let her curves do all the talking. Her hair has been arranged into a classic low bun with a mother-of-pearl hairpin to accommodate a Mariela Marino masterpiece: Il Napoletano, if I remember the auction catalogue correctly – a dainty cream hat holding three brushed-cotton balls of strawberry, chocolate and vanilla ice cream with an elegant fan wafer made of lace jutting out from the centre. 'I think Flavio's cousins are quite thirsty.' She waves her flute of champagne in the direction of the stage.

'Sorry, I . . . You look great!' I say, running my eyes over her outfit before turning to Marco. 'I'll be back.'

By the time I have gone back to the bar, refilled my tray with flutes of champagne and provided the band with drinks, Marco is nowhere to be seen. I hold a cold bottle of beer against my cheek and feel a sense of pride as one of Valentina's friends glides across the stage in her lace gown, the fabric pooled like liquid behind her and although I know I should have given her a lower neckline, the cut is perfect.

'There he is!' Signor Zaccardi points up at the cloudless sky as the buzz of a plane fills the air.

I look up to see a Valentina & Flavio banner streaming out behind a small aircraft.

Signor Zaccardi gazes up at the heavens with pride. 'His eyesight doesn't allow him to be a commercial pilot, but—'

'That's Marco?' I gasp.

I think about everything Marco told me in Florence. How addictive the feeling of flying is. The sensation of being at one with the world, a part of the earth's atmosphere. He may not be able to pilot commercial flights, but he's certainly not given up on his dream, and it reinforces the fact that I really shouldn't give up on mine.

Afternoon becomes evening, the sun hanging low over the hills and a gentle breeze blowing through the valley as guests mingling in every nook and cranny of the village square are ushered into the marquee for dinner.

'You will serve the head table.' Enzo nods at Zhané, who has somewhat predictably proven herself to be the most competent host out of the four of us. 'You will take tables two, three and four,' he says to Flora. 'Tables five, six, seven for you.' He looks to Fabrice. 'And . . . Ramona, the table at the back for you.'

I feel a bit like the last girl to be chosen for the school netball team, entrusted to wait one table only and in the shadows at that.

'Let's go!' He claps his hands together charismatically.

I head to my assigned table at the back of the marquee where the village priest, two women from the local knitting club, Signor Zaccardi and a bunch of people I have never met before fawn over Valentina's bridal gown as she leans over to thank them for coming. Over on the next table, Flora is getting along famously with Flavio's cousin who is doubling up as the drummer tonight and, out of the corner of my eye, I can see Fabrice flirting outrageously with the village locksmith. But it's Zhané's table that has got my attention; Marco sitting with his arm around the back of Maria's chair as he throws his head back and laughs. What did he want with me earlier? And why am I pouring wine into a glass that's already full?

'Salute!'

'Cin cin!'

'Congratulazione!'

The chink of glasses and the clink of cutlery ensues as the wedding party enjoys a meal which has me running about like a motorised lunatic, followed by speeches delivered by one of the Best Men and Valentina herself, who gets the giggles halfway through and has to compose herself with a glass of water. It is then Marco's turn to say a few words; the guests belly laugh at his story and I chide myself for not understanding a single goddamned word he's saying. I *really* must learn Italian.

Fabrice wanders over with a beer in his hand. 'You should have seen the Mother of the Groom's face when I told her that Polly Darton was serving her antipasti. I swear she nearly had a heart attack. Look, are you OK to serve coffee to tables five, six and seven if I take a quick comfort break with my locksmith friend?'

I stare at him wide-eyed in horror. The village locksmith is a happily married man, and I can't see that his husband will be too chuffed with this idea.

'They have an arrangement!' he says as though reading my mind, then plants a kiss on my cheek and swaggers off, the pair of them laughing as they dip outside the marquee, the locksmith's husband nowhere to be seen.

As the sun sets and night draws in, the village square becomes a makeshift dance floor, disco lights beaming across the cobbles and illuminating the church behind. An all-inclusive affair, no villager has been forgotten, the butcher serving barbecued pork in the baker's bread buns, the couple from the wine cellar pouring a steady stream of rosé prosecco into champagne flutes provided by Enzo and the tobacconist-cum-vape seller teaming up with staff from the Post Office to build the stage, where the timid woman in charge of overseas parcels bangs out a series of rock songs until she's hoarse. Flavio's cousin retires the band and takes over as DJ, a series of trashy electronic songs blasting through the valley and a group of children throwing shapes across the cobbles.

Zhané and Enzo are deep in conversation about the price of prawns, Flora is still flirting with the drummer and I haven't seen Fabrice since he disappeared with the locksmith a good hour ago. Deciding I've earned the right to get changed out of this unsightly polo shirt, I take a cold bottle of Diet Coke and head up the hill to decompress. It's weird, but when I was here alone it felt as though I belonged in Altaterra – as though by seeking it out solo, I came to understand the village as an inhabitant rather than a visitor and was building a life here. Granted, I will never fully understand the Italian psyche, but I feel an undeniable bond with this place. An attachment. A loyalty and a sense of self as I've got to know the locals and grown to understand how things run on the inside. And yet, with my friends around me, I'm just another English tourist on holiday, my time here transitory.

'Hey.' A voice plucks me from my reverie.

I look down to see Valentina slouched on a stone wall, her dress crumpled and her face tear-stained.

'Are you OK?' I say, crouching down next to her.

Her shoulders sag. 'The singer has lost her voice entirely and dancing the macarena on my wedding day was never part of my fairy tale.'

A laugh escapes my lips. 'The music is pretty diabolical.'

She frowns. 'Seriously, I can't dance to this shit.'

As if to illustrate her point further, Flavio's cousin mixes 'Barbie Girl' in a nineties blast from the past, the bass thumping over the hillside.

'That's it, I'm done.' She pulls the veil off her head and tosses it over the stone wall with a dramatic flail of the arms and I am left wondering what sort of animals live in the field behind us and whether the veil is biodegradable.

I lean over the wall. 'Are you really sure you—'

'And why are you wearing that?' She gestures to my polo shirt and screws her nose up with horror.

Shame rises within me. 'It was the only T-shirt that—'

Her eyes narrow. 'Did Marco not ask you?'

'Ask me what?' I say, but before she can answer, Fabrice's head pops up behind the stone wall, startling both of us, Valentina letting out a scream.

'I think you dropped this,' Fabrice says, handing over her veil, the village locksmith appearing behind him and brushing down his trousers.

'Great wedding!' Fabrice smiles smugly.

Valentina rolls her eyes. 'I'm glad someone is enjoying themselves.'

I grab at Fabrice's elbow as he jumps over the wall. 'Do you think you could persuade Polly to perform tonight? It might just save the day.'

He looks at me like a disgruntled cockatoo. 'Polly Darton is over. Finito. She's in a coma with a great, big, fat "do not resuscitate" sticker on her.'

'Please!' I tug at his sleeve and nod in Valentina's direction. 'No bride should be made to feel like this.'

'Please? I just want somebody who can sing.' Valentina looks up at him with big doe eyes.

'Fabrice, it's ruining her wedding night,' I plead.

'I couldn't even if I wanted to, I don't have anything to wear.' He runs his hands over his uniform.

And it's at that point that my thoughts flit to the redundant DragFest dress that I created, a fizz of excitement coming over me and goosebumps springing up all over my arms and legs. 'Follow me!'

A moment later and we reach the cool confines of my studio, the electronic music down in the village square a distant thud. I stand under the glow of the lightbulb in the cupboard under the secret staircase and untangle the bright yellow net tutu train from the dazzling daffodil-yellow fabric. Smoothing out the feathers, rearranging the plunging, ruffled neckline and straightening the capped sunflower sleeves, I admire the black sequined bodice and feel a sense of pride at the way the Swarovski crystals twinkle like stars in a clear night sky.

Holding up the dress in all its glittering glory, I open the door to the studio and position myself in front of Fabrice. 'OK, you can open your eyes now.'

He peels his hands away from his face, his expression morphing from one of shock into one of unbridled joy. 'Oh my godfathers! You made this?' He reaches out to touch the fabric, awe dancing across his face as he admires it from all angles.

'For DragFest.' I grin from ear to ear.

'This is *incredible*.' He runs his fingers over the daffodil-yellow sash and looks up with tears in his eyes. 'It's everything, Vivienne. It's a work of art.' He paces full circle around it. 'Can I try it on?'

'Only if you give Valentina a song or two?' I stick my tongue out playfully.

'I love it. I really do, but I just . . .' His voice reduces to a squeak. 'Call it an existential crisis or maybe Polly Darton is going through the menopause, but I'm just not sure I've got it in me anymore. If I could turn back time, and not in a Cher way, I'd be all over it, I promise I would, but I'm just not sure I can put myself out there anymore. Life is tough enough as it is without people criticising you constantly and leaving spiteful reviews on social media. Maybe I'm getting softer in my old age and need to grow a thicker skin, but honestly . . .'

I squeeze his shoulder and look him in the eye. 'Fabrice, you told me off for letting one person's opinion derail me from my dreams and called me out for being a sell-out, and you were right. I lost my nerve and gave up on Curvaliscious entirely because it was easier than facing all the hurdles set out in front of me, but I promise I'm already back on the horse.'

'What horse?' He takes the dress from me and holds it up under his chin.

'The size-inclusive apparel one,' I say, ripping off my apron and throwing it to the ground.

'Vivienne, what are you doing?'

'This "uniform" is a case in point. I've been forced to wear a man's polo shirt because the women's shirts don't come in my size. I've had enough. If you won't wear the dress, then I will.' I snatch the gown back off him.

'Oh no, you will not, Vivienne. That's *my* dress!' He snatches it back and marches into the changing room. 'You don't remember what happened to my wig, do you?'

I pull the drawer out from under my worktable and take the blonde beehive out from its box. You can never underestimate the seductive power of a good frock.

Running my fingers through the strands of yellow nylon, I glance at the clock on the wall. 'How's about neither of us give up?'

'What do you mean?' he shouts from the changing room.

'I won't stop making big girl's clothes if you won't stop wearing them.'

'I might need a hand with this, Vivienne!'

'Deal?'

'Deal.'

The curtain slides open to reveal the most amazing version of Polly Darton I have ever seen. Features accentuated, curves emboldened, waist cinched, makeup applied, I can't take my eyes off her.

'How do I look?' She sashays across the room.

'Bold, brave and unbelievably beautiful,' I say, jaw on the floor. And it's at that point, right there in the Altaterra studio standing in front of my friend, that I can finally pinpoint that je ne sais quoi that has been missing from my new line of clothes, resolving to adjust the collection's name to become Bold, Brave & Beautiful.

'And I have just the perfect accessory.' Polly's eyes search my sewing desk. 'Oh, fucksticks, it's gone!'

'What's gone?' I say.

'Queen Bea made me my very own Columba Bianca based on the photos you showed me – you know how good she is with props – and I left it here on your sewing desk when I ran the auction. It was in a hat box and—'

'Was it pink?'

'No, it was white. Columba *Bianca,* darling.'

'No, the box.'

'Yes,' she says thoughtfully. 'I believe it was.'

'Ha!' I squeal.

'Vivienne?' She cocks her head to one side. 'Would you care to tell me what's going on?'

'I think you may just have saved the day!'

'He ran off with your fake!' I say, kissing her forehead and pulling up the straps of the backless royal blue dress prototype I am now wearing and folding up Enzo's polo shirt and apron. 'Raffa thought Bea's replica was the real thing and ran off with it, which means that the real one is—'

'Under the fifth step of the secret staircase.'

'What?' I say, the ground feeling as though it's shifting beneath me.

'My stiletto got stuck in a crack on the fifth step of the staircase earlier and when I looked down, I could see the faint outline of a square that had been cut out, so I had a little poke – you know me, Vivienne, I've never been one for restraint – and hey presto, with a bit of assistance, it came open.'

'And . . .'

'And all I could see was boxes. Hat boxes,' she says, leading me by the hand towards the staircase. 'I mean, I didn't have time, not with the auction about to start but . . .' She bends down on the fifth step, levering out a rectangular piece of wood with her fake nails and giving it a jiggle until it comes out. Reaching down through the gap, she pulls out a circular baby blue box smaller than I'd imagined. Instinctively, I look up, imagining I've heard footsteps, but the only sound I can hear is the hammering of my heart.

Slowly, I lift the lid and there before us sits the most beautiful creation I have ever seen. Diminutive, dainty and deliciously delicate, la Columba Bianca has long, natural white dove and goose feathers, each individually mounted on a small round ivory satin base to create the illusion of the wings of a dove in flight.

'What the focaccia?' Polly looks at me, eyes ablaze with wonder.

'Wow,' I say, twisting it this way and that, the tiny silver beaded feather ends catching the light. 'I can see why she hid it.'

'Come on, I think we've got some celebrating to do!' Polly Darton offers me her arm. 'Would Princess Charming like to take Cinderella to the ball?'

'Yes,' I say, giddy with excitement. 'Yes, she bloody well would!'

CHAPTER TWENTY-FOUR
The whole truth

Polly Darton takes to the stage. Like a sunflower in bloom, she towers above the rest of the band, layers and layers of bright bumblebee-yellow net flowing from the back of the gown in a detachable tutu train that takes up most of the stage. A deep sense of accomplishment comes over me as she swaggers over to the microphone, the slits in the skirt showing off those amazing legs, but it's only when she reaches into the hat box next to her and lifts out Mariela Marino's prize possession that a collective intake of breath fills the air.

'La Columba Bianca?' Valentina screams as Fabrice lifts the delicately crafted, soft feathered white dove hat onto his head, a small triangle of white mesh falling over his face.

La Columba Bianca. La Columba Bianca. Whispers spread.

'Eccolo! Il ladro!' Giuseppina chimes. 'Stop, thief!'

Polly reaches for the mic. 'Ladies and gentlemen, I am Polly Darton, your host for tonight and we are here not only to celebrate the wedding of Valentina and Flavio, but also the re-emergence of Mariela Marino's famous Columba Bianca. It turns out Mr Bergamaschi went home with my fake and this little beauty that we found under the floorboards, locked away with several others, is available for rent.'

'Let me try it!' Giuseppina staggers towards the stage.

'No, me!' Francesca follows, a mass of guests hot on her heels, and it takes fifteen minutes of complete hysteria, people throwing themselves onto the podium in the hope of touching Mariela Marino's masterpiece and a fight breaking out as to who will be the first to wear it, before Signor Zaccardi is forced to take it away, keeping it under lock and key.

'OK, let's party!' Polly announces.

The crowd whoop and cheer as the opening notes of Dolly Parton's '9 to 5' start up and an entire village comes to life. Flavio's father stamps his feet and claps his hands in time to the beat whilst the local baker drags the village priest up to dance and a whole mob of Valentina's friends form two parallel lines as the bride herself shimmies between them, thrusting her hips and tapping her heels to the rhythm. Polly 'stumbles out of bed and tumbles to the kitchen' and a sense of euphoria fills the village square. Flanked by Zhané and Flora, my arms slung over their shoulders, I join the sea of wedding guests who bob up and down in time to the music, joining in on the chorus and the atmosphere is so electric that I feel lucky to be alive.

'Hey!' Marco grabs me by the hand. 'I like your dress!'

340

'Hey!' I say with a look of surprise and try not to act all weird, but the touch of his skin against mine and the urgency with which he is grasping my fingers is doing things to me deep inside, feelings fluttering around my chest that I can't quite harness and thoughts bouncing around my head that I definitely shouldn't be thinking. Instinctively, I look around for Maria but she's nowhere to be seen.

'I wanted to ask you something, but it's a bit late now!' he shouts just before the song explodes into another chorus, two hundred people now belting out the lyrics.

'What?' I struggle to hear over the music.

'I'll tell you after this song!' He abandons the conversation to grip me more tightly, pulling me into his chest and spinning me around.

Obviously I mustn't interpret this act of intimacy as anything other than the light-hearted spirit in which it is intended, so why are the palms of my hands so clammy and why is the moment already running away with me?

Letting go of my hand to take his phone out of his pocket, Marco starts to video the next chorus, the screen swivelling between Polly up on stage, a sea of guests bouncing and jolting beneath her, and our two sweaty, gurning faces singing our hearts out into the camera. Out of the corner of my eye I see Signor Zaccardi swinging Zhané around and behind her, Flora huddled in conversation with Flavio's cousin.

Finally, the song draws to a close, the crowd heckling for an encore. Taking my hand in his, Marco leads me to the shelter of a sycamore tree and, stopping abruptly, turns to face me. Tucking a blond spiral of hair behind his ear, he looks at me earnestly whilst clearing his throat and from the gravity of his expression, I can't work out whether he's going to tell me that someone has been taken critically ill or worse, died.

'Ramona, I wanted to ask if you would be my guest to the wedding. I'm sorry it's too late now, but I couldn't find the right moment.'

'Your guest?' I splutter, feeling a mixture of relief that no one is to be hospitalised, giddiness at the idea of him wanting me as his guest and total mystification.

'Yes.' His eyes twinkle.

'But what about Maria?' I say, looking around for her.

He laughs. 'I may ask my sister for a lot of things, but I don't need to ask for her permission to take someone to a wedding!'

'Your *sister*?' I say, wondering how many beers he's had. 'No, I said *Maria*.'

He stands stock-still. 'Maria *is* my sister.'

'Maria is your sister?' I cry out just as the music cuts out. 'But . . .'

Hands on hips, he looks at me quizzically.

I search his face for a hint of irony. The sign of a joke. A trace of sarcasm. Surely, things have got lost in translation. 'Sorry, I just thought . . . I thought Maria was your *wife*.'

'My wife?' He laughs.

'Or girlfriend,' I append quickly.

'I don't have a wife or girlfriend,' he says, matter of fact.

'But you're having a baby with her!' I blurt out, a torrent of emotions gurgling inside me and rushing to the surface ready to escape.

'Am I?' His eyes widen with surprise.

'You had a baby scan the day we went to Florence!'

He shakes his head and laughs. '*Maria* had the scan. I was helping her.'

'But . . .'

'When a woman chooses to have a baby on her own, without a father, you must give her all the support she needs. My sister is amazingly strong, but still, it's tough alone at times, you know.'

Like shifting jigsaw puzzle pieces around until they fit, I try to look at him through a different lens, recalling the Airbnb hosts being listed as Maria and Marco, the welcome note on the table from the pair of them, the photograph of them together, his confused reaction when I asked him if he's looking forward to becoming a father, and the look of mystification on Maria's face when I'd asked if she didn't mind Marco taking me to Florence. Hadn't she egged it on, telling him to buy me ice cream?

'Oh my God.' I drop my head into my hands.

'You didn't think it a little strange that I wanted to spend time with you instead of my partner?' He gasps with laughter.

I pause for a moment. 'Did you?'

'Did I what?'

'Want to spend time with me?' I say, hopefully.

'Was it not obvious?'

Silence lingers until he grabs my hand and leads me towards the alley that runs alongside the bakery with an urgency I can't quite keep up with, the heels of my sandals getting caught in the cobble cracks as we head all the way up to La Casa dei Cappelli, where he sits me down on the cold, stone steps, takes a deep breath and turns to me. 'Look, I know it wasn't the greatest start when you checked in and I was in my theatre costume and shouting at you as the cleaner . . .'

I cast my mind back to the first time we met, recalling the ghastly harem pants and tie-dyed T-shirt. 'You're an actor?'

'A bad one. I was helping a friend out. Look, I'm sorry. I've really done this very badly,' he says, cupping my hands in his. 'The reason I wanted to cover you with plaster to make un manichino is because I like you. The reason I accompanied you to Florence is because I *really* like you. And the reason I ask the Mayor of Florence to empty the Porcellino to find your jewel is because I like you too much.'

'Sorry?' I say, ruining the moment by realising I've left pins in my dress around the hem and unable to fully focus.

'This.' He dips his hand into his pocket and there, lying in the palm of his hand like forgotten treasure is the small, blue Wedgwood pendant I lost in Florence. My grandma's boomerang, just as polished and perfect as it always was around her neck, the stone cherub entirely unscathed, a new chain sparkling in the dark. Memories of my grandma flicker across my mind's eye. Dressed in tennis whites at my Y11 parents' evening when my mum was ill. Wearing tweed at my cousin's christening. In a pleated jade suit for my eighteenth-birthday outing to the theatre. In her Sunday best for Christmas. Not a single special occasion went by without her wearing this pendant, a tradition which I would dearly love to adopt and pledge never to let it out of my sight again. 'But how did you . . .'

'Please.' He spins me round and lifts my hair off my shoulder, a shiver running down my spine as he attaches the chain around my neck, his sweetness unsettling me and leaving a light spongy feeling in my stomach.

Comforted by the touch of the cold stone against my hot skin, I cast my mind back to Dante's Chiesa di Santa Margherita and in particular the wish that I made when dropping that scrap of paper into the coffin. 'Where did you find it?'

'I wish I could tell you a romantic story like finding the shoe for Cinderella, but the truth is that I phoned and emailed the municipality of Firenze so many times to ask them to check inside the Porcellino for your necklace because I had a feeling maybe it had fallen inside that eventually they got so annoyed with me that they empty the pig to keep me quiet. Two days ago, they posted it to me and I received it this morning. I've been trying to find you all day, but it was never the right moment. With you, Ramona, it feels as though it's never the right moment.'

'Thank you! Thank you so much.' I grab hold of his shoulders and give him a peck on the cheek.

'OK, so I screwed up the moment when I first met you, then I screwed up the question about you being my guest today, but hopefully I won't screw this up,' he says, leaning in to kiss me.

My stomach squirms with delight. His lips are soft but persistent, his touch gentle but firm, tiny fireworks popping and fizzing throughout my body as his hands find the nape of my neck and travel down my spine to the small of my back. I lean into him, breathing in the musk of his skin and the sweet honey smell of his hair, my senses heightened in the here and now, and the whoops and whistles of the wedding party down in the village square fading into the distance.

345

'You OK?' He lifts his head to check in on me.

'Never better.' I draw him closer.

'Molto bene.' A wide grin stretches across his face before he leans in to kiss me again, this time more tenderly, his tongue taking time to explore my mouth, his fingers tracing the outline of my dress across my breastbone and a million tiny goosebumps springing up all over me. His movements are slow but assured, the heat of his body against mine doing something to me deep inside, releasing a landslide of lust and longing, and I wish this moment could last forever.

Red-faced and woozy, we head back down to the wedding party and over to the dance floor, where Polly greets us from the stage with a flash of white teeth and a knowing wink. The music slows and the undulating rhythm of 'Jolene' starts up, Marco holding me tight, his chest pressed against mine and his breath heavy on my neck. I drink him in. The contours of his shoulders. The cut of his jacket. The beating of his heart, our eyes sharing a conversation of their own as we twist and turn, my arms draped around his neck, his hands around my waist, and I take time to savour the moment and appreciate just how happy I am.

'Just friends, hey?' Zhané leans over to whisper in my ear, breaking away with a wink and a smile to shimmy into her next dance move alongside Giuseppina.

'Special friends.' I wrinkle my nose in delight.

'Like Flora over there!' She nods her head in the direction of the car park.

Out of the corner of my eye, I catch Flora snogging Flavio's cousin whilst Valentina and Maria appear next to us on the dance floor, twirling each other in slow circles and exchanging looks of glee. Pressed against Marco and surrounded by friends old and new, I can't remember the last time I felt in such high spirits, the spell only partially broken when the song draws to a close, Polly taking a sip of water and primping her beehive, and Francesca seizing the moment to steal the limelight.

'Where did you buy your dress?' she says.

'It's bespoke, darling. A Ramona Matthews special.'

'Ramona made this dress?' Francesca wades through the crowd towards the stage and hauls herself up the steps, her heel tips clacking against the wooden panels as she makes her way across to Polly's podium to finger the fabric. 'Can she make one for me?'

'And me!' Giuseppina follows, hot on her heels. 'I can never find anything like this in my size.'

Polly treats them to a twirl, the butcher inserting his finger and thumb into his mouth and whistling. 'They say that the clothes do not maketh the man, but let me tell you, they sure as hell maketh the woman.'

Francesca reaches for the gown. 'Seriously, this is what I've been looking for forever, but there is nothing like this for people like me.'

'People like *you*?' Giuseppina scoffs.

Francesca lowers her voice. 'The larger lady.'

I watch through Zhané's phone as she zooms in and captures the whole exchange on camera.

'The larger lady!' Giuseppina repeats, Francesca scowling like a cornered street cat and just as I'm wondering whether we should all take shelter from the fisticuffs that are about to unfold, against all odds Giuseppina takes her hand in an act of solidarity. 'People like *us*.'

Francesca turns to Giuseppina in surprise, her face softening.

'It's true,' Giuseppina goes on. 'Designers think that when you become a certain size, that's it. Paf. Finito. You are for the rubbish dump and so they don't make clothes that fit the larger ladies, but large ladies like to celebrate just like everyone else.'

'Hear, hear.' Polly Darton reclaims the microphone, jutting one hip forward and inviting the audience to admire her fishnet stockings.

The butcher rubs his thigh and lets out a throaty growl.

'Big girls with big dreams need Ramona Matthews in their life,' she goes on, Zhané continuing to record every word.

Hearing this exchange, it feels as though my heart might just burst. If only I'd taken Giuseppina and Francesca to my House of Dreams pitch! My shoulders relax, a euphoric rush of endorphins surging through my whole body, and at that moment, right there on a makeshift dance floor in a small village in the middle of Tuscany, everything clicks into place: Fabrice has got his mojo back. Women are celebrating my clothes and I am enjoying the Tuscan wedding of a lifetime in the company of my oldest and newest friends. I look up at Marco: and one particularly special friend.

'Get the three queens off the stage and let's dance!' a man hollers from the back.

Giuseppina and Francesca share a look of revulsion.

'We are not drag queens!' Giuseppina spits, horrified.

Polly cajoles them off stage with the back of her hand and takes to the microphone for the last dance of the night.

'Good to see you two together.' Maria throws her arms around Marco and I, squeezing us against each other as though we are joint winners on a first-place podium, and squeals with joy.

I study her face, recognising the shape of her brow as that of Marco's. Up close, the similarities are uncanny. The heart-shaped face. The fine nose. The high cheekbones. Although their eyes couldn't be more different if they tried – hers so dark brown they are almost black, and his the ice blue of a glacier. Shaking my head in wonder, I clasp Marco's hand a little more tightly.

'*Finally!*' She laughs.

Marco scratches his chin in contemplation. 'The hasty cat made the kittens blind.'

'Sorry?' I say, lost.

'It's an Italian expression. Some things you cannot rush,' Maria explains, bursting into Phil Collins' 'You Can't Hurry Love' and turning to me. 'You know he's been in love with you since the day he camped outside your apartment to protect you from Raffa?'

I raise a playful eyebrow in his direction and push down the warm, fuzzy feeling in my stomach. 'Is that true?'

'I guess,' he says bashfully. 'Come on, let's go before my sister can embarrass me with more confessions.'

'Extending your Airbnb booking! Making excuses to come to the apartment with new customers for wedding costumes! The trip to Florence!' she calls out after us as Marco leads me away from the crowd and towards the cobbled lane that climbs the hill.

'I guess it did take a while.' He laughs.

Butterflies flutter beneath my ribcage as I pluck up the courage to ask if he'll leave the wedding to walk me home, but by the time I've worked out how to phrase it with just the right amount of nuance to keep it coy yet casual, I realise that we are already halfway there.

As we approach the garden gate, I try to remember what sort of disarray I've left the flat in and whether my knickers might be sprawled crotch-side up on the bathroom floor, but figure that when it comes around to maintaining a respectable landlord/tenant relationship, that ship has already sailed. 'I don't suppose you'd like to come in for a coffee?'

He raises an eyebrow. 'It's a little too late for coffee.'

'A snog and a biscuit?' I giggle.

'A snog?' His face crumples with confusion.

'I'll show you.' I grin.

I take him by the hand and lead him down the garden path, both physically and metaphorically, the hoot of an owl and the cluck of a disgruntled hen guiding us through the long grass as the moon disappears behind the terracotta roof and a dozen twinkling stars shine down on us from the clear night sky.

In the morning, I wake up to find Marco gone. My stomach drops. Aren't all happy-ever-afters a work of fiction? The reality being that in the sober light of day he'll have come to his senses and questioned what the fuck he has got himself into with the overweight girl he rented his flat to and realise that he's made a grave mistake. It's so formulaic that it's almost laughable I allowed myself to get swept along. Good old Ramona. Always the friend, never the girlfriend. I bury my head under the covers. The scent of his skin lingers on the sheets, the cotton rumpled in a way that still bears the imprint of his body. I look across at the empty space that he occupied all night, his limbs wrapped around mine, my back cocooned by his chest, and sigh.

Dragging myself out of bed, I tiptoe downstairs so as not to wake the girls, yet when I reach the living room, it is only Zhané that is laid out on the sofa bed. I muster a smile. At least Flora got lucky! Feeling crushed, forlorn and more than a tiny bit humiliated, I switch on the kettle and lift a single cup out of the cupboard – I really thought Marco was better than all that. Wasn't he supposed to have liked me for a while? Didn't we just share something really special? And just when I'm psychoanalysing every move we made last night, the door springs open and in steps Marco with a bunch of flowers fresh from the hillside and a bag of pastries. Awash with joy and relief, I resist the urge to race over and shower him with kisses, and instead reach for a second cup, Zhané still dead to the world.

'You've looked online?' Marco says, getting plates and knives out of the kitchen cupboards and setting the table outside.

'No . . .'

'Ramona Matthews has gone viral!' He takes his phone out of his pocket.

'What?'

'Who is Giovanni Columbo?' He frowns.

'Gio—give it here!' I reach for the handset and there on Instagram is the video of Fabrice, Giuseppina and Francesca uploaded by Zhané, who has thought to tag every fashion house under the sun, adding Giovanni Columbo for good measure, although the caption she has chosen suggests that @RamonaMatthews has a brand-new range of clothes out!

What was she *thinking*? 'One thousand, five hundred and three likes? Flipping heck!'

'It's my gift to you.' Zhané murmurs from her slumber. 'I fell asleep when we reached a thousand.'

'That's not all,' Marco says, snatching back his phone. 'DragFest has a new sponsor.'

'What?' Zhané springs up off the sofa.

'*La Casa dei Cappelli*.' Marco reads from the news feed on his phone. '*Raffaele Bergamaschi has offered full corporate sponsorship to Europe's largest annual drag carnival, DragFest, following widespread interest in his hat emporium. A set of photographs posted on Instagram where Mariela Marino's head pieces were paraded by drag queens as part of a village wedding in Tuscany have piqued the interest of thousands of people around the world.*'

'Raffa is going to sponsor DragFest?' I take hold of his phone and let out a laugh at the strapline that has been appended below the photo of Polly Darton, Giuseppina and Francesca, citing the three of them as 'experienced, exuberant and extraordinary drag queens'. 'Well, wonders never cease,' I chuckle, looking over at Zhané, who is scraping her hair into a ponytail and stepping into sandals.

'I'm going to find Fabrice!' she announces, grabbing her bag and making a beeline for the door.

Out on the terrace, not only has Marco laid out fresh croissants, but he has also arranged a platter of ripe figs and unwrapped cheeses. My mouth waters. And as I sit down next to him, the sun on my skin, a cuckoo singing from the branches of a nearby peach tree and the gentle tinkle of Signora Abbadelli's wind charm fluttering in the breeze, a deep sense of belonging comes over me and it strikes me that I can't imagine a life away from Tuscany. I take a bite of gorgonzola, its salty, full flavour infusing my mouth, leaving a delicious aftertaste that leaves me wanting more. Before us, a patchwork of golden fields stretches out to the horizon – a mosaic of oranges, purples, yellows and greens – and I can't imagine life without this beautiful landscape that I have come to fall in love with. The ancient Tuscan road winding down to the valley. The dark spires of cypress trees framing fields like loyal guards. The mishmash of rusty red rooftops. The violet hue of lavender. Honey hay bales. Mustard seed and mulberry. Wild orchids and tangled grapevines.

'I've been thinking . . . Maybe you should stay here a while,' Marco says as though reading my mind, his foot finding mine under the table.

Leaning my head against his shoulder and reaching for my grandma's pendant, a smile spreads across my lips. 'Maybe I should.'

EPILOGUE

Three years later

I look out of our bedroom window, the medieval city streets of Florence sprawled out below like an ornate toy town, and trace the River Arno with my finger against the cold glass pane, shadowing its twists and turns as it snakes its way through clusters of red terracotta roofs, church steeples, palace domes and museum towers until it runs out of sight towards the Ligurian Sea. A flutter of exhilaration starts up in my chest. Sometimes it's mind-blowing to think that I, Ramona Matthews, am living in the homeland of artists like Botticelli, Leonardo da Vinci and Michelangelo. Roaming the same streets. Looking out at the same river. I take a moment to drink in the view. Even from two kilometres away Il Duomo looks every bit as magnificent as it did the very first day I laid eyes on it.

The smell of freshly baked bread infuses the apartment – that's one of the good things about living above a bakery – and intermingles with the aroma of ground coffee beans, a blend that Marco has insisted on buying ever since my mum and dad introduced him to the Monmouth Coffee Company on a trip back to London last autumn. I look at my watch. Eight o'clock.

'Busy day ahead?' Marco stands behind me, wrapping his arms around my middle and resting his chin on my shoulder.

'And some!' I spin around for him to massage away a small knot in my upper back. 'I think we're going to have to take on extra staff at the rate we're growing.'

'A good problem to have.' He smiles.

I run my finger over the embroidered lettering on his shirt and wonder whether I should have given 'Marco's River Cruises' a couple of sunshine motifs to dot the i's, but decide that might be one too many shades of cheesy. 'Right, I'd better go otherwise Fabrice will be locked out.'

'A presto!' He presses his lips against mine and I still feel that fizz of excitement three years on from our very first kiss.

'Arrivederci!'

A moment later and I am on my pushbike, sailing down the hill in the low winter sun, beyond the Boboli Gardens, along the river and through the narrow alleys behind the Uffizi Gallery until it becomes too painful to cycle with all the bouncing and juddering over uneven cobbles. Dismounting, I push my bike past the Pizzateca, through the Uffizi courtyard and over to il Porcellino, where I park my wheels against the wall and, gathering my grandma's pendant in one hand so as not to snag it on the pig's snout, rub the pig's head – not to make a wish but to thank him for making mine come true.

Further ahead, the smell of cinnamon pastries fills the cobbled square of Via Roma, commuters darting this way and that to the sound of Radio Toscana, which bursts out of a small gelateria – here, it's never too early for ice cream. I chain my bike outside Gucci, enjoying the sense of satisfaction that comes from walking towards my own shop and wondering which incarnation of Fabrice I'll get today; the clean-cut, short back and sides, stylish, suited-and-booted British gentleman or his new alter ego, Fabrizia, an infinitely dazzling pencil-skirted siren with statement black bob modelled on *Pulp Fiction*'s Mia Wallace in preparation for this year's DragFest, which is scheduled to take place in Copenhagen.

My phone jingles, a fresh wave of panic overcoming me at the thought of another message from the DragFest graphic design team regarding the digital format of the RM logo, no doubt quoting insufficient bleed size and incorrect aspect ratios. Sponsoring DragFest is an honour and a privilege and something that I could only have dreamed of three years ago when Raffa somewhat predictably pulled out as soon as payment was due, but here I am now, funding one of the greatest festivals in the world which, now televised, is proving to be a win-win, Ramona Matthews getting its name out globally and DragFest bigger and better than ever. I guess the one saving grace is that Raffa at least stuck to his guns with opening La Casa dei Cappelli as a hat library, putting it firmly on the map with all the free publicity generated by his brief flirtation with sponsoring DragFest. Visitors have dramatically increased each year, preserving his grandmother's dream and boosting the local economy. And who knows; it may not have even been Raffa who pulled the plug on DragFest– another rumour floating around is that Giuseppina put a halt to La Casa dei Cappelli signing the contract, neither wanting her beloved village associated with the art of Drag nor hundreds of resplendent drag queens descending on the village each year. Whatever happened, things seem to have worked out OK.

Time to address that logo design. Yet when I look down at my phone screen, it's nothing of the sort. Instead, there sits an email from the Devil in Lycra herself. Seeing her name makes my blood run cold. I thought that chapter of my life was over and would rather gargle with bleach than revisit it. With trepidation, I open the mail.

From: Setayesh.Akhtar@Iceland.co.uk
Subject: Happy Christmas and Congratulations

Hi Ramona,

I just wanted to send you my warmest congratulations on your Christmas range. The whole collection looks stunning. I also wanted to say sorry for being an out-and-out bitch. I know you knew Aart and I were seeing each other and he kind of got me the gig at House of Dreams and, to be totally honest, I guess I was ashamed. Not all of us are as talented as you and some of us need a leg up(/over!!) from time to time.

You probably heard that I was let go shortly after falling pregnant with Aart's babies – twins, it turns out. Single parenting has been tough, I won't lie, but Artemis and Theodora are good kids. I just wish Aart would show an interest. You'll have seen that he's married to an eighteen-year-old Swedish model now.

Anyway, just wanted to say sorry and Happy Christmas,

Setayesh x

Emotion prickles in my nostrils. Never in my wildest dreams did I think I'd be feeling sorry for the Devil in Lycra herself and yet here I am, wishing I'd spent less time getting worked up about her conniving ways and more time getting angry about The Horse taking advantage of his young, female employees.

To: Setayesh.Akhtar@Iceland.co.uk

Subject: Happy Christmas and Congratulations

Hi Setayesh,

I'm sorry, too. I should have spoken up.

Happy Christmas xx

I guess you never know what goes on behind closed doors.

Lifted by the energy of good karma, I walk past Prada and Fendi, Valentino and Armani, studying their Christmas window displays and smiling – they don't have anything quite as eye-catching as the silver sequined plunge-neck, batwing-sleeved, ruched-waist, button key-holed back evening gown I made for Fabrizia last year; a dress which sent things next level for me and helped her win DragFest. I chuckle, a feeling of joy sweeping over me at the memory of her gliding through the streets of Amsterdam on the top deck of a glittery bus, waving theatrically at her fans like the Queen (God rest her soul) addressing her peoples from the balcony of Buckingham Palace – a magic moment for all of us, and a dream fulfilled for Fabrice, who finally handed in his notice at Pomfrey & Wibble.

Turning the cold, heavy keys around in my pocket, I bend down to unlock the metal shutter which glides over the shop window at the touch of a button, culminating in a slow reveal of Fabrice's silver dress, flanked by two pieces fresh out of my Christmas collection. I stifle a giggle; these days I don't have to make my own mannequins! The metal shutter reaches its resting place above the shop window with a click, my eye drawn to the swirly gold lettering set on a black background and the same warm, fuzzy feeling I get every day returning as I look up at my shop sign. Ditching the Curvaliscious name was something I agonised, Zhané eventually persuading me that 'Ramona Matthews' was more grown-up, aspirational and solid than 'Curvaliscious' and pointing out that it was my name that went viral. And, so far, the decision has paid off – with a store opening in London next spring and plans for another in Paris the following year, 'Ramona Matthews' is here to stay.

Bounding into the shop and performing my customary early morning twirl of gratitude, I cast my eyes over row upon row of size-inclusive apparel and my heart sings all over again. Whether it's my silver-glitter jumpsuit with gathered bodice panel and beaded tie waist, or my plum wide-legged trouser suit coupled with a charcoal felted wool cape, seeing these designs become a reality makes me feel complete. And as my first customer of the day, a big girl with big dreams of finding something she can wear to a celebrity book launch, comes through the door, I feel alive, emboldened and empowered all over again. Isn't that how life should be?

ACKNOWLEDGEMENTS

Thank you to my original agent, Felicity Trew, for matchmaking me with Bonnier and championing this Tuscan adventure from the get-go. I would also like to thank the editorial team at Bonnier for their guidance, eagle-eyes and trust – especially Sarah Bauer and Laura Gerrard whose notes were invaluable. This brings me on to thanking my agent, Julia Silk, for taking me on and championing *What the Focaccia* in all its Plus Size glory.

I'd also like to thank fellow writer, Bruce Jones, for his feedback on my first draft and for pointing out that I had actually written two starts – rectified in the edit – you are a trooper, Bruce, and I wish you all the best with your masterpieces.

In the acknowledgements of my last novel, *You Had Me at Halloumi*, I mentioned that I wrote the book during lockdown and that whilst it was brilliant escapism to transport myself to sunny climes and turquoise seas, the stress of home schooling, working a comms job in a bank and writing around the clock just about finished me off. This time round, *What the Focaccia* was written when we were semi-locked-down in the UK, but at least the schools stayed open. Thank you to teachers and school staff for doing such an amazing job and the hugest respect for those with children who are still at home because the transition back was too much.

A good storyline beyond the arc of romance needs inspiration and this is where my friend, Stephane V, comes in. I am so very grateful to have met Stephane all those years ago on *that* project. If he hadn't approached me with a half-written pantomime, there wouldn't have been a Murder on the Eurostar, Cattle Class or Eurostar academy and therefore I wouldn't have gone on to write stage-plays, performed at the Edinburgh Festival Fringe and become the published author I am today. Imagine, if we hadn't performed in Paris (Sailor, Sailor), written on the beach in Camargue (Mets de l'huile) and created Agatha Frisky. Imagine then, that you hadn't returned to France and become the award-winning fashion designer and costumier that you are today (https://www.stephanevcouture.com), dressed me up in your atelier and inspired this entire storyline.

With writing comes unconscious thought. Thank you to all my friends and family who have unknowingly influenced my characters and narrative, injecting humour, thought and chaos throughout. Lee I hear your voice when I write Zhané. The *trompe l'oeil* hee is for Steph and my book club ladies. You'll probably find nuggets you recognise throughout.

And most importantly, thank you to my family. Thank you to my boys, Alfie and Oscar, for overlooking the stuff open in Word before heading to Safari, and for being genuinely chuffed when something good happens with the writing. And thank you to Adam for reading all of my drafts, being my champion and having faith way more unwavering than mine. Florence was bloody amazing, thank you.